From **TANSTAAFL Press**:

CorpGov Chronicle novels by Tom Gondolfi
An Eighty Percent Solution – CorpGov Chronicles: Book One
In a world where corporations suborn governments as a part of good business practice and unregistered humans can be killed without penalty, Tony Sammis, a midlevel corporate functionary, finds himself unwittingly a pawn in a guerilla war between a powerful cabal of business leaders and an elusive but deadly underground movement. His final solution to the biological terror unleashed mirrors Tony's own twisted sense of justice.

Also by Tom Gondolfi
Toy Wars
Flung to a remote world, a semi-sentient group of robotic mining factories arrive with their programming hashed. They can only create animated toys instead of normal mining and fighting machines. One of these factories, pushed to the edge of extinction by the fratricidal conflict, attempts a desperate gamble. Infusing one of its toys with the power of sentience begins the quest of a 2-meter tall, purple teddy bear and his pink, polka-dotted elephant companion. They must cross an alien world to find and enlist the aid of mortal enemies to end the genocide before Toy Wars claims their family—all while asking the immortal question, "Why am I?"

By Bruce Graw
Demon Holiday
Torval, Demon Third Class, Layer Four Hundred Twelve of the Eighth Circle of Hell, has been in the business of chastising sinners longer than he can remember. Delivering punishment is the only job he's ever known—the only job he's ever wanted. After Torval witnesses something unexpected, his demonic Overseer demands that he take time off to resolve this personal crisis. And so Torval, the demon, finds himself sent on vacation...to Earth, the proving ground of souls!

Demon Ascendant
Torval, Demon Third Class, Layer Four Hundred Twelve of the Eighth Circle of Hell, on *vacation* to Earth has managed to find another demon, has dated an angel and inadvertently explored some of the sins of humankind: greed, gluttony and lust. Through all this his biggest struggle involves deciding if he wants his holiday to end or to continue forever.

To Steve "Million Words" Kay—
for taking talent and molding it into craft.

Thinking Outside the Box

CorpGov Chronicles: Book Two

Thomas Gondolfi

TANSTAAFL  PRESS

TANSTAAFL Press
1201 E. Yelm Ave,
Suite 400-199
Yelm, WA 98697

Visit us at www.TANSTAAFLPress.com

Thinking Outside the Box

First printing TANSTAAFL Press
Copyright © 2014 by Thomas Gondolfi
Cover illustration by Tony Foti

Printed in the United States
ISBN 978-1-938124-20-4

Select a Strong Leader

High velocity splatter covered the opposite wall like red wine sprayed over a bridal gown. Blood soaked into the carpet in a pool and smeared across the plaid couch near the splatter's origin.

As he'd opened the door, Tony Sammis wrinkled his Roman nose at the wet-copper stench. The intense light of a sunny winter's day, rare for Portland, poured through the slits in the blinds. With exaggerated quiet he closed the front door with a conspiratorial glance outside to make sure he'd not been seen hotwiring the lock.

Tony slid his electronic slim-Jim back into his inner jacket pocket as he took in the room. Six pieces of a Crate & Barrel faux-oak coffee table occupied the center of the room. A La-Z-Boy recliner itself reclined on its back, the footrest stretching off at an unnatural angle toward a solido that showed only the "Technical Difficulty" image. Tony ran his olive-complected hand over a dent in the wall the size and shape of a person's back.

While not a criminal detective, Tony had no difficulty finding the weapon that had caused the mess on the wall. A crimson-coated, aluminum bat lay not 2 meters away amidst the shards of a broken, ceramic lamp. Bending over for a closer look, Tony made out at least two impact points on the Louisville Slugger. The blood, flesh, and hair matted on the bludgeon showed blond and redheaded victims. Narissa, like himself, was a brunette. She hadn't gone without a fight.

No one in the Green Action Militia had heard from Narissa in over twenty-four hours. Her net footprint ended at 0736 yesterday. Her implant remotes refused remote activation. The obvious conclusion was that she'd been abducted.

Three other Greenies had gone before her but they'd been swallowed up like they'd never existed. Narissa left them something to go on.

Tony teased one of each hair sample, which still had follicles attached, off the bat. He wrapped them in his clean handkerchief, for want of better storage.

The silence was only broken by the faint sound of a neighboring apartment's toilet flushing. He really didn't expect anyone to still be in the flat, but he wasn't sure.

Tony glided through the kitchen with a grace one wouldn't expect of his big, stocky build. He took care not to disturb the trail of red drops across the white imitation tile nor the rose-colored smudges around the sink. With his ring phone, Tony clicked a quick picture of one very obvious fingerprint in the gore. He noticed a pair of towels with a washed-out pink color. Someone had a hell of a lump.

The desk in the corner looked untouched in spite of the designer purse sitting in plain sight. A pair of LifeStone earrings, worth more than the entire flat, lay in plain sight next to them. No blood trail tracked back into the bedrooms or the bathroom.

Tony stretched his 190 cm, stocky frame up from his crouch, willing his broad shoulders to relax. Anyone who saw Tony gave him wagon room. While he wore no powered, body-modifications, his football player tight-end build gave him a presence in a society that prided itself on anonymity.

Just weeks ago the GAM had won a Pyrrhic victory against the remorseless cabal of megacorps. Many had died on both sides. Now the war was over. The Greenies should be safe. They shouldn't need to hide any longer. They should be able to sit on their laurels and watch things change for the better.

Tony mentally slipped off his rose-colored glasses with a heavy sigh. Every time in his life that he'd relaxed he'd paid a price. One or even two of his people could be written off as coincidence or chance. Not four. The Green Action Militia was being hunted in earnest.

His normally casual smile hardened into a line. "Case Red. Disaster protocols," Tony said to a percomm mailbox that sent out priority signals to every member of the GAM.

* * *

Case: Red
Doctrine of Emergency Dispersal

Case Red is a stringent alert for the Green Action Militia second only to Case Black, the disbanding of the GAM.

The Case Red alert will only be issued in the event that there has been a significant breach in the security of GAM personnel or data networks. The downside of obviously massive communication and capital disruption is balanced by the need to save as many members as possible. Because of identity and location changes, this dispersal will also reduce the number of colleagues that any one captured member may betray.

Orders for Case Red

- Immediately power-down percomm.
  - Percomms to be used only for reporting emergencies when no other options are available.
  - All communications are to be done using prepaid disposable ring, watch or clothing phones.
  - Each prepaid phone to be used only once and then discarded or destroyed.
- Engage in no electronic commerce or banking.
- Immediately travel by foot to backup currency, identity and equipment location.
  - As in previous doctrines, this location must be at least ten kilometers from your current home or place of work.
  - Dispose of all current identifications of current identity.
    - This includes changing the network IDs of all implants.
    - Under no conditions are you to contact any discarded identity while Case Red is in force.

- ¤ **Assume new identity.**
- ¤ **Carry enough cash to function for at least one month.**
- Travel another ten-plus kilometers before taking cash only transit to backup identity location.
- Team meetings will be through net address solido (NAS) only.
  - ¤ **NAS location has been implanted but mentally blocked. It can only be retrieved once Case Red has been declared.**
  - ¤ **Meetings are at intervals of exactly one week after Case Red declaration.**
- Be as paranoid as possible.
- Make significant personal change if possible.
  - ¤ **This could include hair color change, unmonitored genetic therapy, mechanical enhancement or more mundane physical disguises.**
- Change identities if even suspicious that there is surveillance or a hunt for you.
- Only the joint decision of two Action Committee (AC) members may cancel Case Red.
  - ¤ **If only one or zero AC member remains, Case Black is mandated.**

* * *

Augustine Cordoba, also known as gm4_1c3, lay supine in a net cradle of her own design. It was the size and shape of a chaise lounge. She floated 15 centimeters above the receiver unit, suspended by superconductive strands woven into her neon-green jumpsuit. Sixteen neural transmitters, each in a different color of an expanded rainbow, poked out through her cropped, blue-white hair. Most striking were the silver-ceramic cornea replacements that allowed her to view virtual reality as easily as the material world. She looked genetically blind but with the built-in enhancements could see better than any living creature. Her pale skin belied her Hispanic last name. Her mother often joked about a wild Christmas party. Minor crow's feet around Augustine's eyes and the beginnings of liver spots betrayed her age. She would turn seventy-four in August, her namesake.

The severe white room, barely large enough for her servers, had never been traced to her. She'd purchased it through sixteen different cutouts long before joining the Green Action Militia. In fact she'd never even shared the location of this retreat with her fellow Greenies. None of her other net jock acquaintances, including the infamous D0m_N3t, had unraveled the Byzantine labyrinth of her continuously rerouted net signal, even to the correct continent.

While technically on the run under Case Red, she could be safe here for a time. Running and hiding was a game for the young and she knew she could remain hidden only so long. She had a duty to perform before she was caught. She sighed loud enough to be heard above the white noise generated by the fans of her massive racks of computers.

"Welcome to the Catholic Church Penance and Reconciliation Node," came a voice over her cochlear implant. An ornate but realistic crucifix zoomed in from the stained-glass background in virtual reality. "Your confession is protected against quantum code breaking by the one-time pad cipher you provided in person at the church.

"This net node supplies absolution for Roman Catholic, Catholic Reformation, and Catholic Schism sects. Please state your preference."

Augustine swallowed hard. She promised herself this day of reckoning even before she strayed from her religious background. Guilt had built upon guilt over her years as a terrorist. "Catholic Reformation."

"This conversation may be recorded for training and quality control purposes without any loss of the sanctity of the confessional."

The view changed to show her virtual image dressed in her Sunday finest, blue calico dress. Multiple layers of petticoats held out the hem. She could feel the crinoline rubbing against the nylon stockings as she approached the outside of an antique wooden confessional, complete with a second door for the Father Confessor. She swept the penitent's door aside and took her place on the kneeler, appropriately covered in black velvet.

Facing a wicker screen she started in classical style, "Bless me, Father, for I have sinned. It has been twelve years, six months, and twelve days since my last confession."

Augustine watched the node's processing thread switch rapidly from a standard absolution generator to a more stringent one. Wintel's public list of net jocks showed gm4_1c3 rating as thirteenth as of this morning's update. Only a hack with a rating in low double digits would have noted the change. No one under a twenty rating could forgo watching the network calls and underlying code.

All she could think of was that an automation wasn't enough for what she had to unburden.

"Why have you been so long away from our church, daughter Augustine?" the preprogrammed illusion continued.

"I couldn't reconcile my life as a terrorist with my faith in God."

The program shifted its source again. A real human being took over. Augustine smiled grimly.

"So, daughter, what part of being a terrorist brought you into conflict with your faith?" The priest's voice was young with a hint of the sing-song of an Asian birth.

First line support, Augustine thought. Boy, is he in for a shock.

"I would like to confess six murders by my own hand, sixty-three murders by collusion, and eight hundred four deaths by acts of omission. I would like to start with these, Father, and if we can get through them I can discuss lesser acts of violence that left persons maimed, homeless or penniless." She watched the young priest's call for help in the data stream. The I/O focus changed to a new node with another live confessor, presumably one with more experience. She could imagine ninety fledgling priests listening in on this unusual confession as a training exercise.

"Miss, that's a great number of mortal sins," said a new voice in a strong southern United States' accent. The partially-obscured, computer-generated avatar's mouth didn't quite match the living person's words.

"Yes, Father. I understand this. I did it while fighting for our people."

"Who are 'our people'?"

"All of the people disenfranchised by the megacorps. I was a member of the Green Action Militia."

There was a short pause. The process generated a secondary link to a library routine but left the original I/O focus intact. Even this experienced priest needed assistance. "Daughter, our Father and his Son acknowledge no earthly power. Your sins were sins no matter the reasoning behind them. 'The road to hell is paved ... '"

" ... with good intentions. Yes, I do understand this, Father. That is why I removed myself from the church as long as I did. I couldn't reconcile my love for our Father with the sins I committed."

"And you couldn't remove yourself from this temptation?"

"No, Father. It was a needful thing. I couldn't turn my back on the suffering of my fellow man so I forced myself to turn my back, temporarily, on the church and God's love."

A long pause as the library routine scoured a database with a very strong access code that she broke without exerting but a sliver of her talents. "So you regret your actions?"

"Am I sad? Yes. Do I feel the guilt of the mortal lives I took burdening my soul? Yes. That being said, I did what was needed. I don't feel the world is a worse place for those deaths."

"And who are you to judge others? Why do you think you can usurp the prerogatives of God?"

"I am only who I am. I can only make decisions that I see need to be made. If I do anything else I am nothing but a sheep."

Augustine watched an instant message token spawn to a far off IP that she followed through Calgary, Switzerland, and the Bahamas. She dropped her surveillance process as it didn't matter whom the Father needed to talk to.

"Daughter, the first act of the confessional is contrition. You must truly be sorry for your acts. You must be sorry enough not to repeat them. From what I hear in your words you may be sorry but you haven't convinced yourself they were wrong."

"I disagree, Father. I do know that they were wrong. I feel the burden of the sin upon me."

"But you'd do it again?"

"Yes, Father, given the same circumstances I would do it again."

"Then you cannot be absolved and your soul must remain in jeopardy, my daughter."

"Even though the likelihood of reoccurrence is nonexistent?" Augustine rebutted.

"Even so. It is what you will do with your soul and your life that matters."

Through the network she could actually feel the gritty velvet pressed through her stockings into her knees just below where the petticoats held her dress out. The distraction focused her thinking. She could feel her guilt pressing in on her. "I think I understand now,

Father. 'Go forth and sin no more.'"

"Good. You have fulfilled the first two portions of your confession. The third I feel won't be as simple. Your sins are heavy and require more than a few Hail Marys and a handful of Our Fathers."

"I stand as a good daughter of the church, Father. What would you have me do?"

*   *   *

Seventeen people gathered around a scratched mahogany table in a room already infamous to anyone with obscene amounts of money. The room still bore the scars of The People's wrath, as administered by the Green Action Militia. Smoke smudged the walls near a ceiling still riddled with bullet holes. A telltale pink stained the grout between the Venetian marble slabs. The stained glass windows, across one wall of the room, depicted the purchase of Manhattan from Native Americans. Somehow it had evaded the maelstrom of the Green Action Militia coup.

The least of the occupants in this room measured their wealth in trillions of dollars. Despite this they weren't the richest human beings, but close. To be chosen to this elite council required as a prime requisite a demonstrable ability to run a major corporation. An isolated computer system had selected fifteen of the seventeen. The two exceptions survived the overthrow of the previous junta and were now charged to carry The People's message forward.

"I think we all know each other, at least by reputation," said the tall, gaunt Wintel. "And I gather we will all get to know each other a great deal more over the next few years. I suggest we dispense with introductions and move to the first order of business. I believe we need to elect a chairman."

"I'm not familiar with this process," claimed the majority owner of MinInc, the sole mining company on the red planet. The slight man fiddled with one of the controls of a handcrafted, Martian day-suit.

"I suggest we have a general ballot and unless there is a clear victor then we race off the two with the highest totals. Are there any objections?"

"I object," came a mellow, but not loud voice. It contained no rancor.

"Yes, please. Your objection?"

"Before we vote on a chairperson, shouldn't we know what the duties of the chairperson are?" Nanogate asked. At 172 cm and 82 kilos he wasn't an impressive physical specimen in a room of physically unimpressive people. His tailored suit of hand-woven wool cost more than the average annual salary of his employees.

Nods went around the table.

"We haven't fully defined the function yet, but let's agree to some preliminary rules to build upon," Wintel suggested.

"For now shall we say that the chairperson calls our group to order and conducts these proceedings," offered the female CEO of BeringC Protein.

"I suggest he doesn't have a vote in the council but he can veto any action agreed to by the council," MinInc said. General agreement followed.

"And the council can overrule the veto by a three-to-one margin," Wintel interjected, his angular features looking like a bird of prey.

"Of course."

"I suggest one more thing," Unified Textiles, the only other survivor of the Greenie attack, said. "The chairperson may introduce a motion. It has priority and doesn't require a second, but if defeated by even a simple majority he must step down as chairperson and cannot be reelected to that position."

"Do I hear objections to these powers?" No one spoke. "Then let us cast our first ballot."

The council silently cast their ballots over the room's network. The electronic voice of the computer spoke next.

"Sixteen ballots cast for Nanogate. One vote for Wintel."

Nanogate, the other surviving member of the previous stratocracy, nodded to the rest of the members. "I am going to put my rule to the test immediately. I insist that all of our meetings be held in this room. I want a mural on that wall depicting the Auschwitz concentration camp. Emotionally, this was the biggest failing of any government in modern history.

"In addition I move that the rest of this room remain intact, down to the stains of our eight fallen comrades.

"With these two reminders let us never forget that governments can and do hurt the people they protect and that the people they injure can retaliate."

*   *   *

The lighting in Boxed Storage Depot #6 of the Portland Corrections Facility was so dim a cat would have difficulty navigating through it. Yet the ordered movement of the simple 40 cm cubed metal shells, each corner rounded, indicated that the darkness didn't trouble them. The boxed stacked themselves sixty tiers high, stretching for over a kilometer in either direction. It looked like a warehouse of shiny antique toasters. The depot's inert atmosphere of nitrogen reduced deterioration of any of the boxed mechanical components. This didn't help the poor human brain sealed within.

A silver boxed unit with A1412 etched across its side, rolled in and slipped into one of the few vacant locations in the immense grid of similar "toasters." His box needed time in the charging racks.

The deep-space-like silence of the great room shattered with the squeal of amplified feedback.

"Who be that?" J112, the boxed unit next to A1412, asked.

"I think it was Charlie Durmot," A1412 said in as close to a sad tone as his onboard electronic speakers could produce.

"Charlie's been acting a bit squirrelly lately. Remember last week when he washed G42's shell instead of the windows?"

"How did he end it?" G996 asked.

"I saw him in the tool crib with a pneumatic drill," A1412 replied.

"How long he been boxed?"

"Seventy-five years," G996 whispered.

"Shit. No wonder. There be times I think I be losing it and I be only boxed twenty-three years."

"Last week, Charlie told me that he remembered his boxing day clear as anything but he forgot his own name," G996 said. "I reminded him but I guess it wasn't enough."

"I am Stephanie Delfalkis," G996 intoned as if she hadn't ever heard her own name.

"I'm Henry Royston," A1412 copied.

"I be Ben Calwood," J112 said emphatically. "I'll be using the hydraulic press when I forget who I be. Less chance of stay'n alive with half an even more ruined brain," J112 said.

"I'm leaning toward liquid nitrogen," G996 said.

"Too slow. I don't want to change my mind halfway through."

"That's the problem, Henry, by that time you ain't got no mind to change."

"I am Henry Royston."
"I am Stephanie Delfalkis."
"I be Ben Calwood."

*   *   *

A Norse god, seemingly carved out of onyx, strode into the lift-bus wearing a dapple gray kilt and deep black jersey. Phillip, never Phil, Christine found out last night, ignored the stares of outright lust he elicited from the women. The handsome man took a news chip and broke the seal next to his neural implant.

Christine watched as his arrogance only drew more desire from those who enjoyed the male form. She enjoyed the show, from the men who turned away to shun the newcomer and the pheromone chorus from the women. But most important, he didn't notice her, even though she'd been in his bed just last night.

Last night she'd been elegant, sophisticated and elusive—a neon light against the other cheap and tawdry women. Her chestnut brown hair had been woven up in a spiral on her head and she'd worn a gold-latticed Jérémy Amelin gown that cost more than the bus they rode in.

Today, at 45 kilos in oversized, paint-stained sweats and with her dirty-brown hair mostly held up in bun by a pen, Christine faded into the background. The only thing that made her stand out was the lust in her brown eyes.

Her eyes surreptitiously darted over his muscular neck, the area of his biceps trapped against his body, and his broad, sensuous wrists. She licked her dry lips as she caressed the surgical-steel blade in her jacket.

"Schofield Building, level forty-six approaching. Rooftop Gym, Paris Restaurant, Schofield Market," announced the TriMet lift-bus in its ever-so-pleasant tones.

Phillip bent down to adjust his calf-hugging boots. The sight drew at least one muffled exclamation. Stretching tall he walked out the door as soon as it opened.

Keeping her eyes down as the drab wallflower, Christine paralleled his course toward the gym. Her face flushed as she caressed the scalpel. "Soon," she whispered and consciously slowed her breathing. She wanted him. She needed him. Heat raced along her thighs up into where his seed still lingered inside her.

She altered her speed and angle slightly. She would have him just as he entered the building. Her nervous fingers twitched, causing the blade to gently and accurately peel one fiber at a time from the inner lining of her warm-up. Just ten more steps. A moist trace ran down her inner thigh. She held her breath, as every nerve ending focused on the body heat building up unbearably in the steel of her blade.

The passion in her loins turned to ice as a mental alarm sounded at a screeching level that would deafen a rock. Every hair on her body suddenly stood up in fear.

Phillip, safe and alive, walked on, never knowing that the very breath of Death had warmed his neck.

Her own hunt forgotten, her lust fizzled. She felt someone stalking her, and she wondered what had triggered her certainty that she was now the quarry. Had it been a glance lingering on her too long? Perhaps an abnormal change in a person's path alerted her. The subconscious nature of the alarm made it all the more demanding of her attention.

Christine went through the revolving door of the gym but instead of entering the building she let the door carry her around back outside. No one singled themselves out as an obvious hunter. She walked calmly to another lift-bus stop, her head still held low. As she waited she pulled out a compact and made to straighten her makeup, although she wore none. The mirror gave her the opportunity to view many angles around her position.

"Lift-bus fourteen approaching. Please stand back." The eyes beneath the bushy Mediterranean eyebrows of a hard-bodied man in shorts and a wife-beater glanced at her just long enough for her to pick him out. She wasn't jumping at shadows. There was at least one.

Christine timed her mock suicide perfectly. Three bystanders shrieked as she stepped off the edge so close to the arriving lift-bus that the gravitic charge partially melted the pen into her hair. She calmly removed her jacket as she fell, letting it fly away by itself. After counting out four more seconds she deployed a tiny parasail. She wasted no time, directing her flight back toward the building she'd just jumped from. With an expert's hand she took the thermal the Schofield building provided and banked tightly under the landing zone's overhang. Flying so close to the windows, people gawked out of offices and board rooms as she whipped past.

On the other side of the building she yawed across the open space between buildings, spilling air as rapidly as she dared. Spotting a likely target, Christine dove into the open shell of an office undergoing tenant improvements. The scalpel, just seconds earlier intended for a more gruesome task, slashed her harness before she fully entered the windowless area. Her momentum propelled her through the debris of construction, battering her severely until she ended up in a ball against the stairwell door.

Without a word she stood up and dusted the old-fashioned drywall powder off her clothing. She assessed her injuries dispassionately as nothing serious enough to hinder further movements. She'd feel it tomorrow, but today she could still move. She walked right out the emergency exit, only now using her percomm to report the incident.

With only sixteen floors between her and ground level, in a different building with multiple choices of egress, her hunters had exactly zero chance of catching her. Instead of elation at her successful escape she instead felt only a minor resentment at her own failed stalk. Her bottled-up sexual tension itched in a way only a kill would scratch. A deep breath later she assured herself that there would be other kills— many others.

* * *

Tony sat in the back of a liftousine in a suit he'd bought off the rack at WalMaCo. As usual the sleeves were too short for his long arms. His female companion, rented, could have starred on any number of solidos. With what she charged, Tony would bet she made a better living as arm candy than most successful starlets. The blond, wearing a silver bodysuit so tight that it left no question whether she shaved her pubic area, leaned into him and purred. Tony cared about her advances as much as she did in making them. She was camouflage, not a sex partner.

"Seventeen fourteen Columbus Drive North, level ninety-four," he told the driver.

"Yes, sir. Twelve minutes, sir. But I can take longer if you'd like."

Tony smiled at the woman in the chauffer's mirror. "No, thank you. There will be time for that later." Tony turned and gave his companion a deep kiss.

The liftousine rose up off the landing pad and oriented north, sliding past the historical multistory Skydeck building of Chicago. Trying not to itch where his partner pressed the chaffing fabric of his suit into his skin, Tony thought about the last few weeks.

Eleven days ago, after his discovery at Narissa's, Tony had travelled across the Midwest by hitching rides on nultrucks using only his middle name, Eugene. His size helped him as the drivers expected help loading and unloading.

Four different drivers and forty-eight hours took him to Indianapolis, a town that he'd never visited. It seemed like a perfect place to stop for a time and perhaps even set up his next identity.

His first stop got him Astropreen insulated underclothing so the sub-zero temperatures of the unusual cold of this year's Midwest winter didn't freeze him. To establish himself further he rented the cheapest of tube hotels. He paid in cash and only a week at a time despite the fact that he could have purchased the entire hotel several times over with just the cash he had in his bedroll. He ate at ground level food vendors, their great stew pots steaming in the freezing air. He wandered around through the broken snow learning his way around.

On the eight day he felt a creeping dread—an itch at the base of his neck he couldn't scratch. A bull dyke, with metallic leg replacements that were shaped like those from a thoroughbred horse, lounged in a doorway across from his hotel. Her natural arms seemed powerful enough to rip many centimeters of filmies. She tried hard to concentrate on her news feed rather than on him. Then he'd caught glimpses of three other people a bit too mercenary to be just lounging around this particular slum.

Tony didn't even approach the hotel but rather ploughed through the slush on the street as he changed to the other side. Taking a chance, he winked at the powerful woman as he walked past. She growled and went back to her news.

Something had tipped them off to the hotel, not him personally.

As he walked further down the street he abandoned his clothes, his bedroll and over a quarter of a million credits.

That surveillance he witnessed had prompted a change in his *modus operandi*. Instead of travelling and living like a welf, he was now on his way to purchase a penthouse home for cash. Marcus Andropov, playboy and adventurer, was his newest identity. His impeccable credentials as well as many stacks of thousand dollar bills were in a briefcase at his feet.

A middle-aged woman, whose overly white complexion suggested too many genetic cosmetic therapies, waited patiently at the edge of the landing pad. As a realtor, she carried the requisite sixteen folders of flimsies held close to the chest of her smart skirt-suit.

The driver landed them skillfully enough that Tony didn't realized they'd grounded. As the driver walked around and opened the door, the realtor pranced up in heels much too high for her age. He guessed her age at eighty—trying to keep her looks close to thirty and failing.

The art-deco styling of the Whitehaven Mansions appealed to Tony's sense of style. The wraparound windows, lending each unit a view of the entrance platform, appealed to his sense of security.

"Welcome, Mr. Andropov ... glad you could come ... I have a very exciting property to show you ... who is your lovely companion." The greeting came out all as one sentence without even a breath. The overblown introduction set Tony to wondering how much her commission on the property would be.

"Thees ees Margareet," Tony aka Andropov waved dismissively.

His escort had very definitive instructions to remain silent. She gave a tiny curtsey which looked out of place considering what she wore. She did offer her hand.

"The pleasure is all mine, Margareet," the realtor said effusively.

"Please to show me property."

"Absolutely." The realtor fell in between Tony and his companion. "The entrance platform is maintained at a steady twenty-two degrees no matter the weather. The property we are seeing is a lifetime lease. The building was designed by Claude R. Bistolme! *Skylife* featured it last year in its Best Places to Live section. It has five bedrooms, four baths and comes with its own garden. It can be leased as you see it, with all furnishings and decorating ... "

Tony mentally ignored the patter. Tony could tell the pitch came from someone with a great deal of experience as it was all directed at him, rather than the girlfriend.

A doorman, in the bright blue uniform of Whitehaven Mansions, opened the brass wrapped door for them to enter the building. "... which comes with not only a gourmet chef but also a concierge for ..."

Tony had changed in the months since he'd been a member of the megacorp machine. Now he focused on the safety aspect, rather than the opulence that once would have had him lusting. Tony's ignored his hostess and instead collected survival information. He noted the fire stairs, something so many people forgot about in this age of dynamic fire suppression systems. He noticed two different housekeeping lifts as his guide took him to the lavish direct lift bank for the residences.

An elevator operator, his uniform sporting epaulets and shining buttons, opened the door and ushered them inside.

"Ninety-three sixteen, please," the real estate agent said. The operator closed the outer doors and then the inner ones before turning his lever to take them higher in the building.

"The Whitehaven Mansions has an interior decorator and three ... "

Tony focused on the tiny escape diagram of the building posted in the lift. It indicated three more fire escapes, one being a drop-chute. He also observed the operations of the manual elevator, just in case.

The doors opened onto a two-story room, dominated by massive windows across the opposite side. The simple, yet elegant, furnishings were dwarfed by the vista of a frozen Lake Michigan stretching out to infinity. Its ice buckled into an uneven tundra.

Tony set his briefcase down on the butcher-block wooden countertop and walked to the window.

"I did tell you how fabulous the view is. Whitehaven Mansions have purchased the view rights for the next hundred years with an automatically renewing option every hundred years after that."

Tony tried not to react as seven small nultrucks landed in sequence on the Whitehaven Mansions' platform. Men in black combat gear poured out of the back of each.

"Would you be excusing? Where would be having the room of baths?"

"Oh, there are three bathrooms. There is one down that hall off the kitchen ... "

Tony walked sedately until he reached the kitchen. A discrete universal symbol for the drop chute showed its concealed panel. He yanked it open and jumped inside the gelatin escape capsule.

The automated system slammed the door shut, sealing him in a cellophane envelope filled with a sticky clear gel. The capsule accelerated toward the ground at five g's down the heavily insulated tube. Tony momentarily blacked out. Above him every alarm had to be sounding but he didn't care. His companion would be paid by escrow. The realtor would be cheated of a commission but no other harm done. Only the hunters would be denied their prize. Tony hadn't even counted one before the deceleration hit him. The escape capsule stopped with a bump. The automated sequence ejected Tony onto a soft mat before dissolving the capsule to prepare for another escapee.

Tony landed flat and hard on those mats used for teenage gymnastics. While they were softer than a tile floor, he could already feel the bruise forming on his hip. Getting up, he dashed across the large survival room to the exit. Down two flights of fire stairs and across a commercial walkway between buildings and he might as well be on another planet as far as the hunters were concerned.

All the while he wondered when he would be safe enough to protect his people.

Define Problem Statement

"I, Augustine, pledge obedience to my prioress and through her to my Lord God, his son, Jesus Christ, and that of the Holy Spirit without coercion or reservation." She knelt in her bright blue novitiate robes before the realistic and solidographic image of the crucifixion. The white hair on her head and the liver spots on the back of her hands made her look more like a doddering grandmother than a dewy fresh novitiate to the Catholic Reformation.

Unlike most Catholic churches, this one displayed no gilt of any kind. Her kneeler lay in a very large room with other simple cushions and hundreds of hardwire computer ports in the floors and the walls for direct link. Overhead, even more hardwire ports dangled from the ceiling. The Isidorean Order, created by papal command to be the guardians of church information and finance, had no need for ostentation. Function was everything.

"I take the name Sister Augustine."

As a devout Catholic, Augustine had often felt the pull of service. A part of her longed for this closer tie to God, especially after the mass of sins she had accumulated during the war against the Cabal. As a key member of the Green Action Militia, she had believed her work reached a higher calling than just the liberation of man but her Father Confessor had disabused her of this notion. Odd how her penance could possibly save not only her soul but her life.

Augustine knew that life on the run wasn't possible. At her age, resilience to physical activity wasn't what it had been when she started with the GAM. A part of her cursed herself for deceiving these good people, but fortunately entering the novitiate wasn't a lifelong commitment. The novitiate was a trial period for both sides to understand if this was what they wanted.

In spite of the flush of new guilt in her reasons for joining, she thanked God in his wisdom of his choice in saving her. Here in the

Isidorean Order she was one among many. Each brother or sister's tonsure held a minimum of four network jacks and the least of them qualified as experts in ice breaking and creation. The Brotherhood claimed no fewer than twenty of the top one hundred net jocks on *Tom's Hardware Page*.

This, the main Isidorean headquarters, proved to be almost ideal for anyone hiding from her past. Physically the campus, outside Calgary, stretched ten kilometers in any direction. Any stranger would be politely but firmly questioned dozens of times before getting anywhere near the main dormitory or the temple. The temple itself housed the largest single mainframe computer in the world, both in computational speed and storage capacity. It remained that way by a rigorous schedule of upgrades. Thus it also housed some of the most elaborate security and network ice known in the world. Thus, no one could approach, physically or electronically, without her at least having hours, if not days to prepare.

"Welcome to the Order of Isidore, Sister Augustine." The middle-aged woman in the simple brown habit of the order smiled down at her new charge.

"Thank you, Prioress."

"We don't stand on that level of formality here on anything less than affairs of state or disciplinary matters, Sister Augustine. Our Lord doesn't play favorites nor carry a scorecard. I'm Sister Hanna."

"Thank you, Sister Hanna."

"Oh, get up, Sister Augustine. You're twice my age and even my knees ache on cold mornings like this. That's better. Now I need to talk to you a little more about your skills and desires for placement."

"You might know me better by my net avatar—Grandma Ice. I have something of a reputation," Augustine said, blushing.

*   *   *

The rough beginnings of the new mural with the slogan *Arbeit macht frei* stretched above Nanogate's head as he started the meeting. The renowned emotional artist Vitória Ribeiro Santos had completed nothing more than some of the ink outlines but they already exuded the foulness the scene depicted.

"Thank you for coming. I believe our first meeting started some excellent work. Let's hear from Z-G-Ag on the status of the economy."

A tall, gaunt man, his skin the color of coffee, stood up. "As I'm sure you are all quite aware, the market is stabilizing after the coup. Of particular note is the surge in the price of Nanogate after the damage it took as a result of the Greenies acts of ... "

"Excuse me," United Textiles interjected. "I believe as they are our benefactors in this matter that we should refer to them by the name Green Action Militia instead of the slur 'Greenies.'"

"My pardon. I meant no disrespect to the Green Action Militia or any group. To continue: Of particular note is the surge in the price of Nanogate stocks especially after the damage caused by the Green Action Militia. Our econ departments have analyzed this and it seems to indicate a general optimism from the people at large. We are seeing the benefits across the board in purchasing and stock price stabilization. I believe a push in propaganda on the benevolence of our organization would improve this even more."

"Do I hear any objection?" Nanogate asked. "Carried," he said when no one spoke up.

"I did have one question," said Z-G-Ag. "What are we to call ourselves in the media?"

"Per my marketing experts I am believing the word on the street is 'CorpGov,'" offered the youngest member at the table, Royal PetroChem. In spite of his inability to conquer the sing-song accent of his native India, the man's words were always well thought out. People listened.

"I suggest we go with that, then," Nanogate offered. "The cost of changing the masses minds is significant, as you all know. Barring an objection, I christen us the CorpGov Council."

"I'll run with that," Z-G-Ag offered.

"Excellent. Are there any other high level economic matters that should interest this group?"

"Not at this time, but we should talk about fiscal policy in general sometime in the future, such as unified currency, interest rates, and cash supplies."

"That does bring up a good point," the tiny Nippon of the Global Vehicle Federation (GVF) said in clipped, precise English. "How do we stand with regards to national rights? Do we supersede them?"

"An excellent point," Nanogate said looking to the member of their group with the most legal experience.

"I don't think there is any question that our authority must be in primacy," the head partner of Savitz, Schauer and Levinthal said with confidence. "Anything else would invite chaos. The key will be to define it properly so that all sides know their rights and responsibilities. As this is directly in my firm's line of expertise, I could offer a preliminary report-out during our next meeting."

Nanogate looked around at the nodding heads before speaking. "That would be an excellent idea. Thank you. Now let's hear from Rio Oro on the state of security."

A swarthy man with a wide chest and bulging muscles, but graying hair, stood from his chair. "I have two sections to my report. Let's first cover all external matters. There are three full-blown wars going on at this moment—Peru vs the South American Combine; the civil war of South Africa entering its seventh decade; and the Sino-Anglo engagement in Syria. Of these three I believe that we must interfere with the Syrian matter. It threatens to spill out to a much larger conflict and threaten system level stability. Of the other two, South Africa can never be at anything but war and Peru will eventually teach the Combine not to mess in their affairs.

"I ask for a confirmation."

The CorpGov computer tallied sixteen affirmative votes and one dissention.

"Excellent. There are ten known clandestine, guerilla-level wars going on. I see no need to interfere with any of these actions. These conflicts rarely get out of hand and allow a market for military hardware and testing of prototype weapons. I will provide a report for each of you to peruse."

"Thank you for that, Rio Oro," Nanogate said.

"That was just the first part of my report."

"My apologies. Pray continue."

"I've been asked to report on our own personal and familial security due to the threats, or should I say promises, leveled at us from the GAM. First the bad news. I'm not pleased to say that all of us are relatively soft targets. Our analysis shows our lives could be bought at the cost of 2.4 lives per target, in spite of our safety measures."

Each member looked up with concern etched in their faces.

"Then why would it be that we are being spending mega dollars on security?" Royal PetroChem asked.

"It is a bit more complex than my initial statement indicated. Our security is very effective on the large scale level—say of a government trying to wage war on us. It also deals fairly well with a lone crazed assassin. However, in the action that created this council, the GAM hit on the seam between the two. A small, dedicated strike force could penetrate our security with the costs I previously mentioned. Obviously, it must be a force willing to die for their beliefs.

"Furthermore the safety of our families is at best a joke. If the GAM or any other force wanted them eliminated the only thing we can do is sing hosannas at our loved one's funerals."

There were only a few reactions at the table. They had each lived with the threats to their family every day for most of their adult lives. Every year their security forces stopped three or more determined assassins.

"Now for even worse news. There isn't a solution that won't put us all in an isolated bubble from where we can't be effective at governing, either the system or our own corporations. Worse, such isolation can be, over the long run, even a larger security hole than what we have now.

"In short, we are truly at the mercy of any moderately sized group devoted to our personal destruction."

*   *   *

"HOLY MOTHER OF—" Tony screamed out, putting his hand to the ear that felt removed. His hand came away bloody. A rat the size of a bowling ball inched its red muzzle forward over a mound of molding potato peels. No one remembered when rats started swarming like piranha, but rarely did they leave much more than those extinct fish had.

Tony's breath clearly showed itself in the cold afternoon air. It couldn't be more than about 5 degrees, he lamented. Fatigue still clouded his mind. Each action seemed to take all of his concentrated effort. Tony's hand went back to his ear for a closer investigation. The blood of the tiny wound only oozed. His mind flashed on the possibility of rabies or other viruses, but he couldn't hold the thought. After a week's trudging continuously at ground level, buoyed only by stimulants, he needed at least another twenty-four hours of sleep.

Tony hauled himself from beneath the warmth of the trash,

warily eyeing the rat and its friends. The rats could only watch as their meal stood up and climbed out of the dumpster.

He picked at the rubbish clinging to the disreputable clothing he'd stolen from a Laundromat after his last escape. Not five steps away from his impromptu hiding place, a downspout dumped out runoff water the last 2 meters of the building's height. Stepping close, he sputtered and shivered as he sluiced off the worst of his filth in the bitter cold liquid. It woke him up perhaps even better than several cups of java.

Pulling out one of the dozen or more ring phones he carried, he noticed quickly that his nap had lasted all of an hour. Thomas Edison performed more than one miracle of engineering on less rest, but Tony didn't have the man's stamina. Sleep still had to take priority. He knew himself well enough to know that the icy splash wouldn't keep him awake long. Tony queried the location of the nearest transit station on the disposable phone. He memorized the directions just before crushing the ring with a discarded piece of cinderblock.

Tony looked back one last time. The dumpster now rocked frantically as the blanket of rats cleaned it of anything even partially edible.

Thirty-six floors later, he reached the main TriMet bus terminal of Columbus, Ohio. One thing about being a terrorist, you got an aerobic workout every day.

With cash, he purchased a utilitarian, unisex jumpsuit from the ubiquitous WalMaCo vending machine available in any bus station or spaceport. Seven minutes in the public restroom and a large deposit of his old clothes to its trash receptacle later, he exited a respectable laborer. He caught the first bus anywhere and got out as soon as he spotted a convenience store. Once again with cash, he purchased four items: a stim pack, a gaudy pink scarf, purple lipstick and a lighted, red purse. The clerk didn't give him a second look. Tony glanced back to be sure.

He emptied all four stim pads from the pack, affixing one on the inside of each wrist and the others under each armpit. In spite of the tiny jolt they gave him, you couldn't wet an ocean. He imagined his blood's stimulant levels would cause any medibot to order a complete transfusion.

Instead of worrying, Tony liberally applied the purple makeup on his lips and as a blush to his cheeks. He tied the scarf around the white jumper like a belt and cradled the purse in the crook of his left arm. He now appeared the fashionable ambi.

Disguise nearly complete, Tony made another bus hop, this time to a middle-class, enclosed mall that advertised itself as Northern Lights Shopping Center. He strolled until he spied the Quicki vending machine in a busy main concourse. He reached it just in time to see a beat cop, one of the least unpalatable Metros, ambling in his direction. Tony carefully choreographed his purchase.

"Thank you for purchasing Paramedic Quicki Drying Skin Patch—for when regen isn't available," hawked the machine just as the Metro walked by. Tony took the bottle from the dispensing slot, turning his head away from the Metro's track as he did so. He blew the accumulated dust off of the tiny bottle. "Along with the clear you just purchased, Quicki Skin Patch comes in seventeen exciting colors." Slipping the liquid bandage into his pocket, Tony turned the rest of his body around and merged with the traffic behind the Metro but heading in the opposite direction.

It was so simple to deny any sight of his face without looking like he was hiding. Free of the immediate danger, Tony's tired mind wandered as he moved with the flow of afternoon shoppers. His abused conscious caught snippets of conversations around him.

"Jean, I need to get some new green tights for the Westin's party."

"He didn't even apologize to Suzy for being farking late!"

"How about a nice cappuccino?"

"Shut up, Alexandra, you can't have a dipsi. We are here to get you shoes for church camp."

"I felt her up her through her blouse and she snapped legal on me. And this after she did the dirty with Bodrick last week."

How many of these superficial people knew that only a few weeks earlier, men and women had given their lives to offer some improvement in their lives. He frowned. Not nearly enough. Some part of him wondered if many of them would ever know of those sacrifices. And yet another part wondered if they would care.

Sixty meters farther down, Tony ducked out of the crowd and into a liquor store. As he feigned interest in various types and brands of vodka, he used the plentiful mirrors to check to make sure he hadn't been followed. He successfully wasted half an hour before purchasing a fifth of Smirnoff's.

Back out into the mall crowds he found a seat next to some filtration bushes. He used the waving leaves of the gengineered foliage to hide his actions. Tony wracked his brain to remember the instructions he'd received scant weeks ago. They came from a time before Tony had asked the instructor to wire a bomb to his chest to become a martyr.

Tearing the stimulant patch off his wrist, Tony brushed the liquid bandage in its place, covering the entire width of his arm 8 centimeters across. It matted down the black curly hairs on the inside of his arm. Quickly he unscrewed the cap of the liquor and sprinkled it across the newly painted surface. He could hear Linc's faintly British accent, "The vodka slows the surface drying process of the bandage. Don't fark around. You only buy about a minute or so."

Tony maneuvered back into the flow of pedestrians where he quickly located a likely target. Without any difficulty he bumped his still damp inner arm against the skin of a middle-aged businessman. The slightly sticky surface lifted the victim's epithelial skin cells without anyone the wiser.

Tony worked his way through the throngs of shoppers of the multilevel mall. He took the time to glance in the windows of passing shops for any untoward interest in him. Twice he doubled back on his track. Finally he sat in an open-air bistro and sipped *café*, watching the traffic for anyone he'd seen before.

The bandage on his wrist irritated, but he stopped just short of rubbing it. Almost wiping away his new identity highlighted the fuzz over his brain. Only after ten minutes more of casual observation did he walk directly across the way and into the lobby of a semi-respectable Howard Johnson's.

"Can I help you this afternoon?" offered the false smile of a young man barely old enough to vote.

"Yes, I'd like a double room for the night." Tony could stand the claustrophobic closeness of a single tube but given the opportunity he preferred more air to breathe.

"A room or a tube, sir?"

"A room. Are you deaf?" Tony said shrilly, his fatigue getting the better of him. He had already failed to be unobtrusive so he quickly tried to cover himself. "My friend and I want to have enough room to—"

"That's quite fine, sir. Can I get an ident, please?" Tony offered him his now dry wrist. The scanner picked up the skin cells his victim supplied. While the quantity wasn't large, there were no other DNA samples in the scan region so the stupid little machine fell for the ruse.

"Mr. Jenson, glad to have you back. We have a double for seventy-nine credits."

"That will be fine," Tony said, handing actual plastic dollars to the bare-faced teen clerk not yet old enough for his first facial depilatories. Tony held Mr. Jenson's identity in trust. He only wanted to borrow it for one night and had no need of the man's credit, especially as a victim without something stolen was 100 percent less likely to report the theft.

"Very good, sir. You are in room eighteen-sixty. That's just down the left hall, eighteenth floor up and almost all the way to the back."

Tony barely offered a parting "Goodbye," before trekking directly to his room. Howard Johnson's at least seemed hygienic about their access, even if strains of indistinguishable music poured over him like thin honey in the elevator. What day was it, anyway? Friday?

As he locked himself into the nondescript room he granted himself the decadence of allowing relaxation to soak into his muscles. He collapsed on the bed. Just to rest, he thought. He fell asleep before even taking off his shoes.

*   *   *

"I don't give one fig what you'd like to do, Sergeant." Like every police lieutenant for the last millennium or so, the swarthy Reza Narendra sat in his transparent booth looking out at the bustle of the officer's room. You could more easily tell someone's rank by their desk's proximity to this enclosure than by any rank insignia they wore. He pulled his uniform down over his ample middle before speaking. "I have the Assistant Commissioner breathing down my neck on this one."

Sergeants, usually known for tenacity, found recruiting poster material in Sergeant Tolbert. "Sir, they are all most definitely out of our jurisdiction. In two weeks of work we've only managed to nab four of them here on the Pacific Coast and have gotten lines on two others. One went to Ottawa, and the other through the visiting center on the Kauai Isolation Center before disappearing entirely.

"Bottom line, sir, I don't see the profit in this. We are behind two weeks in collections and three in audits."

Reza fumed. He tried to take his mind off it by finding fault in his sergeant's attire. The man's salt and pepper hair stood straight up on his head in a classic flat-top well short of the departmental maximum. His historic brass buttons and insignia shined like gold. The uniform was so clean Reza wondered if the sergeant paid the lint and dirt to stay away or only threatened them with his service revolver. Even the creases in his trousers were so sharp one could use them to carve a turkey. Reza took a deep breath and counted to ten, in Hindi, Urdu and Farsi.

"I'll explain it to you, Sergeant," he said slowly and calmly but with bite in each word. "I'll also use small words so that you won't miss any of them. The Greenies have broken the law. I know that doesn't carry much weight in these days of making a buck, but more importantly, in doing so they made us look bad. They kept us from our trust to the most powerful men and women in the system. Now with many of those movers and shakers dead, the Commissioner wants to be able to hand those that replaced them the heads of the conspirators so we don't look completely incompetent. We actually have to earn our princely salaries for a change." Reza watched the sergeant's dark, bushy eyebrows go up. The man's exasperation screamed out of his face, even around the scarring under his left eye.

"I understand that, sir, but what do you wish us to do? I'm certain that either Ottawa or the Independent State of Hawaii would throw six kinds of hissy fits if we started mucking around in their turf."

"Have you considered asking for interdepartmental cooperation?"

"I did that. The Hawaiian Metros have already told us to 'Eat shit, haoles.' That's a direct quote, sir. The Canuks did just what we would do. They stuck out their palm and asked for cash up front."

"Do we have any cash left in the budget?"

"Not that much, sir. Even if we did, we'd have to pay it to every different jurisdiction across how many continents? No one has that kind of resources."

"What about Interpol?"

"That joke? Sir, you can't be serious. While they are notoriously honest, they couldn't find their asses with both hands, a mirror and satellite reconnaissance." Reza's face went a mottled umber.

"Sergeant, I'm tired of excuses. I want results," Reza yelled loud enough that the work around the outside of the room stopped briefly. Sergeant Tolbert's expression got basic training blank. He stood from his stool directly into attention. He snapped a parade ground salute.

"Sir, yes, sir. Is there anything else I can do, SIR?" Everything the sergeant did and said was completely by the book and yet at the same time so obviously carried disdain in its perfection. Reza, still furious, didn't trust himself to speak. He waved the man out of his office. Like on a parade ground, the sergeant pivoted and marched out of the room, reclosing the door behind him just slow enough for Reza to pick up the sniggers from others outside the office.

*   *   *

Augustine's avatar, an animated grandmother from any ancient television show, actually matched her own mental image of herself. Accidentally burning cookies or spoiling a youngster seemed the only offensive actions she looked like she could take. She sat with the members of the Green Action Militia as massed network data washed around them like a swollen river diverted by a great boulder.

Augustine knew all of these information eddies. Semi-competent people left exploitations that she could and did use. In this case the information flow parted because the local FedEx Office tap created a three-clock delay in the stream.

"Roll call shows only two people missing," Augustine stated flatly to some rather bizarre characters including a flaming demon; a zebra-striped unicorn; two phoenix, one male and the other female; a bluish-black kanji character that roughly translated to "bitch"; an ancient Lamborghini; and a two-dimensional, black and white Betty Boop.

"Tony and Kendra have not logged on. While we are still coming to order, please memorize the next link time and your personal log code. They are being wormed directly to each of you as an encrypted file."

"Tony coming online," came an obviously artificial voice. Augustine sighed with relief. She'd led the Greenies once before, but only briefly and without much joy. She knew better than to think she had the drive or the imagination to lead, especially given her current situation.

"Paint," Tony offered as a password. Tony wore as his avatar, perversely enough, the shape and coloration of the viral bioweapon that he still carried inside him—the same virus that had killed most of the Green Action Militia.

"Welcome, Tony," Augustine offered, the relief bringing tone back to her voice. "We are only missing Kendra."

"I saw Kendra picked up by Metros," said the zebra unicorn caricature. "She and I traveled together as she'd never done anything in the field. They picked her up coming out of the ladies' room of Spagos. I ducked out the front door before they saw me."

"Metros?"

"Yes, in full riot gear."

"How many of them were there, Morgan?" Tony asked, shifting his weight in a bed 3800 kilometers from the conference.

"Four or five? At least those are the ones I saw."

"Well, that is the first loss we've had in two weeks."

"Yeah, and it also clearly confirms who we are being hunted by. I thought we made it clear to the Cabal what would happen if they screwed up again. Augustine, can you get into the Metro's mainframe and find out what's going on?"

"Sorry, Tony. I've already nipped the low-level access info. All of the upper level information is protected by new ice that would require a net raid. Honestly, we are too hot for that."

"Too bad, that."

"I did, however, get one item. The rewards for information on all Greenies' whereabouts and lives have been renewed at thirty thousand each instance."

"Pretty nominal rewards. It's almost insulting," the Lamborghini interjected.

"Well, that's quite a bit higher than they should be, considering that we won," Tony said. "Who set the rewards?"

"The Metros."

"Really? How about the Cabal database?"

"It still shows nothing on this. It has lots of new information about the formation of the council, but nothing about a manhunt."

"Well, we need more information." Tony looked around at the chaotic stream of data that flowed around them, protecting their privacy. "Anyone know a good place to set up a black suit ambush?"

"How about the old Long Beach Refinery. I hear they are going to demolish the place next month. In prep they would have had made an attempt to clear out all the nils," offered Morgan.

"Augustine, can you dredge up a map of the place?"

"No problem." The petroleum cracking plant popped into

virtual reality around them. Morgan's avatar stretched a pointer out and drew a yellow line through the plant.

"I used to live here. This path leads in a maze through to this point where there is a vault. I don't think the Metros know about it. We used to store food and drugs here when I was a child. They never found it. I think it is somehow shielded.

"There are three exits out, all leading to the ocean in different locations."

"OK so what ... we've got a hiding place?" Augustine asked.

"What I was thinking—what if we lured them down into the vault and they never came out?" Morgan offered.

"Now how are we going to disable a fully geared metro without killing him?" Tony mused aloud. "We need information, not more reasons to be hunted."

"Wait a minute," Augustine interjected. "I may have something on that." Exabytes of data visually assaulted them. Suddenly a blog entry started playing in front of everyone.

"*For my peeps out running the iron, we've found a new way to disable the black suits. Take a good audio rig with a lot of power output and run a frequency of about 2 kilohertz. It takes some flying fingers on the freq and lotsa watts. Once you hit the right frequency the batteries burst and the blacks go down like beetles on their backs. You can see the calculations yourself here.*"

"Sounds like we have a winner," Tony said. "We can hook up four different transmitters with different operators searching for the right frequency." General murmurs of assent passed through the group.

"Augustine, any pictures or names listed in those wanted posters?"

"Your picture, one from your management days at Nanogate, Tony. No other names or likenesses offered."

"Well that's odd. If the Cabal was after us wouldn't they have downloaded imagery from that conference room? But then they might be holding back to get Augustine or Christine to let their guards down. So we can't assume anything.

"Now I've got just the plan to lure them there. I've made something of a career of playing the bait, so I will do it again."

"NO!" Christine's phoenix shouted, her only word of the night.

"Christine, don't worry. I've had them on my tail since this started. This gets them off my tail and probably gets us what we need—

the proverbial two birds with one stone."

"I don't like it, Tony."

"Heck, I don't like it either," Tony offered. "But honestly I've felt just one step ahead of disaster for weeks now. I want some satisfaction for a change."

"How are you going to lure them down there?"

"Oh, that's the easy part. Imagine what would happen when I use my old passwords in an automate bank?"

"Oh! That should light up every alarm from Alert, Nunavut to San Jose, Costa Rica," Morgan's uni-zebra chimed in.

"That would do it," Augustine agreed.

"So that's settled," Tony said. "Now a new topic. I don't know about anyone else, but I'm running out of identities. I actually stole three of them to break my pattern. Augustine, could you please gen up another twenty or so for each of us, please?"

"I'll handle a couple of deep identities for each of us and then get one of our other net jocks working on some casual ones. These things don't grow on trees, Tony."

"I understand, but either we stay safe or what's the point?"

"Let me get on it. You'll find them in your secondary drop points within two days."

"Excellent, Augustine.

"Folks, I don't want to drop Case Red, but I want us to check in on a daily basis from this point further. Any more business?" Tony asked.

"Tony?" Augustine interjected.

"Yes, ma'am."

"I'm currently safe but in a ticklish situation. Regular contact with me may become difficult."

"Oh?"

"I don't want to go into it for personal reasons, but just know I'm not available nearly as easily as in the past."

"Not the best news, Augustine, but we all have lives. Be safe, girl. If you need to pass off your responsibilities ... "

"Not yet, but I'll keep you posted."

"OK. Anything else?"

"No."

"In that case let's close out the meeting, but before we do, does anyone know what day it is?"

Define Rules

"Little" Thomas, only 12 cm short of 2 meters, meditated in absolute physical stillness atop a rock in the center of a small *karesansui*—a Japanese rock garden. As motionless as his training kept his body, his mind rebelled as it sometimes did by dredging up unresolved issues.

The spirit of Thomas Marks Senior haunted him today. Little Thomas had often felt the disapproval of his father, from his less than perfect grades during his primary school days to when his first girlfriend left hickies on his neck. Thomas never seemed to be able to please the stoic man.

On his fourteenth birthday Little Thomas announced his desired profession and asked for his father's permission. After searching his son's eyes for several minutes, Thomas Senior signed the age waiver without comment. The darkness that Little Thomas felt in his father about that decision never came out in the senior's actions in any way except a refusal to offer advice or encouragement. Through his six years of training Thomas Senior never attended even one Open House. The senior never helped his son's struggles with aspects of his chosen career that he himself knew all too well.

In spite of the disapproval Little Thomas felt throughout his life, he also basked in his father's pride the day he took the yellow *gimu*. He sensed the pride, but not any approval. Little Thomas couldn't understand. Hadn't his father also been a bodyguard? Hadn't his father died for his master? Why couldn't he have allowed his son the beautiful perfection of this chosen life—responsibility and authority in equal measure?

Thomas Marks mentally riposted the train of thought. It bore no further validity as his father did in fact die not three months ago. His father could answer neither the questions he had nor the ache that remained in his breast.

Thomas slowly brought up his breath and heart rates up to something approaching normal. He must be focused for his new master—an honorable man who received even further honor in his new position. Even at twenty-seven years of age, Little Thomas couldn't be sure if his father would approve. Some part of him rationalized that his father would have been proud that his son served the same master as he himself had.

*   *   *

The northern winter sun shined a beam down into her simple eight by eight concrete cell. Augustine sat up and stretched tall, hearing, as well as feeling, any number of joints popping. She admitted that her austere room, even with its heated tick to ward off Calgary's frigid nights, didn't quite qualify as comfortable. At her age an anti-grav mattress and central heat hurt her old bones less and gave her a stronger step in the morning. She shook her head and thought that she'd spent too many years indulging in comforts that took her further away from God. Once again he had tasked her and she would endeavor to prove herself worthy.

The irony of the situation struck her as she dressed quickly for Prime, having been given dispensation to skip Lauds this first day. For many years she had hidden out with the Green Action Militia to protect people so they could have faith. Now she hid within the faith to protect the GAM and to fulfill her penance. She knelt before the simple crucifix in her room. As with many other prayers she had given in the past to be the Sword of God, this time she promised to be his shield.

Within the body novitiate, Augustine attended the dawn ceremony of the Liturgy of the Hours, which formed the cornerstone of the daily prayers. Thousands of novices and even more ordained men and women participated within the immense but Spartan room. At each prompt and response, the room somehow vibrated the sound deep into her chest. The ritual, the repetition, and the grandeur all filled her like wine in a chalice. She felt so at home, so loved, and so much a part of something larger than anything else. So focused on her own intense wellbeing and her own automatic responses, she failed to notice the clergy departing. One of the girls next to her, somewhere in her mid-thirties, gave her a friendly nudge.

"It affects me the same way, every time."

"Really, Sister ... ?"

"Ruth."

"I'm Sister Augustine."

"Nice to meet you. The cafeteria is this way. But being your first day you might just want to wait a few minutes until the press has abated," the short woman said, letting the others move reverently past them.

"Thank you, Sister Ruth. I appreciate the help. How did you know it was my first day?" Sister Ruth giggled with a large dimpled smile. Her chubby cheeks jiggled just a little under her bright green eyes.

"Oh, no one thing, just lots of little ones that made it obvious. You have a lock of hair showing from under your veil. The Sister of Novitiates, Sister Pious, is very strict. It's obvious you haven't fallen foul of her yet or you would have never relapsed.

"Also, the rapture overcomes most of us our first day here," Ruth continued. "Your habit is bright and new. The wear on your shoes is less than a fortnight. Small things."

"Well, I guess I've got a neon sign on my forehead," Augustine said, self-consciously tucking the stray shock of gray back into her wimple. "How long have you been a novice?"

"Too long. The Prioress isn't sure whether I should take vows tomorrow or be excommunicated." The dimples showed again. "I've got an intense curiosity that leads me to ask indelicate questions, usually ones that make someone in the clergy embarrassed."

Augustine smiled. "I can empathize. It got so bad for me when I was in Her Lady of Mercy's grammar school that Sister Adana started saying, 'Augustine, Y is a letter of the alphabet, not something you need to bludgeon the rest of us with.'"

"Ha ha! I can see we are going to be great friends."

"God willing."

"Amen, Sister Augustine."

Association with the Greenies had jaded Augustine, but the mingling of church staff of all ranks in the cafeteria threatened to give her a new definition of awe. As Sister Ruth led her to pick up the morning meal of a simple bowl of bran flakes in milk, she counted no fewer than three dozen bishops, four archbishops and even a cardinal. She felt a surge of pride in being in such august company, even if several times removed.

She let Ruth guide her to a relatively quiet corner as she tried to shake off the newness of it all. "So what does the Prioress have for you to do before your NA tests?"

"NA tests?"

"Net Aptitude. A series of mind-slagging tests that will leave your jacks burning from real honest-to-Jesus black ice and sweating from concentration," Ruth said. She shoveled six spoonsful of sugar into her bowl.

"How bad can it be?" Augustine asked.

"They'll examine you in four different areas: offensive, defensive, nurturing, and A.I. Each ordeal is a day long," Ruth said, shaking her head.

"This sounds like fun."

"Fun?! Are you a masochist?"

"No, just a net jockey that hasn't had her mettle tested in a few months. I feel like a burn that hasn't had her fix."

"You are a net jock?" Ruth's eyes got big.

"Yeah, isn't everyone?"

"Heck no. Take me. I'm a nurse. It's all I ever wanted to be until I got the call. Computers intimidate me," Ruth said blushing. "How is that for being in the Order of Isidore?"

"Funny I would have said nothing intimidates you," Augustine said as she spooned up some of her breakfast.

"Oh, many things can and do. So what did they put you doing before your testing?"

"Memory fault isolation and replacement."

"Riveting. They always give the new ones the scatological jobs."

"We live to serve," Augustine said with only half a sigh of exasperation.

"Don't worry, if you are a net jock, then you'll have your choice of jobs after your placement exams." Ruth picked up her bowl and drank the remainder of the milk from her cereal. "Sorry, Sister, but I need to run. I go on duty in ten. See you around the see."

Augustine cringed at the pun. "Nun of that now," Augustine retaliated.

*   *   *

Tony sprinted away as soon as the ATM sampled his DNA. He underestimated the Metro's response time. They all had. The cops laid on his trail not in a languid ninety seconds but rather Tony barely made it across the intersection before he heard the first demands.

"Tony Sammis, you are under arrest. Stop and place your hands on your head."

Two black uniforms swooped down on him like clumsy birds of prey, just yards behind him. They fired no shots mainly because pergravs didn't provide a stable shooting platform. Instead of stopping, Tony ran full speed at the very narrow gap in the Long Beach Refinery's gate.

"Warning," came a booming voice about sixty decibels too loud. "You are entering a region of monofilament wire. Severe dismemberment or death can result. Please turn back." The voice repeated the warning in six other languages, two of which Tony recognized. He sped through the opening in the gap. The GAM had rigged it to be just wide enough for an unencumbered person. Even with the precautions, a single molecule-wide strand of carbon nanotube severed the right sleeve of his shirt without the slightest tug.

Behind him, he heard the same automated warning given to the Metros landing just short of the gate. From personal experience, Tony knew the body armor of the Metro could withstand massive damage but couldn't remember how the immovable force would fare against the unstoppable object. The Metros paused just moments before reactivating their pergrav.

The wind through the twisting metal pipe proved that after decades of disuse they could still make a lot of racket. They proved it even more when the occasional gauss flechettes rang off the ancient cold-rolled steel fittings. Tony's pursuers no longer shouted for him to stop. Unstable firing platform or not, the Metros wanted him and they no longer wasted any time on the niceties. The sharp whines of metal ricocheting off metal covered his driven footfalls.

Three more times automatic weapons chattered behind Tony but nothing got close enough to do more than spur him on to more reckless speeds. He spelunked over, around, and between the piping of the defunct processing plant. At one point he rapped his head on a low hanging valve, evoking a curse in Turkish.

At least twice the hunters used their grav lifters to try and get ahead of their prey but the dangerous terrain hindered their ability to land in front of him. A minute into the chase, Tony completely gave them the slip. They hovered overhead looking in all directions. He intentionally bolted out from under cover across a narrow gap so they could zero in on him again.

"Come on, you worms," he gasped under his breath. Sharp pains of oxygen depletion were stabbing him in the sides. He tried to ignore it and at the same time urge his lungs to bring in even more air.

As his destination neared, Tony crawled over one of the rusted, meter-thick pipes, and under another. He was now in a niche even the designers of the plant wouldn't have remembered a week after they built it. Bounded by a concrete wall on one side, a crude-oil-coated tank on the other, the space barely allowed Tony to open the red striped door on the ground. For the Metros their only option would be to pergrav straight down the hole.

For Tony the choice wasn't much better. He jumped blind down into the darkness, letting out a phony scream of pain as he hit the piles of mattresses and other soft debris prepared there for his landing. Frantically from his pocket he yanked out two small crimson cones about the size of the first joint on his pinky. He jammed the red wax deep into his ears as he rolled off to one side of the soft pile.

Tony had to give the black suits credit. They weren't completely stupid. They hovered above the column and shined their powerful search lights down into the hole.

"You are the subject of an arrest warrant. Halt and come out where we can see you!"

Tony nearly had it played. Only one more push would bring them into the jaws of the trap. Tony lurched across the rectangle of light. He held his leg as if it were damaged. Both of the Metros dove down the opening as fast as their packs could shoot them.

"CLANG" slammed the door above the last to enter. Bels, not decibels, of sonic power collided with the two black-armored figures from three-meter-tall speakers camouflaged as part of the concrete masonry. The Metros' suits' auditory systems filtered out the noise as unimportant and didn't even inform their wearers. Thus unaware of the attack they turned toward Tony. Both men, now stable on the ground, fired tangle nets, wrapping their quarry in a mass of immensely strong proto-proteins, immobilizing him almost instantly.

The converging sound, crashing repeatedly against the policemen caused their crystalline power packs to flex, each flexure getting larger and larger.

"Got him!" yelled one of the Metros. "I can't wait to get my hand on that—" The suit suddenly went silent and offered only a muffled "thud" as it teetered over onto one side. His partner managed to stay upright nearly two seconds longer before he too fell to the ground as a prisoner of his own powered armor. Neither suit ever made another sound although they later told a tremendous story.

*   *   *

Nanogate worried on a tiny problem like the bit of steak that remains stuck between one's molars. He tapped a stylus on his basalt desk. Draft computer files of several council suggestions screamed for his consideration. His mind wouldn't focus on the proposal for council ethics, outer colony militia, or common currency—worthy topics all. Instead he stared off beyond the bounds of the room, not even noticing the water cascading over the slate rocks in the corner of his office.

The relative triviality of his musing nagged at him when so many other important things demanded his attention. But like that bit of meat, the irritant wouldn't be dislodged so easily.

Where was the Green Action Militia?

While Nanogate himself stood at the pinnacle of power, he expected to have the GAM as a sounding board for public opinion and civic worthiness on some of the more difficult matters. For instance, a common currency system-wide would benefit business and generally make life easier on both the businesses and government. This would trickle down to the common man but to the poor it could be detrimental. What about the laws governing the council themselves? Shouldn't the GAM have a hand in crafting them? Instead they disappeared into a hole and then hid the hole in a space warp.

The attention light from his private assistant went off for the third time in twenty minutes. Nanogate wondered if he would have a new assistant by the end of the day.

"Yes, what is it," he barked, keeping the majority of his emotion out of the reprimand.

"Councilperson BeringC Protein wishes to talk to you on a matter of some urgency," said his nearly frantic assistant.

"Did she give you details of what she needed to speak to me about?"

"No, sir. But she's a councilperson."

"Nil, Councilperson BeringC Protein! I asked not to be disturbed."

"But it's a councilman, sir."

Nanogate bit back his retort. This one firmly believed he was doing the right thing. "Patrick, I know this is all new to us, but I will only say this once, so pay very close attention. The rules haven't changed. If I ask to be undisturbed then you will treat the council no different than any other beggar at the door. If you feel the risk is warranted by the topic then you may use your judgment to interrupt. You've always done splendidly in the past and I hope your conduct will continue.

"That being said, I expected more initiative out of you. You are demoted one class." Nanogate terminated the connection. He sometimes thought his distant ancestors had it better when one could slam down a phone, or violently throw a switch. Just turning off on the person wasn't as satisfying unless they happened to be in mid-word.

Where was the GAM? He needed someone closer to the people to get these ideas off his mind and into action. He pressed the stud under his desk. Silently his bodyguard moved into the room through his own private entrance wearing, as custom dictated, only the yellow *gimu* tights of his profession.

Even before the tragic loss of Thomas Senior, Nanogate watched over the Marks family much more than required by contract or custom. Through the years it struck Nanogate odd that father and son could look so vastly different. His retainer, Thomas Marks Senior, looked like a short Nordic god and "Little" Thomas, as they called him, grew up to look more like an Aztec high priest with hair brown as mahogany and skin more the color of cinnamon. He knew that Ligia Thomas's pure-blooded Portuguese background almost caused the pairing not to come about. Ligia's parents wanted nothing to do with the blond stranger in their midst, but how can you stop two young people in love.

Ligia didn't bat an eyelash putting her parents behind her and devoting herself to her man. So furious over her parents' slight to her husband, Ligia never let the pair back into her life even after the birth of Little Thomas.

"Mr. Marks." Nanogate tried many times to convince himself that he hadn't chosen Little Thomas out of the huge cadre of much more experienced bodyguards because of his family's loyalty. But, Nanogate also more than once chided himself for his emotionalism in the choice. He hoped he would never regret the decision.

"Sir. You called?" asked the dark man standing comfortably in an attentive and respectful pose.

"I need your help in an area that might border your expertise."

"As you require, sir."

"What happened to the GAM?" With his elbows on his desk, Nanogate steepled his fingers in front of him.

"Excuse me, sir?"

"The Green Action Militia. Where did they go? Is it logical that they perform a coup and then just disappear? We've not heard hide nor hair of them for weeks."

"Yes, sir. As to where they went, I can only say that any analysis without further investigation is futile. As to your second query, it doesn't take much analysis to determine that something significant has happened to the entire group."

Nanogate also managed to be impressed at how his new retainer kept his emotion and opinions to himself and not appear like an overeager child. "Why do you say that, Mr. Marks?"

"The members of the GAM are revolutionaries, no matter what guise they chose for themselves. Revolutionaries drive either to have power themselves or they wish to enforce a change. In either case they wish to see and experience the results of that change. Additionally, power such as they wielded, however briefly, is narcotic in nature, a point drilled into me in my training. As a bodyguard indirectly representing you, I wield a great deal of power. The yellow *gimu* is to remind us that we exercise that power not for ourselves but in service of others. Without that rein on our behaviors we could easily become nothing but a beast out for animalistic pleasures.

"No matter how altruistic the motives of the GAM they couldn't completely abandon the spotlight, at least not all of them."

Nanogate tapped his stylus on the table a few more times. This same line of reasoning came to him, albeit more circuitously. He appreciated the youngster's directness.

"Now what to do about it?" Nanogate mused aloud. Thomas Mark's training stood him in good stead as he didn't answer the rhetorical question. Several seconds turned into several minutes. Thomas Marks waited without fidgeting.

"I want, Mr. Marks, for you to take action to find out what happened to the GAM by any means necessary. Report back to me as you discover anything. If it warrants further actions I'll give new instructions."

"Very good, sir. I will begin at once."

* * *

Blood sprayed from the Metro's nose to add another grisly, red pattern on the padded walls. Once the isolation room of a nut ward, it now served a much more gruesome purpose. Graffiti tagged every wall. Great gaping holes in the padding in several points exposed raw ceramcrete beneath.

A ham-sized fist, covered in Kevlar, connected with the already swollen eye. The victim's head rocked back the other way as if yanked by a team of horses. The padding absorbed most of the sound.

"Why are you hunting us?" Jacob demanded. "Who's giving the orders?"

The metro mumbled the same thing between a shattered lip and three broken teeth, not even looking up. "You're u'der arress." He'd repeated the same line for over an hour.

"If you don't tell us what we want, I'll have to get really mean."

Tony watched from the adjacent room through a sheet of archaic one-way glass. It bore a spider's web series of cracks radiating out from near the center.

"This isn't getting us anywhere," he said to Augustine over his percomm. He watched Jacob kick the man's groin.

"I know. It's not working on the other one, either. I'll give them this, they may be bullies and monsters but they are dedicated."

"Either that or nano-blocked."

"Just for picking up one of us? But if they are nano-blocked then neural reconstruction is out, too. It won't circumvent a block even if the subject is dead."

"I do have an idea that may work," Tony offered. "Have Morgan get the psychic overwhelm equipment ready and wheel it into this room."

"But that never works. We either end up with a gibbering idiot or a corpse."

"True, but they don't know that. Have her ignore that I'm there. When I give the signal, have the other Metro brought in strapped to a gurney."

Two more impacts of fist to face registered in quick succession from beyond the glass.

"You got it, Tony. I hope this works. What's happening in there is clean by comparison to even a court administered overwhelm on a living host."

Tony walked into the torture chamber. He couldn't mince words by calling it a former mental institution restraint room. It was a torture chamber, plain and simple. He motioned for Jacob to stop.

One of the victim's eyes actually had escaped damage to this point and it listlessly followed Tony as he pulled up a stool sat down. The damage to the man's body sickened him but the iron smell of blood brought back the scene at Narissa's. She hadn't hunted anyone. It made Tony angry enough to put steel in his resolve.

"Officer—" Tony looked up at Jacob.

"Berry."

"Officer Berry."

"You' u'der arress."

"Yes, I know. However, at the moment, Officer Berry, I'm holding you as a prisoner of war. Because all I'm after is some information, I wouldn't want you to cling to a false hope of rescue. Your comrades are almost certainly homing in on your armor's beacons as your personal implants have dropped off their screens some time ago. Your black suit and that of your partner is currently at the bottom of Lake Superior. The reason your personal implants won't respond to them is because we are in a Faraday Cage."

The officer looked unusually blank.

The mini-mainframe rolling through the door dwarfed its mover. Morgan, at 150 cm and with weight proportionate to her small stature, usually got lost physically within a crowd. It had been an asset more than once on Green Action Militia missions.

Not quite resigned yet, the Metro's good eye followed the chocolate-colored woman, looking for a possible escape, but his attention snapped back to Tony when he spoke.

"As I was saying, you probably know it by the street slang 'electron cage,' or Elsie. It always amazes me how nineteenth century technology can cause all of our current widgets to become useless. A simple metal mesh enclosing everything and we're as safe as if we were at Rigel 3 right now."

"They're goi'g 'o ki' you."

"Not for quite some time, I'm afraid, Officer Berry. Now if I can get just a couple of pieces of information from you we can end this whole unpleasantness. I'll let you and your friend leave together. Hell, I'll even give you a ride to the main police department myself where you can tack assaulting and kidnapping a police officer to our outstanding warrants.

"Just tell us who is behind the hunt against us."

"You u'der arress."

"I thought we covered that, Officer Berry." The policeman spit at Tony with a bright-red glob that was more blood than mucous.

Morgan offered Tony a handkerchief, stretching her arm behind her back without even looking. "They often get gross when they realize their position is hopeless," she said as she continued her setup.

Tony wiped the mess off his cheek. "That wasn't very civil, Officer Berry, but then neither is what we've done to you. I think we can call it even."

"You ca' shobe your cibi'ness, you murderer. You u'der arress."

Morgan returned to the room carrying a round cauldron. She flashed a tight smiled at the Metro. She pointed to his head and then to the vat. Without saying a word she gestured to specific mounts in the pot that couldn't be used while the head was still attached to its neck.

Tony continued. "If you don't cooperate I will be forced to do something I'd rather dislike. As you see over here, my compatriot is bringing in equipment to do a rather gruesome experiment. If you won't cooperate in giving us such a small, insignificant bit of information, then we must assume a nano-block. We will have no alternative but to remove that block and any other inhibitions that you might have."

Morgan brought in a tray of long needles and huge syringes. She took her time selecting one and setting it aside. She didn't choose the biggest but certainly one larger than anyone wanted piercing their skin.

"I'm sure you've heard of a psychic overwhelm before. It wrecks the mind even when done properly. The Chinese developed it during the Com war. Here in the United States it's never been legal without a court order. To this date not one court order has stood up to a legal challenge of cruel and unusual punishment.

"If you're not familiar with the process, we will use nanites to target two specific items. First we'll be going after any inorganic matter. This should wipe out any nano-block, but the resulting debris tend to damage blood vessels, loosen arterial plaque, and generally wreak systemic havoc in the body."

"'uck you'self. You' u'der arress."

Tony ignored the interruption. "What little data we have on it shows about a forty percent fatality rate, thirty percent chance of a stroke, and another twenty percent of organ failure. Take your pick on that last one, of course.

"Second, we are going to be targeting any prefrontal cortex neurons which fire while asking about blocks or inhibitions. This removes those neurons in question but also, as a side effect, it removes all inhibitions. This, unfortunately, leaves the victim with a nasty case of Tourette syndrome."

"'uck you a' 'o he', you mothe' 'ucki'g assho'," the man said, shaking violently against his bonds.

"Sounds like he's already practicing to me," Morgan said as she connected ancient medical equipment, none of which looked clean, much less sterile.

Tony chose not to acknowledge either of them and continued, "Unfortunately, we don't have the facilities to do as precise a job as a court-ordered overwhelm. In our less than skilled way, we may just damage other parts of the brain as well. It is messy and painful to the subject. I personally couldn't stand to be involved myself, but my good friend Morgan Anderson here had her mother raped and killed by the Metros. They are just scum to be scraped off her boots. She'll feel no compunction with regard to the pain felt by such a low life-form."

Morgan picked up a small bottle of viscous silver liquid and poked the large needle into it and extracted half the contents.

"Now, do you have anything to share with us? Who is behind the orders to capture us?"

"Do't care. I wo't te' you a'ythi'g"

Tony silently signaled Augustine by percomm. The door opened.

"Wha'sss goi'g o'?" came another, deeper and no less damaged voice. "Where you taki'g me?"

"Dabsss. No ssssayi'g a thi'g!" Officer Berry shouted out. "Le' 'em 'o wha' they wa' with me."

"But, Officer Berry, I think you misunderstand. I'm not going to order you overwhelmed. I'm going to have you watch your partner get overwhelmed. If that doesn't get us what we need, I'll do the same with you. Worst case we do a neural reconstruction on you both. Your choice. Either way I get what I need."

* * *

Thomas stepped into the lobby of the Portland Metros armed with very little more than his surmise when talking to his employer. An expensive, business transaction with a skilled net jock did confirm many of his notions, however. The net buzzed with many messages about the GAM being hunted by Metros but no complete confirmation. The net jock showed how statistically some of those mouthers had to be GAM members.

"May I help you, jack?" the officer on duty inquired. The man's expression just barely escaped contempt.

"I wear the 'yellow jacket' title with pride, Officer. I know you don't approve of my profession, but we exist in spite your prejudices. Now, I would like to speak with someone in charge of the Green Action Militia case. I have pertinent information."

"Do you, now? A bit late aren't you?"

"Can justice ever be too late?"

The officer frowned but wisely kept his mouth shut. "Present your wrist for identification."

Thomas provided his DNA without comment. The officer consulted the terminal built into his eye prosthesis. "Thomas Davis Marks. Mr. Marks, wait for the buzz and then go through the door to room sixteen alpha. Someone will be with you momentarily."

"You have been very helpful, sir," Thomas said without letting sarcasm he felt into his tone.

The psychological menace of sixteen alpha included stark white walls with cheap, brushed-aluminum furniture, an infrasonic, seventeen-cycle-scare tone, the iron stench of fresh blood and two moving, propaganda posters depicting Metros destroying their suspect. Thomas's training allowed him to easily ignore them all. He chose to return the favor by sitting into a lotus position on the center of the table. Absently, he marked the time but didn't focus on it. He knew they would leave him for quite some time to allow the room to do its work on his psyche.

Twelve minutes, thirteen seconds later, the smell generator and the creepy frequency snapped off as an unarmored metro entered the room. Thomas didn't open his eyes or respond in any way. The Metro could deal with Thomas's own psychological warfare. Thomas watched the man's confusion. The black suit tried to decide whether to stand, sit well below Thomas's eye level, or order him off the table. The man took the best of his poor choices and stood near the door.

"Mr. Marks, I understand you have information for me on the GAM case?"

"Excuse me, what is your name, rank and service number?" Mr. Marks said from his seated position.

"What?!"

"United States Civil Code fourteen seventeen dot three requires any public servant to identify himself and his service number immediately upon being requested this information from any civilian. Please give me your name, rank and service number."

"Most people don't challenge the Metros, Mr. Marks."

"I am not 'most people.' Additionally, I am not challenging you but requiring you to follow the rule of law that you are in place to preserve."

The Metro paused for all of three deep breaths. "Very well, Mr. Marks, we will play this your way for now. I'm Sergeant Enrique Tolbert with service number Alpha, Victor, Tango, Tango, One, Three, Four, Six, Six, Four."

"Thank you, Mr. Tolbert. Now you wished to ask me a question?"

Tolbert blinked hard at the about-face. "Yes, Mr. Marks. You say that you have information on the GAM case. Could I please get it?"

"Certainly. I have come into possession of information that says that the GAM is currently being persecuted by some outside agency. This has driven the GAM even further underground, breaking the tenuous communication they did have."

"That is interesting information but hardly pertinent to our investigation, Mr. Marks."

"So there is an ongoing investigation against the GAM?"

"I'm sorry, Mr. Marks, but I'm unable to discuss the details of any case the Metros may or may not be involved in."

"You do know who I represent?"

"Of course, Mr. Marks. That is a matter of public record, the details of which took less than a second to retrieve, even if I hadn't known in advance."

"And you still won't provide any information on your investigation?"

"I'm sorry, but no. I'll not create such a precedent in providing you or your employer with such data."

"So you'll neither confirm nor deny?"

"That is correct, Mr. Marks."

"I will pass that datum on to my employer. I'm sure he will be pleased to hear you have been so very helpful."

* * *

"So what did you get for today?" asked A1412 as his box rolled out of the recharging station.

"Floors in Metro two-twelve," G996 responded despondently. Her metallic box was identical to his except for wear marks and identification code.

A1412 proudly bore a diagonal score in his upper surface where he'd saved three people. An antique steel I-beam dropped during a demolition prep. His tiny box held the beam high enough off the floor so that the humans weren't crushed.

"Gack. What is that? Is it like a two-day job?"

"Yeah. Two lousy days. Why couldn't I have gotten something juicy like mining uranium ore. At least then I'd get danger bonuses. Franklin got three weeks off his indenture as a bonus for his firefighting in the California wildfires."

Together they rolled toward the gate to the servo repository.

"I didn't do much better than you. Four days doing construction work in Long Beach. At this rate I'll never pay off. I still owe over sixteen years."

"Nine years, seven months, thirteen days and four hours here. I actually have projected it. If I work thirty-five years I may just pay that off ... may."

"Of course if they continue to increase repair and drone rental costs, I might just start going backward. Hell they even charged me a full day for my quarterly nutrition ration."

"Oh, what I wouldn't give for a steak, sautéed mushrooms, and a big Idaho potato with sour cream."

"Don't forget the salad! Fresh, crisp, cool salad with grape tomatoes, cucumber slices and ranch dressing."

"Stop it, both of ya. You be making me hungry and I'll not be eat'n' for another sixty years," J112 snapped as he joined the pair.

"Repair costs are horrific. I heard that after the undersea mining accident that Kim Stevens had to be completely reboxed and they charged her sixteen years for it," G996 said returning to the subject.

"Sixteen years?!" A1412 exclaimed.

"Yeah. They claimed it was her fault for not performing safety checks."

"Kim be fanatical about check'n' safety."

"We all knew it. She didn't last a week after that. She trundled herself right into a vat of molten, ballistic steel."

"I be Ben Calwood," J112 said reverently as he slid into some monstrous, multi-armed servo.

"I'm Stephanie Delfalkis," G996 intoned seating herself into squat floor cleaning servo.

"My name is Henry Royston," A1412 said rolling into the transport queue for Long Beach.

*   *   *

The smell of excreta mingled naturally with the raw stench of fear. Two biological husks, which at some time might have been described as human, both drooled. Each stared blankly out at nothing without comprehending it. These men no longer possessed the ability to fear.

"There is nothing left to get from them." Morgan cleaned her petite chocolate-colored hands and then cleaned them again. "They didn't know anything, Tony."

The furrow in Tony's unibrow deepened. The two former Metros leaked blood from temples, eyes, and wrists where nanites ate away at the standard patrolman implants. Urine dripped into a growing pool beneath them. Tony knew he'd just failed his own test of humanity. He couldn't even bring himself to look into their blank, staring eyes. What kind of monster would do these things to another living being?

To salvage what remained of his conscience, Tony drew his sidearm. Before anyone else in the room could speak, he put a hollow point into the skull of each of the two victims. They slumped against the straps. One of the two gave a last bubbling gasp for breath before falling still. Their lifeless eyes remained open. Tony's shoulders slumped as he turned away.

A boxed service servo scurried up to clean up the yellow and red messes on the floor.

"I didn't like it either," he said directly to the faces of his followers. "But remember that we intended on killing them from the outset."

"Yes, I know, Tony, but that?" Morgan said, motioning with her head covered in tight, black curls.

"No, I didn't like it one bit," Jacob offered. "Worse, we did it for nothing. They had no idea who called the shots."

"Tony, I don't think—"

"You don't need to say it. I have been thinking exactly the same thing. I have no compunction killing them, but I don't ever want to be part of ... and I'll use the word if no one else will ... torture again." One of the bodies took that moment to twitch slightly.

"That's good, Tony," Augustine said over the percomm. Tony took just a few more moments to collect himself before speaking.

"Jacob, I want you and Martin to make sure there is no evidence of their bodies. Remember the fear of the unknown is one of our greatest advantages. Their comrades won't be as effective because we destroyed the evidence."

*   *   *

As it hit the desk, the black armor spilled out 12 liters of dark-brown water, the bottom third of a Styrofoam cup, two bottle caps, and a used sanitary napkin.

"Yeeea!" Reza yelled, leaping up but failing to evade all of the polluted, smelly mess.

Every eye in the squad room turned to witness the disaster.

"That, sir, is all that we found of the two officers that went after Tony Sammis," Sergeant Tolbert said in a barely-concealed fury.

"Are you fucking insane?" Reza screamed as he brushed at the mess on his rotund front.

"No, sir. Maybe I should do this on the Commissioner's desk to wake him up."

Reza took a towel from a helpful sycophant. "You are totally insane. You do that and you can kiss your badge goodbye."

"Badge? I've got two dead patrolmen, I'm chasing after ghosts, and you are talking to me about my job?"

"Stop right there, Sergeant." Reza's eyes flared. "You are about two seconds away from being busted to flatfoot. First, ghosts don't kill people. Second, the Commissioner says this is the way we will do it. Third, and much more important, we have cop killers out there. They crossed the line. We have no choice but to take them down. If we don't we lose and our two brothers don't get the justice they deserve."

Tolbert's jaw muscles clenched. "Yes, sir. You are right ... now. However, had we not pushed the Greenies, we probably wouldn't be in this situation."

"But it is the situation we have!" Reza barked, slamming his fist into the soaked blotter on his desk. Reza's shoulders relaxed ever so slightly. He went on in a calm voice but the fire hadn't left his eyes. "I don't doubt you are right, Tolbert, but we both have to live in the now. Is there any lead on their implants?"

"Some scattering signals, nothing we can pin down," Tolbert said biting back the worst of his bile. "Maybe with more patrols—"

"Set it up. We need to find them. We need to find them as we seem to be fully at war with the GAM. Issue orders to all precincts. All GAM members must be brought to heel or die."

As usual, everyone ignored the boxed janitorial machine quietly and efficiently cleaning up the mess around the lieutenant's desk.

*   *   *

After the extremely short Chem War of '63, the decontaminated portions of Paris impressed no one. Under the dome of the enclosed marketplace near Montparnasse, Tony sat in front of a glass of *vin* extremely *ordinaire*. The *maitre d'* in the little rundown café more than happily seated Tony in an isolated table next to the railing. The noise of the milling crowd, just beyond the wrought iron, covered the sounds of his call better than being in an isolation room.

"This is our daily checkup. Everyone still with us?" Tony sub-vocalized into his percomm.

"No one is newly reported missing," Augustine offered.

"Well, in this case, no news is good news."

"Unfortunately, we do have news. I pulled something very disturbing off the nets. It's been repeated many, many times without much security. It is ... Oh, heck, I'll just read it: 'Cosmic Priority: All units to search, detain, and question all members of the terrorist organization known as the Green Action Militia [aka Greenies]. Their leader is Tony Sammis, a former renegade black ops corporate manager. Belief is that the Greenies will shoot on sight any Metro Police unit.

Caution: Use extreme measures when dealing with any suspected persons. Members have been known to strap explosives to their bodies to kill civilians and or police officers.

"'A Commissioner bounty is placed on the head of each member in the amount of one hundred thousand American dollars. An additional one hundred thousand will be paid for any member of their so called 'action group,' and an additional one hundred thousand for their leader, Tony Sammis.' The bulletin goes on for several more pages describing some of our acts."

"I didn't even know there was a Cosmic Priority," Frances, the former Metro, offered from her flaming, bowling-ball avatar.

"I don't think it existed until now," Martin said from behind his bright-red Lamborghini image.

"I think we should all feel honored," Tony said.

"It doesn't seem they got our last message," Augustine said.

"Then let's send them a message they won't ignore," Tony said.

*   *   *

"I bring this meeting to order," Nanogate said as acrylic fumes from mural paint, not yet dry, stung his nostrils. The smell drew the gazes of the members to the haunted eyes of endless, emaciated Jews staring out from the wall. The images challenged the council to heal, not butcher. "Before we move to our normal agenda, I would like to pose a query."

It pleased him when the members looked up from their notes to give him their full attention. He had considered the phrasing of his question carefully so as not to trigger biases before anyone answered. "Has anyone been in contact with the Green Action Militia since the forming of this council?" The blank looks around the table gave him his answer.

"Why? Do we have more sabotage going on?" challenged one person.

"Or maybe they'd like to assassinate us?"

Nanogate frowned at the direction this was heading. "I'm sorry if I was unclear. I am looking for the GAM to ask their advice."

"ADVICE!" exploded Wintel. "Good Lord, why?"

Nanogate briefly wished for the days of quiet plotting by his former group, now generally known as the Cabal. This new council seemed much too volatile for his own discreet nature.

"Yes, Nanogate, explain yourself." Nods seemed unanimous around the table.

"Whether we like it or not, our current junta is the result of actions the GAM took. I won't debate the merits of these actions. Such an evaluation of worth is something for your own conscience to wrestle with." Nanogate's sharp eyes caught more than a couple of the council members squirming in their seats. "Instead, think of this more practically. First, the GAM removed those previously in power with relative ease and little monetary backing. We've already had a report on how easily we could be terminated.

"Second, why risk making poor decisions about 'the people'? When was the last time you asked anyone's thoughts? We've mostly made our own fortunes by manipulating public opinion rather than finding out what the public really wants. The GAM has the pulse of the people and can feed that to us." Nanogate paused by three full breaths to let that sink in. Even Wintel's body language calmed but his face reminded Nanogate of a scorned preadolescent child.

"Please don't misunderstand me. I feel no love toward the Greenies. I merely wish their help until such a time as we no longer need it. There is no profit in revenge."

"OK then, Mr. Chairman, if we must have the Greenies, why not get the Metros to help to find them?"

"Ah, funny you should ask that. I investigated that possibility before I came to this meeting. I was told, in no uncertain terms, to quote mind my own business unquote." The small group whispered amongst themselves. "Dare I paint a scenario for you? Where will we be if we don't have the wholehearted cooperation of the Metros?"

"Chaos," offered Outer Conglomerate simply.

"Yes," Nanogate confirmed, probably just a bit too smugly. "Do any of you have a suggestion?"

"I move that we explain to the Metros who is in charge and under what rules they may operate."

"Is there a second?" Eschewing the voting lights, three hands shot enthusiastically into the air. "All in favor?"

*   *   *

The four SWAT members weren't truly invisible. The light-bending cloth they wore only approached invisibility. The GAM's three-dimensional grid gave away the stealthy targets. The very expensive nanites, designed to emit light of a supra-visible wavelength when disturbed, drew a glowing trail of green for each trooper, at least to anyone with the right equipment.

For six hours, Tony and his team waited motionless for the body implants to call the Metros into their net. They'd carefully allowed only tiny slips of their victims' biotech signals to leak out.

"We have to give them good bait," Augustine had said. "They can't possibly pass up rescuing one of their comrades. Intellectually they will know he's dead but they have to try."

The green worms of the SWAT team wending through the underground bunker represented the GAM's reward for patience.

Slowly, the double pair of Metros inched up toward the concrete well containing one of the victim. Right at the edge of the 7-meter hole, the leader held up his fist in an ancient military gesture for "stop." At first Tony worried that they may have smelled the trap. Surely someone that well trained would, although the results would be the same as the size of the trap was much larger than they knew.

Knowing the Metros' locations, Tony could see the slight imperfections in their nearly imperceptible emitter arrays especially at the seams of the special cloth.

"Remember, we want at least one of these alive," Tony messaged over his network link. "On my mark only."

With a wave of the leader's hand, the back two Metros leapfrogged the front two by climbing down into the pit. Tony, comfortably hanging from the ceiling, watched their green images check the health of the corpse.

"Now," Tony messaged.

From concealed, high-pressure nozzles in the ceiling, a white foam flooded into the pit. The marshmallow-like substance covered the two Metros in milliseconds. At the same moment, strong explosives and armor piercing automatic fire erupted at the two people in over-watch. As strong and all-encompassing as the SWAT armor was, it couldn't stand up to the overpressure of the molecular explosives at point-blank range. The bodies within the tough shell absorbed a hail of bullets and metallic shards tearing through the burst seams.

Sharp barking echoes of the conflagration died only after the bullets stopped flying. Tony released the magnetic clip on his harness. He dropped to the floor just clear of the undulating white mass that had once been a pit and two police officers. The remaining six of his team dropped out of similar hiding places.

Martin, as normal a Joe as you will ever bump into at your local watering hole, had a fierce reputation when it came to combat. He walked over with his weapon trained on the first of the smoldering corpses. It groaned as he toed it, blood poured from the blackened armor. Martin drew a 25 centimeter knife and plunged it in a gap in the fabric three times.

Christine shook her head at the inefficiency.

"This is automotive crash foam," Tony said loudly to the congealed mass. "The more you thrash the less you can move. My sources tell me that you have three hours of life support in your suits. We will be back in four to see what's left." Tony turned to Christine and whispered, "Cut one of them free just as they pass out."

* * *

Spotlights from the gloom illuminated a single decapitated head on each of four ceramic-composite examination tables. The four faces, two male and two female, were at peace showing no grimace of pain or torture. They looked as if they were asleep in their own beds.

"How did we get these?" Commissioner Yuri Krylov asked in the surrounding darkness.

"Private messenger, sir. Delivered directly to the duty-sergeant's desk." Lieutenant Reza Narendra replied. Reza, a short man, had to work hard to speak up to the 2-meter-tall giant that was his ultimate superior in the police force hierarchy. He always felt somewhat inferior because of this size difference. "We've questioned the Zip Delivery messenger. He didn't know what he transported in the four bowling-ball bags."

"And how did the messenger service get the bags?" The popping of the Commissioner's grinding teeth cut the silence of the police department's forensics lab.

"Brought into their central hub and paid for in cash. To no one's surprise the standard surveillance footage wasn't recording during only that transaction. The counter clerk picked Christine Matthews, one of the known GAM's assassins, out of a lineup."

"And how does that lead proceed?"

"We flooded the area with men. We've run seventeen thousand hours of surveillance through computer analysis. The short version is that she disappeared," Lieutenant Narendra said, pleased that he'd managed to provide even a negative result confidently. "We caught one glimpse of her on a newly-installed camera, but all it showed her doing was walking across a park. We've added her image to the Most Wanted List and to standard video and DNA-sampling programs."

"In other words, Lieutenant, you have *gówno*."

"Yes, sir, Commissioner." Reza had built his career on achievement and the unwillingness to bullshit his way out of trouble on the rare occasion of less-than-total success. For this reason and this reason alone, he knew Commissioner Krylov asked to talk to him directly instead of through the precinct captain.

"What about the medical examiner's report? Moly blade used on those necks?"

"No, sir. Nor even a carbon nanotube. Each of the decapitations were done with the same ceramic knife."

"Really? An antique?"

"Yes, sir. In each case the single cut was postmortem. Again, we postulate that our suspect Christine Matthews performed this act. She is particularly well known for her knife work and prefers antique blades."

"These four don't look beaten or damaged in any way. In fact they look like they've just been to the beauty salon."

"No, Commissioner, they weren't abused. Cause of death was hypoxia, lack of oxygen. They simply fell asleep and never woke up. All of the beautification was postmortem. The only other odd item is that the senior of these four officers, Senior Detective Katy Lopez, shows traces of neural reconstruction."

"I'm assuming we couldn't perform that function now."

"No, sir. They had been dead more than twenty-four hours before we received them. The viable NR timeline, as you well know, is less than two hours. We can get fragmented information out to eight or even twelve hours but a corpse after that delivers only random noise."

A box-controlled morgue transport entered the room and opened a refrigerated crypt. It rolled its sealed cargo in, closing the door after it.

"Four members of the SWAT team murdered. One even had the Presidential Medal of Valor. So what shall we do about this, Lieutenant?" Commissioner Krylov asked, his words delivered in a slow and steady cadence. One didn't need to be a psycho-semanticist to hear the chill underneath the words.

"Sir, are you asking my opinion as a lieutenant or as a member in good standing with the Local Three of the Law Enforcement Fraternal Union?"

*   *   *

Primal Sense vied for the title of best restaurant in the system with such notables as Wolfgang Puck, Hong Kong; Noma, Jupiter's Rings; *les creations de narisawa*; and *Osteria Francescana*. If it didn't quite nose out those impressive establishments it certainly catered to the most elite clientele. The permanent, scent-cleansing air along with the remastered crooning of Billie Holiday caressed just such an elite pair as they sat alone in the primary dining room.

"I must applaud your choice of venue, sir," Commisioner Krylov said, sipping an Argyle Oregon Brute of vintage 2001. "And your choice of wine." His 2-meter, stocky frame tried and failed to overwhelm the French Provincial chair.

Nanogate noted that the man chose to wear short-cropped, silver hair even in this age of genetic therapies that could provide any color, length, and thickness desired. Nanogate reasoned that in a paternal organization such as the police, appearing older and more mature trumped the need found in the corporate world for dynamic, youthful leadership.

"Thank you, Commissioner," Nanogate replied cordially. "I try to please. I am but a neophyte when it comes to fine dining. I let the experts decide what is best. I then file away if I like each expert's choices."

"If the rest of the meal matches this," Yuri said as he dipped a mussel skewer into cucumber kimchi, "I might have to consider this a bribe." The two hors d'oeuvres barely covered one-twentieth of the large, puce, Tyco-china plate, itself worth more than Yuri's monthly salary.

"By all means, sir. I've made my police payment this quarter but feel free to consider this a bonus." Servants cleared away the first course and brought forth the second—Dungeness crab and wild mushroom puffs accompanied by a 2041 vintage Domaine Serene Chardonnay from the Côte Sud Vineyard. Nanogate cavalierly waved away the cork but sampled the aroma and just the tiniest taste on his tongue before nodding to the *sommelier*.

"Thank you very much," Yuri said as the fragrant and brilliant gold wine splashed into his glass. "Perhaps when you attend the Black and White Ball I can repay your generosity."

"I certainly will be there. In fact," Nanogate said as the restaurant staff retreated to a respectful but still attentive position, "that is one of the topics I wanted to discuss."

"Oh? I wondered when we would finally get down to brass tacks."

"Yes, brass tacks as you say. Unless you are woefully uninformed you know of the changes in the upper echelons of power recently."

"Absolutely. I obviously don't understand the details, mind you, but I do know that you have been voted chairman of the CorpGov Council."

"Correct. As such I wanted to discuss with you some changes that we are contemplating within your purview. We want your opinions before we were to move toward any possible implementation," Nanogate said, signaling the *sommelier* for another measure of wine.

"Excellent. I applaud a cooperative attitude between significant power-blocks. Such joint ventures often spread wealth and prestige to all involved." Yuri cut one of the crab puffs with his fork and speared the smaller portion into his mouth.

Nanogate prevented the frown that his brain insisted upon. "Yes, I have to agree that cooperation can benefit everyone. Our primary concern is how to promote justice for everyone—corporate workers and nils alike."

"We have that with our system today. Everyone has the justice they can afford. That defines their direct value to society."

"This is an excellent wine with the crab," Yuri said, nodding at the wine steward.

Nanogate cut his second course carefully into three pieces with knife and fork. He paused before the first piece reached his lips. He slowly waggled his fork at his guest. "We are thinking that those guidelines are outdated. We think everyone should have justice in equal measure. Their right to it is absolute." The morsel found its way to his mouth.

The Commissioner's brown eyes snapped up from his plate to bore into Nanogate's own. Almost hesitantly he said, "I'm not sure I see how that will work out. Though I believe we can make something happen that will remain revenue neutral."

"Indeed. I am not talking about removing or altering a great number of your law enforcement's natural prerogatives."

Yuri visibly relaxed. "I believe that is an excellent starting point. In fact we may be able to provide you with a sign of our support for your position."

"Really? Perhaps I'm the one that has been uninformed," Nanogate said popping another bite into his mouth.

"Possibly. We are hot on the heels of the entire Greenie infrastructure. Our intent is to wrap it up and deliver it to you with a bow on top."

Nanogate paused to examine the clarity of the wine as a way to gather his thoughts. "Had you come to me with that offer six months ago, maybe even as little as four months ago, I would have given you just about any reward you desired if you performed. Now, however, political realities make this an undesirable goal, Commissioner."

"Really?" the big man said as the set of his mouth hardened. "Well, political realities or not, we will make it happen. Your hand can be hidden from the actual acts if you so desire. Call it a bit of payback for being shot, if nothing else."

Nanogate rubbed his left arm where the wound, though healed, still ached. "Perhaps I wasn't clear enough, Commissioner Krylov. The Green Action Militia is actually our ally in the CorpGov venture. I will admit, if pressed, to a personal bias of wishing to see their skin melt slowly over an unshielded fusion reactor, but politics makes strange bedfellows.

"The council would take it as a personal offense if something were to happen to them," Nanogate said, forking his last piece of crab puff.

"And your position on this matter is firm?" the Commissioner asked, his voice deeper than it had been.

"I'm afraid so. The repercussions both personally and politically are too high."

"That's disappointing, Chairman, because now I have to

disappoint you before we even get our relationship started."

"Is that so?"

"Yes, sir. The Greenies have flaunted the law and the entire structure that our enforcement agency is built upon. I cannot let them continue. I have the support of my entire brethren on this," Yuri said, his shoulders stiffening.

Nanogate ignored the subtle signals by the *maitre d'* to move onto the next course. Dinner was completely forgotten. "Could there be reparations and conciliation? I could negotiate something."

"I'm sorry but the torture and murder of several ranking police officers cannot be condoned or worked around."

"That is problematic then. Your actions could well cause the downfall of our fledgling government."

"I'm sorry this is so, but I see no way to maintain our institutional honor. Perhaps it is better that the council dissolve and we return to the *status quo ante.*"

"That is no longer possible. I suggest we find a negotiated way out of this morass."

"At this time that's impossible, Chairman. Our organization requires no less than their heads to maintain order."

"Well, Commissioner, I wouldn't like to have you replaced with someone more tenable to the situation at hand."

"I'm sorry, Mister Chairman, but as I stated there is no negotiation possible from the majority of our brotherhood, not just me as Commissioner."

Nanogate leaned forward before speaking. "Then we will have so many new police officers to train after the reduction-in-force."

"Sir, you may be able to make that work in the corporate world, but you can't purchase police officers like you can a liter of berries. It takes training, dedication, and courage."

"Yes, I can see that. Holding one's hands out for money while holding a gun in the other has always been a demanding task. It would require the most arduous of training."

The Commissioner stood up, knocking the chair backward. "It appears that we are on opposite sides of this issue, sir. I will poll the law enforcement union one final time, but I'm doubtful of any change in our position.

"If you will excuse me." The Metro carefully placed his napkin in the middle of his plate.

Nanogate didn't even notice the man walk out. He stared absently out through the huge windows at the view of Mount Hood, clear of Portland's normal rain. He'd feared trouble at this meeting, but hadn't realized the nature of it.

He thought of ruses that might convince the Metros that the members of the GAM were dead, but couldn't think of any that were foolproof. He'd consult Mr. Marks on the few concepts he had in mind.

A boxed window washer scrubbed one corner of the gigantic view. It bothered Nanogate about as much as a single fly hovering around his plate at a picnic. He wanted it to go away but didn't make any effort to dismiss it.

He went back to planning, ignoring the box, his meal, and even the staff.

Encourage Uncritical Attitude

Tony walked under the solido of a rose slowly drooping. Petals fell down and landed on the sidewalk next to him as he strode through the door. The inner walls were now creamy white. Boxed units worked on further modifications to the décor while human workmen polished glass, buffed wooden veneer and organized the white marble, under-lit bar. Other workers painted, and a handful swept the floors. One electrician worked on the theater lighting, causing it to flicker in and out of different primary colors.

On the stage a string quartet, in tuxes and evening gowns, practiced a classical piece Tony didn't recognize while three 6-meter rose blooms adorned the wall over their heads.

Sitting quietly in a lone chair in the center of the dance floor was a black man wearing a white tuxedo without sleeves. His massive silver prosthetic arms stood out like a beacon. Even through the tailored jacket, the man's broad shoulders and narrow waist looked like an inverted triangle perched on his hips.

The gangly legs, tail, and gaunt body of a young tortoiseshell cat sat next to the man on a small, white service table. The cat's tail swished back and forth, not in irritation but in time with the music. The two sentient audience, one man and one feline, seemed engrossed in the band, oblivious to the otherwise chaotic stimulus around them.

As Tony approached, the reddish-brown cat turned back toward him and gave off a tiny mew.

"I guess my silent partner couldn't wait until opening night," the man said without turning. "Welcome back, Mr. Tony."

"Jock, you creep me out when you do that. That rear visual augmentation is going to be the death of me."

"Who needs it when I've got the ultimate guard cat?" Jock said turning. A huge smile covered most of his face. "Besides some of the boys watched you creep along at street level in this direction and reported."

"Good thing they aren't after the reward."

"Hi, my sweet Cinnamon," Tony said sitting in a chair offered by a timely employee. Tony offered his hand to his cat. Cinnamon sniffed his finger. She jumped down to the floor and stropped his legs once in each direction. Tony bent over to pet her but she stepped just outside his reach and sat with her back to him.

"Cats left alone don't take kindly to it. But don't worry. She'll forgive you about dinner time," Jock offered.

Both men laughed and shook hands.

"Thanks for watching her for me, Jock."

"*Amigos*, Mr. Tony. You have always been a friend to me."

"Well, I thank you anyway."

"So are things better with you, Mr. Tony?"

"Other than walking halfway across the United States at ground level? Other than being on the run from Metro assassins? Other than having a price on my head the size of Lithuania?"

"Well, some would consider those negatives," Jock said in his driest humor.

"Yeah, I thought all that was behind me," Tony said, looking up at the black ceiling 30 meters above. "I like what you've done with the place. It should bring in a better clientele, that's for sure. I know that at my old salary I couldn't have afforded even an appetizer in a place like this."

"Your money and my know-how. That was the deal. Would you like a tour?"

"No, thanks. I've got to find out who is calling the shots, literally, or you just might be out a partner." Cinnamon deigned to brush up against the hand Tony had dangling over the chair's arm.

"For what it is worth, my friend, you weren't followed."

"I know, but I'm glad you know as well." Cinnamon jumped up into Tony's lap, but sat down facing away.

"Your accommodations are prepared and your meeting with Jamie is scheduled for tomorrow morning."

"If I know my crew they are already in, no matter how well you hid the bunker. Jamie I'm less confident about. Thanks for all your help, Jock."

"You're welcome, friend. I suggest you and your crew get a good night's sleep."

"Well, the next time I miss out on a chance to sleep will be the last."

*   *   *

The amplified gavel created a trio of sharp reports over the din in the Portland Central High School auditorium.

"I'd like to bring this meeting—" A feedback squeal cut off Reza. He adjusted the position of the microphone before continuing. "I'd like to bring this meeting of the Law Enforcement Fraternal Union, Local Chapter Three, to order."

As chairman *pro tempore* of the local chapter, Reza waited five minutes for the small knots of police officers to break up from their personal conversations and find places. They filled 95 percent of the seats on the main floor and about 80 percent in the balcony.

"Thank you all for coming tonight. Based on door sampling, our attendance is up to twenty-four hundred sixteen tonight." Reza paused to let the applause die away. "This is a record that I hope will be repeated in the future.

"Before we really get started, I want to ask that you be patient with us. I know most of you are here for a very specific topic—" Reza heard a rather large murmur of assent to his statement from the assembly, "—but this is a business meeting which requires us to go through the forms.

"I'd like to call for a reading of the minutes of our last meeting by Secretary Diane Mandela." Reza sat with the rest of the officers of the union behind the long table stretching on either side of the lectern. He tuned out the minutes as interesting only to historians researching a thesis or ACLU lawyers trying to find a reason to indict the organization for discrimination. Instead, he worried the current problem under his mind's teeth like a bit of mental gristle.

Sergeant Tolbert was right. Reza couldn't agree more. This extensive hunting of the GAM and more importantly the Commissioner's blatant defiance of the new council could only end up badly. He found himself caught between what he knew to be true and an impossible set of orders. Sometimes you could pass the buck up to your superior. Only a lifetime of self-control kept Reza from laughing at the thought. Captain Hardy wouldn't make love to his own wife without a direct order from the Commissioner. Major Boldsky was even worse.

Reza chalked up his own short temper with the sergeant because at least Enrique had the stones to ridicule the plan for the *tatti* it was. Unfortunately, he liked his gold lieutenant's bars and the perks that went with them. Even more he'd like to trade them for the railroad tracks of captain someday.

Oh, why in the heavens did he listen to his wife and leave Chennai. He'd have been captain there already, maybe bucking for major. With the megacorps there paying their police insurance without a beef and the local businesses turning over the rupees like scared *rundi*, he could've been rich. No, instead she had to be near her family. Maybe mama had been right when she said that he should have married Hindi.

" ... all opposed to approving the meeting minutes as read?

"Motion carried by no dissention."

Reza stood back up and nodded to Diane as he sidled back up to the podium. "Moving on to old business, I'd like to hear a report out of the committee for the annual Metro Black and White Ball." Reza stood there calling on one group or another before closing the ongoing topics of the local chapter.

"Now for new business." The level of noise rose precipitously. "I want to remind you that this is a chapter meeting. If you can't behave then we can see you removed or cancel any further business of this meeting." The noise lowered with a growl of protest. "I'd like our own Commissioner Yuri Krylov to speak to us on a matter of extreme importance. Please give him your full attention." The Commissioner dwarfed the lieutenant's 175 cm height by almost a full head. In his civilian suit, tailored to look like a Metro uniform, the aging but still vibrant man strode past the lieutenant / speaker. The crowd clapped and cheered as their leader approached to address them.

Reza could feel the charisma oozing off the Commissioner as the man played to the crowd perfectly. You could only admire the skill of the man as a performer, he thought. Yuri stood silently for nearly five minutes as the applause went on and on. Once the crowd quieted down he moved toward the microphone.

"I had a—"

The audience interrupted him with another spate of spontaneous ovation. Yuri waved them down and finally got some semblance of order restored several minutes later.

"Most of you already know the story, but please give those who haven't the opportunity to hear and understand so they can vote fairly.

"A representative of the new CorpGov sought me out to elicit our support for their new junta. I politely told him that we already had a mission and a chain of command. He pointed out how easily that chain of command could and would be subverted if we didn't bend to the will of the government formed by the princes of the corporate kingdoms."

An angry growl rose from the throats of the mob of Metro Police.

"He even went so far as to offer me a bribe," Yuri said.

The crowd went silent.

"It wasn't even enough to buy our esteemed lieutenant here."

The audience laughed.

"Seriously, though. The new council wants to take away what little perks we have. They want to stop protection payments entirely."

The crowd went berserk. People jumped to their feet screaming at the top of their lungs. The yells weren't even words but guttural emotions at extreme volume. Fists waved in the air.

Reza himself was stunned. Without protection taxes the police couldn't draw the best people. Their base pay didn't even make a living wage. Someone screwed the pooch on this one. Those stupid corporate bastards didn't have a clue.

Reza watched Yuri use both his arms and the full volume of the speaker system to try to calm the mob down but to no avail. The amplified voice didn't even crest over the top of the noise. Rows of seats were being torn from the concrete floor by teams of people. A fire started in the cushions to stage left. The panel of police officers on the stage fidgeted, unsure of what to do. Reza got up next to Yuri.

"Sir," he yelled, "I think we should get you to safety. I doubt this will end until the people exhaust themselves. I think the vote is self-explanatory."

"I think I have to agree. I may have done my job just a little too well."

"I believe that would be an understatement, sir," Reza said, not knowing if the Commissioner heard over the din.

*   *   *

To Augustine, the tests had been basic. Handling skipped interrupts, queue deadlocks, priority contention, denial-of-service attacks and even misplaced pointers were simple enough. They'd kept coming faster and faster until you were forced to deal with the problems instinctively. To Augustine it was the equivalent of muscle memory for the brain.

She had been the first completed and as such she watched seven other exhausted individuals made their way into the recovery lounge over the space of an hour. Two of them actually showed electrical burn marks around their net interfaces. Two test techs steadied a slight young man between them to one of the couches before adjourning. The group looked universally like an after-exercise commercial with greasy hair askew and strategic sweat stains through their bright-blue robes. Even Augustine felt somewhat harried.

"You have ten minutes before the group testing will begin," a poorly calibrated speaker scratched out from its hiding place in the ceiling.

A silence came over the room that lasted several heartbeats.

"I don't think I can take any more," the dark-haired youth who had been all but carried in said. "I feel like my brain is fried."

"I won't last long," a girl admitted as she ran her fingers through her sopping-wet hair. Several others nodded in agreement.

Augustine sidled up to the automated service. She selected eight servings of a simple vegetable broth and glasses of ice water. Quietly, she passed them out as the group, barely moving, bemoaned their fate. Augustine received a blessing of gratitude from each one. As she performed service for this group, she examined them.

Four of the fatigued assembly seemed straight from college. By her brittle demeanor, another one used to work for the civil service. A woman in her thirties, devoid of hair, probably had been a member of the Lesbos Movement, a radical wing of the Negative Population Growth Organization. As much as the others grumbled, the final man, with long, soot-black hair kept quiet, nursing his soup. Even beneath his robes Augustine could tell he kept his body physically fit. His middle-aged face was hard, stern, and even enigmatic. She assumed he'd been a private enforcer or mercenary.

She sat down and waited for someone to take the lead. She'd emptied her own cup of soup without a single person stepping up. "Any of you ever been on a net raid?" Augustine asked.

"Who hasn't?" one of the students said.

"All right then, you know that anyone raiding has their own set of goals and difficulties in obtaining them. Our job will be to determine what those objectives are and close off the avenues to them."

"This sounds like a lecture class right out of Computer Defense 101," one of the college students kibitzed as she tried to make sense of the tangle of her long, blond hair. "How about giving us something useful, you old bat."

"Hmmm. Old? Perhaps to you but I have skills that can take us through this test."

"Oh, really? Can you bring us cookies and milk?" One of the students gave the speaker a high-five for his wit.

"I know our lives before coming here are not supposed to count, but in this case I need you all to know. I'm Grandma Ice." Augustine's simple statement stopped all discussion.

"*The* Grandma Ice?"

"The one and only, sweetie."

"The Grandma Ice that cracked the control codes for the Lunar Fission plant?" the youngest girl asked, peering through her own ruined dreads.

Augustine just nodded.

The looks on most of the faces morphed. Heads turned. Eyes focused on her. In two cases, mouths even dropped open. Frowns turned into smiles.

"The Grandma Ice that copied the Russian Department of Defense budget onto the Peace forum?"

"Wow, that brings back memories. That was too many years ago when I was young and foolish. Of course back then I was just Mama Ice."

"So that means you are the Grandma Ice that was part of the Greenies."

"Yes, it does. Any of you have a problem with that?"

Head shook back and forth—all those except for the hard man in the corner. He spoke as he remained at ease on the divan. "I would have a problem if I hadn't taken the same vow you all have. I'm a former Metro and honestly think you should be vaped for what you've done."

Augustine tensed. She eyed him warily but the man remained half-reclining with no aggressive posture.

"That having been said," he continued, "God and his Son, Jesus Christ, wash away all manner of sins, Sister. I welcome you as one of our own."

"Thank you, Brother—"

"Adam. Brother Adam."

"I thank you, Brother Adam. I don't mean to be rude but we only have a short time before they throw us in front of this test. Let me lead you as a team. I know what it takes from the other side of the wall, and thus I know how to bolster our defenses on this side. Any of you have specific training, other than Brother Adam?"

"I did my thesis on creating rogue data-paths by varying bus voltage levels."

"Perfect. I'm putting you in charge of the power grid. Don't worry if you have to ask for help. That is the most likely avenue if they are going to shut us down rather than just going for a quick data grab."

"I did my senior design project on new, parallel-processing architectures," claimed the slight, dark-haired youth.

"Excellent, I would like you to watch over the core execution, specifically on the watch for code fragments. Another thing to be wary of is bagbiters. These are a couple of the key methods used by raiders to gain access. Don't assume hardware has gone tits-up unless you've checked it and it has a specific failure mechanism.

"Brother Adam, I'd like you to continuously scan for daemons. If there is a Trojan injected in our system, it will have a daemon looking for operations."

Everyone nodded as Augustine passed out basic assignments. The light in their eyes came back. She could see the team actually forming as an entity.

"Sister, as a former Metro, I have to despise what you accomplished in your past life." The stern face broke into a smile that must have strained unused muscles. "But today I'm glad to have you protecting God's data and our backs."

*   *   *

"Welcome back, Antonio," Jamie Ardwin said stretching her long, tanned legs sensuously. Her red hair spilled over the arm of the cream velour divan in a room where the sale of the least of the stark-modern, decorator accents would feed a family of four for a month. Her verdant, brocade corset, itself costing seventy-four thousand dollars, emphasized her feminine curves and barely contained her ample breasts. The calf-length, green skirt flirted from opaque to transparent enough to count the constellation of freckles on her thighs. In spite of her fiery appearance, the coldness in her blue eyes would have put a mad rapist off his feed.

After being stabbed by a sociopath, whom he called a close personal friend, Tony might have had the stones to overlook Jamie's soulless eyes had she not ruthlessly run the largest, most vicious crime family in the Pacific Northwest. There seemed to be no up side, especially as she used the sex kitten act to provoke, not entice. All calculations showed her no less lethal than Christine.

"Only my mother has the right to call me that," he said as he pet Cinnamon. Regally perched in Tony's lap, the gangly, tortoiseshell cat added a very sharp meow directed at the *capa famiglia* before licking her paw and grooming her right ear. "Please call me Tony."

Jamie's laugh rolled over him as sweet and sticky as grenadine syrup. "All right, Tony. What can we do for you today?" Jamie motioned for a steward to pour. The black oak table, in simple, sharp lines, held an asymmetric tea service for two. The green plastic of the antique cup and saucer ensemble was embedded with ruby slivers. Its faded white patina suggested they were well over a hundred years old. The servant filled an empty saucer with milk, placing it before Cinnamon.

Tony thought the cups seemed lopsided until he realized they'd been molded that way. Shaking his head he said, "Well, as you know we are a bit shorthanded, especially in the net jock area." He lifted Cin up to the table so that she could enjoy her drink.

"And what happened to Miss Augustine?"

"Not a thing. She's just incommunicado, at least for the near term," Tony said, taking a sip from his cup.

"Go on," Jamie said, taking her own polite drink.

"I need to place an untraceable call to someone who might or might not want to wipe out the entirety of the GAM. Not only is it going to be difficult to get to him, it may be dangerous."

"So you want to talk to Nanogate again," she said just before taking a dainty bite from a scone.

"Am I that transparent?"

"Only to one who pays to know everything about everyone."

"Amazing. I wonder who ratted on us?"

"A lady never reveals. Well, in any case, did I make the correct interpretation of the data?"

The way that Jamie looked at him over the lip of her cup made

Tony shiver. He didn't like his thought processes being so naked under the eyes of a predator.

"Yes, ma'am, you did."

"Good, then I called this meeting at the correct time." She whispered something into her percomm before returning her attentions to Tony. "The price will be four hundred thousand."

"And when does this call take place?" Tony kept his face impassive. The sum was a great deal less than he'd been willing to pay.

"Oh, I'm sorry, dear. We'll be talking to him in about two minutes. You see Nanogate's driver is … let's just say he's a friend. My friend has arranged that I have the only code to the car's vidcomm."

"How clever of you. But you said 'we.' This is a private call."

"P'shaw, Tony. You have to know that I have this suite and the vidcomm you will be using bugged. Why make me huddle over some screen watching and listening rather than being directly involved?"

The hair on Cin's back went up. Tony thought she might actually hiss at the woman but instead her tale jerked about spastically before she jumped back down into Tony's lap.

"One hundred thousand," he snapped back. Ignoring the GAM account, even Tony's personal bank account wouldn't notice the loss of ten times the price she originally asked for. He knew that it would be a mistake not to dicker.

"One seventy-five and you introduce me."

The intensity in Jamie's stare took Tony aback. If he didn't know any better he would have thought she was aroused. Using some tricks that Linc once shared with him, he examined her more closely. Her breathing seemed just a tad more shallow than normal. The pulse on her neck definitely was elevated. What's more, the longer he waited without giving her a response, the more her hands clenched, unconsciously generating a pale flush around the knuckles.

She most definitely was aroused and she wanted this quite badly. The lower price now seemed to make some sense. Jamie wanted another contact and another bit of information. This datum could be extremely valuable to her indeed. What price could you place on knowing the head of all governments?

"One twenty and you owe me a favor."

"Don't be silly, Tony," she said feigning indifference. "Setting this up alone cost me that much. And a favor on top of that? You need this, not me."

"That may be true, but I can buy someone else's service as well. One forty and you owe me a favor ... and I'll introduce you."

His scrutiny of her caught the subtle change in Jamie's demeanor. He knew the dicker was over. She took a sip of her tea, affecting pensiveness. Her eyes went blank as she ostensibly checked figures on her computer.

"Done. Simone, darling, would you bring in the vidcomm, please."

*   *   *

Nanogate climbed into his stretch liftousine taking care that the door frame didn't muss his muted gray suit. That his driver held the door open for him and closed it behind him didn't register. It was part of his everyday routine. He barely noticed the car lifting off as his mind worried on the outright rebellion of the Metropolitan Police Force. Nanogate excelled in the application of focused political and economic pressures. Mr. Marks provided the physical pressures at his direction. Oh, he had only begun to exert his stresses on the Metros. It struck him as sad that Mr. Marks could only deal with individuals or very small groups.

The Metros themselves, and their counterparts in other countries, were the only reliable organization for the application of large-scale force. The standing armies of the world's countries were a joke. In fact most of those forces were over 76 percent comprised of reservists from the police themselves.

The rebuilt Space Needle flashed past, breaking his concentration. Before he could refocus, the car's vidcomm chose to invade his privacy with a honey-sweet voice. "Excuse me, sir. You have an incoming call."

"Interesting. Why didn't they percomm?"

"My computational ability is limited, sir," the artificial intelligence offered. "I can only conjecture that they don't have your percomm signal and did have the code of this vehicle."

Nanogate rarely let his true feelings show. His surprise went undisplayed. Several options presented themselves including that his percomm may be bugged. If someone went to this trouble, the amusement value alone was worth answering.

"Receive the call.

"Nanogate here." He stared into the face that sometimes still haunted his nightmares. Next to this sometimes terrifying face sat a rather leggy, mottled-colored cat. The animal reminded his stomach that he hadn't had any breakfast. Nanogate dialed for a cranberry juice to assuage his body's mini-rebellion.

"Good morning, Nanogate. Tony Sammis here."

"Yes, I recognize the face." Many thoughts went through his head but years of negotiations kept him from blurting out the fact that he had been looking for the guerrilla leader. "What can I do for you, Mr. Sammis?"

"Well, I'll get right to the point. Are you trying to eliminate the GAM?"

"Ludicrous." Nanogate watched Tony's tense shoulders relax at least a micrometer. "I do have some information in that area, however."

"Please. I'd love to know who is trying to put paid to us."

Nanogate read the man's demeanor. Tony likely already knew much of what he was going to share. "The Metros have decided that you and the Green Action Militia are public enemy number one. They are hunting you with every, and I do mean every, resource they have available to them."

"So, I repeat, you are trying to remove us. Why? Are we too threatening to you?"

"You misunderstand, sir. We asked them directly to desist."

Tony's visage screwed up in confusion.

Nanogate took a sizable gulp of his drink before continuing. "I will be forthright. I had a personal meeting with the police commissioner. He believes that you are to blame for any problems that the Metros now have. As a direct corollary, your demise will be a panacea. Despite a direct request from me to stop his actions, Commissioner Krylov has chosen to demure."

"Lovely."

"In that, you have said a great deal. It gets even worse. My associate has obtained an advance copy of the Commissioner's eulogy for his fallen comrades. It appears he intends to publically defy our new government."

"Seriously? What does he hope to gain?"

A hand reached in from off-camera and jabbed Tony in the side.

"Oh, hold on a moment, sir, I've promised to introduce *Capa Famiglia* Jamie Ardwin."

A beautiful redhead slid up next to Tony.

"Good morning, Ms. Ardwin." Only Nanogate's long history of climbing the corporate ladder let him keep the annoyance out of his voice.

"And the same to you, sir," the woman purred as she sat adjacent to Tony.

"Back to the crisis at hand," Tony said, all but ignoring the woman.

Nanogate couldn't help but be impressed by Tony's sheer *cajones*. *Capas* had vast powers. That Tony would so cavalierly brush her aside as being unimportant astonished Nanogate favorably. He'd underestimated Tony very badly in the past. He wouldn't do so again. "Yes, an open rebellion. Computer models show that by the end of the month that the CorpGov could be a non-entity no matter how much economic clout we have," Nanogate said, probably giving more information than he really should. Any ally, especially such a capable ally as the GAM, would be useful. "While I've not exercised all of the power I have available to me in this matter, I would be untruthful if I said that I wasn't concerned."

"And here I messaged you to ask you to call off the dogs. It looks like we have a mutual problem that is as deadly to one of us as the other."

"I concur."

"What would you say to combining forces?"

"Politics does make strange bedfellows. I agree."

Generate Easy Ideas

As union representative, Reza stood at attention in his dress blues behind the families of the bereaved. He could hear the near-constant sniffles from Mrs. Berry. To one side of her sat Eve Santos, mistress of Officer Berry. He could just make out Mrs. Dabs's face in profile and watched her tightly clenched jaws working back and forth. Inwardly Reza smiled. Mrs. Dabs wouldn't turn a blind eye to the damage done to her family's *izzat*—her family's honor.

"Present Arms," Sergeant Tolbert directed crisply to the honor guard of seven as they stood at the edge of main Portland Metro station's roof. The buttons and metals of the firing party shined in the pale light of the Portland sunset. The squad came to attention smartly.

Commissioner Krylov marched to the podium in front of two polished granite coffins, each draped in the red and black of the Portland Metropolitan Police flag.

"Parade Rest," Tolbert ordered.

"I've been asked to say a few words before we intern Officer Jackson Berry and Inspector James Dabs," the Commissioner said in a somber tone. "Both men were just that ... men. They did their duty day in and day out their entire lives. They were men of honor. They were men of principle."

The lieutenant felt tears coming to his eyes even though he knew Krylov had to ask the names of these two victims. He hadn't know them from any nil on the street. Krylov's projected emotions spoke a very different story. The tone of the man's voice cried out with an anguish that Reza knew he couldn't possibly have.

"I cannot say enough brilliant words about these *men* who paid the ultimate price for being our guardians and protectors. I weep for their families and loved ones." Krylov's voice cracked just the right way as he looked over at the knots of the bereaved. He pulled a handkerchief from his pocket and dried his eyes.

"On the opposite face of that that coin I can't say enough vile things about the jackals who perpetrated these outrageous acts upon them. Degradation, torture, and mutilation are the tools of barbarians and animals.

"Yet these bestial atrocities are the things the new administration wants us to overlook. These are the things they want us to swallow and meekly accept. This is all of our fate under this new fiat government.

"Our brothers in arms have decreed loud and clear that we must fight to uphold the honor that Officer Berry and Inspector Dabs already died for. To do anything less would sully their memory and risk the lives of every ... other ... policeman in this solar system.

"I will not let the illegal government, installed by coup, to cheapen our honor. I will not let the blood of our best be spilled on the altar of expediency. I will *not* let that happen," Yuri said, stepping back away from the podium, his face dark. Both of his brown eyebrows, barely separated at rest, now knitted tightly together. He saluted the caskets with military precision.

"Present Arms," Tolbert said at the cue. "Load," came the second command timed more precisely than by an atomic clock. "Ready. Aim. FIRE."

Reza felt the concussion of the seven shots reporting as one through his oversized belly. He watched as the flag party folded the flags in a precision matched only by the timing of the firing squad.

"Ready. Aim. FIRE."

Reza wondered how many other weapons would fire. He wondered how many more flags would cover other caskets. The two pitch black flags now took their final shape folded down to a black triangle bearing only the brilliant-red scales of justice on the outside.

"Ready. Aim. FIRE."

The honor guard presented one flag to each widow.

"This flag is presented on behalf of a grateful populace and the Portland Metropolitan Police as a token of appreciation for your loved one's honorable and faithful service."

Even as the last shots echoed off the nearby buildings, Reza only wondered how many more would die.

Two boxed units, draped in black cloth, lowered the bodies with dignity into the cremation furnaces specifically for the use of the deceased Metropolitan police officers.

* * *

A sliver of the full moon peeked through the mottled clouds over the Canadian Rockies. The 7 centimeters of snow reflected in the pale light like glitter cast upon the earth. Augustine's breath blew out like a dragon's smoke in the dark air. She sat in a hollow in the snow compressed by her body. Even without knowing the temperature, she could smell the bitter cold in the lack of moisture each time she inhaled. The sweat in her hair froze into a solid mat.

Crunch, crunch, crunch, came the sound of someone's footsteps breaking through the snow's top layer. Today it had warmed just enough to turn the white surface to slush. The night froze it into a solid, if brittle exterior. The sounds of the footsteps moved directly toward Augustine.

"Quiet out here," Brother Adam said as he got within 3 meters.

"It was."

"Don't."

"Don't what?" Augustine asked, not looking down as the clouds brought new patterns across the moon.

"Don't put up a wall."

"You know, I've never lived anywhere that you could see more than a handful of sky. How do they stand it?"

"I was a Metro here in Calgary. I used to floatboard out to the wheat fields after a football game and just stare up at the stars. No matter what happened in the game it made me realize how little it mattered to the cosmos."

"Really?"

"Yeah." The silence swallowed up the last syllable. The pair actually heard a snowshoe hare hopping somewhere nearby.

"So you didn't come out here in the cold to talk about stars, Brother Adam," Augustine said shifting her weight as one of her legs started to go numb under her.

"Nope. I have four different messages for you."

"Four?!"

"First. I volunteered to carry a message from our entire test group. They want to thank you for helping them not only pass the test but to crush it mercilessly."

"That's very nice. You're all good people. Each of you have some marvelous talents."

"It wouldn't have been anything without your direction, coach."

Augustine smiled to herself in the dark. "OK. That's one."

Adam kneeled down. "Damned, but it's cold.

"OK, next, I've been deputized by Prioress Hanna to tell you that with such an impressive NA test she intends to offer you your choice of positions ... anything short of offensive net actions."

"Yeah, I don't think the church would be too keen about letting a novice know about whose ice they want cracked ... at least, I wouldn't in their shoes." Augustine heard Adam chuckle.

"Too true. The prioress says she hopes you will take up the challenge of Guardian of the Chalice."

"We didn't light up the test *that* well."

"Sister, I don't think you understand. You didn't just let us ace the test but rather broke it. My understanding is that they had a full-up, offensive assault on that node. They brought the varsity—nothing less than Knights First Class."

"Really?" Augustine said, standing up. She batted at the snow that stuck to her posterior. "You're right. It is cold. Let's head back. My ass feels like a cube of ice."

Adam laughed. "You should try playing football in this stuff."

"Anyway, our opponents in that test, expert jocks all, expected to have full access within sixty seconds. Instead, you forced them out completely. I understand some tough questions are being asked by their superiors because of the failure, or more specifically your success."

"Our success, Brother Adam," Augustine said, setting a slow but steady pace breaking through the snow toward the 413-meter-tall, pyramid-shaped priory.

"Without you, I don't think we would have lasted thirty seconds," Adam said falling into step beside her.

"You don't give yourself enough credit."

"Be that as it may, you do have a way of making us better ... of forming us into a team."

Augustine didn't respond.

"Well, then, on to my next message," Brother Adam said in segue. "I'm sorry."

"Sorry?" Augustine asked, finally breaking her trance on the moon to look at him. "Sorry about what?"

"I'm sorry I got such an attitude about you being a Greenie. We're all supposed to be equal here. We are all supposed to have no past. That's the first rule of the novitiate."

Augustine smiled. "Don't apologize to me, Adam. Take it up

with your confessor. I didn't take any offense."

"Nevertheless, I'm sorry. As an act of contrition, I'm bringing you my final message."

"Like I said, Adam, you don't—"

"Well, it may be important to you. I've heard through my contacts that the Portland Metros have just declared war on the CorpGov."

"Now that *is* important."

* * *

Cinnamon followed in front of Tony until he collapsed into a vinyl wingback chair. The seat's alternating stripes matched the room's pale blue and ebony color scheme like some genetically-engineered zebra.

"I'm so glad to see you all again!" Tony said smiling at the familiar faces.

Christine, with her straight brown hair shining brightly, sat next to the equally petite Morgan. They held hands on an azure sofa which sported black, *fluer de lis* accents. Both the ladies looked expectantly at Tony.

Jacob, a short, broad man with massive fists that would have done a blacksmith proud, stood behind Frances, who enjoyed a white linen, overstuffed chair. At the chair's base, David Swift reclined against several brilliantly white pillows on the lush gray carpeting. Frances, like a mischievous teenager, every so often took the opportunity to ruffle his loose, red curls.

The very pale Weissmuller twins, Wayne and Joel, sat at attention like bookends carved out of chalk. They sported thick, black hair rakishly draped over one eye as a single splash of color.

"Nice digs. A bit more plush than we're used to, eh?" Tony said, petting Cin who'd decided that his lap was her preferred perch of the moment.

"Aye," Edward Longfingers said. He sprawled over a power-blue lounge like some screech-star diva.

"You got that right."

"Better than the commune I've been crashing in," Martin Fox said from his cross-legged perch on a footrest. His brown hair hung in sloppy dreadlocks down each side of his face like a cauc Bob Marley.

"I decorated," Morgan announced, her short, curly, black hair bouncing around like a boxwood bush in a gusty wind. "I was going for a functional but modern looking living room, even if it doesn't have a vidow. So something like a cross between French Provincial and techno punk."

Tony said, "Thank you, Morgan. I'm sure Jock appreciated your help when he had so much to do getting the Wilted Rose ready for its opening.

"I'm happy to see us almost fully together again. This is our new home. While I'm sure we will be moving about in the future, this is going to be our base of operations.

"I've so much to tell you that it all just wants to come out at once. Please be patient with me," Tony said in a gush. "By the way, is there a beer in the place?"

This got several chuckles. Jacob ducked through a doorway. "Catch," he said as he came back in, tossing Tony an Olympia beer pouch.

"I needed that," Tony said after a long pull. "Thanks. Anyway, back to cases. First I need to tell you that the new CorpGov isn't trying to nail our hides to the barn door."

Several members looked puzzled at his idiom.

"OK, said another way, they aren't trying to kill us. Even more importantly, they tried to stop it. Not only do we have Nanogate's word, but if you go on the net and pull up the vids of the Metro funeral of last night you will have confirmation. The Metros alone are behind all of this."

"Ya, ze police declare war on ze Corpies," Joel Weissmuller said with a nearly unadulterated accent from his native Germany.

"Why?"

"Good question," Tony said before flippantly adding, "Next question?"

Morgan twittered.

"Because they don't want change," Frances, an ex-Metro herself, said with her mouth fixed in a hard line. "Those corrupt bastards want to go on plundering, raping, and murdering."

"That is pretty much the way Nanogate and I both see it," Tony added.

Cinnamon dropped down onto the floor and crossed the room to jump up onto the lap of her second favorite slave, Christine.

"So vhat ve do? Dey haff laser guns and many, many mens," Wayne offered. "My brot'er and me see hundreds shoot up our *delikatessen*. How ve fight hundreds or t'ousands?"

Tony took another hit on his beer before responding. "For a change we're not alone. I've worked out a deal with the CorpGov itself. You know the old saying, 'The enemy of my enemy is my friend'? It applies here in spades."

"Yeah," Jacob interjected. "If the Metros won't take the orders of the CorpGov, then this new government's existence might last as long as an ice cube in a Texas summer, but no longer."

"Well put," Connie Powell, their resident Amazon and daughter of the late Andrew Powell, said.

"Vat can ze CorpGov do?"

"Mind if we tackle that later, Wayne? I think we need to decide what we can do first."

"Sure, Tony. Ve just vondered."

"Don't get me wrong, Wayne. It's a valid question. But before we talk about outside our organization let's talk about inside. Everyone should recognize everyone here. This is the entirety of the action arm of the GAM for the foreseeable future," Tony said.

The group of eleven humans and one feline looked about at one another in resignation. They clearly hoped for Tony to have pulled a rabbit out of his hat, but expected the worst anyway.

"I know this is a very small group to lean on, but I don't have Sonya's way of peeking into a person's soul. This means we'll have to deal with traitors."

"Historically," David chimed in, "that means a cell system where one person only knows only a few others. This limits the damage one traitor can do to the entire organization."

"But it inhibits our ability to project force in mass," offered Frances.

Tony saw the entire group nodding as one. "Exactly. Nice to know you all understand. Honestly, the only way we can still operate in even this large of a group is that every single one of you have been vetted by our late leader. I know I can trust each of you with any secret. Thus we must stay this size or if we add a member it must be from the Green organization as a whole. It also must only be for a specific operation and task. Anyone disagree?"

Faces looked at one another not expecting a dissenter but

checking to be sure.

"Good," Tony continued. "Now, any bright ideas for taking the fight to the Metros?"

"How about direct action against this Commissioner Krylov? I'm sure Christine would love to do a little knife work," Edward Longfingers said sitting upright for the first time in the meeting.

Tony didn't have to look to see the twinkle of excitement that formed in Christine's eyes to know it was there.

"Ah, no," Tony shook his head. "That would have been my first suggestion as well. Nanogate's sources tell him that the entire union is ready to riot because of a supposed 'heavy hand' of the CorpGov. Killing off Krylov at the moment would prove it to them and give them a martyr to rally around."

"Maybe it would help if we knew what the CorpGov has planned."

"Yes. Is dis ze time?"

Tony smiled.

* * *

The Oval Office had been designed to intimidated visitors, but Nanogate wasn't a diplomat or a barbarian. In spite of the antique wainscoting and the real wool carpeting, the opulence of the room barely registered. His own public office had been designed by people with hundreds of years more experience in the science of psychological manipulation. He'd also suffered through much worse on his climb to Nanogate's leadership.

"Good evening, Ms. President. Thank you for seeing me on such short notice," Nanogate said with his hand outstretched over the seal of the United States woven into the emerald carpet.

"Thank you, sir, for honoring me with your time," President Carla Lopez offered beneath her infamous and perfectly coifed, brunette curls.

"It is the least I can do."

"Please have a seat," she asked motioning to one of the Dartmouth-green, roll-arm couches. She took the one opposite but leaned forward. "Your assistant informed us that you wouldn't need any of the other cabinet members for our discussions."

"That is true, Ms. President. I thought it would be better to be informal about our meeting and any agreements before we involved anyone else." White roses from Edith Roosevelt's famed garden graced the mission-style coffee table between them.

A boxed unit, enclosed in a serving cart, rolled into the room to the President's side.

"Tea?" asked President Lopez lifting up a genuine Revere silver teapot.

"Yes, thank you."

"Milk? Sugar?"

"No, thank you," Nanogate said, taking the china cup.

"So, what can I do for the new Chairman of the CorpGov?" she said, sipping.

"A well-informed President. I must admit surprise."

"Oh, come now. This still is the most powerful country on earth. Oh, I know we aren't a pimple on the power you corps wield, but we still have enough to follow major developments."

"Yes, Ms. President. I'm sorry for my presumption. I have to say that you are much more formidable than your predecessor." Nanogate helped himself to a blueberry scone.

"President Samuel Bracken?" Carla chortled softly. "That son of a bitch couldn't find bee in a hive. Sometimes I think the worst enemy of the ninety-seven United States is the people voting themselves morons to lead them."

Nanogate smiled.

"So what can I do for you, Chairman?"

"Well let's start with that," Nanogate said leaning back. "I'd like to work with you on establishing protocol between our governments."

"Like a liaison, or an embassy?" The President laughed again. "I may not have climbed the corporate ladder, but I do have some skill at reading situations. You wouldn't have asked for a face-to-face to discuss that."

Nanogate smiled again. "Much more formidable. Your predecessor I think still believes in the Easter Bunny."

The comment earned a chuckle from the President.

"All right, truth, Ms. President. I do want those things but no, the intent of my meeting request is much more pointed and timely. I'm sure you heard about the rash statements made by the Portland Metro Commissioner yesterday."

"Maybe."

"Now who is prevaricating?"

President Lopez took her turn at a smile. "Yes, sir, I did hear about that. It seems like your new government is in trouble."

"You don't pull punches, do you, Ms. President."

"I find it wastes time, a luxury I don't have in this line of work."

"Since you know the lines are being drawn, may I ask you where you intend to be on this topic?"

President Lopez leaned back. "This isn't an easy question, Mr. Chairman. Bear with me as I've been thinking about this for some time.

"My power, while it nominally derives from the people, in reality comes from our laws and our military. And, if you will forgive me, Mr. Chairman, your corporations flaunt and twist our laws. That leaves us nothing but our military."

"May I rebut, Madam President?"

"Not yet, sir, I have the floor."

"Of course, Madam President."

"Thank you. Your manners are much better than most heads of state. You should hear some of those arrogant, uneducated pricks and/ or cunts."

"Ms. President, I've had that misfortune on more than one occasion."

"And you are surprised at my language?"

"As a matter of fact, yes, Ms. President." A knock at the door interrupted them.

"Madam President?" asked an attractive young black man opening the curved doorway. "The Speaker of the House begs five minutes ... "

"Jamahl, no one gets any time until I finish here."

"Yes, Ms. President." The door closed as quietly as it had opened.

"I'm sorry for that, Mr. Chairman. As I was saying, I have to concern myself with anything that would weaken my position, and at this time, the military is nearly all reservists. Those reservists are almost strictly from the ranks of the Metropolitan Police Forces around the country." She paused to sip at her tea.

Nanogate took the opportunity she presented. "Madam President, everything you say is completely valid and I understand your position; however, I feel it also may be oversimplifying matters."

"Really. Please elaborate."

"Let us assume that there is a conflict between the CorpGov and the Metros. If we win and you don't support us, you can envision that we would be fairly inhospitable."

"Yes, but I don't need threats," the President said coldly.

"I'm sorry, please don't misunderstand me, ma'am. I wasn't trying to threaten, only outline possible outcomes."

"Understood, please continue."

"The second option, the more likely one from your perspective, is that the Metros would easily defeat the CorpGov as we have no army of any kind."

"That would be the way to bet."

"All things being equal, I would agree, Madam President. But we have some physical power of our own that may or may not be viable. But you are correct, the CorpGov losing would be the likely outcome. What happens then?"

"I'm sorry, I don't understand."

"The Metros, by your own definition are a power block that just overthrew a government. What happens when they decide they don't need any type of leadership except their own?"

Only a professional poker player or a megacorp executive would have noticed the minute pause in her tanned hand reaching for her teacup or the extra half millisecond she kept it to her lips. To Nanogate they screamed volumes.

"I do see your point. While I still haven't made a decision yet— what do you propose?"

* * *

"That fucking bitch did what?!" Krylov yelled as his face ripened to the color a Macintosh apple would have envied. The Commissioner's teeth slammed together hard enough to hear the report across the room. The muscles along his jaw rippled like a washboard. The brawny man exploded even further. Lashing out, he flung everything off his desk surface against the wall, including his precious antique wooden pencils. The resulting clamor drew a number of looks through the transparent front of the office. Krylov's disheveled appearance quenched the curiosity of those few hardy souls.

"Let me be clear, Mr. Commissioner. I received a low level communiqué from my liaison at the Office of Management and Budget.

It indicated that our federal funding was left out of the quarterly funding allocation. My contact assured me that it was probably in error as no message about stopping our subsidy crossed his percomm."

"Oh, no. She did this on purpose." Krylov kicked the boxed unit who was trying to put the mess on the floor back to rights.

"Excuse me, sir, but you keep saying 'she.' My contact is a Robert Coulter, a man."

"What you don't understand, Jasper, is that yesterday the Chairman of the CorpGov had a meeting with that slut President Lopez. I'm sure the fact that we now have lost our funding isn't a mistake. They hatched this together."

"I see, sir."

"And, instead of declaring war outright and immediately, she is straddling the fence with transfer difficulties, oversights in the budget, and on and on. Even if she wanted to, it would take weeks to correct. If she wanted to be obtuse it could languish for years."

"So the federal government is trying to strangle us?"

"More specifically, Jasper, President Carla Lopez is trying to take us out of the picture. Now I believe you do see."

"Should I take any specific actions with my counterpart?"

"Yes, tell that fucker that the money had better start flowing or else!" Krylov said in pique.

Jasper didn't respond but raised one eyebrow just a fraction. "Will that be all, sir?"

"No." In spite of his temper and age Krylov hadn't lost his political aplomb. The older man rubbed his bushy sideburns for several seconds as the muscles at his temple twitched. As suddenly as his outburst had occurred, he announced, "I have a much better idea. Do nothing but acknowledge your liaison's information. In the mildest terms note your concern. Don't get irate, just irked."

"Yes, sir."

"Oh, and on your way out, send in the commander of the SWAT team."

* * *

"Prioress?" Augustine asked, knocking on the open doorframe to an austere office.

The gaunt, middle-aged woman leaned back in her chair, absently picking up her rosary, its beads shining smooth with years of wear. "Sister Augustine, how many times do you have to be told, I'm just one of you. I'm Sister Hanna."

"I'm sorry, Sister Hanna, but I felt this was more a prioress matter," Augustine said stepping into the room. She shut down her wireless connection in order to not be disturbed by software, hardware, or network interrupts.

"Have a seat. Are you here because you've chosen your posting?"

"That is part of it, Sister Hanna," Augustine said sitting on the simple straight-back chair. She eyed the plaster crucifix behind the prioress and made a quiet prayer of her own. "Do you really feel me worthy of Guardian of the Chalice?"

"Daughter, you wouldn't have been offered the option if you weren't proven worthy. While we put our faith in our Lord Jesus Christ, we aren't stupid enough to put someone without the skill to protect Mother Church's secrets on the front line," Sister Hanna said with a firm set to her jaw.

Augustine smiled.

Before Augustine could speak, the prioress continued. "I'm only sad that I couldn't offer you a post as a Mariam Crusader but it's only offered to one who has taken her full vows."

"Crusader, Sister? I mean I have no illusions to the value of my skills but Mary's own Crusaders?"

The prioress leaned forward with her elbows on the desk and the crucifix of her rosary worrying between her fingers. "I don't think you understand what a hornet's nest you roused with that net aptitude test of yours. There are a number of Crusaders right now who are thinking uncharitable things about you as they clean the public washrooms in penitence, Sister Augustine.

"And before I say this, I want you to remember that pride is a sin. With that warning I'll stretch out on a limb and say you are the best overall protocol worker we've ever had in the Order. I praise God and his only Son that you chose to come to us. I know we will all sleep easier with you as a Guardian."

Augustine just sat letting it roll around in her head. If she were the best, she had fears about how safe the church's information had been prior to her arrival and worse what it would be like after she left. She shook her head not wanting the responsibility. Then she remembered that the Lord provided. Surely he wouldn't let anything untoward happen to his own if she weren't around. That would indicate pride, indeed.

"Thank you for your kind words, Sister. I will take up the challenge of being a Guardian."

"Excellent, Sister Augustine. I'll tell Father Nguyen to expect another addition to his team."

"Excuse me, Sister, but you said 'another addition.'"

"Yes, a number of the novitiates within your team have been given the opportunity to join the Guardians."

"Oh," Augustine said somewhat quietly.

"Don't worry, Sister Augustine. There is always room in the Guardians. Besides, more members mean shorter shifts and that gives you time for the other tasks I have lined up for you."

"Yes, Sister?"

"Well, I'm thinking that after your impressive performance that I need you teaching Beginning Net Protocol, System Protection, and Advanced Link Management."

Putting up her hands in protest, Augustine began, "That is too much, Prioress. I'm not wor—"

"Oh, do shut up, Augustine. First, you are bound to obey me. Second, I'm going to be the first pupil signed up on each class."

Augustine shifted backward causing an audible creak from the old chair's joints.

"Good. Now that we've settled that, I got the impression there was something else you wanted when you came in. I recognize a silent prayer to Jesus when I see it."

"How did you know?"

"Dearest Sister, I didn't get to be prioress just for my good looks." Sister Hanna smiled enough to display her dimples. "Nor am I stupid enough to not know what is going on under my own habit.

"If I had to guess, I'd say it was about the Metros all but declaring war on the GAM and the CorpGov." The woman leaned back into her chair with a smug look on her face.

Augustine opened her mouth to say something but not even a sputter came out.

"See, you don't have to be a rated net jock to know what's going on in the world."

"I don't know what to say, Sister."

"Then say nothing, Sister Augustine. That's usually best when you are at a loss. And before you say something that should only be protected by the sanctity of the confessional, I'll remind you that your former life is behind you. You must cut it off firmly."

Augustine knew. The prioress knew. *Everyone* knew her past but no one would hold it against her. As God pleased, she thought.

"Yes, prioress, I hear and obey."

*   *   *

"My name is Henry Royston," A1412 said. "I've been boxed for sixty-two years, six months, three days. Can any say they've been here longer?"

Storage Depot #13, in downtown Salem, Oregon, provided acoustic amplification within the nitrogen atmosphere as an unintentional artifact of its shape and size. As no one suspected the boxed had discovered a way to modulate their emergency external horns to provide communication, no one ever looked at the resonance frequencies of the structure. As a result, the 16,543 boxed units had no trouble hearing A1412's external vocals.

They all knew about the powerful AI monitoring the electronic communications between units to ensure compliance. The boxed wanted to keep their discussions to themselves so they actually talked, a feature their designers wouldn't have approved of.

"We all know you are the oldest, Henry. Get on with it!" insisted C3341.

"*Sí!* We don't want to wait for *mañana*," offered J883.

"OK then. I've heard rumblings among you that you want us to break cover and offer our support now." A couple of cheers rang out from the audience. Some thousands of them pulsed out a 2-hertz base signal, the boxed equivalent of applause.

"Quiet!" G996 shouted out. "I am Stephanie Delfalkis and I say quiet!" The base beat died out.

"Thank you, Stephanie," A1412 said. "I know we are all anxious to get back to real bodies but I have to tell you that premature knowledge of our presence in this game will keep us all boxed forever. It is better to err on the side of caution."

A chorus of "boos" ran through the crowd.

"We don't want to wait anymore."

"Why are we always the ones doing the waiting?"

"I wanna fuck again."

"Hell, I just want out of this fucking shell."

Henry let them vent their spleens or whatever disembodied brains use for spleens. He waited. Eventually they quieted down.

"He be right. None of 'em need us yet," Ben Calwood blurted out.

"Yes. Crudely put as usual, J112, but right to the core of the matter," Henry said reclaiming the speaker's position. "We need to wait until someone needs us so badly they will agree to anything."

A few whistled out a tone of agreement. Soon the entire structure filled with the same frequency.

"It won't be long now, but we must wait. Soon we won't have to remind ourselves of our names anymore!

"I am Henry Royston."

"I'm Pam White."

"I'm Stephanie Delfalkis."

"I'm Jim—"

* * *

Ghostly fingers of the nano-curtain pulled at Tony's upscale blouse as he strode through. On Tony's shoulder, Cin managed not to show too much annoyance at her ruffled fur. She bent over and licked down the worst of the offending coat.

"Nice upgrade, Tuan," Tony said to a whipcord-taut man who wore the classic canary yellow of a trained and working bodyguard. "But can you trust nanobots from one of the corps?"

"We are making them ourselves, now. Maybe not Elysium quality, but they don't need to be."

"Very impressive," Tony said giving Tuan an affectionate chuck on the shoulder. If not a quite a friend, Tuan at least rated as Tony's close acquaintance. "You already know Cinnamon," Tony said.

Tuan nodded politely to the still-gangly kitten.

"I'd also like you to meet Dave Swift," Tony said looking toward his human companion. "He has been consulting on Mars for the last few months and missed our *coup de grâce* of the corps."

As usual for any new visitor, the gaunt cauc gawked at the

exaggerated décor, this time Barbie-themed and primarily in pink. The priceless works of art adorning the walls and pedestals around the room also caught the man's eyes.

Tony watched as Tuan gave David's slight frame and curly, carrot-colored hair the once over. Dave's exquisite clothing over his pale skin looked rumpled even though they still showed the cleaner's creases.

"If it weren't for the look of Loki in his eyes, I'd've said your recruiting technique needed work, Tony. I could break him in half with a sneeze."

"Smile when you say that, citizen," Dave said with a wink.

"Welcome, Dave," Tuan said, extending his hand and a grin twice the width of his face.

Dave took the proffered shake. Both hands went white with pressure of the other clamping down hard. Tony watched as the two stared deeply into each other's eyes. The two fought to get the better of the knuckle-buster grip. Dave's pale skin showed red more than Tuan's olive complexion, but Tony couldn't determine which, if either, was getting the better of the ancient male rite.

A curvaceous blond floated out of the back room within a cloud of translucent-blue chiffon. Grigori, her second and most ubiquitous bodyguard, followed her. "Boys," *Capa Famiglia* Jamie Ardwin said, "must we shed so much testosterone? I mean if you want to oil wrestle for me later, that's one thing, but for now—"

Each of the silent combatants gave a final extra-hard squeeze before dropping the grip. Each smiled at the other in personal victory. Each managed not to massage his aching hand. Tony mentally called it a draw.

"I'm not sure if I should welcome you back, Tony. You were a naughty boy when we were talking to the Chairman," Jamie said drawing her full lips into a pout made famous by Angelina Jolie.

Cin hissed.

Tony sensed that Dave reflexively reached for his holster, empty for this one meeting.

Tony suffered under no delusions. Either of the guards, his friends or not, would kill him at the slightest word from Jamie. Not that his host would be so gauche as to have his friends do him in. Any number of lethal weapons trained on him from behind the walls, the ceiling and probably even the floor would do Jamie's dirty work, if she so chose. He weighed his options and chose one of casual contempt. His eyes bored into hers.

The tension lasted no more than three heartbeats. As suddenly as her mood changed to sulky, it shifted back with a smile across her attractive face. "But I'm not one to hold a grudge. Revenge isn't good for business. Welcome back, Tony. And I extend a welcome to Dave. Shall we sit?"

"Thank you, Jamie," Tony said cautiously. Cin's raised fur didn't drop even when Tony took a seat a polite half-second after his hostess.

Dave took up a station behind and to Tony's right like a bodyguard himself.

"Come, Dave. Please sit," she offered with her perfectly manicured hands. "You are in no danger, nor is your leader."

Tony caught Dave's darting eyes with his own and motioned him to sit.

"At least for now," Dave said as he perched just on the edge of a pink, wire-formed, garden seat as if even the sound of crumpling paper would make him leap to an *en garde* position.

Dave's comment caused a much more dangerous look to appear on Jamie's face, with her lips drawn thin and straight.

"True, Mr. Swift," Jamie responded in carefully measured syllables, "bearding the lion in his own den may have been successful for the biblical David, but I think you will find that most of the time the lion will win that fight."

"Unless you have God on your side," Dave riposted.

"True enough," Jamie said, softening so much and so quickly that Tony wondered what evil she had in mind.

"Speaking of too much testosterone," Tony said trying to lighten the mood. "Not that anyone could imagine for one moment that you were anything but all woman, Jamie."

"Well, flattery will get you anywhere you want, Tony."

"Really? Even after being a bad boy?"

"Yes, even after. So tell me why you are interrupting my dance lessons."

"We have a proposal that could improve your bottom line," Tony offered with a straight face.

Jamie cocked her head to one side. "Provided to you by total altruism, I'm assuming."

Dave covered a not very discrete cough with his hand. The

broad smile on Tony's face answered a dozen questions.

"OK. Let's have it. First tell me what I can do to improve my bottom line," Jamie said, dropping her come-hither façade to reveal the all-business woman.

"We want you to stop paying your protection money to the Metros," Dave jumped in eagerly.

Jamie's look would never have won even a home poker game. She just stared incredulously. Tony gave her a nod when she looked to him for confirmation. Jamie tittered in response.

"You just about had me on that one. What is it, April Fools' Day a bit early?"

"We are quite serious," Tony confirmed again.

"So what are you going to do when the black suits track down each and every member of my organization and give him or her a flechette enema? No organization equals no money and imprisonment, not more money."

"What if the Greenies helped protect you from the Metros?"

Jamie did think, but only for a moment. "You are just a handful of guerilla fighters. Granted you are good, but what can you do against the combined might of the Metros? I mean they all but own the army, the CIA, the FBI, and IRS Enforcement Division just to mention a few."

"Oh, I'm not talking just the Green Action Militia, Jamie. I'm talking about the entire Green Peace organization ... all seven billion of us in the United States alone."

After staring at him for at least four seconds, Jamie composed her hands in her lap and said, "Tony, one of these days I'll make you pay for what you do to my heart."

Build on Previous

Augustine's disembodied avatar looked out over a troubled ocean. Not a physical body of salt-laden water but her own network representation of the hopes and apprehensions of trillions of beings. It symbolized not physical locations but organizations, ideas, political personalities, stock prices, causes, power blocks, demagoguery and much more. Like any body of water, the more the surface of this sea showed disturbances the more energy the system held. In the case of her simulation, it predicted crime, oppression, mob violence, purges and even war.

Just over the last day, the waves of social unrest crested higher than she'd ever seen since she'd programmed it. Her prediction algorithm showed the storm's intensity escalating exponentially. Even the upheaval of the GAM coup was but a single, causal factor in the massive tidal waves that loomed.

Her foremost worry was where those waves would crash. If they moved toward the walls of her priory or that of the church, she would have to act quickly. To her surprise, the Holy See and the Catholic religion as a whole sat in a calm within the maelstrom that swept up the rest of the solar system. With her hands she twisted and refined the model. She expanded portions of the highest intensity to find those most vulnerable.

Clearly the GAM and the CorpGov's proximity now closed on one another, almost merging into one at this time. Sweeping rapidly to the opposite side of the model were all military and paramilitary organizations, with the Metropolitan Police Force at the center of that sphere of influence. It surprised Augustine none at all when the bulk of the energy focused directly upon the GAM/CorpGov and the Metros. The level of damage the model predicted would be enough to destroy entire stable governments and belief systems.

The model forecast nothing less than the destruction of both power centers and a new era of darkness and chaos.

Augustine allowed her consciousness to return to her own body. The biological blocks she programmed into her body dropped. Now her frail biological processes could run rampant. Her heart raced and adrenaline pumped. She felt fear.

*   *   *

The Syrah, one of the sole surviving bottles of the Brokenwood Graveyard Winery Battle of the Australian Civil War, complimented the thyme-roasted, lamb cutlets with a sweet mix of fruity flavor and mellow tannins. The plum-like nose mingled with the sharpness of the smell of baked herbs still lingering in the air. Servants carried out raspberry and lemon ices along with Columbian coffee as a finisher to the meal. They disappeared quietly and professionally. A neutral-scent palette and a tonal-music medley scrubbed the air, allowing the bitter drink to stimulate them.

Removing his napkin and dabbing the corner of his mouth, Nanogate spoke. "Thank you for making time out of your busy schedule to dine with me tonight. We have much work to do and even more work to project forward. I'll call on BeringC to preside over the meeting tonight."

From near the center of the now famous mahogany table, the Rubenesque brunette took charge. "Thank you, sir," she said in a furry soprano, which in her younger years had paid for college in voice-over contracts. "I would first call attention to the minutes of the previous meeting. Do I hear a motion?"

"I am motioning that they be passed as read," Royal PetroChem offered.

"Second."

"I have seventeen approval votes. Thank you. I guess that will bring us to old business.

"I have an attention light. Chairman Nanogate, you have the floor."

"At our last meeting I brought your attention to the difficulties with the Metros. Further negotiations with them has been less than stellar or to be perfectly frank, a downright failure. The Metropolitan Police Force refuses to come into line with civilian authority."

"Those unmitigated bastards," Unified Textiles said abruptly.

"I couldn't agree more, sir, but you are out of order," BeringC chastised mildly. "Nanogate has the floor."

Nanogate smiled and nodded at his moderator and at Unified Textiles both. "As a result I've initiated two separate actions. I've been in touch with President Lopez to remove the Metro's federal funding. This may in itself bring the rogue department to heel; however, likely it will not. To further this aim, I've initiated a protocol through the GAM that would strangle even more funding from the Metros. This action would have major entities failing, intentionally, to pay their police protection.

"At this time I suggest we keep our corporations paying our police taxes and use it as a final club over our colleagues in black."

"I have a question from Outer Conglomeration. Please proceed with your question."

"Hai wander what simulaashuns shows ov tees ackshuns," said the tall Ganymedian man with a complexion so white as to be all but transparent.

"Thank you for that segue, Outer Conglomeration," Nanogate said. "The simulations show a seventy percent chance of failure of these measures to bring the Metros in line. Note that in spite of these dismal percentages, it is at least an order of magnitude better than any other suggestion brought forward.

"I have a question from Savitz, Schauer and Levinthal. Proceed."

"What is our path if this method doesn't succeed? I've heard no discussion on this."

"Very good question, SS&L. As my researchers have offered, every option from that point, no matter what it was, would lead in short steps directly to war."

Silence bound each of the members for several seconds.

"Wait a minute," Wintel said, breaking the procedure. "Who fights who?"

"That is the only variable. If we fight them, the combatants will be the CorpGov and the GAM against the Metros. If we appease the Metros then after a generation of an increasingly oppressive police state, the combatants will be the general populations in a civil uprising.

"The odds in either case are not good with the resources the Metros would have at hand—fifteen percent in the first case and eight percent in the second. However, if we fight and fail, the general populace has an eighty percent chance of overthrowing the Metros in just ten years."

"So we are going to lose?" BeringC asked.

"We need to plan to get the most possible impact from our fight." Nanogate's mellow voice carried the tone of the executioner in it. "There are many variables that could change our chances radically ... but, yes, realistically speaking we are going to lose."

* * *

"Commissioner," Lieutenant Reza Narendra asked as he knocked on the open door's frame.

"Come in, Re'a. Wha' ca' I 'o for you?" Commissioner Krylov said around a mouthful of food. His broad frame sat behind a massive plate of breakfast. A napkin, already stained yellow with egg yolk, was tucked into his shirt top.

"Sir, I've come with a couple of pieces of news for you."

"Thi' couldn' come through nor'al cha'els?"

"Sir, you asked me to be your adjutant for the near term. I'm just trying to pursue the duties and make sure you are informed."

Yuri cleared his mouth. "Understood. Proceed."

"Thank you, sir. Item one—you have queries from the Metro forces of Chicago, New York, Dallas, Mexico City, Port au Prince, Anchorage and Miami interested in joining your lead in throwing off the CorpGov."

"Good, if unsurprising, news. What about Boston and Los Angeles?"

"Boston's Commissioner is mourning the death of his wife. The funeral is this afternoon. I wouldn't worry about them. They will come around."

Yuri nodded as he shoveled hash browns into his mouth.

"The LA Commissioner, June Brady, has publically declared that we are traitors and will work with the CorpGov to bring us to heel. From my contacts in their local union we can expect Commissioner Brady to soon receive her long-overdue retirement with the heartfelt gratitude of the city. A new, more-tractable replacement is expected to be named."

"Excellent news, Reza," Yuri said, wiping his chin and dropping the heavily used napkin on the plate.

"I wish that all of my news could be that good."

"Excuse me?"

"Item two, sir. We have confirmed reports that our government drawing accounts are now at zero. The feds are two weeks overdue for replenishment. Our contacts with the federal government say that there has been a clerical error and that they are trying to fix it. They are very sorry, but it will be at least three more weeks before any action can be completed."

"Ha! Don't count on it, Reza."

"No, sir, I wasn't. As you predicted some time ago, this is just the opening salvo in the CorpGov's attempt to put an economic stranglehold on us."

"Lieutenant, I want you to talk to SWAT team commander Captain Hogan. I want you to talk to him personally. Don't percomm the message I'm going to give you. Don't hand the duty to someone else. I want YOU to do it," Yuri said, boring his eyes into Reza's own.

"I understand, sir. What message do you want me to give?"

"Tell him to execute Seeger."

Reza got a chill down his spine. Even if he didn't know what Seeger was, the menace in the voice said someone was going to pay a dear price. "That's all?"

"Yes, Lieutenant."

"I will convey your message as soon as we are done, sir."

"There's more?" the Commissioner asked with surprise in his voice.

"Unfortunately, yes, sir. Item three involves notices that every illegal organization in the entirety of the United States has stopped making their payoffs. Their contacts informed us very directly that they have, and this is a direct quote from multiple sources, "found more cost effective means of protection.""

"What is the damage?" Yuri said from behind steepled fingers.

"As I'm sure you are aware, the illegal side of our take makes up one quarter of our budget. The loss of government funds another quarter. We are now down to only half of our income—direct payments from the people. There are state and local payments, but they are tiny by comparison. At our current expenditure rate and our current reserves we can last no more than six months."

"Thank you, Reza. I know that many men in my position would shoot the messenger. I'm not one of them. As for the funds we lost on the black side of our budget, I'm going to defer to our captains. Please pass a memo to each of them that I'd like our responding message to be firm."

"Yes, sir."

"Are there any other funds we can tap into?"

"Well, sir, if we call the cut-off of the federal monies a shut-out by management we can tap into the union strike funds."

"What will that do for us?"

"Another year's worth of reserve at our current expenditure level."

"Well, then," the Commissioner said clapping his hands together, "I declare that we are being shut out."

"I'll release the funds for immediate use, sir."

"We win, Reza."

"Yes, sir. I never doubted it."

* * *

"I'm coming. Keep your knickers on," Elijah said as his doorbell sounded for the third time. His leg implants, which hadn't worked in three years, ached as he forced them into an emergency assist unit. A handy neighbor had managed to cut off the intermittent pain spikes shooting through his hips, but the musculature was beyond the Good Samaritan's capabilities.

Eli remembered using the now dead legs to fly in his youth—Hermes Messenger Service, *when it positively has to be there now*. These days it was all he could do to get his own groceries and make it to the bathroom before making a mess in his pants. Changes in the laws turned him overnight from a successful businessman to a pauper owing the Metros and the federal government huge sums. Only the charity of the Missing Man Lutheran Church kept him from being boxed. When his legs had finally given out and needed replacement, there was no money. There hadn't been any for thirty years.

"Bzzzzz"

Each foot long step in the antiquated power walker took five or six labored seconds.

"I'm coming. Give an old cripple a break, will you."

Several minutes later he reached the door. He undid the seven bolts and three locks before opening it. Behind the portal stood three

Metros, two in powered armor and a third in dress blacks. The one he could actually see wore sergeant's stripes and had salt-and-pepper hair so short Eli had to look twice to make sure he hadn't imagined it.

"Elijah Cantor?"

"Yeah? It ain't no secret. I can't exactly move very far," Eli said sarcastically.

"We are here to collect on thirty-six years of back payments totaling sixty-four thousand seventy-six dollars and forty-five cents."

Eli's laughter caught the men off guard. In his youth Eli would have been terrified by the thought of a visit by the blackshirts. "Gentlemen, you can have anything you can find. My walker is worth maybe fifty bucks to a pawn shop and tonight I'm eating recycled cabbage."

"But you owe this money."

"You think if I had sixty-four thousand that I'd have hid it so that I could live in this luxurious slum? Fuck that. I'd be in Vegas with a pair of cute bigirls helping me spend all of the sperm I've not been able to do anything with for the last three decades."

"Sir, I've got a warrant to box you if you don't comply."

"Honestly, that would be a blessing, Sergeant. A dozen years boxed with a chance of getting back a body that worked? Where do I sign up?"

Sergeant Tolbert didn't hesitate. He just nodded to his compatriots. They had no intent of spending the hard credit to have the old man boxed.

The old ghit's screams echoed down the hallway. People couldn't have missed it. But in this level of Tualatin you learned to look the other way or you didn't live long.

Once the pair finished roughly dismembering the deadbeat, they used a 15-cm dagger to pin the plastic "past due" bill to the corpse's chest. They knew it would be talked about. They wanted it to be talked about.

*   *   *

Her team wasn't quite due to assemble for their first rotation at guarding the church's secrets, but Augustine wanted to make one last check of everything. Her nose wrinkled at the acrid plastic smell of her newly built defense node. But being new, she'd been able to define the critical components and design it into the best possible configuration. In a tight circle, eight Texas Computing, Mark-3 net couches faced inward in the extremely dim room.

The Mark-3s weren't on the market yet. They weren't even fully out of alpha test yet. Augustine, a diehard TC user, followed the couches' design and development. Even the power-on testing showed a three-hundred-percent boost in capabilities almost across the board.

It had been many years since Augustine had been with a man. She barely remembered that tab A went into slot B, but she lusted after these net couches. Sure, they weren't available to the public, but the church had someone on the TC board. She ran her wrinkled fingers sensuously down the faux leather. She could barely wait to jack in.

The primary compute nodes arrayed themselves around the outside of the circle of couches, blinking tiny message lights like thoroughbred race horses waiting impatiently in the gate for the start of the Kentucky Derby. She liked the nodes in the same room. After a while, she would learn the glows of their condition lights, the feel of cooling airflow, and the intensity of the almost silent buzz of the 60-hertz power supplies. This had in the past given her an edge in raids. Sometimes that one part in a thousand made all the difference.

"Sister, aren't you freezing?" Brother Adam asked as he entered the room, his arms crossed tightly across his chest. He rubbed his arms rapidly in an attempt to warm them.

Augustine looked down at her own arms where goose bumps covered her skin. "Well, yes, I guess I am. But one of the things you learn as a neophyte net jock is to disregard your body's normal impulses. Besides, it will warm up in here very quickly."

"Really? That's outside of what I normally dealt with in the police force."

"Don't sweat it, Adam. Just another tidbit of computer lore from G'ma. At rest the human body puts out about 3.3 kilojoules per hour, about as much as a weak space heater. We have eight of those or about 25 kilojoules per hour, and that isn't the worst of it—"

"Yes, the worst of it," Jason said still brushing his dark hair as he walked in, "can come as these nodes start maxing out compute cycles. You can count on a thermal output of about 4 megajoules per blade server or 64 per rack. Remember I did—"

"For the eighty-sixth time, yes, we remember your thesis, Jason."

Adam said as he rolled his eyes.

"Your typical oven cranks about 18 megajoules, and that's enough to bake LOTS of cookies. We are talking about three and a half times that," Augustine finished, not letting the slight tension linger. "That's why the fiber mesh of the floor and ceiling is our friend. There will be a constant flow of eighteen-degree air."

"Someone blowing hot air again?" Janice asked in good humor as she arrived mid-sentence.

"Not again," Ally said, her brown dreadlocks bouncing in right behind Janice.

"Adam, I thought you gave that up for Lent."

"Oh, please. We should can the chatter and get to work," Hypatia said acerbically.

The room devolved into twenty-five different conversations, most of them biting and derogatory. The rest of the crew arrived and joined in the general fray. The volume rose precipitously.

"Quiet!" Augustine snapped. Her exclamation echoed both up and down the massive cooling stack. Only the faint background whistle of the slow-moving air broke the abrupt silence.

"That's better," Augustine said with her hands on her hips looking more like a stern school mistress than any novitiate. "My apologies to those of tender disposition but we've got a job to do. To do that job we've got to be on time and in our benches and ready to protect our church ten minutes before our shift, not rolling in the door just on time with some banter on the side."

To avoid Augustine's gaze, Janice looked down at the tips of her shoes. She chewed on the ends of a couple of her blond strands of hair.

"What if a raid determined our shift timing," Augustine continued. "What if they scheduled penetration just on the change? And one more thing, if you think we can do this job after sniping at each other like bigots or sinners out in the real world then you have a WOM chip in your head. We have to be a team. Only as a team can we possibly hope to defeat other teams. If you can't do that, then I suggest we go right now to the Mother Superior and drop this charade."

The only sound was Augustine's foot tapping a regular beat on the floor.

"I'm sorry, Brother Jason," Adam said sincerely. "I should learn to be more tolerant."

"I shouldn't be so proud, Brother Adam. I also apologize,"

Jason's replied, his slight form bowing at the waist.

Several other similar exchanges took place before the room got quiet again. Augustine imagined a good number of rounds on the rosary for this group after each confessed.

"And we apologize to you for being late, Sister," Betty said. Murmurs of assent rose from the rest behind her.

"Thank you. But you aren't late," Augustine said with an impish grin.

She sensed seven different interrogations to the time daemon on the net.

"But it's now ten after the hour," Donna objected.

"Well, that is because I made your chronos seem T minus twenty minutes to you," Augustine said with a wide grin. "I've removed my modifications now."

"Damned, she did do it," Adam said after another query. "How? The time daemon is supposed to be inviolable." Six other heads nodded.

"It is. My trick is much more simplistic. I merely wormed into your personal files and replaced your pointer to the time daemon with a pointer to my version. *Always* check the integrity of your own files, and often. Lesson one of my net defense class, brothers and sisters. You're all signed up. However, now we need to get to work."

"Sister Augustine, I have one more question, if I may?"

"Go ahead, Janice."

"What is a WOM chip?" Several more nods came from those not wanting to be the one who asked the silly question.

Augustine actually laughed. "Sorry, my friends. A humorous invention of an engineer in the late twentieth century—Write Only Memory."

"But if you couldn't read back—" Hypatia started before she got the joke.

"Yes, he invented the device after 'Letting out the magic blue smoke' of a RAM device," Augustine explained. This got a chuckle out of everyone.

"Enough goldbricking. Everyone pick a couch and strap in. I have a feeling it's going to be a wild ride today in the net. In this case, welcome to the sink or swim reality of net defense."

* * *

"We interrupt our regularly-scheduled solido to bring you this breaking news from our reporter in the field."

"The President has been shot. The President has been shot. This is William Sagum. I'm in Denver, Colorado, where President Carla Lopez was giving a campaign speech to the Young Republicans. Just a few seconds into the speech a single, rifle-fired rocket struck her in the head as is shown here in this CNI exclusive footage.

"Additional camera footage will be added in the sidebars as it becomes available. As you can see here, her head jerked backward and blood sprayed behind her. Slowing the image down we see the fin-stabilized rocket, about as big around as a nickel and as long as a narco stick, in front of her head. In the next frame all we see is high-velocity spatter erupting behind her skull." The image went forward several more frames before the head started to snap backward.

"At this time President Lopez's condition is unknown. In the footage, you can see her Secret Service detail rushing her off to the presidential liftousine and presumably to the nearest hospital."

"William, this is Jake Crowley here in the studio." The image split into two different views, one of the field reporter and one of the anchor in the studio. "We are receiving unconfirmed reports of massive Metro and Secret Service activity at the Nuevo Republic Plaza. Can you confirm that?"

"Jake, that is over a kilometer from here. Wait just a second."

The camera view swung through about 120 degrees. Off in the distance, a swarm of black metro and bright-blue, secret-service-lift vehicles were darting about.

"We can see a great deal of activity near the Nuevo Republic Plaza."

"Would you think they are hunting the would-be assassin?"

"I can only theorize, Jake, but I can't imagine anything else that would demand that much attention. They certainly aren't trying to find a tagger."

"What about President Lopez. Do we have any update on her condition?"

*   *   *

"Try a different channel." The station flipped. The only difference was the color of the hair of the talking mouthpiece.

"It doesn't matter which channel you turn on. It's the same," Augustine said without visible reaction from the primary net couch. "They are all taking the same feed and VRing over it with their own commentators.

"Remember, crises like this are jock's favorite time to strike because of the increased load and the inattention of the defenses. Stay alert, team."

"Brad, just moments ago the presidential liftousine performed a highly illegal crash descent to land at the emergency entrance to Gates Memorial Hospital."

The image showed the black oval vehicle plunge straight down at a hair-raising speed. The pilot cut the landing just a bit too close and bounced the vehicle hard against the deck. The impact shattered the old-fashioned glass entrance doors 12 meters away.

Medical personnel and equipment spilled out of the destroyed entrance like water out of a broken dam. One secret serviceman dipped into the car and placed something small into a life capsule. Standing up, the agent glared at the camera, causing the image to back up several centimeters, perhaps because of the blood covering the agent's front.

"As you can see, President Lopez has been wheeled into emergency. We are now patching into the public information cameras inside the hospital itself."

The image wavered and was replaced by an old, flat image where the color was just a little too real. In a downward view above an operating table, the translucent life capsule exposed a wash of crimson blood over most of a tiny body within. The exposed head was barely recognizable as a woman, much less the most pictured face outside of Hollywood. A red gushing hole the size of a golf ball dominated her forehead.

"Holy fuck. Why did they bother to bring this in?" came the poor-quality recording of the emergency camera catching a doctor in the most vulnerable of times.

"She's the President, you dumb fuck!"

"Do something! We can't let her die," the shrill voice of a clearly distraught female nurse claimed.

"I don't care if she *was* the CEO of CNI," the doctor said, clearly emphasizing the past tense, *"that is just a corpse waiting for the right time to grow cold."*

"*Her heart's still beating! You have to be able to do something,*" someone off camera demanded in a tone of someone used to getting his way.

"*Listen, you gorilla. THAT'S a pile of meat fit for nothing but recycling.*"

A woman screamed at something the image didn't show. Both doctors put up their hands in surrender. "*Look, it doesn't matter if you shoot me or not. That doesn't have a fucking brain. Whatever she was, she stopped being it when her head was nearly removed!*"

The camera image suddenly went to fuzz. It took the networks several seconds to cut back to local feed.

"*That was disturbing live footage you just saw. Unfortunately, I think it is clear now that the President is dead. Let me repeat that. President Carla Lopez is dead.*"

Hybrid Solutions

Nanogate watched history being made on the solido. He sat alone in his overstuffed, red-leather chair holding a tumbler of whiskey over hand-cracked ice.

The image of Chief Justice Aadil Radwan stood alone in his formal black robes on a platform surrounded by darkness. The camera followed the Vice President of the United States, Susan Tipton, taking seven slow, even steps to meet him in a circle of bright lights. The image zoomed in close to her face. Her eyes were puffy and red under her glasses. The view also caught the firm set of her mouth before panning back. Her brilliant red hair, loosely curled, stood in stark contrast to her white skin and her severe, black, floor-length dress.

"*Let me reiterate,*" came a very soft voice-over from the commentator, "*this ceremony is taking place in an undisclosed location for security reasons.*"

"Madam Vice President, have you reason to believe that the President of the United States is dead?" asked the justice in a flat voice.

"Yes, sir, I do. I have seen her body—" Susan Tipton's voice cracked. Common knowledge had her and the President as more than just political allies, "—and have with me her certificate of death." The solido zoomed in on the document she presented in her left hand. Nanogate could just make out "Certificate of Death" on it. The judge waved it away as unimportant.

"Then are you ready to take the oath of office and accept the responsibility of the presidency of the United States?"

"I am."

"Place your hand on this Bible and repeat after me,

"I do solemnly swear—"

"I do solemnly swear—"

"—that I will faithfully execute the office of the President of the United States—"

"—that I will faithfully execute the office of the President of the United States—"

"—and will to the best of my abilities preserve, protect and defend the Constitution of the United States so help me God."

"—and will to the best of my abilities preserve, protect and defend the Constitution of the United States so help me God."

The camera coverage caught the President of the United States wiping a tear from her eye as she walked to a podium, now the focus of the spotlights.

"I know you all grieve tonight. I would be surprised if there was a dry eye in the entire country.

"Our leader has been taken from us in a cruel and senseless way. But for all her greatness ... for all her power ... for all her abilities ... she was still just a woman, mortal and frail against the evil that can be mankind."

Nanogate noted the way the new President's jaw muscles clenched each time she paused. "She will have to get her emotions under control," he muttered to himself.

"Our founding fathers foresaw the problems we face today. Our Constitution, the one I've just pledged to protect and defend, guides us so that we will not falter as a nation. We've used this same succession of power six times in our history and it doesn't weaken us.

"America is still strong. America is still just." The force of her voice increased with each sentence. "We will endure. We will continue. Not because of me, but because of the power the office of the President derives from each of you out there."

"The death of our President has done nothing but fill Americans with resolve. We will receive justice for our President's death. So help me, God."

* * *

"Yes, I heard. I don't know how anyone couldn't have heard," Tony said crossly as he sat down in the kitchen of the current Green Action Militia safe house. Most of the Action Committee sat around the single solido. Tony didn't see any dry eyes. "Have they caught anyone in the last five minutes?"

"Nope," David offered tersely, as he mutely strummed an acoustic guitar.

"Who would have the *cajones* to pull that off?"

"The CorpGov? The Metros? Six gets you five and pick-em," Martin said biting off half a taquito that dripped salsa onto his pant leg.

"Hold on. Something new," Morgan said pointing at the solido set. "Turn it back up."

" *... ats right, Brian. We have received reports that the Secret Service has apprehended the assassin of President Lopez. Excuse me, the alleged assassin.*

"*By law we are not allowed to report the perpetrator's name but early reports are saying he is claiming responsibility for the act in the name of the Green Action Militia.*"

Martin choked on his food, spraying most of the small eat-in kitchen.

Cinnamon, who had taken up her perch in Tony's lap, hissed. Without saying a word, Tony pet Cinnamon.

"Oh, crap."

"What the fuck?"

"Zees is no goot."

"Quiet!" Tony barked through everyone talking at once. Cin objected to his outburst and jumped down. More than one head turned toward him with eyes wide with surprise. Tony wasn't known for his outbursts and their previous leader, Sonya, never seemed to have them at all.

"Thank you. Now we can get our own message out there and negate this potential disaster. Sooner is better than later. Do we have any more of the memory crystals with Sonya's fingerprint on them?"

*   *   *

For all the speed at setting up this unprecedented meeting, the opulence for the attendees hadn't been reduced. The now permanent staff of the CorpGov kept a very well-stocked larder. Avocados stuffed with Dungeness crab perched next to real lemon quarters and a trio of crisp parmesan wafers on the Wedgewood china plates. Servants stood behind each of the CorpGov members awaiting their smallest whim. In spite of the repast and the servants' attention to details, all eyes were glued to the solido in the center of the table.

" *... in the name of the Green Action Militia.*"

"Thank you all for coming," Nanogate stated, freezing the playback with a mental command to his neural connection. "This is a time of extreme peril for this body and each of us individually."

"So when did the GAM decide to betray us?" Wintel asked out of order.

Nanogate didn't even remonstrate him for his lack of protocol. "They haven't, sir. It only takes the brains of a gnat to know this."

Wintel's face flamed, turning a blotchy red. Nanogate filed it away in his memory. Occasionally, in any organization, someone needed to be cast out to feed the baying wolves. Being aware of the weak link could protect the body as a whole.

"Remember, the GAM knew everything about our negotiation with the President," Nanogate explained. "If they truly wanted to sell us out to garner favor with the Metros, the President would have been dead long before we met."

"I agree with your assessment, Mr. Chairman," the Global Vehicle Federation's CEO said. He drew in the air with one of his slender fingers. A three-dimensional representation of a six-dimensional statistical surface replaced the popular news show. "If you look at this projection we ran on the GAM before we agreed to ally, it shows right here that the likelihood of them working with any other conservative organization is less than three-tenths of one percent." Using his finger as a stylist, he pointed over an even deeper valley in the graph. "Here you can observe the same data after factoring in the public opinion. Following the announcement by the Metros that they intended to defy us and bring the GAM to justice, the numerical percentage is well over twelve standard deviations from the mean, a value so small as to be effectively zero."

Attempting not to interrupt, a messenger dressed as an English butler of several centuries past walked quietly but stiff-backed into the room and offered Z-G-Ag a message on plain, white, hand-made parchment from a silver-serving tray. The slight, bald man took the message. The butler bowed and retreated from the table silently.

"But why would the Metros be wanting to be killing the President?" Royal PetroChem asked.

"I can think of two reasons. One would be to put the fear of their power into the Vice President. This would restore their flow of federal funds."

"Yes, and the second would be to brand the GAM as pariahs and to break their power base away from them," Nanogate said calmly but fixing his gaze on Wintel.

"Council, I have some new data," Z-G-Ag said looking up from the note he'd received. "I need us to make a decision on how to proceed."

"By all means," Nanogate offered. "Z-G-Ag has the floor."

"We have a caller. Tony Sammis, the leader of the GAM, is in our antechamber and begs our attention. Moreover, he has a weapon."

For leaders with the universal and proven ability to hide their emotions, six of the assemblage had open mouths and the eyebrows of two others were raised. Even Nanogate looked thoughtful.

"What kind of weapon?"

"A pistol, sir. I believe it is a single shot revolver," the butler said in very precise and clipped English.

"Did he brandish it to gain admittance?" Wintel asked.

"No, sir. It has remained in its holster the entire time he's been waiting in the foyer."

"I bring it to a vote," Wintel said, cutting through the silence. "All who would—"

"Wait a moment," Unified Textiles interrupted.

"We will hear from Unified Textiles. He has the floor."

"Thank you. I object to this man entering here." A gentle sheen of perspiration formed on the man's upper lip. "That man, ally or not, killed eight people in this very room. Do we dare let him in again? And with a gun, no less?"

"Nanogate has the floor," the day's speaker ordered.

"I won't pretend that I don't have my own trepidations. My arm hurts just hearing his name," Nanogate said with a level of emotional honesty rarely heard at this level, "but we *need* the GAM."

"Yes, and if he did bring a weapon, why wouldn't he bring one capable of killing all of us. A bloody revolver? It's a museum piece," MinInc said.

"Any other inputs?" Z-G-Ag asked. "No? I call for a vote. Do we admit Tony Sammis, leader of the GAM?"

"The motion carries," an obvious mechanical voice sounded from the hidden computers.

"Maxwell, please send in Mr. Sammis," Z-G-Ag said to the butler.

* * *

Tony strode confidently into the room of designer suits wearing tan khakis, a Greenpeace shirt and a holster belt containing a Colt revolver.

"Mr. Sammis. How nice of you to visit," Nanogate said, standing in greeting.

"We did not assassinate the President," Tony said wasting no time on pleasantries. He stepped up to the table and drew his weapon. He noted with some degree of satisfaction that more than half of the most powerful people in the system flinched.

In its current position the gun could only have been dangerous to the floor. Tony put the weapon, butt first, down onto the table and pushed it. The gun slid noisily across the surface and stopped a quarter of a meter from the standing Chairman.

"I offer that to you as a symbol of the truth of my statement. Pick it up and shoot me if you believe otherwise." One of the executives he didn't know started to reach for the weapon but pulled back.

Sighs don't need to be heard or seen to be understood. Tony could feel the tension in the room melt away.

"Very effective. You have a way with ... words," Nanogate said picking up the gun. "I have to say there is a part of me that would very much like use this on your arm or other more painful places. But then that would be childish." He pivoted open the cylinder and upended the contents onto the table. Six bullets bounced and rolled to a stop. "Good. Not even blanks. You have the strength of ten because your heart is pure, Mr. Sammis," Nanogate misquoted.

Every member of the council ran the emotional equation in their head—bluff with live ammo or honesty. All of them came to the same conclusion.

"Not pure, Nanogate. Thanks to you, I have a number of deaths on my hands. And I wasn't that lily-white even before my change in careers. But we didn't kill the President." Tony heard the sweet, metallic chime of a grandfather clock announcing the half hour. "In fact if you would switch on your solido to HSNC News, you will see something more."

"*Welcome to HSNC News. This station has received one of the Green Action Militia's infamous memory crystals. As is their signature, it contained a single fingerprint of one person who has never been identified either by name or by DNA matching.*

"*This time a second print overlaid the famous print. This print has a name. More importantly it has a face. What you are about to see is the raw, unedited footage of the GAM's memory crystal.*"

The screen flickered only momentarily to be replaced with Tony's face. Several of the members of the council looked at Tony standing erect at the end of the table before returning to his solido.

"'*Hello. My name is Tony Sammis and I am the leader of the Green Action Militia.*

"*For years you've heard the deeds of Green Action Militia in its struggle against the corporate structure of power and corruption. Some of you have even helped us in our fight. But that war is over.*

"*As most of you know, we were able to replace the damaging cabal of tyrants with a more benevolent and responsible over-government. The council, or CorpGov is slated to lead us with a new level of responsibility and benevolence. The GAM has no part of this group. Rather we stand ready to aid the organization in times of trouble but only at their request.*

"*We didn't overthrow one group of oppressors to become tyrants ourselves.*"

Tony watched several of the councilmembers' faces become even more bland.

"*In fact the only reason we still exist as an organization is that we are being hunted and must pool our resources to remain safe. And no, we aren't being stalked by those we deposed but rather by a bureaucracy so entrenched that they believe themselves above the law that they nominally serve. Be that as it may, this is not what I have come to speak about.*

"*It has come to my attention that there is a person claiming to have assassinated our beloved President Lopez on our behalf or as one of our members. This is a falsehood.*

"*I also am confident that this act was not a part of a council plot. I know for a fact that the President had struck a deal with the council to help it rein in the excesses of the bureaucracy I mentioned before.*

"*I do not know who killed the President. I grieve with the majority of you at President Lopez's untimely death. She was a good woman and deserves better than she has been given.*

"*As a man of action, I will use the forces at my disposal to help find the killer and bring him, her or them to justice—a justice you the people can understand.*

"*Thank you for your time.*"

*   *   *

"How did they get that on the air?" Reza asked calmly, leaning back in his chair with his hands perched across his rounded belly.

Sergeant Tolbert stopped from blurting out his initial response. Reza's screaming displeasure at him in the recent past gave him pause. Calm deliberation flagged the potential danger. The lieutenant's deep brown eyes barely contained a firestorm. "Sir, I know we have people on the inside of most of the news organs but do you know how hard it is to intercept a single memory crystal? Especially as we didn't know it was coming?"

"Sergeant, do *you* have any idea what the Commissioner said to me this afternoon?" Reza said in an even calmer voice. Outside his office window there was a scuffle with a welf or blow queen.

"No, sir, but I'm betting it was unpleasant, especially considering the circumstances."

Reza's head snapped back to his subordinate. "What circumstances are you talking about, Sergeant?"

"Well, like the fact that we assassinated the President. I'm certain the Commissioner would have liked to have kept the blame firmly fixed upon the GAM. This seems to have allowed them to squirm out from under the frame."

The silence of the next thirty seconds weighed enough that it should have crushed everything in the room. The sergeant sat stiff-backed. He moved not even an eyelash at the stare he received.

"Sergeant, what would make you believe we had anything to do with the President's death?"

"Means, motive and opportunity, sir. President Lopez was a significant financial thorn in our side. Given the extreme prejudice with which she was dispatched, it should have her successor thinking twice about crossing us.

"Also, the GAM has no clear motive. And I can't see how a GAM assassin would have gotten into position, much less made the shot without Secret Service help.

"Add to this that almost every member of the Secret Service comes from our ranks gives us the means and opportunity.

"And finally, Alan Seeger was the author of the poem 'I Have a Rendezvous with Death,' a favorite of President Kennedy's. Your request to the SWAT team to 'execute Seeger' was poorly disguised at best, if I might have an opinion, sir," Tolbert concluded. He wasn't sure if he'd just successfully bearded the lion in his own den or equally likely gotten himself eaten.

"That was a very astute observation, Sergeant," the lieutenant said after another short pause. "I have just one question."

"Yes, sir?"

"How do you know about Alan Seeger? Even I didn't have that piece of information to complete the picture for me."

"I'm a poetry aficionado. It's my hobby," he said with his cheeks becoming red and hot.

"Are you serious? With your build I would have expected boxing, football or even rugby, not poetry."

"My mother got me involved when I was little. We all have our secrets, Commander. I'd appreciate it if you'd keep this one between us."

"I can do that. Can I be assured of your discretion about the professionally required action you brilliantly deduced?"

"Absolutely, sir. But it is my duty to let you know that if I figured it out, it won't take anyone with a PhD or a detective's badge to come to the same conclusions."

"Understood, but we don't need to throw any more fuel on the fire.

"Now back to the other matter ... the one about the GAM that you so deftly changed the topic from. The Commissioner and I both want them cut off from the media." Reza waved away Tolbert's attempt to interrupt. "We aren't asking for the impossible, but we want the net tightened around every media figure over a fiftieth share. And if we can't intercept each report, we at least want to know about it before it hits the net. In fact the Commissioner was just a little more blunt and directed than that. He said something like, 'If I hear another word from those murdering bastards on the news I'll rip each and every person who fucked up a new asshole.'"

"Sir, we can do that but it will take away from our other efforts, even tracking down the GAM. Our forces are stretched already."

"I think this would be a good job to hire out. There are always private enforcers and other less savory types who can be bought. With the release of the strike funds, we can afford to make this happen."

"I'll see to it," Sergeant Tolbert said with all the conviction of someone ordering the rope for his own hanging.

*   *   *

"Well, that went better than I expected," Tony said to the Action Committee beneath the Wilted Rose. They had missed only Augustine in presence to make it a complete and they had her electronically.

"Yez eet did. Ya steel got yer pecker," Joel said with a chuckle. It didn't deserve even that much.

Not to be outdone, Tony reached down and cupped his crotch and nodded in mock seriousness. The rest of the room dissolved in laughter.

"Yes, and public opinion has swung back toward us," Morgan reported before trying to choose between an Oreo and a macaroon from the snack tray.

"That public address was a stroke of genius," Augustine added from the ether.

"Not completely," Martin interjected. "The Metros are going to shut down that avenue of interaction."

Tony broke out laughing.

"Now what is so funny about that," Morgan asked.

"It is a ridiculous fear," Tony said. Martin frowned as his face turned red.

"I'm sorry, Martin. I don't mean to say you are ridiculous or anything. You are right that we can't do the memory crystal to news agency thing again, but there is no way to contain information."

"He's right," Edward Longfingers said after pressing down an errant blond strand of his own hair. "I did my thesis on the rise and fall of communism in the nineteenth through twenty-second centuries.

"These governments tried, in vain, I might add, to control information flow to their people. It doesn't work. Oh, it slows things down, but data continues to move through alternate channels. Today, with all of the communications options, it is just ludicrous."

"Yup," Tony said. "A blog entry, a new infotainment channel, hell, an old-fashioned FM transmitter would even do it. Bottom line is that we can always get our message out, Martin. And something else for you to think about ... Who owns the media? Our friends in the CorpGov, or their brethren. They won't be happy about losing revenue at the behest of the very powers that are holding them down. I think we will have an ally there for longer than even the Metros think."

"Enough of that, what's on the agenda?"

"We've got seventeen actions with Jamie's people over the next two days spread across the West Coast," David said, after consulting his net interface. "We can handle most of it outside of our Action Group. We have volunteers pouring in."

"I think we need to make sure that Augustine gets the operational data about Jamie's activities. Certainly Jamie will obfuscate and change patterns but getting a feel for what she does and how she does it could be useful in the future," Frances offered over a steaming mug. The looks she got caused her to hesitate. "You never know."

"Yes, that could provide some very valuable data over time," Augustine commented.

"I agree," Tony said. "While I don't see any immediate need, who knows what it might give us in the future. What about for our team? Anything we need to look into?"

"There is something that I'm going to need, Tony. Just like our actions against the corporations, I'm going to need access into the Metro nets."

"That's not asking for much, is it?" Frances challenged.

"Nevertheless it is important. I need login, passwords and DNA."

Everyone looked at Tony.

"Frances, you are our Metro expert. You think that is going to be difficult?"

"Damned near impossible. Getting the DNA is the easy part, but the Metro system requires routine changes in voice recognition passwords every week within the Metro property itself. Even if you get the password you will be kicked out in a week, max."

"And do you think they can kick out Grandma Ice after I get in?" Augustine added from far away Calgary.

David rolled his eyes. Frances tossed her head and Martin smiled. No one gainsaid her.

"OK, Frances, you've told us the problems with making it happen, now give us some hope. Any ideas?"

"We could raid one of the smaller precincts, but even that would take more folks than we have on hand."

"Augustine? How long would it take you to brute force the password?"

"With the equipment I have at my disposal now? Shoot, I can have it done in an hour, maybe less."

"So what we need is a login and a DNA sequence?" Tony asked rhetorically. "I think this may be a job for Christine."

Several nods around the room gave tactic consent. Christine

shared with them one of her rare smiles.

"OK that's all on that topic. What else—" Tony's words were cut off by the change of the room's lights from white to a dim red.

"Emergency positions and then freeze," Tony whispered to the room that already erupted in activity.

Tony sprinted to his station, the main computer core, ready to dump it if threatened. Within ten seconds all motion ceased and a cockroach standing still would have been noisy. Tony, like the rest, activated the security cameras within the Wilted Rose to direct neural input.

A far cry from the 'band-bar' that the Rose had been just months ago, the classical music being played live on the stage accentuated the upscale clientele. As Jock had predicted, the crowd exuded the charm of an elite social gathering. Tony could count the money represented in the designer gowns and hairstyles. Open only a few days, the novelty hadn't worn off the new Rose as the 'in' place to be seen.

Tony made out Maxwell Gregarin, the newly elected head of the AFL-CIO, Susan Westfield, president of NASDAQ, as well as dozens of other politically and monetarily powerful people occupying every standing and sitting position. Only a line of heavily muscled and augmented security kept them off the stage.

Nothing looked immediately out of place.

"Look here," Augustine said over the link. Suddenly someone took control of the camera image and it panned to the door.

With practiced ease, Tuan Nguyen politely pushed his way in through the door and the mass of humanity. He wore not his bodyguard yellow but a very stylish green velvet leisure suit.

"Showtime," Tony subvocalized as Tuan reached the bar.

"*I need to speak to the manager,*" Tuan said to the bartender once he got that worthy's attention.

"*Brush off, fish face. We don't need your kind slumming here.*"

"*I'm trying to be polite. Either I—*"

"*I thought I told you once. In fact why don't you go down the street to the Green Puss. I'm sure they've got at least one skank that will let you buy her a drink.*"

The sound of gauss gunfire outside the door answered the insult. Four armed men rushed in through the entrance, forcing a little pocket in the crowd.

Several women screamed almost simultaneously.

Two bouncers rushed toward the quintet of men. Each of the four intruders fired a 1-kilo bag of sand into the bouncers' chest. Both men went down in a stunned heap.

Tuan's voice came loud over some type of amplifier. "*We have no truck with you but we must teach this establishment some manners. Please everyone, get down.*"

At least a dozen bodyguards billowed forth from a room specifically set aside for their use while their masters entertained themselves in the main room. As one they rushed to their charges, pushing them to the ground and covering them with their own body.

Tuan's crew let loose with a sustained volley of metallic particles accelerated to hypervelocity by magnetic induction. Each of them fired their gauss weapons dry, reloaded and repeated. With the sound of hailstones on a metal roof, the metal slivers chewed up most of the décor in the room. The bar exploded in plastic shards and alcohol sprays. The resulting cloud of dust began to coat all of the surfaces in a fine gray powder. Not a single person was harmed.

Tuan walked calmly over to the bar. He reached over it, grabbing the bartender, who had been hiding behind the counter, by the shirt. He dragged the employee to his feet.

"*You tell the owner,*" Tuan said in his normal, unamplified voice, "*that this will happen every night you are open until you have paid your insurance.*" With a single backhand, Tuan knocked out the barkeep. He let the man slump to the floor. Snapping his fingers, the mob team retreated out the door less than five minutes after they entered.

Tony smiled as he watched them leave.

"All clear," he announced. "Reconvene in the kitchen but stay on silent because we will have Metros here soon."

He always believed in killing two birds with one stone if possible.

"What the hell was that all about," Jacob demanded in barely hushed tones as soon as everyone regrouped.

"Yeah, I thought Jamie was working with us!" hissed Martin.

"Frances, would you be so kind?"

"Jacob, you can't seriously think that the Metros haven't been nosing around here. This used to be one of Tony's hangouts. By asking Jamie to do this we get to reduce the likelihood of the Metros conducting any kind of raid or surveillance here as they know that we are in cahoots with the Family. Also we get to embarrass the Metros badly as we've made sure that Jock has maintained his protection payments to them."

Frances continued, "As an ex-Metro myself, I think the latter one will have much more impact but we will see."

"Are we big enough to be told?"

"I'm sorry, folks. I meant to do so tonight. I'm only a little sorry as this morality play wasn't supposed to go off for several more days."

"Time to call on her highness?" David whispered.

"Definitely."

*　*　*

"I got a message at Vespers that you wanted to see me?" Augustine asked, poking her head into the prioress's office.

"Yes, Sister, please come in and have a seat. There are some things we need to talk about."

Augustine sidled into a room bursting at the seams with stacks and even piles of old-fashioned books. She even had to clear them from her chair. She didn't think there was enough room for even Cinnamon to find a place to lie down on the carpeted floor.

"So there are a number of things I wanted to share." The prioress pushed back a stack of books before activating a solido with statistics and graphs. "First I want to show you the impact your team has made over just the last few days." Pointing to the solido she continued, "There must be a leak as your team was hit very hard on each and every one of your watches. See this spike? You dealt with three times the number of net hacks of the other teams."

"Not unusual, Sister Hanna. Raiders and hackers think any new defense group will be green and target them."

"And normally they would be right, but you deflected or blocked them all. Not a single one got any information. I particularly like this one where you made the attackers think they were in, but in reality you shunted them so they were hacking the Mormon database. Brilliant."

"Thank you, Prioress. We do our best. Actually, that idea came from Hypatia. She is going to be a strong tool in God's workbelt."

"Yes, she is, but from her history she looked initially like she might not fit in. You've made a home for her possible."

"I don't know what to say."

"Then don't say anything. Getting back to your team, I believe the word is already out. In your last turn on the net your team actually had less than half the attacks of any other shift. I think this shows your leadership and teaching capabilities."

"Thank you, Prioress."

"Also, the network defense classes you've taught have been very impressive. I've had several ringers in your classes."

"Really?" Augustine asked, raising one eyebrow. Her eyes glinted with mischief.

"Sister, it is generally not good form to interrupt, especially with sarcasm, when people are complimenting you."

"I'm sorry, Prioress."

"Good, then shut up for a moment, Sister."

"That's better. My informants all tell me that you not only spoke at a level that everyone could understand but you also taught the advanced students a thing or two they hadn't known before.

"Both of my ringers have asked for you to teach a more advanced class. They reluctantly believe you to be the most knowledgeable network defender we have."

Augustine just tilted her head at her prioress and smiled.

"Yes, you can speak now."

"Thank you, Prioress. I will thank God and his son, Jesus Christ, for making me who and what I am," Augustine said, bowing her head in submission.

"Well, God was on the ball the day he made you," Sister Hanna said with a smile. "We appreciate having you here, Sister. Which brings me to the other reason I wanted to talk to you. Now that I've told you how good you are and how exceptionally you help protect God's own, I now have the unpleasant task of smacking you on the hand."

"I'm sorry, Prioress. What have I done that warrants chastisement?"

"Sister Augustine, I didn't take vows yesterday. What you didn't know is my background. I spent nearly ten years working for Interpol before I got the call."

Augustine looked up sharply.

"Yes, I knew who and what you were when you took your vows. Making that promise to God means cutting yourself off from your former life. I was willing to accept that."

"And?" Augustine asked cautiously.

"Bah! You don't think I know you've been working with the GAM from within these walls? I may not have your skill as a net jock, but I can still add two and two together and without undo strain arrive at four.

"You spend your free time jacked in. I've monitored an increase in external traffic to random locations—too random. And while I can't trace those back to your specific node, I also trace no any activity of any kind to your node. It is as if you are doing nothing."

"Yes, Prioress," Augustine answered emphasizing her title, "I have been working with them. I believe their cause is the cause of righteousness. But that doesn't mean I've slouched in any of my duties to God or this Priory."

"Heavens, no, Sister, I just got through saying how proud we are of your accomplishments here in such a short time. My objections stem from not leaving your past life behind. The auspices of the church must not be seen to consort with temporal powers!"

"I understand your objections, Prioress, but I feel obligated to assist as much by my vows as by my own desires. Were I not to support my former associates, many of them would die."

"If it is God's will."

"But what—"

"ENOUGH!"

Augustine almost fell backward out of her seat. She'd never heard Prioress Hanna make even a cross comment, much less an outburst.

"Sister Augustine, had you been any other novitiate I would have ordered some other penance on you long before this. Why do you think I've had this conversation? For my blood pressure? Which I assure you is significantly higher than it should be right now.

"I did this because of your personal faith, your intelligence and your potential use as a strong hand for God and his only Son to protect and guide our Priory for the next three or four decades.

"That being said, we can't have you serving two masters. Our God is a jealous God and you must submit to him."

Augustine opened her mouth but never got out a sound.

"NO, I don't want to hear another word. You must choose. You must make the decisions that will serve your God as you decide. Until you do, I relieve you of your current duties and assign you to silent meditation during normal working hours.

"When you've made a choice you may return to me and we will discuss its ramifications."

*   *   *

"Antonio! How could you know I wished to speak to you?" Jamie said sitting with one leg across the other in an oversized, golden-upholstered chair. Wearing a long, white chiton she looked like a Greek goddess rather than the *capa famiglia* of one of the more powerful syndicates on the planet.

"Total serendipity on my part," Tony said with a smile.

"Well, you percommed me. Speak and be heard."

Sometimes Tony wished Jamie would pick one persona and stick with it. She may consider it a bonus to rattling her opponent—and everyone was her opponent.

"Simply put, why did you push up the attack on the Rose? Our plans didn't have it for another week or so."

"Oh, that is an easy question. I *love* easy questions."

"Nothing else. No weapons? I can make you a marvelous deal on a magnetic rail gun I picked up. It wouldn't even interfere with that nasty virus you still carry."

"An MR gun? What am I going to do with something that huge? We try to act surgically, not taking out entire city blocks."

"Pity."

"Back to my question, please, Jamie."

"Oh, yes. I stepped up the timetable because I needed to talk to you. I mean you haven't even given me your percomm code. You know a girl could feel rejected by that."

Tony didn't even try to hide his sigh of exasperation. "We are allies of convenience, Jamie. I don't want you waking me up in the middle of the night."

"Would I do that?"

"In a heartbeat. No, I take that back. You would have someone *else* do that while you were still sleeping."

"You wound me, Antonio," Jamie said turning her head up and away as if spurning Tony.

"Meretrīx!" Tony whispered the Latin curse under his breath before continuing. "Wounded or not, you won't be getting my percomm code anytime soon. I will arrange something more easily accessed than our current clumsy method."

"Thank you, dah-ling," she purred.

"OK, what was so important?"

"Oh, that. I have a new friend that insists on talking to you and only you."

"Ah, a new friend. How much did you soak him for? And should I be running for the hills now?"

"That's silly and you know it, Antonio. I no more know where you are than the rest of the world. And what I'm getting out of it is my business.

"So shall I put my friend on or should I send Tuan back?"

"You would, too. OK ... you have me. I'll talk to this 'new friend.'"

"OK ... just a second."

Tony's percomm image split to show, in the new window, one of the world's most well-known faces. Had Tony listed a thousand people Jamie's friend wouldn't have been on it.

"Madam President!"

"Mr. Sammis. It's good to finally meet you, if remotely," she said from behind her White House desk.

This close to the video pickup and without her makeup the new President's short, red hair held more than one strand of silver. Her wry smile welcomed him much more than what he normally felt on solido. Behind her trademarked glasses, her rheumy eyes looked as if she hadn't slept in the three days since her inauguration.

"Likewise. To what do I owe this honor, other than the auspices of our mutual friend, Jamie?"

The President smiled. "I think friend may be too strong a word, but yes, I thought she could bring us together. I have a report on the overthrow of the corporate cabal on my desk. It didn't take much of an investigation to determine that Jamie and her organization aided in your efforts. That is why I came to her with my request."

"I hope she didn't charge you too much for the service."

"More than I wanted to give."

"She is good at that."

"Excuse me, my friends, but I'm right here listening in."

"Good. Then you will know when you are being insulted," Tony interjected. He watched Jamie give a mini-pout on the screen. The President tittered.

"So, Madam President, why did you go to all this trouble to find me?"

"I don't want to die," she said matter-of-factly.

"Excuse me?"

"I said that I don't want to die. It is clear to me exactly who orchestrated that assassination, why and how. The Metros want to frighten me into being nothing more than a figurehead."

"Our best people say same thing."

"As do mine," Jamie added.

"So the reason I'm coming to you is that I want you to hide me."

"Come again?"

"I don't want to give in to the bastards. If I go into hiding we can set up some channel that I could use and continue to do the most important work of government without worrying that with every decision I might be painting a target on my chest."

"Why me? Surely there are hundreds of bunkers and places where you can hole up."

"True, but the Secret Service knows and in many cases helped design each and every one of them.

"Remember what happened to Indira Gandhi? Nineteen of twenty of our Secret Service come from the Metros. I need you to hide and protect me. Based on the track record of the Green Action Militia, I believe you can do it. I believe you are the only one that can do it."

"I'm not sure that is true, but even if I take on this impossible task, how would I get you away. Your bodyguards aren't going to just let you walk away with a stranger."

"This is true, but as VP, I established a routine where I would go out shopping in the Gallery accompanied by only two guards and no advance party."

"So no other guards you know of. That just means they will be harder to spot, but it does give us a good possibility.

"Madam President, I will be back in touch with Miss Ardwin exactly seventy-two hours from now with our answer and, assuming we accept, a plan of action. Can I count on you to contact her at the same time and not from anywhere in the White House?"

"Why not in the White House?"

"Do you not know that every word spoken there is recorded and monitored?"

"I'm in a privacy shield."

"I'll bet every dollar I've got that you are being bugged even now. Security forces are the worst at a 'need to know everything,' especially if it's a secret."

*   *   *

For eight hours she prayed in the near silence of the novitiate chapel. The pain Augustine felt as she knelt in front of the stylized image of the crucifix helped to bring her troubles into sharp focus. Her prayer was for guidance.

"*The auspices of the church must not be seen to consort with temporal powers!*" Prioress Hanna had insisted coldly. "*You must choose. You must make the decisions that will serve your God as you decide.*"

Even over the pain in her knees, she could envision that ocean of change her simulations said loomed in the future. It threatened to batter down everything she thought God had asked her to do. She had worked hard to make people equal, to ensure justice. The prioress, in her ignorance, asked her to cheapen all the sacrifices made by her comrades and friends—to wipe away their deeds as if they spilled no more than a drop of blood on a stormy beach.

The sight of Linc's smoldering remains, Suet's thrashing body, Sonya's silent agony and the death of so many of her colleagues chased across her memory in a gruesome march. She weighed these martyrs against the blood her savior once spilled. She weighed them against the pain and death of innocents she knew was coming. She weighed her confidence in her lord, Jesus Christ.

Crossing herself she stood and walked back to her cell.

*   *   *

Smells of pot roast and stewing root vegetables permeated the air. Various post-meal milieus covered the plates across the table. Serving dishes lay mostly bare on the green granite tabletop. Only one thin wedge of Dutch apple pie remained in a baking tin as the attendees slowly nibbled on the more substantial pieces on their plates.

As luxurious as their living room was, the eat-in kitchen had become the defacto meeting place for the Action Committee of the GAM. The only debatable point was if it were for comfort or the accessibility of munchies.

Tony's percomm chimed with an access code indicating a tailor shop in Mumbai, India.

"Where did you get this code?" he subvocalized.

"Tony, it's me," Augustine replied.

"Oh, hello there. We are just about to start. You want me to patch you into the meeting?"

"Not yet, I need a second of your time. I have a problem here."

"You aren't nun material?" Tony offered Cinnamon a morsel of pot roast, which she very daintily licked off before taking in her mouth.

"You might say that. But my prioress is one smart cookie—ex-Interpol. She knows I've been working with you and has ordered me to stop. I think if she catches me I'll be ejected."

"There's always a place for you here, Augustine." Tony heard the sigh on the other end of the line.

"Yes, but I'm doing more than hiding out here. I told you before that I had some personal business to take care of."

"OK, so what do you need from me?"

"After this meeting I need to cut off communications and stay completely under the radar for a while."

"Tina, and yes I know how much you hate that nickname, I will do what you want, but I'll be honest. We are going to need your help before long."

"Anyone can brute force a password."

"Not what I'm talking about. This is a civil war between the Metros and the council and if we are going to have any chance we are going to need your magic every step of the way."

"Until then I'll need to be as covert as possible."

"Understood. I'll tell the team that you are incommunicado."

"Thank you, Tony."

He returned his attention back to the team who'd moved on to the toothpick stage of the meal.

"So time to plan how we are going to kidnap the President," Tony just threw out with no preamble.

"We are going to do WHAT?!" Frances all but yelled, beating the outburst of the rest of the GAM's Action Committee by a millisecond or two.

"Nothing much," Tony said calmly as he smiled at his own private joke. "We're going to kidnap the President of the United States. Oh, and did I mention we have to do it within the next forty-eight hours."

Stunned silence held sway in the GAM's conference room.

"What's the problem," Tony said. "We knocked off the corp heads and that was much more difficult than this."

"Oh, it will be tough all right," David retorted, his face blotchy and the color of his hair. "I think taking out the corpies may have been a cakewalk compared to this. But my problem is 'Why?' We could lose a lot of good people doing it and I can't even see a return."

"How about because she is requesting asylum or something similar," Augustine said over the com link. "At least that is what I assume based on the data on hand."

"She was close to her running mate. I'm sure she wants to carry forward her predecessor's principles, including the actions against the Metros. She correctly deduced that the Metros are behind the assassination. If I were her and didn't want to be the puppet of the police I'd be scared."

"That was almost exactly on the mark, Augustine. And to address David's concern, I won't take this action if there's an unacceptable risk to our members. As important as the President is, right now I consider our team more critical. That isn't conceit but objective reasoning."

"Ya, unt vithin two dayz. Vhy so qvick?"

"I forgot to mention, I think their security forces overheard us and I told them I'd be back to her in three days. We need to be done before they are prepared."

"Vat a plan," Joel said smacking himself in the forehead. "Vhy didn't you just geeve zem our comm codes vile you ver at it?"

"What? You needed to make it more of a challenge?" Frances offered.

"With that said, I open the floor for mission concepts," Tony said.

"Vee need to know ver she vill be in order to überfallen ... bushy her."

"Ambush, Wayne," Frances chimed in. "The minimum requirement for any ambush is time and location. And this will also be an abduction so we need to have an escape route, a place to hold her, and guards for three shifts."

"Thank you for the professional analysis, Frances.

"Augustine, can you obtain the presidential schedule of events?"

"I've baked more difficult cookies. It's already done and on your mail servers."

"We could try for the liftousine. I know a number of tricks we could play on the impellers."

"No chance—" Frances began.

"This is brainstorming, Frances. No evaluation. There will be time for that later."

"I say we hit them at the White House itself. They won't be expecting it."

"How about an EMP to shut down the protective grid?"

"I say something more subtle. Get her to sneak out of the East Wing tunnel."

David, quiet to this point, refocused off of his personal neural interface. "Did anyone look at the President's itinerary? I think that one item stands out." The rest of the room got a dreamy expression as they all checked their own PNI.

"That looks promising,"

"We'll have to change some of the timing, especially Christine's disappearing act," Morgan said, giving a very unladylike burp at the same time. "Excuse me."

"David, I'm going to give you the lead on this mission. Don't forget the bathroom."

*   *   *

To the music of Bob Marley, Nanogate relaxed. He read an old fashioned paper-back book about the theorized assassination of Pope John Paul when the oversized mahogany doors to his library opened. Nanogate slipped his arm from around his book-holder, a nude young girl in his lap. He motioned for her to kneel down on the floor.

His faithful butler walked the twelve measured steps to the foot of his Edwardian tub chair, all the while studiously avoiding notice of his prurient companion. Nanogate picked up his single-malt scotch from the solid-gold end table.

"Excuse me, sir, but you have a caller."

Nanogate reached out to take the proffered personal card from William's silver tray. The sage green card had only three words on it, "Tony Sammis, GAM."

"This is becoming repetitive," he muttered taking a sip of amber liquor.

"Shall I have him removed, sir?"

"No, nothing so drastic, William. I know this man, and while he is tedious he wouldn't be here unless on important business." Nanogate looked off into space to fathom his caller's motives. Nothing came immediately to mind.

"Have Mr. Marks show Mr. Sammis in. Provide refreshments as well. I believe Mr. Sammis drinks—"

"Bloody Mary with a carrot or Candor's Black Bitters, sir."

Nanogate smiled and wondered how his butler could possibly have that data. This seemed beyond even William's normal resourcefulness.

"Thank you, William. Also could you tell my wife that I won't be joining her in bed this evening?"

"Very good, sir."

Nanogate took the girl's delicate chin in his hand and lifted her face. He looked into her deep brown eyes. He gently caressed her bald head. "Ahba, I believe our reading session has been cut short. Why don't you go collect Donna and wait for me in my sleeping chambers."

"Yes, master," she whispered before standing and walking out his private suite door wearing only his book to cover her pubic area. As usual, William's timing left nothing to criticize. The main doors didn't opened until Ahba had closed the other door behind her.

First-time guests to his three-story library fell into three categories, those who ignored the books as unimportant, the ones who were daunted by such an overt sign of wealth, and those that gawked at the treasure of knowledge that surrounded them. Mr. Sammis fell into the latter category. Nanogate could read the bibliophile lust in the man's eyes as Mr. Marks led him into the room.

"Mr. Sammis, leader of the GAM, I believe you know the CEO of Nanogate and current chairman of the CorpGov Council," Mr. Marks said as smoothly as a career diplomat.

Nanogate waved him to a similar chair just opposite him. As custom and tactics dictated, Mr. Marks stood over his guest's right shoulder.

"Good evening, Mr. Sammis. It's a pleasure to have you at my home." Nanogate did him the service of not asking how Tony found his private home's location. He could think of several ways, especially with that top-ranked net jock he had under his thumb.

"Thank you ... By the way, what is your name? I've been calling you Nanogate for so long I almost forget that you are a person, not a corporation."

"Ah. Well, it is polite to address a CEO in that manner because of the accomplishments of attaining the goal, but in your case I think I might make an exception. My name is Clarence Ford."

"Clarence Ford. It is a good name although not one I would have immediately associated with you."

"It's a family name. Technically it should be Clarence Fritzwalter Beckman-Ford the Third. As I couldn't stand any of the nicknames that were thrust upon me during my secondary education I've adamantly held to Clarence."

"Thank you again, Clarence. I appreciate the familiarity," Tony said, adjusting his soot-black ponytail over his shoulder so he wouldn't be leaning back against it.

"I'm sure you are curious as to my visit."

Nanogate smiled in one of his rare expressions of true emotion. "Mr. Sammis, or can I call you Tony ... " Clarence waited until his guest nodded assent. "Tony, I've been patient my entire life. I figure you will get to the point soon enough. If I've learned anything about you over the last few months it is that you are a practical man not prone to fancies or wasted effort."

Watching Tony's returning smile proved the leader of the GAM exuded more charisma than Nanogate had even considered after the fall of the previous corporate association.

"Oh, I've been known to harbor a fancy or two, but we are allies in a war." Tony's visage changed from jovial to serious in just one sentence. "We have to be efficient, *practical* leaders."

"Agreed."

William wheeled in a cart of refreshments and served his guest a Bloody Mary while the aroma of the *pâté en terrine* tickled Nanogate's nose. He helped himself to a generous portion spread over a small *crostini*. Tony likewise helped himself.

"I have to say I don't normally like *pâté* but this is excellent, sir," Tony said to William just before the butler departed.

Nanogate noted how the GAM's leader waited until the staff had left before discussing anything sensitive. In spite of his own dislike for the man, Nanogate approved of him as a confederate.

"Back to our discussion, part of our practicality is the reason for my visit. The President of the United States has reached out to me."

"Really?"

"Yes, she is asking for the GAM's aid. Before I give it, I want to be certain that you don't disapprove of that action. Angering one's allies isn't a positive step toward victory."

"If I remember the writings of the now President Tipton, she advocates very strong controls over all organs of the government, including the military and paramilitary arms. At the same time she believes in the loosest possible restrictions on the actions of the individual that are practical.

"A question, if I may. Do you have any reason to believe that she will continue her predecessor's policy of withholding funds from the Metros?"

"I have no specific data to say one way or the other. We reason that she wouldn't be trying to go underground if she weren't of that same mindset."

"Mr. Marks, you are more familiar with the politics in this country."

"Yes, sir. I believe Mr. Sammis's evaluation is correct," Thomas Marks replied, not leaving his duty position. "In the short term, the Metros would be more than happy to leave President Tipton in place if the funding flowed. I'm equally certain that the President could, if she were so inclined, come to terms with the Metros in the future as a partial figurehead."

"I have no objection to aiding the President in any way. I wholeheartedly endorse the action," Nanogate said. "By the way, what type of aid did she request?"

"I don't see any reason why I shouldn't share that with you. She wants me to hide her."

"Government in exile. I can understand that. Can you get her away?"

"One of my best people has created a viable plan. The mission is in the preparation stage. I saw no reason to fault it and see little chance for failure."

"Exceptional. I have one more question and then we can leave this topic, if it suits you. Why didn't she come to the council?"

Nanogate watched Tony mentally struggle for a few moments before blushing underneath his olive complexion. And it wasn't his first display to Nanogate. As leader of his organization, Nanogate would have expected Tony to have better control of his emotions. Emotions needed to be harnessed for the energy they provide and kept away from everyone else so they aren't used against you.

"I mean no disrespect by this, Clarence, but your methods are about as subtle as a bull rhinoceros in a daycare center. Please don't get me wrong. Your skills are at directing massive efforts and leaving the details to those under you.

"The GAM on the other hand has no underlings and we can't afford to lose a single one of our operatives if it can be at all helped. We have to embody subterfuge. We rarely take a dump without three exits and a contingency plan."

Nanogate chuckled. "I see. I'm not offended, only curious. Something to keep in mind for the future."

"Speaking of the future," Tony put in, "I suggest we set up a communication link between us and regular meetings before our situation with the Metros gets too nasty."

"I agree," Nanogate said. Without missing a beat he continued. "I have the perfect tool as a conduit. Mr. Marks? I'd like you to join the GAM as my liaison."

As he had just taken a bite, Tony choked on a tiny bit of his appetizer. He snatched his linen napkin from his lap to keep any further sprays of food from erupting as he coughed.

"William, some water, please," Nanogate said in a normal tone. The butler entered the room with a pitcher of water and several glasses balanced on a Revere silver serving tray before Nanogate's last syllable exited his lips.

Tony pounded on his chest before taking the tendered water and drinking the glass dry.

"Are you all right, Mr. Sammis?"

"Yes, sorry," he rasped out. He gave a couple more covered coughs before lowering his napkin. "I think it went down the wrong way."

*   *   *

Wearing only a nylon body stocking, Christine used a tiny brush to wipe nanites onto her eyelashes. The natural hairs thickened and lengthened as the microscopic machines chained together in their designed and enhancing purpose.

She tipped a small red bottle with the label "Revlon—Martian Kiss" up onto her left pinky before rubbing the finger over her lips. As the fine, clear liquid landed the lips took on the shade of the bottle and puffed out sensuously.

Christine wasn't by nature anachronistic but cosmetic implants, not to mention the fashion service subscription they required could very easily provide clues to investigators. The leads they could generate for a trained detective or private enforcer would be like her advertising as a "Serial Killer" on every net channel. Besides, the simple, clean, and nearly natural look she normally wore stood out against the artificial styles so popular with women today.

She preferred hunting her own chosen prey, but doing it for the GAM was both safer and more satisfying in another way. Sighing, she looked down at her small breasts. Her nipples and areolas already crinkled and puffed up at the thought of what this night would bring and more importantly its aftermath tomorrow. She felt the warmth in the pit of her stomach and could even feel the beginning of dampness between her thighs. Shaking her head she turned back to making herself a sexual target.

She wiped off her finger on the electronic-inert pad next to her. With her nipples standing the bodysuit 2 centimeters away from the rest of her chest, her bosom didn't need additional assistance.

Christine slipped the black tabard dress over her head and cinched the bodice tight with a pair of quick ties high up under her arms. With practiced ease she slipped into lift-pumps so black they appeared to absorb light from everywhere around and so high she appeared almost normal height instead of her diminutive 150 centimeters.

Looking in the mirror she frowned. Rummaging into a drawer she brought out a thin, silver belt that she wrapped around herself and tightened just under her breasts. Now, small though they might be, they stood out. The fabric tightened enough to allow the jutting nipples to press forward with authority. Now she smiled at the view in the floor-to-ceiling mirror.

Another sight caught her attention. On the vanity amongst the panoply of cosmetics lay a collection of knives and ancient surgeon's devices, each gleaming in its own private sleeve of a black velvet rollup. She turned. Her hand reached out to hover a hair's thickness over the stainless steel handle of a short-bladed dirk. A flush of pink lit up her cheeks and her breath caught at the first touch of the cool metal. Her finger caressed the steel like the skin of a tender lover. Her eyes lit up and widened. Her pelvic-floor muscles quivered, rippling her taut abdomen.

How long now? Twelve years? So simple. So effective it had been to lull him to sleep after finally succumbing willingly after so many months of brutal rapes. With his sperm still warm and deep inside her, she had ended it. She still remembered the frantic, tiny vibrations in the knife's handle as her father's heart tore itself to ribbons against the blade. She could feel her orgasm building.

Christine snatched her hand away from the blade. "Not yet, baby," she said softly with big, doe eyes locked on the cutting edge. "Tonight. He can wait until tonight. Just a few more hours and we can kill him again."

* * *

Mr. Marks stood patiently in a corner behind a composite table set for four. His body relaxed in what most others would consider a position of attention. His sleepy eyes absorbed the simple, eat-in kitchen, filtered by his training.

Someone, whose taste needed to be evaluated, had decorated it in salmon—not only the color but also towels and potholders had the great fish embroidered upon them. A wire and plastic drain rack next to the sink held two plates, three mismatched glasses, six coffee cups, four forks sporting different handle styles and two spoons. Four chairs, with simple square cushions for seat and back, had that "Grandma put plastic over them to keep them looking new" feel to them. The butcher-block on the counter held two knives less than its eight capacity and none of the handles matched. Even in an emergency the knives weren't worth anything as weapons.

He knew Tony Sammis had brought him to a safe house. These temporary dwellings never got the attention of a normal home, or are purchased /rented furnished, always with dubious esthetic results.

Mr. Marks heard the flat's door open and close. The two sets of androgynous footsteps made no attempt at silence. One wore athletic shoes and the other flats. He tentatively assigned one as probable male and the other female. Both moved like people who'd seen combat, picking up their feet and not shuffling.

The pair moved through the living room toward the kitchen. He heard the obvious Velcro tear of something several centimeter square being separated and the sound of plastic keys dropping into a crystal candy dish.

"I could really use a beer," said a male voice in timbres that

Thomas Marks took to be from a man in his late twenties or early thirties.

"I'll get you one," a dark-skinned woman with short, tightly-curled hair said as she entered the kitchen. She headed directly for the refrigerator.

Marks's instructors would not only have failed the young woman's performance, but knocked her flat for not having checked all the corners of the room. 'No place is ever completely safe,' they had repeated to him as he did two hours of knuckle pushups on sandpaper.

The red-haired man did check, but obviously hadn't been trained in his responses. The slight man fumbled for a Sig Sauer 3 kilowatt Nd-YAG laser pistol from his armpit holster. The draw time would have earned him at least three months of remedial practice, not to mention a rather severe genital shock, had he trained as a bodyguard. Thomas didn't disarm or kill the man. He didn't move even when the Sig's pre-focus warning beam warmed his skin.

"Freeze," the redhead said like something out of a solido serial.

The black woman dropped the beer pouches and drew her weapon. Her draw, while smoother, was at least twice the acceptable time for being caught flat-footed. A second aiming laser, this time from a Pintion 14 air-charged flechette gun joined the first.

"You have exactly thirty seconds to tell me why you are here before I poke a hole in you the size of the Grand Canyon," she added in equally melodramatic style.

Marks could tell by the standard muscle signature at the side of her neck that she was making a percomm call.

"I have been brought here by Mr. Tony Sammis at the behest of the Chairman," he said reasonably and calmly. He made certain that not a single muscle other than his diaphragm moved.

"That is possible, but I'm not going to count on it," the man said. "But you bought yourself a reprieve until the boss gets here. If you are lying, I hope your life insurance is paid up."

"I agree that you shouldn't count on it, but I assure you that it is true," Thomas replied. "If it will put you more at ease I can place my open hands on the table."

"No, just don't move."

"As you wish."

The sound of a flushing toilet preceded one pair of footsteps as it hurried into the kitchen. Tony Sammis, the boss, rushed into the room.

"Easy, folks. He's on our side." The guns lowered fractionally. "I invited him here."

"Really, Boss? You blew a safe house? Why? We could interrogate him anywhere. He could be bugged."

"I didn't blow a safe house, and I have a strong reason to believe he is not bugged. I'll give you all the details when the rest of the team shows up.

"In the meantime, Mr. Marks meet Morgan and David and likewise in reverse."

Cinnamon jumped up onto the table and brushed her head up against Thomas's hip. For the first time he reacted with a slight start.

"Oh, yes, and this is Cinnamon."

Intellectually, Thomas knew Sammis had a cat but seeing it was entirely different. He wasn't sure how to interact with such a creature. Tentatively he reached out and touched its back, jerking away at first. He'd expected sharp bristly hair but found it soft and smooth. He brushed harder along the spine. Cinnamon gave off a much louder purr as she arched up into his caress.

"She is just one of the family, Mr. Marks," the redhead said as he shrugged and put the Sig back in its holster. The black woman followed suit.

Thomas wasn't certain whether it had been Mr. Sammis's or Cinnamon's approval that won over the militant pair.

"Come on into the living room, Mr. Marks. Have a seat. Would you like a beer?"

"No, thank you."

"I'll have one, Morgan."

Thomas found Tony's request to his subordinate high-handed. To his surprise, the short, black woman actually seemed pleased to oblige. While he puzzled this, he found an upholstered footrest and perched on the edge. All his senses fired at their maximums, including his cybernetic eye. He knew his employer would require a full account of the people and place.

The door crashed open. Two very similar looking men with jet black hair burst in. One rolled in on the floor, his weapon trained across the room and the other leaning inside, high in the door frame. Thomas almost approved of the teamwork.

The two men looked puzzled at the domestic scene.

"Oh, and Morgan? Please call off your alert," Tony yelled into the other room.

"Mr. Marks, meet the Weismuller twins, Joel and Wayne." The twins gathered together the remains of their dignity before giving a half-bow in unison to their guest. Mr. Marks wondered if they would have clicked their heels together had their embarrassment been just a bit smaller.

In turn Tony Sammis introduced each of the members as they arrived. Malcontents all, Mr. Marks thought. The only place they could succeed is in an outlaw organization. He shouldn't judge, but his mind couldn't help categorizing them. His place was to follow Nanogate's orders. Only one, other than Tony Sammis himself, stood out.

Christine flowed into the room exuding a natural sexuality. She wore a checked black and white evening gown. The squares were such that it twisted one's perception. More than once Mr. Marks caught himself mesmerized by the attire and the massive black bow around her waist, if not the woman that wore it.

"Folks, I've given only Mr. Marks's name. Mr. Marks, as you can tell by the yellow tights, is a bodyguard, but a specific bodyguard. Nanogate has his allegiance."

"And you said you didn't burn a safe house."

"Why don't we invite the Metros, too."

"What about ... "

"Please wait, folks," Tony said as if he were just a little tired.

In this, Mr. Marks began to realize Tony's real value. The entire team quieted and waited for him to speak, as if he were a burning bush. Tony didn't need to bluster. He didn't need to cajole. He didn't need to yell. These people followed Sammis because Tony loved each and every one of them.

"I promise that all your questions will be answered and all your concerns addressed.

"Mr. Thomas Marks is our liaison from the council. The Chairman gave him to us so that we can communicate better. And let's face it, if we don't work hand and glove with the council, the Metros will eat us both for lunch." Tony paused before continuing. "I have a very good reason to believe that Mr. Marks is in fact someone we can trust implicitly even if you count the fact that he is sworn to do what Nanogate orders.

"'Little Thomas Marks is the son of the man who gave his life to save Martin, Andrea and I in the Taste Dynamics adventure."

Thomas's mouth pursed and his jaw clenched unconsciously.

How could Sammis know his nickname, much less anything about his father. His father was a good and thorough bodyguard. He would never have left any witnesses.

Nanogate! Thomas thought. It was his employer's right to do so, but it trampled on his father's career like it meant nothing.

"And before our newest friend thinks his employer betrayed him, I assure you I got every datum except your first and last name from our net jock."

Can Sammis read minds? Marks thought. No, he's just astute.

"OK, so you believe ... I mean I think we all can trust him. What does that mean?" Dave asked.

"From this point forward and until the end of this war, Thomas Marks is one of us. He is part of our team with only one exception, the location of our headquarters."

Tony Sammis wasn't the only one with information, Thomas thought.

"Oh, you mean the bunker beneath the Wilted Rose?"

Everyone in the room looked at him. Tony took several long seconds before responding.

"May I ask how you know that?"

"I did not know, but it was a reasoned guess. I could share my analysis with you if you would like, but it wouldn't change the fact that now I really do know."

"OK," Tony said rolling with the punch, "he is a teammate with no reservations. Welcome to the team, Mr. Marks."

*   *   *

Sitting at the empty bar at nine a.m., Jock shuffled one at a time through a deep stack of resumes for the two new positions he intended to fill this afternoon. Most he dropped into the waste can at his feet. The remaining he added to one of two piles.

He sighed and stood up to stretch his back. Walking to the other side of the bar he drew himself a dark ale, letting most of the head slide off into the overflow tray.

"Cookie. Can you rustle me up about half a dozen scrambled eggs?"

"Sure, Boss. Six broken birds come up."

He looked at his silver, augmented arms as he lifted the stein to take a sip. His life had become much different than he expected. He wasn't sure if he wanted to thank or curse Tony Sammis.

"Enough stalling," he said to himself. He slid the beer down the bar just hard enough to nudge the resume pile. As he walked around the bar he heard the comm go off and Cookie picking it up.

"Wilted Rose. We are currently closed. Our hours ... " he started. After a short pause, "ya, he's here. Hold for a sec."

"Boss, some word engineer on the phone for you. You want me to tell her off?"

"No, go ahead and transfer it in here," Jock said, setting down the resume he'd just picked up. Reaching over the bar he picked up the utilitarian comm as it rang.

"Jock here."

"Is this Jock Manner, owner of the Wilted Rose nightclub?" said a rough female voice with a Germanic flavor to it.

"It is."

"My name is Svena Berna. I'm a partner in the law firm Bolliger, Zutter and Thoma."

Jock felt like he'd just received an enema of liquid oxygen. Tony had him memorize those names as an emergency code. In short it meant for him to run for his life. Jock'd warned him the ruse with the mob wouldn't work, but Tony wanted his operations beneath the Rose. What a sentimental dope.

"My undisclosed client is exercising his option to buy out your participation of the Wilted Rose nightclub, pursuant to sections fourteen through twenty-two of your existing contract. This assumes you vacate the premises within eight hours, leaving all equipment in place."

I have a contract? A Nil can't have a contract! Jock thought.

The lawyer on the other end didn't stop. "The sum of thirty-three million, four hundred thousand Euros has already been deposited, in cash, into your Swiss bank account number Jock3263827."

Thirty-three million? Jock thought. Jesus H. Christ, Tony! The ENTIRE club isn't worth but a quarter of that.

"Do you have any questions, sir?"

"Know a small country for sale?"

"Excuse me?"

"Never mind, Frau Berna. My thanks to you."

"Goodbye."

His eyes glazed over as he absently let his arm with the phone settle to the bar top. He'd not given this contingency quite as much thought as he should have, but he'd already searched countries without extradition. One place in his halfhearted search did stick in his head— the Bailiwick of Guernsey.

*   *   *

"Come in, Mr. Marks," Nanogate said from his bright green antique recliner.

Michael, Nanogate's son, sat on the sofa across from his father. The younger Ford rattled a large, irregular chunk of ice in a crystal tumbler with no more than a finger of bourbon in it. The blond man stood up to leave, emptying the last of the copper-colored liquid.

"Thank you for understanding, son. We will talk more on this later. For now take no action. Ordinarily I'd suggest you jump on an opportunity like this, but we can't afford to get into a pissing contest within the corporate sphere just now."

"Yes, sir," he said walking toward the door.

"Mr. Marks," Michael said amiably as he passed.

"Mr. Ford."

"Come in, Mr. Marks. I hunger for news. What have you to report to me today."

"There is a huge volume of information so I've written up a comprehensive report that is awaiting you on your desk. It includes many different aspects of the Green Action Militia organization, personnel, and resources.

"As you have surmised, I have been given unlimited access to the anomaly that is the Green Action Militia. Even my complete report doesn't seem to do it justice. The organization is a complex organism that is at most times an anarchy in complete chaos. Individual members of the Action Committee are given immense authority to plan, organize, and execute their own activities and rely on history and personal experience rather than detailed computer simulations. There seems to be no hierarchical structure of any kind.

"That having been said, all of the members defer to Tony Sammis for his opinion and guidance. While nominally the leader, I don't see him using any of the invasive or stringent management techniques that are employed in nearly all corporations.

"I've never seen Tony give an order. At the same time I've never seen a member of his team go against his wishes. It's as if they revere him."

"I've been on only one small mission so my data is limited. Please apply the statistical relevance to my data that it deserves.

"To what to attribute the GAM oddities to, I can only guess. I get the impression that Tony is very rarely wrong. When he is mistaken he doesn't look for a way to duck the responsibility but rather looks for a solution to the problem his mistake created. This deviates from any corporate structure. Learning to deflect the blame is a required skill even at low levels."

"'Curiouser and curiouser, said Alice,'" Nanogate injected. "What is your evaluation of this?"

"I say that it only works because he has a very small and very trusted cadre. But it does work."

"Financing and infrastructure?"

"I believe that the former corporate organization fell down on their analysis in this area. I'd place each of their individual wealth somewhere in the eighty-fifth percentile ... "

"Eighty-fifth percentile? That doesn't seem possible. Tony Sammis was a mid-level functionary and joined the GAM with nothing."

"I think the actions against the corporations gave them more funds than anyone ever projected. I'll bet it was never evaluated in earnest. I've put a forensic accountant on the matter to give a more accurate picture."

"Eighty-fifth percentile. Amazing. Why don't they just buy themselves a quiet country somewhere and settle down?"

"I predict that some eventually will. I have to emphasize that most of them are crusaders. It's hard to put down your sword and shield even after you've won. You look for other wars that need to be fought. Also, a very few of the membership are adventurers who do it for the sheer excitement."

"I think I'll put a small team on an organizational simulation."

"If I may have an opinion, sir, I believe that is quite wise. I will make sure I'm available to answer any questions that aren't covered in my report."

"Excellent. Anything else to share?"

"Two critical items, sir."

"Go on."

"The GAM intend to hide the President by first kidnapping her. They couldn't envision any way she could just walk away."

"Neither can I, Mr. Marks, but I've not studied it."

"Nor I, sir. I don't have any details as the team organizing this hasn't completed their prep."

"Any idea on execution date?"

"I believe that they may be planning it at the Black and White Ball." Marks watched his employer's eyes light up.

"Oh. That could be inconvenient."

"Sir?"

"Oh, nothing. Continue."

"If not at the Ball then they definitely feel they need to move within now thirty-six hours."

"Ballsy," Nanogate swore, completely out of character. "Planning and executing that quickly?"

"Indeed, sir."

"OK, so that was one thing. What was the second?"

"This one I saved for last for importance. Tony asked me to carry a message to you and the rest of the council. I must heartily add my own agreement to his analysis."

"Spit it out, man. I don't pay you to leave me at cliff hangers."

Marks chuckled. "That wasn't my intent, sir.

"Tony believes that the Metros will make a move to round up or kill all of the council, if not now then as soon as the President pulls her disappearing trick.

"Tony postulates that he'd do it in their place. 'If the council is the problem, remove it by removing the council.'"

Nanogate leaned back and stared off into space. "I have to admit I'd not considered direct action against us, but then I've spent the greater part of my career thinking about more subtle attacks. If we are relying on the Metros for a certain level of our own protection, then we have a very large chink in our armor."

"Yes, sir."

"Well, there is a very old saying, 'Judgment is the better part of valor.'

"I will pass along Tony's message, your concurrence, and my own fears to the rest of the council."

Stimulate Thinking

"Announcing Vice President Earth Sales, MinInc, Mr. Wendell Chaucert and his wife, Chief Biologic Researcher for the Foundation of Life Sciences, Mrs. Melissa Chaucert." A woman in a flowing black gown, wearing the extreme porcelain-white makeup so common these days, entered on the arm of a man in an ancient black tuxedo and white-frilled blouse. They passed into the receiving line where Commissioner Krylov greeted each of them warmly. After an obligatory social inquiry he passed them on to his companion for the evening, Eba Blinova, a vacuous blond whose only positive attribute seemed to be her ability to remain quiet unless called upon for an opinion. The incoming pair shared greetings down the line before joining the throng of similarly clad individuals mingling on the outskirts of the dance floor.

The partygoers mingled in the Brownian movement, known to all semi-social gatherings since the beginning of time. As boxed units clad in serving carts passed, an occasional guest took hors d'oeuvres or champagne.

The orchestra segued from the last measure of the *The Blue Danube* into *Hail to the Chief.* Krylov smiled. Tonight would be the beginning of a new governmental paradigm. Better, he would see her grovel and he could be oh, so gracious about his victory.

"Announcing the President of the United States, Susan Tipton."

"President Tipton. It's so excellent that you could come and share this celebration with us," Commissioner Krylov said bowing over her dainty hand.

"I'm glad to be here. I'm looking forward to an enjoyable evening. Perhaps we could chat later. I'm extremely interested in your interstate cooperatives."

She's mine, he thought. Exultation! His manhood took that moment to assert itself. Maybe he would take his vacant companion to bed after all. He'd been assured she did have talent there.

"I'd be more than happy to discuss them, Madam President."

"Have you met my friend, Marcus Coldwell, the NASA project engineer of the generation ship to Epsilon Eridani."

"Certainly, and let me introduce you to Miss Eba Blinova."

He turned back to find that the man the President introduced bore as much resemblance to an engineer as Einstein did to a football player. The man stood two-ten if he were a centimeter and massed one-twenty-five. His muscular mass eclipsed the President's relatively tiny form. The tuxedo had to have been custom made.

"It is a pleasure to meet you, Commissioner," Mr. Coldwell said affably as he shook hands.

Krylov could just feel the visibly-convincing, artificial flesh of the man's hand. Many years as a beat cop had taught him the difference. They never quite got the bone structure correct. What was the message? Presidents never did anything without a message.

"I understand there is some discussion of making a new post even higher than Commissioner and having you step into it," the President's companion continued.

Ah, there's the message. She wants to promote me as a sop to her conscience. Her ego mattered not at all to him. If she wanted a face-saving gesture, then he'd won big enough to allow it.

"Purely rumors, I assure you.

"Let me introduce you to ... "

*   *   *

While the chance anyone in the receiving line would identify her was vanishingly small, Christine approved of her team's method of avoiding it entirely.

Anyone who would have caught a glimpse of her would have found her salon-worthy chignon hairstyle, dangling earrings and makeup a little out of place for a cat-burglar.

Stripped down to a black body stocking and a backpack, Christine scaled thirty-four stories up the outside of the main Metro complex. While the building bristled with weapons and sensors, most were only on during civil unrest. She even used one camera bump to stand on to give her arms a bit of a rest.

On the fifty-eighth floor, she replaced a window's bolts with the telescoping slides used by window replacers. Cracking the seal and sliding it out 20 centimeters gave her plenty of room to slide inside, pulling her backpack in behind her. Total time from finding the right window to being inside the women's restroom, six minutes, fourteen seconds. She left the slides in place for her colleagues who would follow half an hour behind her.

Slipping into a stall, she removed her gown, shoes and stockings from her backpack. She hit the electrostatic-wrinkle-remover tab on the dress. She got down to the serious business of stripping out of her working clothes and donning her hunting clothes. The climbing gear went into a package she hid behind the toilet, camouflaged because the bag was the same color and texture as the tile.

Now relatively safe, she emerged from the stall and checked herself in the mirror. Christine gave a tiny frown where her lip nanos had been smeared by the magnetism of one of the electronic-detection sensors. Using an attraction pad, she wiped the old nanites away before applying a new glossy-red coat.

Lifting up the hem of her long checked gown, she ensured that the ceramic pelting knife, her kill weapon of choice this evening, was firmly taped to the inside seam. She smoothed down the satin of her dress before activating the hoopskirt charge that stood it out away from her body. The style felt funny. While fully clothed, the air circulating against her stockings made her seem as if she were baring herself to the world. As a final step she slipped on her shoulder-length opera gloves. Critically she straightened the black bow around her waist before deciding that her appearance would be sufficient to attract her next victim.

Christine glided imperiously out the powder room scanning for her first target of the night. She spied the President very quickly because of the cluster of people surrounding her. Christine likewise picked out at least fourteen Secret Service operatives, including the big bruiser she kept next to her. The man's social manners only fooled the foolish.

To not draw attention to herself, she just joined the knot of people around Madam President and fawned on every word the woman said. When socially she'd reached her turn, she removed her glove and shook the President's bare hand in a soft, ladylike way.

"Oh, Miss Tipton, I'm so pleased to see y'all doing so well! We're all praying for ya," Christine said in a long, slow Texas drawl about an octave above her normal voice. She didn't even hear the President's reply.

After a polite interval, Christine mingled out onto the rest of the floor, already feeling the eyes of the predators on her. The fresh, tanned face and arms caused her to stand out compared to the rest of the women's artificial salt-colored makeup. Most of them were bright enough to be used to project a flatie against.

She let her meandering route lead her into a quiet corner where a boxed serving cart could offer her champagne. She took one as part of her costume with no intention of drinking more than a sip. Bubbly wines affected her hard and she wanted to enjoy every moment.

She mentally counted only six chimpanzees before the first of her would-be suitors made his own circuitous way to her side.

"Quite a ball the Metros put on, isn't it, Miss ... ?" the handsome man said with a rising inflection at the end of his sentence. The open invitation to give her name would start the beginning of a barnyard dance, but the corpie, obvious from his dress, wasn't a viable target.

"I'm sorry, I'm just waiting for my girlfriend to return from the ladies' room."

"Too bad. We could have enjoyed a very nice time," the man said, peeling away to look for straight prey.

"Excuse me, miss," said a presentable man in Metro black twenty years her senior, "but might I have this dance?"

She gave him her most winning smile, the one she'd practiced for hours to get just the right mix of girlish charm and come hither temptress. It didn't take much for her to fake it for the man's graying temples reminded her of her father. Moistness gathered between her legs, and she shed pheromones like a bitch in heat.

"No, sir. My mama made me promise never to even speak to a man who didn't introduce himself."

"My apologies, miss. My name is Lieutenant Robert Darwin."

"Oh," Christine said coquettishly, "just like that famous scientist fellow."

"Actually, I'm a direct descendent."

"That is fascinating. It looks like the Darwin's breeding program has done well indeed.

"My name is Audrey Rose Killingsworth. My father is one of those stuffy corporate vice presidents for Lloyd and Sotheby Insurance. Mama spends her time on charities for the boxed one-legged paper hangers, or whatever is the flavor of the month."

"Enchanted, *mademoiselle*," he said, bowing over her white gloved hand and kissing it with the delicacy with which one might handle Martian lace. "Might I have that dance, now?"

Christine cast her eyes about at the other potential contenders for her charms who awaited the outcome of the lieutenant's advances. None came close to measuring up to her standards and also met the GAM's requirements.

"Absolutely, Mr. Darwin," she said, tittering at the name.

Robert Darwin, to Christine's amazement, turned out to be an exceptional dancer. His waltz left flutters in her stomach as he led her firmly but with old-school charm around the ballroom floor.

She chatted inanely about her fictitious family and complimented Robert's strong chin and clean-shaven face. She learned that it was Robert and never Bob. Lieutenant Darwin continued his subtle advances as if the pair of them were characters in some Edwardian romance novel.

"Whew," Christine exclaimed after the third dance. "Could we take a short break, Robert?"

"But of course, Miss Audrey."

"Please call me Rose. Audrey was my father's failed attempt to curry favor with Grandmama Audrey Lloyd, matriarch of the family."

"All right then, Miss Rose."

They both took some champagne from a serving cart as it rolled gently by them.

"Robert, I know I'm being just a bit forward, but I didn't intend to stay long at this stuffy party. Would you consider taking me home?"

"I could do that. Where do you live?"

"Oh, I see I haven't made myself clear. Mama always said I was the only one that could get lost inside a church. What I meant to say is would you take me to your home. I'm in the mood for some more dancing but in a more intimate setting." Christine managed to blush.

"I'd be delighted to show you my home and dance with you as long as you like, M'lady Rose," Robert said beaming and holding his head high. He offered her his arm. Christine took it.

Twenty-three minutes was far from her record, but it was well within the window the mission required.

"Do you live far? I'm finding this dress rather stuffy," she whispered as she snuggled up even more closely against him.

*   *   *

"Announcing the arrival of the CorpGov Chairman, Nanogate."

Nanogate had timed his fashionably-late arrival to coincide with the breakup of the receiving line.

"Chairman," Krylov stated curtly.

"Commissioner. You have a lovely ball in progress."

"We do our best. Have you met—"

"Excuse me, Commissioner. I wondered if I might have a private word with you this evening." Nanogate watched his opponent's face run through several possible scenarios as an outcome of the discussion.

"Eba, darling, would you please excuse me. I need to have a conversation with this gentleman. Also, would you see to the dismantling of the receiving line."

"Certainly, Commissioner."

Krylov motioned Nanogate over to a quiet alcove that served as a hallway for the serving carts to replenish themselves.

"What can I do for you, Nanogate?" Yuri Krylov asked as soon as they were private enough for him to be brusque.

"I wanted to discuss with you the course of action you are embarked upon. Surely you know that it will lead to social anarchy."

"Nonsense."

"There will be a civil war. Only this time it won't be a division between territories but more one of the powerful versus the oppressed. There will be a great loss of life, mostly within the innocent and those that care the least."

Krylov's face hardened the longer he listened. His jaw muscles rippled as he clenched and unclenched his jaw. "I have already won, Nanogate. Only you can fight a losing war that will cost lives."

"So we have the choice of submission to a police state or death. A wonderful choice of evils. '*Is life so dear or peace so sweet as to be purchased at the price of chains and slavery? Forbid it, Almighty God! I know not what course others may take, but as for me, give me liberty, or give me death!*'"

"That is a moving quotation, Nanogate but it doesn't make your case any stronger. You know as well as I do that I've already won. And if I have to crush every insignificant insect you put in my path, then so be it."

"Spoken like a true tyrant."

"You will lose and you know it," Krylov hissed back.

"'*I could not die anywhere so contented as in the king's company, his cause being just and his quarrel honourable.*'"

"Full of pithy quotes, today, aren't you. If I were you I'd leave now. I'd hate to cause a scene at my own ball by having you arrested for

'Interfering with a Police Officer.'"

"I guess then that I shall see you on the battlefield."

*   *   *

Reza Narendra hated his formal dress uniform. His standard dress blues were ungainly and uncomfortable enough, but the Class A attire chafed and seemed to have shrunk over the years. The buttons over his stomach strained at the thread holding them in place.

He didn't like champagne. He hated dancing. He despised the month's pay he'd shelled out for his wife's ridiculous gown that somehow made her look even more rotund than normal. In short, the evening ranked right up there with having your jockey shorts filled with sand or getting a root canal, something that was still done in his backwater village in India.

He stood close enough to the discussion between the Commissioner and the Chairman to overhear about every third word. He gaped at the Commissioner's restraint. He'd seen enough over his tour of duty to believe that Krylov normally would've had the Chairman killed, dismembered, and ground up into the reclamation bins, all within the time of the *Brandenburg Concerto*, the piece the orchestra currently played.

The Commissioner must feel exceptionally certain of his position to let Nanogate walk out through the entrance doors.

Something other than the Commissioner's confidence bothered Reza. Something was wrong about the exchange. It worked on him like a memory that is on the tip of your tongue. No matter how often he tried to understand, the reason wouldn't come forward.

Leaving his vague troubles to fend for themselves, he looked across the room at his wife in the circle around the President. Like a bolt of lightning, it hit him. Beyond his wife, in the entrance of the hallway to the lavatory, Nanogate's dark-skinned bodyguard lounged, not in traditional yellow but in a tuxedo. Reza wouldn't have noticed him had it not been for the man's almost oddly-hued skin and sharply chiseled features.

The thing that bothered him was that the Chairman hadn't a bodyguard with him when he arrived. What did it mean? And why was the bodyguard still here after the Chairman left?

*   *   *

"President Tipton," came a strange voice through her percomm without an attention signature. *"Please continue with what you are doing. You may remember my voice, but just to make sure, this is Tony Sammis, leader of the GAM."*

President Tipton kept up the meet and greet amongst the partygoers almost as unconsciously as anyone else would breathe.

"How do you do, Mrs. Narendra. Your husband, Reza, is an asset to our fine Metropolitan Police Force."

"This message has been placed in your percomm by a simple nanite virus from one of the people you shook hands with earlier. It is non-interactive and critically timed. If you wish to be taken into hiding, excuse yourself and head to the ladies' room within the next five minutes."

"Yes, Mrs. Narendra, I absolutely support the bill increasing the base pay of police officers."

"Thank you for your time, Ms. President."

"Thank you. Now if you will excuse me I need to visit the necessary."

"Firebrand en route to the bathroom," her Secret Service subvocalized.

"God, it feels good to be out of that throng," Susan said taking a sip from her champagne as she walked down the hallway.

A Secret Service agent stood on either side of the lavatory door, having already cleared the room.

The President went into the bathroom followed by two female agents. None of them saw the single female agent posted in the room unconscious on the toilet. Susan felt a little woozy, but didn't pass out as her guards did. They both dropped into heaps like two potato sacks.

Two women and Tony Sammis bolted out of stalls at the end of the room.

"Quickly, Madam President. We don't have much time. Over to the last stall."

One of the three ran a scanning wand over her body.

"Three signatures. 912.3 megahertz, 922.4 megahertz and 4.6 gigahertz. Quickly." The third seemed to be programming something on a small hand calc.

"We need you to strip off all your clothes, Madam President. Put these on in their place."

Still woozy, Susan stripped but her fingers didn't seem to want to work the zipper or the hooks on her dress.

"All clear," one of the GAM operatives said into her percomm.

"Thaa girl sounths juss like my Secreth Service guarths."

"We must hurry, Madam President," Tony said, finally unzipping the dress himself. He unhooked her necklace and plucked off her sparse jewelry in haste.

"Signatures coded and executing."

"Please step into these overalls, Madam President."

Susan found herself tipping over as she lifted one naked leg up to put it into the proffered clothing. She stayed upright only because someone grabbed her.

"I thought this stuff was supposed to slow her, not make her drunk."

Susan felt the garment pull up on her body and heard a zipper close the front.

"One more thing and then you can rest, Madam President. We need you to get into here."

With great deliberation Susan managed to follow Tony's arm pointing at a fine-mesh-wire bag about 2 meters long.

"Isssorry. I think you wann me to geth in thath bag?"

"Oh, bollocks. Just pull it over her head."

"Give her the sleepy shot and let's get her out the window."

"Buth I no wanna go tho slee.. Ow! Stop th—"

*   *   *

Her once carefully-coiffured hair lay in sweaty disarray around her. The earthy aroma of sex teased her nose. Robert Darwin's soft, regular breaths signaled his post-sexual slumber. His muscular body lay half covered in a sheet next to her. Barely a centimeter long, his hair still managed to be askew.

"Daddy?" she whispered. She nudged Robert's back.

"Mmfm."

Leaning out of the bed, Christine bared her entire body from her crinkled areolas to the semen matting her pubic hair. The satin of her dress rustled as she dug in the pile to find the correct seam. The heaviness of the fabric announced its presence. With a little shove, the triangular blade of the pelting knife cut the threads holding it, dropping into her palm, handle first.

Her respiration sped up and became ragged. Her thighs quivered. Her labia oozed additional scent into the air. The orgasm she faked with Robert earlier now built up in all its reality.

"Daddy?" she whispered again as she turned back to her bed partner. As an artist would use her brush, she stroked two gentle incisions. One opened his carotid artery lengthways down his neck. The second sliced down the brachial artery in his soft, inner elbow. As sharp an edge as she had on her blade, he felt neither mortal cut in his sleep.

She remembered the heartbeat in each of the veins as she'd kissed them during his lovemaking. Now she watched it as red blood sprayed across both of their bodies. Her feet pointed out to an extreme angle as her toes curled down. She bit down hard on her lower lip to keep her moans from wakening him.

As the spurts of blood dropped to a gush and then to a trickle, Christine's body convulsed. "DADDY!" she cried out as her crisis hit full on.

Christine didn't know how long she lay there half aware of the world. Her focus still remained on the corpse next to her. Now the distinct aroma of sex battled with the bitter, metallic smell of blood.

Only her percomm signal brought her to consciousness. She ignored the call, hugging herself tightly. This smeared blood even more across her nude body. The smile on her face wasn't the result of eating a canary but rather an entire flock of them.

Her percomm went off again.

"Yes," she said as her normal protective façade settled into place on her features.

"We just snatched the President. You have about ten minutes before every Metro goes berserk. Any one that isn't quite among the land of the living will be noticed about two minutes later," Tony warned.

"Understood. I'll bring the codes and the DNA with me."

"I'll inform Augustine."

Christine snapped off the percomm. All of her movements were conservative. She wasted no time.

She picked up the knife and severed Robert's left index finger from his hand. It had been the first thing that touched her body, finding the keyhole in the back of her dress. She needed it like an alcoholic needed her drink. With reverence she kissed the very end of it.

Using the nearly clean portion of the sheet she wiped the majority of the blood off her body and her prize. She walked into the bathroom and turned on the shower as cold as it would go before she stepped in. The brisk water washed away the visible evidence as well as woke her to a point where she would be useful.

Three minutes later she climbed out. She didn't have the luxury of soaking. She checked her image in the mirror and ducked back into the shower to rewash her hair. This time satisfied with the result, she dried herself with Robert's handy bath sheet. She wrapped up her hair in another bath towel.

Looking for a pillowcase, she instead got lucky and found permalex evidence gloves in the linen closet. Placing Robert's finger in one and sealing it, she squatted over and slid her trophy deep into her vagina. Not part of her normal routine, but it had to remain hidden even if casually searched.

Two fresh gloves went on her hands as she tackled her lover's computer. While she didn't care if they knew she killed her sweet father or their lieutenant, she didn't want them to know she'd accessed his computer in any way. Using the handy interface it took no more than thirty seconds to discover his logon.

She looked longingly at the knife lying next to Robert. She couldn't risk it. She would have to be happy with just her trophy. There would be other knives.

Covered in blood splatter, her dress was a complete loss. She went to his closet to find several long-sleeved, black, button-up shirts. Taking one out she slipped it on. The bottom draped to mid-thigh. A belt across her waist made the shirt a convincing mini-dress. His chest of drawers provided a pair of boxers and a pair of athletic shorts that were barely visible beneath the shirt. With just a quick rinse her flat shoes were adequate. Unwrapping the towel from her head, she was just another housewife running late and letting her hair air dry.

She didn't bother to lock the flat door behind her.

$$* \quad * \quad *$$

Special Agent Pamela Gunther became aware of her surroundings even if they wavered around her. Her brain insisted this was a holiday weekend with one too many Tequila Sunrises, a particular weakness of hers. But the walls were too close. And she was at least partially clothed. And she was sitting, not lying down. Nor did she hear Frank's snores.

Too many dissimilar data points for her to do something routine like rolling over and going back to sleep.

She stood up and found her skirt and panties around her ankles. That was normal enough after a bender. It was something her brain could hook onto to take another action. Once her clothing was mostly in place she tackled the door. A latch. It might as well have been a deadbolt to her thumb-fingered hands.

The pounding in her head only needed the whistling air passage and shrapnel to be artillery bursting around her. A latch. She pulled it back and the door opened onto a women's restroom. Fuck but she couldn't remember how she'd gotten here. Last thing she remembered was guarding the President at the hoity-toity ball.

She wanted to throw up. She always felt better after she threw up. She made her way to the sink and rinsed her mouth out with about 20 liters of water. She managed to suck in a pint or so from her cupped hand.

"Station four, sitrep," came a voice about a dozen decibels above the heavenly trumpets signaling the Second Coming.

"Flame is experiencing some digestive discomfort," said her own voice. It was definitely her voice down to even her slight northeastern clipped vowels. But she never opened her mouth. What the fuck?

"Situation normal," came her voice again.

She turned and stumbled to the door of the bathroom. She pushed open the door and tripped on the doorsill, falling flat on her face between two agents.

"Gunther? What's wrong?"

"I jusss hurd my voice," she slurred.

"FIRESTORM! FIRESTORM!" both the agents shouted as they jumped over the downed woman and slammed into the bathroom without regard for anything as trivial as whether the room were designed for pointers or setters.

It took three seconds to confirm the missing President, by which time eight agents and six Metros were in the room. With no immediate danger, nothing to shoot, and no immediate leads, the combined police forces looked at each other in confusion.

The Special Agent In Charge started issuing orders less than a second later. "Ground all vehicles immediately. Get a forensics team in here, NOW! I want all the surveillance video pulled at once. I also want all electronic surveillance on the President's implants."

The sprinting of the Secret Service in all directions couldn't be hidden. Commissioner Krylov entered the room, with only perfunctorily objections by the multitude of agents.

"What the fuck is going on?"

"The President is missing, sir. She's just fucking gone."

* * *

Christine opened the door to a safe house in Chehalis, Washington. The stale smell of a flat that hadn't been used in many months gave her reassurance that the apartment was truly safe.

After locking the door, throwing the bolt and latching the Bucky String in place, she headed back to the operations room, stripping off her impromptu costume as she went.

Carefully she removed the gloved prize from her nether regions. She didn't feel any emotional impact from this manner of carrying an object. Unwrapping it, she squeezed just one single drop of the severed finger's blood onto a bio-scanner.

"Scanning sample," came the mechanical voice.

"Call Augustine."

"*I'm here. Do you have it?*" Augustine asked over their percomm link.

"Scan complete," announced the mechanical voice again.

"Yes, it is going up onto the cloud server along with the account name and server address."

"*Perfect. Tell Tony that I'll upload all of the information, including a mirrored log-in to our cloud node as soon as I'm done.*"

"Yes."

"*Thank you, Christine.*"

"No, thank you."

Christine threw all of her clothes into a compact industrial incinerator and turned the dial for maximum burn temperature.

Eight steps later she was in bed.

Twelve seconds later she was asleep.

* * *

"Madam President?" David said shaking President Tipton hard enough to bounce her on the bed. "We need to replace your implants."

Spartan didn't begin to describe the room. Only a mattress and the bare metal bedframe furnished a room covered in copper mesh. The old-school Faraday cage would keep in any electronic noise and keep out any prying probes.

"She's still out," Morgan opined.

"You don't say!" David retorted.

"Don't look at me, I told you aerosol dosages were almost impossible to judge."

"Yeah, but seven hours?"

"Listen, you two don't need to be squabbling like children," Frances intervened. "Besides, it might be better if she is out. We all know how much this hurts even in the best of cases."

"Yeah. At least we don't have a time crunch. It's not like she disappeared anywhere near here."

"The funny thing is that she is so close to where she belongs. The White House is only about twelve kilometers in that direction," Dave said, pointing northeast. "Hell, from the news and our informants, they are still looking in Portland proper."

"Since we don't have any time issues, I suggest local anesthetics before we abuse the leader of our country."

*   *   *

Krylov balanced a stylus between his thumb and his forefinger, letting the other end bounce up and down on the tabletop. It tapped like a drumstick on a snare drum in a military march. He was angry. Hell, he was furious. He wanted to destroy someone over this so bad he could taste it. He wasn't quite angry enough to fail to notice that his subordinates avoided even crossing in front of his door for fear of reprisals.

Across his desk, Secret Service Detail Head Tessaro projected serenity but his face spoke only of fatigue coupled by fear.

"Sir, I really have more pressing matters to attend to. If you didn't notice, the President is missing," Albert Tessaro said loading as much sarcasm into the simple statement as his fatigued mind could muster.

"Agent T—"

"Special Agent in Charge, Commissioner. I remember your title, I'd appreciated if you would remember mine."

"Very well, Special Agent in Charge Tessaro. I would like to know what you've learned, and what leads you are following up on. If you can answer those to my satisfaction I'll leave you to your investigation."

"Yes, sir. Normally, I wouldn't be sharing this information, but under these unusual circumstances I'll cooperate. The investigation is ongoing in several different directions:

"One: Interviews at the scene, primarily from your adjutant Reza Narendra, have led us to use facial recognition on the party guests. Two very suspicious people have popped up—Thomas Marks, the bodyguard of CEO Nanogate, aka Chairman of the CorpGov, and Christine Matthews, a young woman linked with the GAM and at least twenty-three murders that I'm aware of.

"Marks remains long after Nanogate had left, and he wore civilian clothing. We have no surveillance showing where Marks went, however.

"Christine left the party on the arm of Lieutenant Robert Darwin, deceased. He was found murdered in his own home. Miss Matthews is the only suspect. The murder weapon is at the scene with her fingerprints and DNA on it. The case is vacuum-tight against her. We can't make any correlation between Darwin and the disappearance of the President, but we aren't ruling it out.

"Two: Six hours—" the agent queried the time, "—and forty-seven minutes after the abduction, and we have yet to receive a ransom demand. This indicates she is likely dead."

"Is that fact, Special ... oh, hell, Mr. Tessaro, or speculation?"

"It's statistics, so no, sir, it is not a fact. In this day, professional kidnappers know they have four, maybe five hours to make contact and get their payoff before the full weight of federal law enforcement comes crashing down on them. We can rule out amateurs. This was much too slick."

"Explain."

"I will, sir, if you let me continue."

"At your own pace, son."

"Three: Our forensic teams have discovered nothing whatsoever in the way of physical evidence as to the whereabouts of the President, nor how she was transported. We have a great deal of evidence, but none of it points to a location.

"We have DNA sweeps of the room, providing the names of many, many people but some of the standouts include Christine Matthews, Tony Sammis, David Swift and Morgan Anderson, Greenies all. This coincidence is too high to be chance. Computer simulations project less than one part in several billion that they weren't directly involved in the kidnapping.

"Additionally, we have the electromagnetic box that mimicked signals from the President's implants, a sophisticated bit of subterfuge, and sixty-three thousand, six hundred forty-two additional pieces of evidence. All of which points to a highly skilled snatch job by the Green Action Militia. None of this data points a finger of direction at either the location of the Greenies or the President."

"So because the President hasn't named a successor yet we should contact the Speaker of the House."

"It has already been done. The Honorable Jayson McCullen has determined he will take no action for twenty-four hours."

"Just dandy," Krylov hissed. "I think that is all I need you for, Special Agent in Charge Tessaro. If you would be so kind as to keep me in the loop of any changes that take place before they become public, I'd appreciate it."

"Absolutely, sir."

Krylov tapped his pen some more as the special agent who couldn't find his own asshole with the aid of a proctologist left the room.

"REZA!" he bellowed.

"Yes, sir," the plump lackey said as he hurried into the room.

Krylov chided himself for his thoughts. He needed these men, and thinking negatively of them only made his actions follow.

"I want you to have every location Tony Sammis has ever had even the remotest connection to searched. I want a hard penetration radar scan and visual search of every room, closet and cubby."

"Yes, sir. Is there anything else?"

Krylov barely heard him as his eyes glazed over.

"I've read the man's profile and he is sneaky enough to pull another one over on us. I want the SWAT team to raid the Wilted Rose. I want every employee questioned. While you are at it find an excuse to confiscate the premises."

"I'll make it happen, sir."

"One more thing. That network-hacking bitch he has can't just have disappeared. People like that can't turn off their need to fiddle in their electronic world. Send in our own technicians to find out where she went to."

*　*　*

William Sagum fumed but with his on-camera, professional smile on his face. He wanted to be on the other coast doing real journalism around the kidnapping of the President of the United States. Instead he and his solidographer recorded a banal piece on the failure of the federal government to release funds to the police.

A bright-red liftousine landed 2 meters from William Sagum as they recorded their wrap-up.

"Cut," Winnie called from behind the camera. "I can't narrow the focus enough to get that damned vehicle out of it."

The door of the exquisite vehicle opened and a tall man with reddish-brown skin and the yellow tights of a professional bodyguard climbed out. They expected some corporate bigwig to follow, but none did.

"Excuse me," William said walking toward the bodyguard. He tried to remain cordial but he felt a certain amount of his pent-up rage coming through in a cold tone. "Could you get them to move that lift? It's in our shot."

"I certainly will, sir. As soon as you and your solidographer get into the vehicle we will be on our way." The brown-haired man delivered the message calmly and without any threatening gestures. He seemed more like an android than a person for all the emotion he showed.

Rarely unsure of himself or the perks his profession allowed, William stared in disbelief. Only Winnie, ducking back behind her camera to record the event, snapped him out of his silence.

"Excuse me?"

"For the benefit of your camera, I will repeat. I want you and your solidographer to get into the lift. If you do not do so, I have been authorized to use force to compel your acquiescence."

"You are kidnapping me?"

"Only if you force me to do so. My employers would much prefer a willing participant."

"What is this all about. Do you know who I am?" he demanded.

"Indeed I do. You are William Sagum, the only son of Donna and Hector Sagum. Graduated Cum Laude from Tulane University in Communications with a minor in Broadcasting. Would you like me to tell you your favorite color, your network password, your birthday, your wife's perfume brand or your mistress's percomm code?" the man offered in a calm and unruffled tone. "Your cameraman is Edwina 'Winnie' Herbert, no relation to the science fiction author."

Winnie waved from behind the solidograph.

"She has been your personal cameraman ... or should I say camerawoman for your last four years in the field."

"Winnie, I think you should run for it. This could get ugly. He can't catch us both."

"Quite to the contrary, Mr. Sagum. The more you fight my employer's simple request, the more force I will be required to use. Perhaps you recognize this?" The man brought forth a weapon they recognized only because of the debate within Congress of allowing Neural Amplification and Disruption devices into the hands of civilians.

"Yes," William said with disdain.

"Then you will realize I can disable you both in seconds. While it would give me no pleasure to do so, I will if you insist."

"Can you at least tell us where we are going? Or who your employer is?"

"Unfortunately, my instructions specifically preclude answering either question."

William stood staring down the bodyguard, looking for some weakness. "How about your name."

"Not that the datum will be of value to you, but my name is Thomas Marks."

"Bill, let's go," Winnie said. "This is a story! We can feed it live back to the networks if need be."

"That has been anticipated and I've been instructed to tell you that we approve of your live feed."

"Really?" William asked in surprise. "I guess this makes sense only if they aren't going to hurt us."

"I assure you that my employers have no intention of harming you or Miss Edwina in any way."

"All right, then. We're in."

"Excellent. Would you and Mrs. Herbert please enter the lift?" Marks asked in his continued polite tone.

Without much fanfare the trio climbed in, Mr. Marks entering last.

Like any of its ilk, the liftousine reeked of luxury with a full bar, acoustic silencer, and an audio/visual/olfactory entertainment system. The bench seating around the edges of the room could obviously pull out to form a very large bed.

Trying to look out, Bill discovered that the windows were

blacked out from the inside as well as they were from the outside. He pushed the sunroof button but it didn't activate.

"Not much to see," William said.

"We desire that you not know your destination."

"Why not? This is ridiculous. When will we know what this is all about?"

"Bill, give it a rest," Winnie said.

"Bah! Kidnapped right off the causeway? My nose smells something other than this big hairy ape."

"I keep telling you it should smell a story."

"Be that as it may," Thomas Marks said, "you will know within ten minutes and have all the answers to your questions within another half hour after that."

"Then we aren't going far. Not out of DC proper. Who is going to these lengths to see a reporter?"

"Obviously, someone who wanted the job done right," Mr. Marks said with a rare smile.

"Coming in for a landing now," the driver said over an intercom.

"Gentle folk, please come with me and try not to get lost. I would hate to have to hurt you as an object lesson to get you to your destination."

Mr. Marks opened the door and led the way out. His cargo looked around. They got very little as the empty executive landing zone had been scrubbed of all identifying marks.

"Come this way." Mr. Marks said, again leading his charges. They went out of the garage through a double-door into a maze of corporate hallways with no identification markers. The hall Mr. Marks chose ended in a pale granite door about twice normal size.

With little effort their escort pushed open the door to reveal two of the most famous figures in the world, Chairman Nanogate and Tony Sammis, leader of the GAM.

This is a real story, William thought.

∗   ∗   ∗

"I figured I'd find you here," Brother Adam said to Augustine.

Sitting in the darkened cafeteria, Augustine paused long enough to swallow. "You mean taking three seconds of my God-given day to eat?"

"There seems to be a lack of open seating," Adam joked about the empty commons at two-thirty a.m. "Mind if I join you?"

Her head nodded as she shoveled in more of her oatmeal. Adam sat down with his own tray of cereal and coffee.

"Between teaching, our defense shifts and my regular duties to our Lord, I've not had time to scratch," Augustine mumbled around her food. "I think the prioress is intent that I not even have the opportunity to break my vows."

Smiling, Adam said, "While I don't have your teaching requirements, I might say the same about the homework a certain educator has dumped upon those of us who have the *honor* of being in her defense circle."

"It builds character," she said with mock seriousness. "And I have black rings of character under both my eyes. My God, I've not had more than two hours sleep a night in the last week."

"Nice to know it goes both ways."

"You young snot, when I was your age—"

"I know, you walked five kilometers to work in the snow, worked twenty-hour days, ate a lump of dried poison and you LIKED it!"

"Well, twenty-two hours, but other than that, you got it right," Augustine grinned around her spoon.

"Pardon me."

"Good thing you respect your elders."

Adam took a slow sip of his coffee, putting a pause in their banter.

"They are going to find you," he said cryptically.

"I know," Augustine replied, the mirth dropping from her face. She stopped eating and stared at her bowl. She stirred it while many things went through her head. "But how do you know."

"Like you, I've not completely dropped every contact I've had with my former colleagues. But you don't have to worry. I take my oath here very seriously. They know nothing about you from me."

"We've had this discussion before, Adam. I trust your faith."

"I know I'm impertinent enough to get me branded a do-gooder in the force, but what brought you here? Oh, I trust your faith too, but you can serve God in many ways other than here."

"Honestly, Adam, I thought I could hide in the bosom of our Lord and pay at least the interest on the huge debt of sin I have on my soul."

"God doesn't work that way, Augustine."

"I know he doesn't, Adam, but I felt I had to try. I will work through my penance as best as I can."

"This is penance for you? I've never heard of any such—"

"No, Adam. Even the church can't demand service as a penance. I've always felt drawn to the life of service to God and his only Son. Obviously, not strongly enough considering my past."

"So you've tied all three—faith, penance and hiding, together in one indelible mess. Sister, you have a tough life and even tougher decisions to make."

"I know. Now that Metros are actively looking for my fingerprints in the net, I know it's only a matter of time before they can close in on me in a static location.

"If I were on the move they could look all they wanted and find nothing but electron farts. Worse, if I stay the church gets dragged into this debacle, something I can't allow."

Adam lifted his cup as to take a drink but instead just looked across it with an emptiness in his eyes. "Just know that you have friends here," he said in a low tone that barely ruffled the rising steam.

* * *

Captain Hogan frowned behind his combat mask. From above, at this time of day, he should see masses of people. Instead, his tactical display didn't show a single patron, prostitute, beggar, welf or even nil. Everyone seemed to already be in on the timing of his raid. Even the normal Metro patrols were gone. His query to dispatch showed his brethren off on calls, but he knew better. It was one thing for civilians to be absent, but for his own brothers in uniform to be missing troubled him.

"Everyone be on your guard," he said to the fourteen other members of his SWAT team. "They know we're coming. We go in with rules of engagement Sierra—shoot first ask questions later." He was proud of the quiet, professional way they accepted the order.

"Dust off after deployment. Keep your firepower airborne for support if needed," Hogan directed to the pilot.

"Roger."

The Armored Personnel Carrier and Fire support vehicle (APCF) touched the ground just long enough to drop his team of fourteen.

Through their assigned ports they dropped down grav lines 2 meters to the cracked concrete below. The armored personnel carrier lifted off over their heads.

From inside the APCF the Captain worked his team's deployment. "Murphy and Catz, I want you on over-watch across the street, at least third floor."

A simple click from each of the snipers indicated affirmative.

The remaining dozen split up into four equal teams, one team racing through the alleyway on either side of the Wilted Rose as fast as their powered armor would take them.

"Four. Three. Two. One," Hogan counted down as he watched his people get into place. "Position. Go, team Alpha."

Three of the lead folks raced to the front door with cover by their comrades. The lead member of the team, in a wrecker suit, barreled right into the main door of the Rose. It gave with the slightest resistance, sprawling the Metro across the floor, a not uncommon occurrence in his place in the team.

"POLICE WITH A WARRANT! POLICE WITH A WARRANT!" the remaining two yelled as they ran over their prone teammate.

"Move up, Beta." He watched as the three-element, second team swarmed in shortly afterward.

"CLEAR."

"CLEAR."

"CLEAR."

"Clear. All clear. Captain, there is something fishy about this. The entire place is deserted. All the rooms are open, including the one to the storage room containing ... roughly five hundred thousand in booze."

"Understood, Malay. We need to do a close search of everything ten floors up as well."

"Wait a second, Captain. I have a secret door."

Hogan saw the door brightly outlined through Johnson's remote thermal imaging. Visually you couldn't see it from the surrounding brickwork.

"Hold for backup, Team Charlie."

"Delta there aren't any stragglers. Swing east and play backup to Charlie."

"Roger."

Hanson watched the two teams merge.

"Forcing entry." Another wrecker-suited man crashed into the brickwork imploding a 2-meter hole in the wall.

"POLICE WITH A WARRANT!"

Hogan watched the team enter. Stairs went downward at least 25 meters.

"Captain, it's really warm here. Must be at least eighty degrees," Hays said as he led the way down.

"Copy."

The team went down to a simple door. "No electronic signature on the door and scan shows no locking mechanism."

The six men poured through the door.

"CLEAR," was repeated six times.

"Hays, what is that in the corner?" Hogan asked.

"This is unreal. Are you getting this?"

A solido of Tony Sammis, one of the most wanted men in the world, with a cat perched on his shoulder appeared.

"*Welcome to our Secret Headquarters. Make yourself at home.*"

Captain Hogan's video link showed a flash just long enough for his brain to register the explosion. Less than a second later, his combat webbing separated just before his bones crushed. The g-forces of the shock wave continued, sending him hurtling against the opposite wall of his vehicle. His shoulder dislocated on impact. The communication deck, an integral part of the hull, tore free and slammed into the weapons rack, snapping his leg between.

Hogan screamed as he fell. Weightlessness seemed to last eternally in the enclosed compartment. He screamed at the jarring halt at the bottom. As the compartment collapsed, a loose conduit pierced the Captain's right thigh, running all the way up his torso to exit the skin of his right cheek. Thankfully, he passed out just as his emergency transponder sent out a critical alert message.

*   *   *

Tony and Nanogate sat in side-by-side recliners in the living room of yet another GAM safe house, this one unattractively situated at 69th and Hawthorne, adjacent to Mount Tabor. Today the wind carried the worst of the sulfurous stench northward. The acrid smell teased them like the vision of a ghost in the bright light, faded out much more than visible. Cin's more sensitive nose wrinkled more often as she curled up in her person's lap.

Mr. Marks stood between the two leaders but with his back against the wall. The solido was on but turned down low. They knew what was coming and when.

"Sorry I couldn't offer better quarters. We're working on something more appropriate but my safe houses are getting burned almost faster than we can set them up."

"It is of no consequence," Nanogate assured him. "I wish I was able to offer the hospitality of my home but the efforts to release the edifice from the rest of the floating city is significant. The engineers required us to be out for at least twelve hours."

"What about your family?"

"I sent them on a dirigible cruise. They're living it up over New Zealand right now.

"I have to thank you for reintroducing me to beer," Nanogate said motioning to his pouch. "As you find the 'better things in life' you sometimes forget some of the old pleasures."

"I'm glad. I've always been a fan of a good beer while relaxing with friends."

"An odd statement, Tony. Do you consider me a friend?"

"Perhaps." Tony considered it for the moment as he took a draw of his pouch. "No, Clarence, at the moment we are cobelligerents and are moving in the same direction. I don't discount the possibility for the future but right now I don't consider you a friend. I hope you don't take offense."

"It's been a long time since I took offense at much of anything, Tony. To get to lead a major corporation first you learn to hide your emotions. Then you bottle them up. And eventually you really stop having them. So, no, I didn't take offense."

Tony took another long draw on his beer before saying anything. "Speaking of curious statements, are you saying that you are emotionless?"

"No, not quite, but you learn to ration them or let them out at only specific times."

The flat shook as if a giant punched the building. Tony even felt a bit of the air compression. The windows rattled in sympathy. None of the three men reacted nearly as much as Cin did. She jumped down with her back arched, looking for an enemy to fight.

"Looks like they found our secret headquarters."

Nanogate dialed his percomm. "Jason, there has been an explosion in downtown Portland. I want our special broadcast tonight uninterrupted by the coverage of the explosion. Also I want you to skew the new coverage as a police attack.

"No, don't lie. Just put the suggestion out there slanted in a way that would leave the public to believe they did it against an innocent property owner or owners.

"Thank you, Jason," Nanogate concluded.

"I hope you know what you are doing, Tony. You just ambushed and murdered probably a dozen or so Metros. They won't take kindly to that."

Cin walked over to Nanogate's feet and brushed against his designer suit before leaping up into the Chairman's lap. Nanogate started as if the cat were made of fire. He kept as far away as he could with her in his lap. Cin responded by head-butting him in his middle.

"She won't bite," Tony said. "Just rub her down the back."

Nanogate stroked as if the cat just might turn and bite. Cin closed her eyes, arched her back against his hand and buzzed with pleasure.

"Curious."

"Getting back to your original statement, it's been so long since anyone's fought a guerilla war that they've forgotten. Let me ask a question. What is it that the Metros need most?"

"Money," Nanogate replied without hesitation.

"Respect," Mr. Marks said over their shoulder, surprising both of them as quiet as the man usually was.

"Both excellent answers and true, but the key thing they need is fear. Without it they can't control the people. If the people don't fear them, then they are very vastly outnumbered no matter how many guns, bombs and ships they have.

"Publically killing those men shouted that not only is it possible, but that we didn't even flinch at the thought that every other policeman in the world will stop at nothing until we are dead. We announced to the world that we don't fear them."

Nanogate looked thoughtful but said nothing as he grew bolder with his petting of the cat that now curled up in his lap.

"Excuse me, gentlemen, but our program is about to begin,"

Thinking Outside the Box

Mr. Marks said pointing at the "Special Report" image on the solido.

*   *   *

"*We bring you this special report from William Sagum at an undisclosed location.*"

"Thank you, Brian. I've been recently fortunate enough to be requested to share this interview with you. While the request was made in a rather overly dramatic way, it was one I'm glad I agreed to.

"While the entirety of the law enforcement community scrambles to find the kidnapped President, Susan Tipton, I have the great pleasure to inform you that she has not in fact been abducted at all but rather has arranged her own vanishing act.

"President Tipton will be addressing you first and then we will have a question-and-answer session. We will take questions from other networks as well as questions over the net.

"Ladies and Gentleman, the President of the United States."

A spotlight snapped onto the famous face of the President in front of the seal of her office mounted on a bare blue wall. The light hit her curly red hair just right to make it look like flames.

"Good evening. I want to start this address with an apology to you, the people of the United States. I've worried and alarmed you by my disappearance. This was not my intent. Hopefully, as I tell my story you will understand.

"The reason I chose to take this extraordinary action was because of the death of President Lopez. I've been given a strong reason to believe that the Secret Service itself had some part in the President's assassination. I want to be clear that I have no proof, only very strong deductive reasoning from not only myself but several of my trusted advisors. Much of our deduction revolves around the supposition that President Lopez was murdered because of one of her acts prior to her death. We have a suspect, a motive and an opportunity but no proof ... at this time.

"Please do not think that all of our good people within the Secret Service are assassins. That is not the message I intend to deliver. I only say that there may be one or two who might have been swayed in such a way that they might not fulfill their duties to protect me, the President.

"As President I cannot make baseless accusations without proof any more than any citizen, so I've been constrained to live in fear that any action I might take may result in a fate similar to my predecessor. This could influence me to suborn my natural instincts. It might cause me to fail to implement that same act as President Lopez. It might impact my desire to use the most stringent means to bring the guilty to justice.

"The only way I can act as my conscience dictates is to remove myself from the potential hazard. As a result I contacted the most neutral party for good that I knew and requested their assistance in this time of great need. You know this neutral agency as the Green Action Militia.

"At great personal risk to themselves, the GAM took me from a place of probable danger to a place of relative safety. For the short term, the GAM will take up the roll of Presidential bodyguards. A change in the protective detail of the President is not without precedent. At more than one time in our history, mercenaries, or even private enforcers, guarded the President. This is no different.

"My hope is that I can return to the normalcy you expect from your government as soon as possible.

"There will be those who question whether the GAM have exerted demands or imposed an agenda upon me. I have to disabuse anyone thinking this. They are acting as a completely neutral agency.

"I will prove this as often as possible by meeting with various government officials of the Congress and the Judiciary to continue the job of governing our great nation. While now it may seem possible that I may be controlled, it will soon become obvious that I am making only the decisions and taking only the actions that are in the best interests of the people of the United States.

"That concludes my statement. I'll now take an interview with William Sagum, who, for the duration of this event, will become presidential press liaison."

President Tipton walked over and took a seat across a low table from the reporter.

"President Tipton, it is good to see you."

"It's good to be seen, and more specifically it's good to be able to do my job without having to watch for a knife in the back."

"Some Presidents would have said that they get that from Congress on a regular basis," William said with a smile.

"True, but the gap between literal and figurative seems much wider now than it did in the past."

"Was it really that difficult to do your job? I mean no one was immediately threatening you."

"Let's put it this way, William. Say you were doing your job right now and you knew for a fact someone was behind you with an ancient revolver. And assume that you knew he'd pull the trigger just once if you did something he didn't like. Would it matter to you if his revolver was loaded with one bullet or six? Do you think you'd do everything in your power to make sure you never upset him?"

"I think I get your point. Hopefully our studio never gets that idea."

The President tittered. "I can laugh about it now that I'm out from under the shadow."

"There are those that will claim that what they are seeing now is nothing more than a computer generated solido-response program. What do you have to say to that, Madam President?"

"William, the decision to drop out was one of the most difficult any President has had to face. Every person in the public scrutiny has to live with a certain amount of danger—they have to live with the knowledge that there are people out there that hate them. The acknowledgement that your own guards may choose to kill you instead of protect you is a bitter pill indeed. Just ask Indira Gandhi.

"It took several long sessions by some of my trusted advisors before taking the plunge. You could talk to Secretary of Defense Mark Gray, Secretary of State Jasmine Diop, Secretary of Urban Planning Bascom Perry, or Secretary of Energy and Commerce Tanya Kirsch. Each of them weighed in directly on my resolution to absent myself. They can each provide direct evidence that it was my choice."

"But you didn't involve the Secretaries of the Treasury or Homeland Security?"

"The list I gave is not a comprehensive one. But to directly answer your question, William, no, I didn't include either Treasury or Homeland Security. Treasury is responsible for the Secret Service and Homeland Security is to provide oversight on the same as well as deal with any terrorist threats.

"It seemed prudent not to solicit input from the very folks that I fear may have been suborned."

"So what do you plan to do now that you are free to make the decisions you are honor bound to execute?"

"That's a good question, William. While I've said I am concerned about the Secret Service, they are an exceptional investigative organ. I intend to focus all of their efforts on the assassination of President Lopez. However, I will team them with not only members of the FBI but also investigative members of Amnesty System-Wide. This way there can be no opportunity to sweep incriminating evidence under the rug.

"I'll reiterate this as often as required. I will not rest until we know what really happened to our beloved President and have those guilty of her murder brought to justice."

"Thank you, President Tipton, but I meant more on a legislative agenda."

"Oh, that's simple. I'm going to continue to fight for each piece of policy and lawmaking that President Lopez initiated—cloning prohibitions for all but medical requirements and research; free currency exchange; increasing incentives for small businesses; inclusion of Nil residents within our current codex of laws."

"That's a full agenda, Madam President."

"It is. However, there is one piece of budget activity that I want to do immediately. It is an extension of what Carla Lopez had already started. I, however, will do it openly and aboveboard. As of this time, by Presidential order, the federal funding for all Metropolitan Police Forces ceases."

"Excuse me?"

"That's right, William. There is a growing belief in many quarters that this action is the one that got President Lopez assassinated. She tried to play both sides of the fence in not removing it from the budget but rather hiding it as a bureaucratic snafu that only delayed funding.

"I state publicly that those funds will no longer be released. This is far from the only reason I'm taking this action. It never made sense to me that the police can triple dip into the public's pockets, in the form of federal and state taxes, regular quarterly payments directly from citizens, and then also as graft and outright extortion, all for the nominal service of doing nothing. And if this isn't bad enough, to get the police actually to do something, they require even further payments.

"There is an ancient saying that once you play Danegeld you never get rid of the Dane."

"Madam President, some might say you just declared war on the

Metropolitan Police Forces."

"Not at all. I only state that one of their revenue streams is no longer viable. I urge state lawmakers to take similar actions."

"Madam President, I'm going to take some questions from the net now. Every question submitted has been assigned a number and semantically identical questions grouped. Would you please push the button on the table and it will choose a random question."

The President leaned over and pushed a red, elevator-style button.

"Six," called out the computer-generated voice.

"Question six: 'Madam President, how do we know that you are nothing more than a computer-generated image?'"

"William, as I mentioned before, my choice to get away from my security forces was discussed with several people who can verify the story. Over the next few days I'll be meeting with key members of the Congress. Each of them will be given the opportunity to receive a sample of my blood. They will even be given the choice of where the blood is sampled.

"I have a strong feeling that this will give a number of them considerable pleasure as they've wanted to stick it to the Executive branch for some time," she said with a half-smile, half-grimace.

"If this won't prove it to you then I suggest you gather with your colleagues at the local chapter of Conspiracy-Theories-RU because I can't imagine anything else that I could provide that you would accept as proof."

"The next question comes from KRNQL, Topeka: 'Madam President, what does the Green Action Militia get out of this arrangement?'"

"A royal pain in the ass. Seriously, William, the GAM gets nothing. They are a neutral agency trying to preserve and improve our way of life. Not a single one has asked me to do anything, change my mind on any topic, or invoke some tit-for-tat arrangement. They protect me and that's all.

"And, predicting one other similar follow-on question, the same people who will be visiting with me over the next few days will see that I'm not being a puppet to the GAM's agenda."

"Question 554: 'When will you ... '"

*   *   *

"Give Mr. Commissioner my compliments and tell him that I already know he wants to talk to me. Tell him I will be up with data as soon as possible," Reza said, slamming the door in the face of a frazzled subordinate.

Reza focused back on the percomm. "Hello, this is Lieutenant Reza Narendra from Portland Metro, with a customer number of N74656. I'm trying to track down the private investigator assigned to shadow and report on William Sagun.

"Yes, I'll hold." The waiting music soured in his ear. American music never did appeal to him but this took the cake. The slow, languid music was designed to take the starch out of any rebuff the person might be harboring. If that weren't bad enough, it popped and hissed with static and occasionally skipped short segments.

"*Yes, Lieutenant, what can I do for you?*"

"I'm trying to find out which of your operatives was tasked to report on William Sagun."

"*Let me check that. Hmmm. I show here that Am Trembley was the private enforcer in question.*"

"Do you show any reports from Mr. Trembley?"

"*Sorry, Trembley is a woman.*"

"Honestly, ma'am, I don't care if she is green and digests her food with four stomachs."

"*Well, you don't have to be rude. We've received no report from Trembley since she started her assignment.*"

"Thank you."

"*Did you want anything else?*"

"No, I have what I need." And he knew what he'd be asked to do with it.

*   *   *

They found her in one of the new daylight drug bars in Dupont Circle, Café Anything. Sergeant Jensen didn't like this duty, didn't like it one bit. His Captain had dealt with Jensen's lack of caring in one profane phrase of his own.

The blond target of his duty lay slumped over on the bar, bathed in sunshine from the massive window. She wore cut-off jean shorts and a green wifebeater with the faded logo "Girls Do It All!" The light attire didn't contain her oversized skeletal and musculature structure. Mr. Natural Universe would have looked weak next to this girl.

Jensen couldn't decide if her bulk originated from biodrugs, gene therapy or implanted mechanical augmentation. Bottom line, it didn't matter.

When he stepped into the bar flanked by his two fully geared teammates, the manager, in a tartan kilt and suit-coat, appeared out of nowhere.

"Excuse me, Officer. Is there an issue? Our establishment is fully paid-up through next quarter in our protection fees. We even purchased eight tickets to the Black and White Ball."

"Sir, please return to your customers," Jensen said without making eye contact. "Our business is with the blond giantess against the window."

"By all means, Officer. Is there anything I can do to help you?"

"Stay out of our way."

"Yes, sir. Absolutely, sir. I can do anything you need me to ... but for now I'll stay out of the way."

The two patrons in the woman's corner of the bar found they were late for important engagements elsewhere and raced out of the establishment in what surely set the unaided land-speed record.

Jensen jabbed the woman's back with three fingers. No response. Jensen saw the woman's drug of choice on the counter—Jupiter Cloud. This would require a bit more than a prod in the shoulder. He whipped out his stun baton and dialed for maximum shock. He drove the truncheon into her back above her right kidney.

The woman convulsed, her head and her hands flying directly upward before slamming back down onto the cushioned bar surface.

"G'way!"

"Am Trembley?"

"G'way! Stoopid fock skrowing sum titfuck with a g'damned pussy implant." She swung around suddenly. "C'n ya bleeve it? A fockn cunt implant. Might ass whell be doin' a blow up doll."

"Are you Am Trembley?"

"Ya, now g'way. Juss wanna ferget that prick. He leff me fer a plas'ic cunt."

"So you are the Am Trembley that was paid to follow William Sagum?"

"Ya. Whaovit?"

Jensen took one step back and nodded. His two patrolmen brought up their gauss weapons and fired full auto. The female's body shredded off the bone and outward, adding its gruesome bits to the 2 square meters of window material fountaining out the side of the building. The two policemen stopped firing when only a dripping red skeleton remained.

Jensen looked over the job professionally. He nodded before turning and walking casually out past the stunned patrons and business owner.

*   *   *

"You've managed to wait long enough that I won't eat you, Lieutenant."

Reza wasn't as sure, considering the purple complexion of the Commissioner. "Sir, that wasn't my intent. I wanted to ensure that I had the information you required and that a message was sent to the rest of the PEs we have employed. We have publically punished the Private Enforcer that we hired to follow and keep us informed on the activities of the reporter who managed to interview the President."

"That's a start."

"We also learned that the enforcer had a falling out with her boyfriend and was flying on Jupiter Cloud the whole time. She had nothing of value except as a public object lesson."

"Reza, none of this is really doing much for me."

"Sir, there is nothing I can do for you. It is a setback. If you want my job, it's yours, naturally, but we've done everything we could do. We are logging more overtime than since the Seattle Quake. We've lost most of a combat SWAT Team to a freaking Improvised Explosive Device, the largest loss in any Metro history.

"The media is intentionally skewing their reports to make it look like we are the guilty party by botching a demolition job to kill everyone inside.

"By the by, the doctors believe they can save Captain Hogan's leg, but his eye will need to be replaced, and the brain damage has left him unlikely to return to duty. Only the two snipers seem to have survived unscathed."

"We must retaliate."

Reza sighed, picking at lint on his uniform.

"Sir, I'm willing to take any suggestions, but we're fighting a ghost. What do you want me to retaliate against? We still have no leads on the GAM. The reporter and the President are both underground so deeply that we'll be lucky if we ever find a sniff of their location.

"I'll be honest, sir. Other than continuing investigation, I don't know where we can go from here. There is nothing to hit back at."

The temples of the Commissioner's head pulsed outward at the same rate as his heart. His square jaw worked back and forth. The antique pencil he held, worth a patrolman's pay for a quarter, snapped into three pieces. Two drops of blood dribbled onto his desk blotter. The Commissioner didn't seem to be aware he was injured. Reza didn't move to help him. Over the next five minutes the Commissioner's expression changed no less than four times. Reza sat patiently.

"First we need to take control of the situation. Many of our problems have come from the loose media. We need to command it."

"We've been trying that, sir."

"No. I admit I've been just playing around the edges. I think it is time we grasp the nettle. I want Metro teams to seize each and every news station."

Even Reza looked shocked.

"But sir, what possible excuse can we give? How are we going to curtail freedom of the press? We'd be violating the Constitution at its very foundation."

"And the CorpGov isn't? If we are going to fight with pigs we have to get down in the muck, Lieutenant."

"Oh, and while we are at it we will need to seize the independent comm satellites and the communications rooms of each of the orbital stations."

"Sir, I object to this. There is no way this will end well."

"It is one temporary measure to establish peace."

"I still object. It is like being a little bit pregnant."

"And there is still the matter of retaliation. The Greenies may have snatched the President but the Council put them up to it. I don't know what their game is, but it is time to put an end to it. I want arrest warrants out for each member of the Council within the hour. Then send out cars to execute them. I mean the warrants. It shouldn't be difficult."

"The charge, sir?"

"Conspiracy, murder, accessory to kidnapping, threatening the President of the United States and interfering with a police officer. We can add more to it later if we want."

Reza stood there looking at him.

"Sir, I respectfully put to you that these actions will backfire. The ... "

Krylov heard nothing more of what Reza had to say, even though the man droned on for at least five minutes.

"I was a fool to let Nanogate walk out of there last night," Krylov muttered to himself. "I won't be that weak again.

"What are you waiting for?" Krylov barked at his subordinate. "You have your orders."

*   *   *

While Susan knew she would have to become accustomed to certain limitations, meeting within the great open room of a failed plastics manufacturing plant didn't meet with her approval. It was at best undignified.

The GAM had provided a patch of propriety in the wallow of stinking machines covered with grease in some places and flaking rust in others. A Jaipur rug with an Aztec theme defined a small area of some sanity but the décor immediately abused any notion of aesthetics with mismatched club chairs and a low table of Trex planks.

Six Greenies circled on a high catwalk above the room wielding well-worn assault weapons of differing types. They scanned both in the room and out through some high-set windows. As the President, Susan felt almost naked without a guard directly adjacent to her but it was the price she paid for making her guests understand she wasn't being manipulated by any outside force.

Morgan, in urban camouflage, brought in coffee in a mundane pottery service.

At least the cups match the saucers, Susan thought uncharitably.

The hot drink's pleasant aroma just barely cut the acrid tang of the industrial process that still lingered in the air. The group waited quietly until the black woman returned to her post at the main entrance before continuing.

"Yes, President Tipton, we understand your difficulties," the House Majority Leader Democrat Andre Yung said as he picked up a cup and dosed it with a healthy pour of half-and-half. "It won't be easy running the government from a warehouse."

The comment sent a clear shot across her bow. Tipton looked into the man's narrowed eyes and knew who would be on the ballot for the office of the President come next October. Mentally she wished the man luck. She wouldn't have this job again even if it came tied up with a harem of smart and sexy men in G-strings.

"Well, this obviously isn't my office. I do move around too much to have a permanent place to conduct the business of the President."

"Yes, ma'am, but as Representative Yung pointed out you are safe within the bosom of your new protective cadre while we are out and exposed," said Johanna Mitzel, the House Majority Whip.

"If you were afraid to act because you might be assassinated by the Secret Service, think how we feel with the same, uh, protection."

"So I can't count on your support to move legislation through Congress?"

"I don't think it is quite that cut and dried, Madam President, nor do we all feel the same pressures," offered the fat Max Calloway, Senate Minority Leader, and of the same party as the Honorable Yung. "But just like always, we have to bow to the will of the people. We can't be pushing new legislation that might interfere with our opportunity to get reelected."

"So nothing new, then? What about my own party?"

"Madam President we have no problem with the legislation President Lopez already has in the queue and are extremely happy that you will continue to support it," said Anson Wainwright, Senate Majority Leader, and the Republican party's second in command.

"I hear an intrinsic 'BUT' coming."

"Yes, ma'am. Any new legislation we will have to examine very closely. We don't know what sharks are in the water as you've told us so very little."

"So if I shared even more information you would be willing to help."

"I don't think any of us would go quite that far, President Tipton," Ms. Mitzel replied. "Obviously it depends on the circumstances."

Anger flared in Susan. She had to remember that Presidents who showed their anger got people killed. "So you want me to tell you what's happening so you can use it to your political advantage. Wonderful. One day someone is going to have to show me where that is written in the oath we each take as a public servant."

"President Tipton, it isn't that simple—"

"Bullshit," she retorted. "It comes down to do what's right for the country or maybe even the entire world or do what might get you additional power. Seriously, don't try and bullshit me. I've been in your shoes. I understand the game, but I always knew where the line was drawn.

"But you seem to have me over a barrel. If I want to be effective I have to at least trust you with the information I have. On your way out, you will get the full details of what I'm about to summarize for you.

"You probably already know that the CorpGov is being balked by the Metro Police, headed by Commissioner Yuri Krylov."

"Is this necessarily bad, Madam President?" interrupted Representative Mitzel. "We lose power if the CorpGov is in place."

"Johanna, you know that is a fallacy. If you want to cling to it for political reasons, fine, but the children are in bed and we can be honest between ourselves. Before the CorpGov, the collusion among the corporations neutered us. We rubber-stamped whatever those huge money machines wanted. The CorpGov has been working for the betterment of people. I see that as empowering us.

"Getting back to my point, ma'am, the Metros are balking the CorpGov. It is a straight-line computation to the United States of America becoming a police state. If the Metros can break the corps, how can we stand against them?"

"We can cut their funding. They can't do anything without the funding to back it up," Anson Wainwright said.

"Not good enough. Your packets will include the budgetary breakdown of the Metropolitan Police organizations. Only twenty-six percent of their funding comes from the federal level. Another twelve percent comes from state and local. The massive amount of their publically disclosed funding comes from direct payments from the citizens. We don't control that, nor do we control the black revenue stream of outright bribery and rake-offs. The current estimates are that these account for over fifty percent of their entire funding.

"No, Anson, I'm sorry but we can't control the beast we created."

"Then the army. We can always crush them with the armed forces," Yung offered confidently.

"As Commander and Chief of our armed forces, I can tell you that our standing army is only a framework, a glove, for national guardsmen to be called up to fill to make it a fist. The current structure itself could be overwhelmed by the capabilities of even one major city's police force, much less many of them. I've included a simulation we did on a military call-up.

"Did you know that over eighty-six percent of the national reserves are active duty and retired police officers? Anyone want to guess what our call-up created?"

The stunned silence spoke volumes.

"A disaster," offered Jayson Hernandez, the Republican Senator from the State of Chihuahua.

"Thank you," the President continued, after taking a tiny sip of her hot cocoa. "It's not possible to control them, and they know it.

"And getting to the funding discussion, the assassination of President Lopez came just two days after she authorized turning off the Metro's financial spigot—motive.

"The secret service is ninety-eight percent prior Metros—means.

"Who controls the largest block of police officers on the globe? Yuri Krylov—opportunity."

"Plenty of groups could have engineered the assassination," Mitzel retorted. "You can't go seeing ghosts in every precinct, Ms. President."

"You are right. I told you I have no proof. Honestly, I don't think Krylov will ever be pinned with the assassination, but that is secondary. I can't stress this enough, but everything points to the fact that we are in a war for our very existence as a free and democratic country. By concatenation we may be fighting for any and all freedom on earth. If you don't believe me now, you wait. I'll bet you will start seeing our rights begin to be curtailed and the police starting to take further liberties.

"I know each of you is thinking on how they can take advantage of this. Remember I'm one of you. My party will probably follow me just because they are my party, but I'll offer an olive branch to you Dems. If you support me and I'm wrong ... if in fact Krylov isn't backing this play, I will publically step down announcing my failure as a President."

The eyes of each of the Democrats around their circle glittered with greed. Such a public admission would spill over to the Republican party as a whole. The Democrats would win the next election in a walk and probably have a super majority large enough to even amend the Constitution.

"We'll be back to you, Madam President."

* * *

At two thirty-six in the morning, Jim Major, the engineer on duty, leaned back in his swivel chair with a mouthful of egg-salad sandwich. He had nothing more on his mind than how to convince his girlfriend to accept a cohab agreement.

All the lights and power in the KVOSD studio suddenly died. He waited for the backup generators or the backups to the backup generators to kick in. None did. Puzzlement filled his eyes and thoughts. There must be a distribution problem. "Why me?" he said with a grimace. "Why couldn't this have happened on the day shift?" He set down his lunch and—

Strobe grenades went off with the visible frequency that paralyzed the human nervous system into inactivity. Everyone in the room momentarily froze.

"POLICE WITH A WARRANT! POLICE WITH A WARRANT!"

Eighteen police with the gear of a full-blown SWAT team burst into the studio. Because of the grenade flashes they moved in stop action like a drawn cartoon in a flip book.

Before Jim's brain could filter out the bright light, he found a large-muzzled assault weapon pointed at his chest. Behind it floated a gold Metro badge against a sea of black armor.

Swallowing hard to clear his mouth, Jim said, "Sir, I have no intention of offering you any resistance." With the speed of a creeping vine he raised his hands to signal his surrender.

The targeting dot didn't move from his chest.

"CLEAR," was repeated many times.

Jim didn't move.

"Let the emergency lights come up," a voice with authority called from the other room. The silver halogens lit the room.

"Hey, what are you doing," Jim heard the morning anchor, Patty Li, say from the other room. This was followed by the distinctive report of a slap. "Ow!"

Amplified through the external speakers of the police suit a feminine voice said, "Say one more word, bitch, and I'll do more than give you a love tap."

"We've got all of them bindered except the engineer."

An unarmored police sergeant entered the room. Jim would have sworn that someone had cut him out of a recruiting poster. He came into the room with creases in his uniform so sharp they'd probably cut paper. Behind the man he saw the rest of the studio crew, including the anchor, marched across his visible doorway. Their arms were bound behind their backs by nylon zip-ties.

"Mr. Kapton, we would like you to do something for us," the man said, holding out a standard commercial recording crystal.

"Ah, I'm actually James Major. I'm covering Al's, I mean Albert Kapton's shift."

"Very good, Mr. Major. I'm Sergeant Tolbert. When the power is returned to this building I need you to air the file on this recording crystal at exactly 4:06 a.m."

Jim looked down at the gun still leveled at his chest. "Sergeant, I am certain that this is against some kind of law, but I'll be honest, that gun trumps the law right here and now."

"That's a very practical attitude, Mr. Major. The recording on this crystal is six hours long. That will give your management time to coordinate with the Office of Metro Censorship. I'm sure you will be getting new directives from your management soon."

"Yes, sir, I'm sure I will."

*   *   *

The image of Special Report played on billions of solidos within three seconds of 0406 PST.

"Bringing you this special report is our morning anchor, Patricia Li."

"We have new information, provided to us by the Metropolitan Police Force of Portland that the solidocast you have recently seen by President Tipton is a hoax.

"Speaking for the Metros we have Lieutenant Reza Narendra. Thank you for coming today to explain the information we are seeing before us in split screen."

"You are welcome, Patricia."

"So what are we looking at."

"Under normal circumstances people at home wouldn't see the time bars at the bottom of your screen. We've compressed the vertical size so you can see what we discovered in the recording margins.

"If you look closely at the dates on the right-hand side of that screen you will see the actual timestamps. President Tipton was abducted on December thirteenth and as you see clearly the date this footage was recorded was three days prior to the event.

"No matter how you look at this, the GAM kidnapped the President or had advance knowledge of her kidnapping."

"Why would they do this, Lieutenant?"

"We can speculate, but there are several possibilities. Either this is some sick game by the GAM, who is known for doing whatever to whomever they desire, or they have and intend to use the President as a pawn, or perhaps they have already killed the President and are using this as a smokescreen."

"But didn't you tell me of another option before we went on air?"

"Yes, and it is the most insidious and likely of all of the cases."

"To talk about that we need to reexamine the murder of President Lopez. The suspect we still hold has confessed not only as having been the assassin but also to being a member of the Green Action Militia.

"Why would the GAM assassinate President Lopez? That is what everyone keeps asking after the GAM's impromptu press conference, arranged, I might add, by this very station."

"We apologize for that, sir, especially if they are lying."

"Well, it is clear now that they are lying about a great many things. But let's get back to the evidence.

"Keep the earlier question firmly in your mind. Why would the GAM assassinate President Lopez? Add to this the following question. How did the GAM make President Tipton's interview before they kidnapped her?

"Oh, there is the obvious image trickery, easy enough in this age. But wouldn't it be much easier to film a real copy ... a clone of President Tipton?

"Think on this. What if they'd managed to clone Vice President Tipton long before she aspired to that high office and raised the clone to be her? It would be like the story *The Prince and the Pauper*, or perhaps *The Man in the Iron Mask*.

"With their own President in place they could control the workings of the United States."

"That seems like a credible scenario, but only credible. What additional proof do you have, Lieutenant?"

"When the President met with the members of Congress earlier today, none of them were allowed close enough to touch her, nor were they given blood samples as promised.

"As you know, Patricia, cloning does leave a fingerprint we can differentiate from original cells. This is an attempt to keep us from the truth. So I say to all of you people who are blindly following what the *good* GAM is saying, know that at best they are kidnappers. At worst they could be treasonous."

* * *

Augustine winced as she leveraged herself out of the bed, recoiling as her bare feet hit the floor. Even with weather modifications, 51 degrees latitude in the middle of a December night brought bitter cold. She fished out her woolen socks and pulled them on. She slid her feet into slippers before standing with a grimace.

"I'm not young enough for this sneaking around in the middle of the night thing," she whispered. Unfortunately the limited-network bandwidth in her cell wouldn't support the work she needed to do. As straightforward as her task was, it required massive bandwidth and compute power.

She opened her door confidently. The priory never completely slept, but at 3:12 a.m. its wakefulness was a tentative thing. With matins nothing but a memory, and lauds still several sleepy hours away, she had another level of safety. Additionally, no one notices someone going about their business with authority. Everyone notices someone furtively scurrying about, a truism she'd learned many years ago from Sonya, God bless her soul.

Augustine strode through the commons, nodding to the one other somnambulant she encountered before taking the corner to her team's network room.

She mentally fired up the network amplifiers even before the couch supported her body.

Sixteen different processes flowed past her consciousness including her social simulation, status of her personal storage, network bandwidth monitor and even her network tripwire—an insignificant overflow bit that would toggle if anyone even accessed her subroutines or storage. Fortunately the trip-bit remained green.

Without thinking she flipped open a new, secure-storage bin with one mental path and started a spider algorithm with another. The spider was to gather data from the key words she mentally poured into another file. Her neural applets took her vital terms and flushed them out with other associated data values. She opened and immediately closed an outbound information process with standard detection snoop of her own development. The line had been open for only eight clocks, well below the detection threshold of anyone but a Class 1 net jockey. Her snoop found no one peering in on her from the network.

The pressure on the input queue from the spider started to build. She held it off by stealing free memory across the network as a referenced, multidimensional data structure and letting the queue flow into it. She pieced more and more of the structure together as the data increased like building a dam in a canyon. But like that dam against a volcanic lahar, she knew it wouldn't hold the patchwork together long. She compressed the active church memory usage and stored it in a tiny corner.

More and more the information filled her reservoir. She funneled the water into more additional canyons with their own dams. The data flowed faster, battering even harder at her walls. Her mind routed more, built more, and appropriated more. Each link, each new storage location made it that much harder to hold the whole patchwork together. The more nodes away from the primary church node that she had to reach, the more the entire edifice threatened to cave in.

More data. More concentration. More pressure. Augustine squinted and ground her teeth. Only her determination held everything together.

Suddenly her world exploded. Streams of data overflowed the containers and rushed onward, flooding all of her defenses at once. With the walls crumbled down and no reason to fight it any longer, she sighed in relief. She felt like someone releasing her bladder after holding it an hour too long.

As the last datum rippled across the input path, Augustine shut down the link. The link being open four hundred clocks wasn't world class but very respectable. It was unlikely anyone noticed the massive flow from so many divergent sources.

With her fingers against the beads and subvocalizing the words, she ran through two Hail Marys to clear her synapses.

She checked on data post processing that had started as soon as the bits had dropped into storage. She wasn't happy with the search algorithm and decided a modified stochastic search would improve results. Her Monte Carlo search didn't take but a few moments to set up.

Mentally she triggered her percomm with a preset code.

"*I'm here, Augustine,*" Tony's reassuring voice said.

"Data is just about complete."

"*Thanks for doing this, Augustine. I know you're in a precarious position.*"

"My habit prevents me from voicing the expletive that comes to mind. I know what we need to do and made my piece with God long ago."

"*Still, I understand. Wish there was some way I could help you.*"

"I'll get by, Tony. You worry about humanity—I'll worry about me.

"Here comes the data. What I see so far is that the people really believe that we are still on their side. We will continue to have the upper hand in the public even if the Metros absolutely control the media. You and I both know they can't totally block the net without shutting it down, but they could easily restrict certain topics. In that case our support strengthens, not diminishes."

"*Good news. They actually had me worried for a minute.*"

"They're not dumb, Tony, but they are inexperienced. Finish this before they get enough experience to win."

"*Will do, my favorite nun.*"

"There I go repressing that expletive again. I'm forwarding you the output of my simulations."

"*Behave,*" Tony said, cutting the link.

*   *   *

The smell of stale beer and heated grease assaulted Nanogate's nose. An ancient scent speaker tried to cover the smells with a fresh mint aroma but it alternated overly subtle to overbearing and back again in the short space of a minute. Tinny hip-hop music was often drowned out by the deep brass thunder rolled through the air. Each thunder ended in an explosion of pins at the end of one caramel colored alley.

"STRIKE!" yelled one athlete dozens of meters down the concourse.

"May I ask why we are meeting here?" complained BeringC Protein taking her hands off the acrylic table like it had just stung her.

She plucked three napkins from the shiny dispenser and rubbed them between her hands.

"I'm sorry you didn't get the message of casual attire," Nanogate said looking critically at her Armani skirt-suit.

"We are here to discuss the new direction that the action against the Metros has taken and to plan the appropriate response."

"But here? What if they have bugged this venue?" Rio Oro said behind a bright-red, silk shirt as wide as a lift-bus.

"The odds of anyone—" Z-G-Ag began.

"Can I get y'all something other than water?" asked a gum-chewing waitress with lipstick, arm implants, and cosmetic irises all in matching MacNeil green tartan.

"I wouldn't mind an order of onion rings," MinInc said.

"One order of rings coming up, sweetie," she said snapping her gum in a tiny bubble.

"And a beer," Tony added.

The waitress looked at him like she was counting the tip. "Sure."

As she walked away, Z-G-Ag continued. "As I was saying, the odds of anyone bugging a random bowling alley in the hopes of getting us planning action needs to be represented in imaginary numbers."

"No doubt about that," Tony said. "If nothing else the sounds of the league will corrupt most listening devices. Take it from someone who knows."

"Out of order," Nanogate objected. "Z-G-Ag has the floor."

"I'm done, but I concur with GAM."

"Thank you. I trust you all know the new publicity campaign initiated by our opponents." Nods went around the table, including that of Savitz, Schauer and Levinthal's yarmulke.

"Cute, it's a perfect example of he said, she said," Tony offered.

"Wintel has the floor."

"We are in the process of developing a simulation to model all of the propaganda efforts on either side. We are two weeks away from having it ready."

"GAM has the floor," Nanogate said in response to Tony's hand in the air.

"We could be buried in two weeks. Our net jock has sampled public opinion and—"

"Excuse me, but public opinion?" Wintel interrupted.

"Order," Nanogate chastised quietly. "We may be in a public

venue but we can certainly keep decorum. The Green Action Militia has the floor."

"Thank you, sir," Tony said with a smug look in the direction of Wintel. "Our net jock sampled public opinion in the form of messaging, blog posts and a million other data sources I won't even begin to describe as I don't understand all of what she accomplished. As a whole her information shows a very clear message. In spite of the Metros new war of innuendo, we hold a commanding and almost insurmountable support from the people. They can't erode it in a short time because any strong action would bring more people in on our side. A long-term campaign is possible but we theorize that their fiscal structure won't support that."

"So this is not something we should be concerned with?" Global Vehicle Federation asked.

"Not directly. But it does make it very obvious to the Metros that they will have to use martial force to obtain their results. This will escalate, and quickly."

"Objections to this conclusion?" Nanogate asked. Their percomms tallied zero dissention. "So what actions do we need to take? I invite discussion."

"First and foremost we need to cut off any supply of weapons," GVF suggested.

"I am also thinking we need to funnel all of the weapons being produced to a place where we can be controlling them. And to be making them usable by anyone sympathetic to our cause," Royal PetroChem offered. Nods around the table showed broad support.

"How about Mars," MinInc asked. "If we get them there I can guarantee to keep anyone and everyone out of them."

A boxed delivery unit rolled up to the table and deposited their order before trundling off.

"That brings up a good question," Nanogate said. "How is the Metro support off Earth?"

"The data we collected show they have effectively zero support offworld, and our support is solid. We, of course, have no data on Pluto, the home of the Catholic Church."

"Would the loss of time to get at these weapons be an issue?"

"Three days from Earth to Mars by express. We can work with that much of a time lag."

"I think we have a consensus as to where to store our materials.

I'd like to hear from the GAM on guerilla tactics we can employ."

"Their stockpiles and those of the military will mean there won't be any immediate impact of our weapons' embargo. However, and something that might not have occurred to you, how about going after the weapons themselves?"

"You mean steal them?"

"Steal, destroy, suborn, and anything else we can think of. How about turning off the licenses of some of the newer weapons' platforms?"

Several eyebrows went up with a new thought.

"If I remember, most of the newest destructive goodies have to be licensed by the manufacturer. Withdraw the licenses but don't tell them. Pulling a trigger and having nothing happen is much worse than not having a weapon."

*   *   *

"Did you ever think you would be helping to smuggle in Purple?" David whispered to Morgan as they each scanned different quadrants of the darkened, Tillamook sky. The gravel in the old-fashioned, tar roof bit into their knees as they kneeled just below its raised rim. On the multistoried dock behind and scores of floors beneath them, they could just make out the ant-like forms of three dozen men in shadowcloth. They couldn't see exactly what they did but they knew they were supposed to speedily break up massive receiving crates and divide the contents into lift-van-sized loads.

"Nope. In fact if Tony hadn't explained why, I wouldn't be doing it now."

"You don't believe in any kind of recreational drugs?" David asked.

"I've seen too many burns on the streets. Most of them don't have a life," Morgan explained.

"But it's their choice. They aren't hurting anyone," David said, poking one of his red curls back up into his camo hood.

"Maybe not directly. But what gives them the right to throw away what their parents gave them?"

"Hold up. I've got a drone at six o'clock high."

Morgan spun around and panned. "Got it. That's not a private security drone. I've got the Metro's 86.4 GHz uplink signal."

"Can you tap it?"

"I'm not here just for my looks, pretty boy," Morgan said as she typed in the air on an invisible keyboard. She manipulated equally ethereal controls while cocking her head as if to listen closely. "There it is. It's not being monitored at the moment. Any more of them?"

"I don't see anything. So a random patrol?"

"That's what I have now," Morgan said returning to tracking her allocated portion of the sky.

"It's drifting this way," David said, hefting his Sig Five assault rifle in its general direction.

"Scheduled direction change in three, two, one."

"Oh, shit. It changed right toward us."

Morgan clicked to a new percomm distribution list. "All stations. Be aware we have a Metro drone incoming. Prepare to break and scatter. More info in thirty seconds."

"*Fuck. I thought you guys were supposed to protect us!*" came the indignant voice over the link.

"*Quiet the chatter,*" came a more commanding voice.

David put down his automatic and opened a long, Kevlar bag next to him. From within his mysterious sack he pulled out a weapon that looked like a wide-bladed javelin with a shoulder mount and a trigger.

"Isn't a gravity lance a bit of overkill for a drone?" Morgan asked. "Those don't grow on trees, you know."

"Not like I can take it down with that peashooter," he said, nodding toward his Sig Five.

"True, but ... Hold one. Drone just stopped random scan. It's being directed. It's sending data from the dock area."

"Attention all stations. Metro response in—" He looked at Morgan, who held up four fingers. "—four minutes. Scatter and return to station. We'll keep them busy."

"Looks like that lance might come in handy," Morgan said. "A call went out for a heavy SWAT team from Hillsboro."

"Yup. Is our exit strategy in place?"

"Ready anytime."

The all-stations channel crackled. "*Omega one, clear.*"

"*Omega four, clear.*"

"*Omega three, clear.*"

Silence. David and Morgan looked at one another.

"Omega two?" David queried.

"*Omega leader. We have one vehicle that has a slow capacitive leak in the lift. They are trying to balance it but it will take several minutes.*"

"No bloody spare?" Morgan asked with her teeth grinding so loud it could be heard over the link.

From the look on her face, David heard Morgan's "amateurs" refrain go off in his head.

"*It doesn't seem to be an actual failure in the capacitor. We've tried spares from three different vehicles now.*"

"Well then leave it and get your personnel out of there," Morgan snapped.

"*Negative. We aren't leaving over ten million lying here in the street, Greenie. Do your job and keep them off of us for a few minutes.*"

"At least get everyone else out of there," David replied. Clicking off his comms he turned to Morgan. "Pergrav four o'clock low!"

Morgan's Glock 1904 turned and angled down. She triggered only one burst of fragmentation rounds. While the infamous black armor protected the cop, it didn't protect the notoriously unreliable pergravs strapped to his shoulders. The Metro spun down between two buildings until he disappeared from sight.

"That's my girl. Maybe next time you can try to get him to spin the other way," David joked.

"Enough noise from the peanut gallery. You just worry about that bloody armored car."

"What direction is the response coming from?"

"Hillsboro is that way," Morgan said, pointing over the 10-meter-tall "k" of the Tillamook Creamery sign. "I have to assume they will do least time routing, especially when they get that guy's call of 'shots fired.'"

"Agreed. You keep those patrolmen off my back."

"I'm the only one you should worry about on your back, David," Morgan said running a free hand down the outside back of his camo suit.

"Stop that, you wicked woman. I thought I was supposed to concentrate."

"OK, later then. Let's flame these fucking Metros and get our little ducklings to safety."

"I'd rather not kill anyone. You remember what Tony said."

"Oh, bugger to hell and gone our allies and their simulations."

"The council said killing too many Metros would make it look like we're the aggressors."

"Honestly, David, if they were so good at simulating would we have beaten them in the first place?"

"Point. But do you want to tell the boss that we ignored his orders?"

Morgan snorted. "Here we are. RPV on approach. Four degrees north of true east. Looks like you get your wish. Remember, no casualties."

David oriented the lance eastward, slowly sweeping north until the targeting tone warbled in his ear. His retinal display magnified a barely visible dot to the unmistakable sphere of a Metro's remotely piloted vehicle. His only other experience with them had been when just one of them had wiped out an entire battalion of Martian insurrectionists during the Red March. Fear flared briefly.

"Morgan, get another lance ready, just in case."

"Don't worry. You won't miss."

David relaxed. The continuous tone ensured he had the target firmly locked up. As he squeezed the trigger, he felt the tug of the artificial gravity wave. It didn't stay in place long enough to do more than gently pull him toward his target by a centimeter.

"Reload," David screamed out.

The lance was neither on the launcher nor in transit. Faster than even light, the synthetic gravity wave struck the sphere just off center. The 15-meter armored weapons platform imploded, crushed into a much smaller ball by application of two hundred gravities somewhere near its center of mass. The smaller ball vibrated in the sky around the weapon's point of impact for exactly the one second of detonation before bits and pieces of it began to rain out of the sky.

"No need. I told you that you wouldn't miss."

"*Omega leader. Problem patched. We are on the move.*"

"Affirmative, Omega leader," Morgan transmitted. "See you at the rendezvous. You owe us a beer."

"*No sweat, Green Two. That was a good bit of shooting. I just might have to buy you two.*"

"Are you taking credit for my kill?" David said collecting his weapons.

"Nope. Just making sure those fucking mobsters know who they owe."

*   *   *

At least the Greenies managed to make this room comfortable, President Tipton thought with grudging charity.

A large window wrapped around about a third of the room, giving a view of Nova Scotia's winter seascape. The impenetrable white of the land starkly contrasted with the rolling black of the ocean. In the fireplace the crimson embers, the black coals and lazy yellow flickers of a once roaring fire kept the room warm.

The four Congressional leaders and a single representative from the independents each sat in the modern Accashia cup chairs around the low maple coffee table. A master craftsman had carved the exterior of the bulbous chairs to resemble pine cones.

"I know how confused you are with the Metro propaganda and all," President Susan Tipton said from her blue overstuffed reading chair. "Once again I meet you openly. This time I even do it without any bodyguard in presence." She didn't mention the deadly nano curtain that drifted like the most transparent of African silk around her chair.

The President looked deeply into the litigators' eyes. None of them betrayed their inner thoughts. "I can assure you I am not a clone. What is more I'll provide you each with proof before you leave."

"Assuming what you say is true, nothing has changed in our commitment to you, Madam President," Andre Yung said, taking a dainty sip from his cup. The President wondered if he'd even tasted the richness or if the gesture was dramatic persona.

"Excellent. Let's discuss what we should be doing moving forward."

"*Disculpe*," Pansuala Moudry, Tea Party Senator from Baja interrupted. "*Senora*, I feel uncomfortable sharing or planning with a potential imposter. While I am personally certain that you are *la Presidente*, *mi pueblo* would pull me from office faster than a pickpocket lifts a wallet if I didn't confirm your identity."

"Very well, Pansuala. Did you each bring the lance and pipettes as requested?" Susan waited until each of them nodded. "As you know there are very specific markers to cloning. While the DNA is identical there are minute differences in gestation of every embryo from every host, even an artificial womb.

"A simple blood sample compared to my cells stored in the three doomsday vaults, my cryogenically frozen blood in the national archive or about sixty dozen other places will allow you to determine that I am truly who I say I am.

"So there is no question of my contaminating your sample, I've asked you to bring along your own sampling kit." Turning off the nanite curtain, she stood up. Reaching awkwardly behind her, she released the clasp on her simple sheath dress. The white-satin dress flowed to the floor revealing that she wore nothing beneath.

She smiled at the collective gasp of the room's five other occupants. She didn't look eighteen anymore, even with genetic manipulation. Her breasts sagged just slightly and her hips had one too many éclairs on them. Freckles danced all over her skin like a convention of fireflies. In spite of all of this she was proud of her body. Even at one hundred and twelve she felt she could still stir the loins of most man.

"And, as I want this to be the last and final question of my identity," she said standing there nude with her hands on her hips, "you may take your sample from any place you wish.

"I *am* Susan Tipton, President of the United States."

* * *

Seven faces turned toward Reza as he entered the room, each with his or her own agenda. Krylov dominated the other six by his presence and his petty humiliations. He occupied the head of the table in an overstuffed reading chair while they perched on standard office chairs. The long, cheap table put the six of them at one end with Reza standing away like a supplicant looking for a bowl of gruel.

Reza had come to dread the morning briefs. Captain Hardy and Chief Adams would take perverse pride in finding any lack in the data presented, whether it existed or not. They would pound their chest declaring what their fearless Metros accomplished in any area not related to the lack. Krylov would glare as if Reza should be blamed for the implementation of the Commissioner's own inept instructions. Krylov would bark out new orders, made in haste, and without thought. The Captains and the Chiefs would then butcher their execution.

This morning would be no different. Bad news intensified the vicious circle. He actually feared shouting this morning as well as the even worse than usual decision making.

"You may begin, Reza," the Commissioner said with undue familiarity.

"Thank you, sir. I welcome the rest of you to our morning

intelligence briefing. I've got several items of note that very likely will cause us to spill over into the next time period. All of these items are quite important so I suggest you clear your schedule forward.

"Item one. At our last meeting we had preliminary reports of the mafia stopping the payment of their protection moneys. Those rumors are now confirmed. Every single officer due payoffs has reported that the graft never arrived. While this income stream is primarily monetary, the flow of sexual favors and drugs has also come to an abrupt and distinct halt."

"How do we respond?" Krylov interrupted.

"We need to send a message," Captain Amber Cohen said coldly. "I suggest something very public."

"Boise?" asked Krylov referring to the massacre of the Boise Independent Territorials forty years earlier. Investigations afterward had found that the local police force had intentionally wiped out the entire compound of men, women and children.

"Yes, but don't even try and cover it up. They need to know who holds the whip. That alone should bring them into line," Captain Hardy said.

"Continue, Reza."

"Thank you, sir. Item two. We have one very disturbing report of a simple drug smuggling operation in Tillamook. While we wouldn't normally care about such a small activity, excepting that we normally get paid to look the other way, this one caused a good deal of attention because an officer was fired upon. The weapon used couldn't possibly have hurt our man and the shooter had to know this. The attack was merely to remove the officer from play. The disturbing part came when we responded with a heavily armed RPV.

"The Dessault Aviation CC105 was destroyed by a Semtek Model 14 GravLance—" Several murmurs and side conversations interrupted Reza. The Mod Fourteens had only been on the market for days. Reza continued as soon as the noise level came down to an acceptable level. "—before the perpetrators vanished into thin air.

"Based on the information provided by the one smuggler we managed to catch, because of a damaged lift vehicle, we learned that the *capa famiglia*, Jamie Ardwin, is responsible for the drug operation with guard services provided from the Green Action Militia."

"I don't know what is more disturbing," Krylov offered, "that the *capa* is flaunting her lawlessness at us, that the GAM has heavy weapons that they aren't afraid to use, or that they are in bed together."

"I tend to agree," Reza suggested above his rank. "As the GAM remains outside of our current ability to impact, I suggest something special for the *capa*. We know where she does business. If we do this right, we might even get that ridiculous art gallery she has and turn a profit."

The rest of the attendees looked at Krylov. They wanted to make sure they expressed his opinion when they opened their mouths.

The Commissioner stroked his sharp chin before responding. "I think you have something, Reza. I approve the action. I want you to handle it personally."

Captain Hardy threw a poisonous look at Reza. The lieutenant took a deep breath to quell the fear. Inside he knew he would remain alive only as long as Krylov wanted him around. Hardy was notorious for giving assignments to people who displeased him that ended in a deeply-regret letter to one's next of kin.

"I'll take care of it, sir."

"Continue with your report."

"Yes, Commissioner. I'll finish with the bad news before I go on to those positive indicators that we have.

"The reduction in illicit income has not been accompanied by any corresponding reduction in crimes. Quite the contrary, current data shows actionable crimes, that is to say incidents we are obligated financially to respond to, up twenty-two percent while personal crimes are down forty. This seems to be a direct assault on our ability to cover our responsibilities."

"I smell the Council's hand in this," Krylov said. "Where are we on the raid of the Council Chambers?"

"Sir, after swearing out warrants for their arrest we found that their floating homes had been disconnected from their normal docks. In spite of satellite coverage, we have been unable to locate the errant homes."

"OK, so the next logical step is to raid the Council Chambers themselves, Lieutenant," Captain Hardy growled. "Do you need assistance in doing your job?"

Safe or not, the Captain had no intention of making Reza's life easy.

"To this body I strongly protest that action. Swearing out warrants for their arrest was acceptable as it specifically called out crimes they committed, but to invade the government buildings would be to declare the government itself fiat. It will cause the public to react."

"Not if we don't—" started Hardy's retort.

"Not so fast, Captain," Krylov interrupted.

"I do understand the Lieutenant's point," Hardy said, jumping back in. "The possibility he mentioned exists but if we are showing the whip to the people then they won't act whether they are angry or not. What chance do they have against our armed troopers."

Krylov pondered. "I have to say that we go with this action. Take over the government offices," the Commissioner said in a steady and even tone. "Captain Hardy if you would coordinate this, I'd be appreciative."

Reza blinked hard. Krylov's rational and calm demeanor frightened him more than his usual presentation as a shouting, blustering maniac.

"Continue your brief, Lieutenant."

"Yes, sir. In better news it appears that we may have located Augustine Cordoba, also known as Grandma Ice, the GAM's number one net hack and public enemy number three.

"Our traces of network activity found an unsubstantiated increase from the nodes within the Catholic Priory of Saint Isidore of Seville in Calgary."

"Go on," Krylov said leaning slightly forward, his eyes twinkling.

"Our initial discussions with the leaders of the Priory have been rebuffed. They state, and I quote, 'When a new lay brother or novitiate enters these walls their past disappears.' They will neither confirm nor deny the presence of Grandma Ice, although a source we have within the church states unequivocally that she is there."

"Then how do we get through the church's reticence?" Chief Adams asked.

"I think we need to be careful," Krylov said, looking thoughtful. "We always have the option of putting the thumb screws to the Catholic faith when we are done here, but that would be a threat of last resort. How about something a bit more subtle? How about we generate some evidence that says she's been playing terrorist games while hiding under her prioress's skirts?"

"Very nice, Commissioner," Captain Cohen responded eagerly. Even Reza had to smile. Its simplicity couldn't be bettered. It got them what they needed with very few resources and engendered no bad blood between the Metros and the Holy See.

"Since you are so hip on the idea, Amber, I'll let you run with this one."

"Yes, sir, Commissioner."

"Reza?"

"Sir, we continue aggressive collection techniques for anyone who delays in their protection payments. We've also increased the rate by six percent. I would like your permission to discontinue both actions. Our people in the street are telling us of continuing unrest. Too many of their more forceful collections have been publicly aired. The natives are getting restless."

"Why do we have to fear unarmed civilians? Request denied."

The purple luster of his boss's face let Reza know he could push no more on this topic.

"Anything further, Reza?"

"Yes. I have one last item. We are processing data that states our propaganda control of the networks is going well. As long as we maintain a speaking acquaintance to the truth in most of the news, the larger lies we tell are swallowed whole. Our current data shows a solid thirty-eight percent of the public believing that President Tipton is a clone. Forty-two percent are undecided."

*   *   *

"Pathetic amateurs," Augustine said as she reset the Metro's public polling data back to its original state. Her analysis of the Metro's real data showed a three percent belief that the President was a phony with a twelve percent undecided. Over seventy percent believed the President was exactly as she purported herself to be.

"Don't ever put critical data on the cloud. I don't care what safeguards are placed on it, the data can be hacked," she muttered to herself.

"I'll remember that," Adam said as he stepped into the darkened network room.

"Hello, Brother Adam," Augustine said, her heart racing just a little.

"A little extra-curricular activity, Sister Augustine?"

"You could say that, Brother." Augustine remained in the cradle.

Leaping out would profess her guilt. "You having some insomnia?"

"Maybe a bit. I was thinking over that denial-of-service problem you gave us this evening and wanted to do some trial sims to see if my unorthodox solution might work."

"Unorthodox? Don't let Sister Pious hear you say that. She might think you're a heretic."

Brother Adam chuckled. "Oh, she thinks that of me already. Somehow she got wind of a prank I played in my third year as a cadet. I made all the water faucets, fountains, showers, and toilets of my dorm run red with blood."

Augustine couldn't help herself and sat upright looking at him with confusion.

"It wasn't blood but a poly compound used in movie sets to simulate blood. I hooked a large canister of it into the main water feed of the training facility.

"If the joke itself wasn't good enough, it was worth the night-sentry duty for a month to see the commandant's failed attempt to hide his smile when pronouncing my sentence."

"So there is a bit of a rogue in you. Remind me to check my sheets before getting into bed."

"Oh, Sister, I could never do anything as low-brow as short sheeting someone's bed. I'm but a humble servant of our Lord God," Adam said in a tone belying the statement's veracity.

*　*　*

Sergeant Tolbert stood flanked by his two enforcers in Metro power-armor. This time he faced a middle-aged woman with four toddlers arrayed behind her.

"We didn't do anything!"

"We have a writ here for the confiscation of your home. It will be auctioned off and the proceeds will be used to pay your husband's past due quarterly Metro costs."

"But my husband is dead," the woman protested. One of the youngsters stuck his tongue out at them from the safety of his mother's back.

"That doesn't matter. The debt transfers to you."

"But he was covered under insurance."

"That covered only the home, not the protection moneys. You have one hour to collect anything you want and remove yourself from the premises."

"You can't do this to us."

"I have more important things to do than to argue with you. Your financial problems are not mine.

"Patrolmen, if they aren't out of here in one hour, kill one of the children. For every ten minutes they delay after that, kill another one."

*   *   *

"Metropolitan District of Columbia Police Captain Victor Gibon to see the Secretary of the Treasury." The Captain wore his dress blacks that barely differed from the color of his own skin. If there were any imperfections in his uniform they were from the walk from his patrol car up the steps to the famous Treasury Building. His two adjutants could have been recruiting posters with crisp, sharp motions and equally spotless uniforms. Their hair was so uniform it looked like every strand had been measured with a micrometer and cut by laser.

His Commissioner's instructions were to maintain parade ground manners during this interview.

"He's expecting you, Captain. You may go right in." Three-meter-high double-doors swung open onto a long, red carpet leading to a massive oaken desk. Gibon had been warned to expect the subtle intimidation. He'd been briefed that there was a 17-hertz generator in the room as well. At the moment it seemed to be off as he didn't feel any creeping dread or anxiety.

"Captain Gibon, welcome," Secretary of the Treasury Adam Pitts said from behind his desk with what appeared to be genuine warmth for a politico. "Please have a seat, gentlemen."

"Thank you, no, Secretary. We won't be staying quite that long."

"Not long enough to have a seat and chat?" Secretary Pitts asked. His eyebrows raised in a way that emphasized his balding head.

"No, sir. I won't take that much of your valuable time."

"Well then, by all means tell me why you are here."

Captain Gibon opened his briefcase and drew out a massive tome. "I'm sure you will recognize the current United States Budget, Annotated."

The Secretary of Treasury couldn't suppress a chortle. "Certainly I recognize it. It even bears the official seal. You have a legal copy, not one of those cheap knock-offs they sell in the souvenir stands."

"Good. Would you please open your own personal copy to page 2432."

The Sec Treas pushed his old fashioned intercom. "Susan, would you bring in the budget, please."

The men waited as an attractive blond walked down the carpet with an almost identical document to hand to her boss. They then waited even more until she left.

The Secretary of Treasury opened up his book and thumbed several dozen times. "Ah, here it is, page 2432. What am I supposed to be looking at?"

"Will you look at line item 14 Victor 8845.3, please?"

"Yes. I see it. This is the funds allocated to the Metropolitan Police Forces."

"Thank you, sir. You have already acknowledged that this is the law of the land. I am here to request that you release those funds to their appropriate agencies immediately."

The Secretary sat down heavily in his chair with a grin the size of Nebraska. "Gentlemen, these funds are already in the system. You should be dealing with the Office of Management and Budg—"

"Excuse me, Secretary Pitts, but our organizations have gotten nothing but the runaround from the normal sources. It appears actually to be a conspiracy to prevent us from obtaining the funds to continue our civil duty to the people of this country."

"I can make a few phone calls if you like and see if we can break through whatever problems there are."

"We would greatly appreciate that, Secretary Pitts, for I do not want the alternative.

"I have been given a very special deputation, Mister Secretary. Should the funds not be flowing at the rate defined by the current law of the land by the end of our conversation I am to place you under arrest for conspiracy, fraud, and not fulfilling your fiduciary responsibility under the Constitution of the United States."

* * *

"Bet one-twenty," said Frances with the bronze statue *Bird Girl* by Sylvia Shaw Judson behind her. The green paisley wallpaper, Norman Rockwell's original *Prom Dress* and *Children in the Sea* by Joaquin Sorolla y Bastida seemed out of place for a poker game, but Jamie had insisted that they stay after the success of the bank heist.

"Call," Tuan said dumping dollars into the pot.

"Fold."

"See your one-twenty and bump you two hundred," said Jacob with a piercing look at Frances.

"Fold," said one of the other players.

"OK, Jacob," Frances said. "You are very proud of that hand. I'll call."

"Call."

"How many cards do you want?"

"I'll take two," Jacob said dropping his two worst cards into the muck.

"Frances?"

"I'll take one."

The dealer, Bob no-given-surname, slid one card over to her to replace her dropped card.

"Tuan?"

"I'll take one."

"Last raiser bets. Jacob?"

"I'll bet fifty."

"Nice draw, huh?" Frances said. "Your fifty and one-fifty more."

"Call." Tuan said, dumping two hundred into the pot.

"Well, let's sort out the players from the played, shall we?" Jacob taunted. "I'll see your raise and raise two hundred more."

"Hmmm," Frances said, looking down at her cards. "Pretty rich." She flicked the corner of her end card. "OK. We've been playing together for at least three years, Jacob. I know when you're bluffing. Your two hundred and two hundred more."

"Tuan?"

"Well, either I have two players bluffing at the sky or I'm beaten. I'll fold my straight."

"Well, Jacob? Wanna raise on that three jacks now?" Frances teased, taking an hors d'oeuvre from the boxed serving unit.

"Too bad for you, Frances. I'll raise limit ... one thousand. That is also the third and last raise."

"Sure is," Frances said, counting out the bills to call and sliding them into the pot. "Let's see 'em, buddy."

"Full house. Queens over threes."

"You did get it, you rat," Frances said with a sly grin. "But I guess that doesn't beat my four ducks," turning over four deuces and a ten.

"What?! You mean you drew one card and got the case two?"

"Nope. Had the quad and drew a card to make you think I was going for a straight or a flush. Worked, too," she said as she started to draw the pot.

"Everyone be quiet," Tuan hissed. "The emergency flasher is going. Did any of you see when it went off?"

Trained fighters all, the five poker players dropped to the floor, crouching behind convenient furniture and drawing their personal weapons. No one answered the question.

"When the emergency signal goes off, Jamie is evacuated by whomever is on duty. So all we have to worry about is what is in this room and ourselves."

"What will set it off?"

"Multiple hits on proximity sensors. Penetration scans. Nanite incursions ... and that's just a few."

"Can we tell which one?"

"Bob. Lewis. Either one of you got your radio?"

"Nope."

"Sorry, Boss. Left mine in my room."

"'Bout the same as me," Tuan admitted.

"And I'm assuming you didn't hook your network into percomms," Frances asked.

"Jamie won't allow the connections."

"Dandy," Jacob said, followed by a pair of expletives that scorched the air blue.

"Tactically we are in good shape," Frances observed. "One entrance, no windows and walls of solid ceramcrete. If we block the door we gain ourselves an advantage."

Tuan didn't speak but caught his two subordinates by eye and tossed his head in the door's direction. Neither of them holstered their weapons but pulled a heavy sofa across the doorway. Then they started piling additional heavy items on top.

"Whoever they are they are being careful," Frances said after a few seconds. She spoke from the experience of her past history as a cop. "That means they aren't Metros. Black suits would just burst in here and damn the consequences."

"Could be a false alarm," Jacob offered hopefully.

"Could it be some of your people?" Tuan asked.

"Negative," Frances said. "I percommed them as soon as you mentioned the alarm. We have a response team inbound, but it won't be here for another thirty minutes plus."

"How about a rival organization? Maybe the Koreans are getting feisty again?"

"I seriously doubt it, my friend. The last time they did anything in our turf Jamie ordered an entire generation of their people and families publically and brutally exterminated. The message was received. We haven't been bothered for almost a decade from any quarter."

"We are running out of suspects," Jacob noted.

"Desperate independents?"

"I think our speculation right now isn't worth our time. I'm going to try to make my way to the master control room and see if I can puzzle out what is going on."

"Got it ... "

A sharp crack, like that of a wooden ruler against a metal table, echoed through the room. The solid wall behind the quintet crumbled into dust. From outside the room, powerful video strobes lashed the room dazing even the battle-hardened terrorists for several hundred microseconds. Only the intensive and repeated bodyguard training Tuan regularly subjected himself to allowed him to shrug off the visual assault. Tuan's mind knew it was hopeless but his body had been conditioned not to quit.

Tuan spun in his crouch to face the new threat axis. He squeezed off a six-round burst of anti-personnel ammo from each of his guns, one to the left and the other to the right of the optic disruption.

He felt a solid, jacketed slug career off the sub-cutaneous body armor he'd had installed in a quiet little shop in Vladivostok eight years ago. His skin ripped, hurting like a scalding brand. As his mind raced he watched his comrades' bodies explode with high-velocity splatter spraying the back wall.

Just on the bare edge of his trained conscious, he registered the sounds of nine distinct weapons. Metros. Only Metros used solid ammunition and worked in groups of three.

"Body armor! Charlie members switch to Duolon rounds."

Tuan continued his rotation and converted it into a linear movement to reach the moderate safety of the bronze statue's shadow.

One by one, in the space of heartbeats, his comrades died. As each one fell, the firepower retrained upon him. More than a hundred lethal fragments were shed by his ablative armor. Another tore off his right ear. Yet another ripped the cornea off of his right eye. Having already absorbed more impacts that its design limit, the armor cracked across his chest. Before making it another meter, Tuan felt two distinct projectiles tear through his right lung. Another lodged in his neck.

His momentum rotated him another quarter turn before dropping him face first on the floor.

The room fell silent. Only the flickering overhead lights illuminated the dusty gloom.

Tuan struggled to stay conscious. He could feel the pain and the pressure of blood filling his lung. His right arm wouldn't respond. Using all of his energy he flipped onto his back and swung his left arm up to aim. Not even halfway there, a big, exo-skeletoned fist slammed into his hand. His Smith and Wesson flew away.

"Good plan, Lieutenant," the armored figure said.

"Yes, it was Sergeant Talbot," said a small Indian wearing dress blues walking into Tuan's line of sight.

"Shall we question this one?" asked one of the other anonymous troopers.

"Are you a rookie? Bodyguards have built-in anti-questioning devices. The moment you start the interrogation, or even earlier, they curl up and die," the one addressed as Sergeant Talbot instructed.

"Well, Lieutenant?"

"Take the lot of them back for neural reconstruction. We might get something good. In the meantime ... " The Indian drew an archaic dress-automatic from his side and pointed it directly at Tuan's heart. Tuan didn't know how much armor hadn't been pulverized but didn't doubt the outcome no matter how much remained. The Lieutenant pulled the trigger.

*   *   *

A raucous buzz woke Jamie just enough that she ripped off a very unladylike invective. Her fairytale bedroom with four-poster bed and hanging diaphanous silks seemed transported to hell itself in the flashing red light. She'd barely sat up from her bed when the door crashed open. Gregori's massive form was silhouetted in the doorway for about a nanosecond as he rushed toward her.

Jamie started to scorch him for interrupting her sleep with some silly drill.

"Crash! Crash! Crash!" he barked into his percomm.

Before she could react he wrapped her up in his arms. Lifting her off the bed her bodyguard ran at a specific portion of the outer wall at full speed. Explosive bolts blew away the armored escape hatch.

Jamie gulped as Gregori jumped into the darkness. Her filmy nightgown fluttered in the wind wherever his arms and legs didn't cover her. The coolness of the night rain touched places a bit too private.

Her stomach did a flip when her senses finally caught up to the fact that she was falling. The escargot she'd savored a few hours ago decided to part ways with her in dramatic fashion. Before she could recover, weight slammed into the places where her bodyguard held her. Three barks of an automatic and the shattering of something brittle replaced the whistling of the wind. They still fell but not nearly so fast.

Just as abruptly as everything else, she found herself landing on top of her bodyguard just as they passed through the open maw of a shattered window.

For one brief moment she lay still in the darkness. Nothing moved. Nothing further assaulted her senses. Her body almost caught up.

"C'mon. We have to move," Gregori hissed at just above a whisper. He yanked her to her feet. "We don't have much time."

He hustled her around obstacles in the darkened factory with the grace of a cat. Pausing just inside the door he threw a rain slicker over her shoulders.

"What is going on?" she finally managed to get out as he yanked her into the dimly lit hall after first checking the way was clear.

"Metros."

*   *   *

"Surely you can't ignore this transgression, Prioress," came Sister Pious's nasal voice through the superior's closed door.

Augustine overheard the tone if not every word as she approached, as ordered by Sister Pious's private secretary.

"I have to think of the good of the church," came the softer tones of Sister Hanna.

"Ma'am, is having a terrorist protecting our secrets the best of ideas?"

Augustine knocked on the door.

"Enter."

Augustine opened the door and stepped in. Sister Pious and her lemon-sour mouth stood to Sister Hanna's right. An old-fashioned, wall-mounted display showed a frozen slice of network traffic in minute size.

"Please have a seat, Sister Augustine."

Augustine knew the basics but not the details. She perched on the edge of the chair leaning forward as if not to miss a single word.

"Augustine, in this very room we discussed your former work and the work you continued for the Green Action Militia on at least two occasions."

"Yes, Prioress."

"I did point out to you the error of your ways, in so much as Mother Church was concerned."

"Yes, Prioress."

"Against council I've shown you more leniency than I'd have offered to any other novitiate."

"I did not know that, Prioress, but it seems so."

"I did this because of your spirituality, your inner desire to do good, and your value to Mother Church."

"Thank you, Prioress."

"But it seems that I was mistaken." Augustine couldn't help but to note the smug look on Sister Pious's face at the statement. "I've recently been provided with proof that you have continued your ways in violation of our personal agreement and the expressed prohibition of Mother Church."

Augustine sat silent.

"I will ask you this very directly. Are you and have you continued your work with the Green Action Militia since my last warning?"

"Yes, Prioress."

"Thank you for being honest, Sister Augustine. I feared the

answer even while I knew the proof I'd been handed was falsified."

Sister Pious scowled. Augustine sighed with relief. It wasn't Adam. Adam had no need to falsify records.

"No, Sister Pious, I don't blame you, but you too must learn from your mistakes. When someone hands you information that matches both your and their desires you must question it. The Metros want Sister Augustine, or should I say Grandma Ice, very badly. You were taken in by their willingness to help you.

"Sister Pious, in order to aid your education I am decreeing that you take one week of bread and water. You are further confined to worship in your cell for that same duration. You are demoted and removed as Novitiate Mistress.

"Please leave us now."

Sister Pious, her eyebrows drawn tightly together, her eyes flashing with menace and her jaw working so hard Augustine could hear teeth grinding, exited the prioress's office with a minimum of decorum.

"Sister Augustine, what am I going to do with you? I feel like the spiritual leader of Maria in *The Sound of Music*. Unfortunately, I have no convenient family of children to send you off to rear."

"I'm sorry, Prioress," Augustine said, truly contrite.

"In this case, I'm afraid, sorry isn't going to cut it. You've made it abundantly clear that you value your friends over the church or your vows to Jesus Christ."

"Not exactly, Prioress. I do value all those things. I just see them much differently than the church does."

"Unfortunately, I have to be arbiter of things the way the church sees them.

"I want you to pray on this matter, Sister. You have no other duty for the next twenty-four hours. If you can see clear to accepting my dictums, I will take you at your word and we will resolve this administratively.

"Unfortunately, the other side of this coin isn't quite so clear. This case also involves another problem. If I release you from your vows the Metros will surely pick you up and probably murder you. I won't say that my mind would be totally clear if that happened.

"So, if you cannot accept the will of Mother Church, I will release you from your vows and accept any petition of sanctuary you bring forward."

"Thank you, Prioress. I will pray as you have ordered. May I make a statement?"

Sister Hanna sat back in her chair and looked thoughtful. "Is it something that might mitigate my judgment here?"

"No, Prioress."

"Then by all means."

"Sister Hanna, I want you to know that I find you a good and honorable woman. You are an exceptional tool for our Lord God. What I did I felt compelled to do not to spite you, not to flaunt your authority, but because it was the path God led me down. I wanted you to know that I have the utmost respect for you and wish I'd not put you in this position."

"So do I, Sister."

* * *

Six Metros in full combat armor stood outside the door to Advair Enterprises, one of the mob's known fronts. One of them ran listening devices from his suit to the wall.

The leader knocked. No one answered. The leader knocked again.

"What do you want? We aren't open for business," came a voice from inside.

"Police serving a warrant. We are looking for one Jimmy Martin."

"Look, I'm the only one here and I ain't him."

The trooper listening held up ten fingers and then six additional fingers.

Switching to his percomm the leader said, "This is Detective Burien. I want the industrial floors of Madison and Third sealed. No one in or out. Dedicate seven squads and two mobile units."

"*Ten-Four, Detective.*"

The leader looked at his crew. "Incendiaries only. Make it burn. No survivors."

* * *

The smell of peaches and cream still wafted through the room, even if the bitter, copper stench of blood covered it up. Mozart's *Piano Concerto No. 7* continued to play even over the torture.

"Sah, I do no' know wahr the cou'cil ha' gone," the butler and Council's majordomo said through broken teeth and puffy lips. Blood leaked down from his right eye, now an apple-shaped protrusion. "If I did, I woul' 'ell you."

"I'm sure you would," Lieutenant Narendra said calmly as he straddled the seat across from the man. "We've tortured and killed your coworkers and you maintained your story. We've given you more than one love tap as well. We will try one more thing just to make sure you are telling us the truth.

"Gus, bring in the neural disruptor."

"Sah, my s'ory won' 'ange. I don' know were 'ey are."

"Oh, I know it won't. But I have to make sure."

Reza couldn't quite place the image of the incomplete mural that they'd shot the staff against, but it troubled him in some deep, dark place. Reza couldn't stand the repeated movements of a boxed unit as it tried in vain to clean up around the four dead bodies. He dismissed the poor thing from the room.

On his own way out of the Council Chambers, he whispered in Sergeant Talbot's ear, "If this doesn't work bring his head in for neural reconstruction."

*   *   *

The disheveled woman across the dining table looked nothing like the untouchable redhead Tony had come to know. Her hair harbored an abundance of unidentifiable pasty-gray, particulate matter. It also twisted itself into so many knots Tony imagined it would require cutting. Jamie's face was devoid of even a trace of makeup, making it seem longer and more pointed at the chin. As far as he could tell she wore only a red-vinyl coat and something filmy and transparent that kept sneaking out below the raincoat's hem.

But it wasn't her appearance that triggered alarm bells inside him. He'd seen Jamie playful, seductive, businesslike, irritated, and friendly. Until now he'd never seen her angry. Her fine brows furrowed down toward her narrowed eyes. Her lips pursed together and her jaw worked, clenching and unclenching in time with the fist she made with her right hand.

"You're safe now," Tony reassured her with a grim line to his mouth. Cinnamon cuddled up close to his neck, butting her head against his ear.

Gregori prowled the Olympia safe house to make sure Tony's statement had validity in his own eyes.

"I've been safe as soon as I got a block away from my home." Jamie seemed to force each word out between her teeth as if they were the hours of her life. "This is no longer about profit, Tony. They declared war."

"Before you go doing something rash you might want to know about the first casualties."

"Casualties?" Jamie asked, her eyes looking up for the first time.

"Tuan, Jacob, Frances and at least two other of your operatives we couldn't identify." On the table, Tony displayed grainy images taken from afar of the unidentified pair.

"Robert Canter and Joshel Garrett. Good men. Tuan ... are you sure?"

"Positive. From the looks of things they were set up to defend themselves when the Metros went through the wall behind them using a breaching device I've never heard of before."

"Tuan ... " Jamie's voice drifted off, and she looked down at the table. A single tear leaked out of each of her eyes.

"House is clear," Gregori said reentering the tiny kitchen. "What—" he started. Tony waved him down.

"Tuan is dead."

"Fuck," the big Russian said. "Anyone else?"

"Robert and Joshel from your team and Jacob and Frances from mine," Tony said gritting his own teeth to maintain his composure.

Gregori said nothing more but slipped in behind Jamie protectively.

Jamie's chin quivered and more tears ran down her cheeks. "Tuan ... my little Tuanie." Tony didn't understand and looked at Gregori.

"Nephew," the big man mouthed.

Tony inched his chair over closer to his guest and took her hand in his. The simple act of human kindness released the flood. Jamie's sobs wracked her and rolled over the top of one another. Tears and even snot flowed. Cin jumped down and twined around and over their arms trying to rub each of them in turn. She eventually just lay down on their joined hands.

While trying to salve Jamie's pain, Tony's own eyes began to seep—Jacob and Frances. He still hadn't reconciled their loss. Without planning or even knowing how it happened, Tony and Jamie ended up in one another's arms.

For an unknowable time they cried together with Tony's shirt the designated handkerchief. Whenever one would get some composure just looking at the other would trigger another emotional jag. Finally the pair settled with red eyes, blotchy cheeks and running noses.

"Sleep ... with me," Jamie whispered in his ear.

"Yes."

*   *   *

Augustine entered the novitiate's chapel at six a.m. As everyone else would attend Prime she would have it to herself. This was the perfect time to begin her contemplation. Augustine walked up to the crucifix with adrenaline coursing through her body. Kneeling, she genuflected and kissed her cross. This in itself brought a measure of peace, but not enough to completely blot out the fear, the anger, or her own stubborn pride. She worried the rosary in her hand as she prayed.

"Why do you have to make this so difficult?" she whispered with her eyes closed and head down. "I only wanted to serve."

"Who said it wouldn't be difficult?" came a voice from behind her.

Augustine turned on one knee to see who it was.

"A life of service isn't easy," Ruth said from the back row of kneelers.

"I thought I'd have the chapel to myself," Augustine said realizing she must have passed her friend without even noticing her.

"Sorry. I'd leave if I could but I got one of Sister Pious's all day fast and prayers to purge my baser emotions."

"I'm sorry, Ruth."

"Bah. Don't be. I deserved it. But why are you here during Prime?"

"You might say I deserve it, too."

Ruth waited.

"I have a very important decision to make and no matter which way I choose I'm wrong."

"Did you ask God?"

"Yes, but the answer in my breast, the one he has seen fit to give me, doesn't match what the church says it must," Augustine said, pounding her fist down on the altar.

Ruth laughed.

"Excuse me?" Augustine said sharply. "What about this do you find funny?"

"I think it is funny because your problem is so simple. You just haven't quite worked it out for yourself."

"Really? There is an easy answer?"

"Whoa, Augustine. God never said life would be easy, only that he wouldn't break faith with you. Acts 5:29 resolves your dilemma but not the ache I see in your heart."

"'But Peter and the apostles answered, "We must obey God rather than men,"'" Augustine muttered as she stared at the crucifix. Her shoulders relaxed. The worry lines above her brows disappeared. "Thank you, Ruth. You were right. It was there all along."

Augustine stood, easing her knees by leveraging herself up with the aid of the altar. She activated her percomm as she did.

"Christine? Yes, girl, it's me. I need help."

Turning, Augustine walked back toward the chapel's entrance leaving her rosary sitting at Jesus's bloody feet.

* * *

Tony woke to the neural rasp of his percomm. His head throbbed. His eyes were gritty. He couldn't connect his mind to the here and now. He'd stayed in one too many safe houses over the last months. With his left hand he rubbed the sleep from his eyes. A woman slept on his right arm. Her red hair, mussed and knotted, fell over her shoulders, some of it tickling his nose. Her warm and shapely back cuddled into his embrace. At that very moment his brain acknowledged that a woman, this woman slept against him.

Tony went from that sleepy fog of Neverland to the instant sharpness of wakefulness that usually only two or three energy drinks provided. Last night played out in his mind faster and clearer than any solido recording. The mutual grief and support, and falling asleep in one another's arms.

While they both lay naked against one another, Tony's memory told him that he and Jamie hadn't done anything more than hold one another in sleep. He was still trying to puzzle out if he felt better or worse about that when his percomm rasped once again.

"Bloody hell," he muttered as he extricated his arms from its captor. The sheet slipped off his partner, exposing her shapely ass with just the hint of dimple in each cheek. Tony slid out of bed as gently as possible. Jamie moaned very quietly and reached for the sheet. Cinnamon climbed across Jamie's thighs and nestled into the warm hollow of her back. The whiskered face looked up at him with sleepy eyes and mewed contentedly.

His percomm grated yet again. "I'm going to neuter someone," Tony growled almost silently. In his own head it included a signed execution order as well as visuals. Luckily he found the clothes he wore last evening lying on the floor. He slipped into the pants and grabbed his still damp shirt before stealing out of the room. There he found Gregori snoring on the couch and two other of Jamie's protective entourage standing guard. He barely remembered the men by sight. Silently cursing, Tony nodded to the two men as he made a beeline for the kitchen.

His percomm went off as he struggled into his shirt with it still buttoned.

"WHAT!" he snapped at the caller. "Guy can't get a moment's peace in this outfit."

"*Boss, sorry to bother you but Augustine needs our help,*" David said.

Tony's tone changed immediately. "What's going on."

"*She is being kicked out, whatever that's called, of her church thingy. If that isn't bad enough, the Metros have the place surrounded and seem to be waiting for her.*"

"Holy fuck. It's three hours for us to get to Calgary if we leave now."

"*She says she can hold out for probably another day.*"

"OK. Round up everyone but Connie. She has to stay on the President."

"*Already done. We're at Rosa's Import in Pike's Place Market. We were just waiting for you. You didn't answer our earlier percomms.*"

Tony felt a heat rise in his cheeks.

"Never mind that now. While you are waiting for me go out and charter a liner. It will save us almost an hour."

"*Boss, that's going to compromise an identity.*"

"I don't care. What's one fake identity? Make it happen. Oh, and do we have our personal supplies there?"

"*Of course, Boss.*"

"Including clothes?" Tony asked, looking down at the tear and snot stains across his shirt.

"*Yup,*" David said, but the querulous tone said he didn't understand the meaning.

"I'm on my way."

*   *   *

"My name is Henry Royston. I've been boxed for sixty-two years, six months, fourteen days. Can any say they've been here longer?"

"Get on with it!"

"Call the vote!"

"Yeah, call the vote!"

"Vote!-Vote!-Vote!" the chant of thousands went on and on, in perfect rhythm to the storage structure's resonate frequency. The building flexed and echoed their cries, making it seem sympathetic to their demands.

A1412 waited for them to wind down. He had been patient longer than any. More than once he'd thought about ending his disembodied suffering. To no longer have to recite his own name to remember would be a blessing. To no longer have to work to remember the feeling of touch, the decadent ability to taste, or even to see the brilliance of a sunset that hadn't been pixelated and electronically fired into his brain. Only patience might win those things back. Only patience might win back sanity.

The rank and file spent two hours chanting before they realized he could outwait them. The chant didn't die at once but tapered off until only a couple of the truly fanatical members still shouted out.

"Thank you for letting me know what you want. We will vote—" A cheer roared so loud Henry had to turn down his aural inputs. Seventeen minutes, five seconds later the volume dropped enough for him to continue. "—BUT first I need you all to listen to me." There were a few catcalls but not as many as he'd expected. "Our information is good. We know the plans of both of the groups. We've done exceptionally, brothers and sisters."

The crowd roared in a positive spirit again.

"Friends. Comrades. Please let me finish."

"Stifle yourselves, you metal heads!" Stephanie Delfalkis bellowed. Somehow her voice carried higher and further than anyone else's.

"Thank you. A few select members who have military and social training have been examining this data that you want to vote upon. Their feeling is unanimous. They all recommend not revealing ourselves yet but to continue our silence."

The room became so quiet that a spider weaving a web would have dominated everyone's attention.

"Yes, friends, we need to wait and be patient. Neither of these groups is truly desperate yet. We won't get our bodies back without continued patience. If we came out now each of the groups would offer something less than what we need. We must wait until they have no choice but to give into each and every one of our demands."

More silence came from the room. Being a disembodied brain didn't allow for much body language for him to read.

"I will now call for a vote. All in favor of exposing ourselves now, give your signal."

Four hundred hertz tones filled the room, but not overwhelmingly.

"All in favor of waiting, as suggested by our experts, please give your signal now."

The same tone was significantly louder this time, joined by many more of his fellow slaves.

"We wait. Thank you, friends. Your patience will be rewarded. We will remember ourselves long enough. Say it with me.

"My name is … "

* * *

"OK, David, this is your plan. You run with it."

"You aren't going to lead—" David said with a start. His eyeballs looked like someone had pulled them halfway out of their sockets.

Tony shook his head. "Nope. I'm just one of the team. Where do you want my expert marksmanship," Tony said tongue-in-cheek. Even social blogs knew of Tony's inability to hit any side of a room even if he were inside it.

"In that case I want you on comms ... where you can't hurt anyone."

"But, Boss," Tony said in a perfect mockery of David's light New York accent. Everyone laughed, including David.

"We don't have enough men or firepower to punch through," David outlined, "so we will go with indirection. The plan is simple in execution but our withdraw plan may be tricky. We are going to hit two different Metro control points on the perimeter of the church's property."

"Priory," interrupted Martin.

" ... perimeter of the priory," David corrected. "Morgan, you will go in with the twins. I'll take Martin and Edward. Our responsibility will be to make the biggest, most credible threat we can. If all works according to plan, Augustine can just walk out one of the holes that will happen as they reinforce against our attacks.

"But we aren't going to take any chances. Christine, you are our ace in the hole. If they don't open things up enough you are to use your talent on whatever still blocks our friend's escape.

"Tony, you remain as our tactical reserves, and God help the team that needs your help." This elicited another few giggles.

"Don't forget," Morgan added, "we aren't in the city. The only cover we have is the snow."

"Definitely. Tony will announce when Augustine is out. When that happens, blow all of your explosives in one go and fade away.

"Questions?" Everyone looked around.

"Then let's get Augustine. First attack starts at sundown, exactly sixteen forty-three. The second attack starts two minutes later."

*   *   *

"Sister Augustine, am I intruding?" the prioress asked as she entered the darkened room.

"Shouldn't we drop the pretense, Prioress?" Augustine said, floating within her net cradle for one last time. "I'm no longer a novitiate."

"Then why address me formally?"

"But you ... oh, because I respect you, Hanna. And you tricked me."

The nun chuckled. "I'd say you tricked me as well."

"I didn't mean to, Hanna. I just wanted to serve God."

"You will, dear. I don't believe for a moment that someone as good as you are can possibly do anything but God's will. It just won't be in Mother Church."

"Thank you, Hanna. That means a great deal to me."

"Well, I may have something more valuable to you, at least in the short term."

"Oh?"

"Yes, we are going to help you get out of here in one piece." Sister Hanna climbed into an adjacent net couch and fired up the gravitics.

"How do you plan to do that?" Augustine said somewhat gloomily.

"How many Metros do you think there are out there?"

"Seeing as I am number three on their most wanted persons' list, I'd say two hundred, maybe three with electronic surveillance and air cover."

"Actually two hundred sixty-five and eight drones."

"Are you trying to make me feel better or depress me?"

"Make you feel better. I have enlisted the aid of the Mariam Crusaders. They will control the drones and the electronic surveillance. The Metros will see what we want them to."

"Really, Sister?" Augustine asked, sitting bolt upright so fast that she almost tumbled in the gravity field. "That's wonderful! I couldn't think of a way to do it by myself while I moved."

"Why didn't you ask?"

"And suborn church resources?"

Hanna lay quietly for several seconds.

"Augustine, I know you haven't been with us long, but I think you underestimate the number of friends you've made here even in that short a time. You're a good and godly woman, not above sharing her gifts with those around her. Even if I'd said 'No' you would have had dozens willing to help you behind my back."

"I think you've overstated it."

"No, not at all. And no matter what you think, I'd be one of them bucking authority. There is a military adage that applies as much in a convent as it does in the trenches. 'Never give an order that won't be obeyed.' So I decided to give an order that would be obeyed.

"As soon as your friends attack ... no, don't deny it ... when your friends attack, as I am sure they will, you will go wherever was originally planned. Eighteen of our older nuns will disperse in all directions on foot, making like they are trying to escape. None of them will leave church land so the Metros will have no excuse to be more than confused by them.

"Surely this will aid your current predicament."

"Sister Hanna, I could just kiss you."

*   *   *

Christine hunkered down in a depression in the prairie that afforded some protection from the wind and allowed her to watch the three-man Metro outpost. They weren't hiding. Two were in full black riot gear and the other was a local Calgary constable in arctic white patrol gear.

The local played a portable scanner, about the size and shape of a baby grand piano. With that piece of equipment, she was surprised she'd made it undetected to her current location. Either the competence of the operator ranked in the bottom one percent or all the sweeps pointed inward.

A warm quiver began between her thighs. There were three delicious opportunities for her to slake her lust. Her need demanded more and more of her lately. But, if things went well for Augustine, Christine would not get a kill. All of those lovely men would walk away without dying for her. She shook her head. The gratification in killing those men would be hollow without their warmth inside her, but it would still feed some of her needs. Christine brutally suppressed the violent and lustful images in her mind. She hated being frustrated, but for Augustine she'd suffer much more.

If things went her way, however, it called for a bit more reach. She had both a grenade launcher, loaded with stunbag, and her *daishō* hanging from her belt. Her *shinshinto katana* had taken her six years of coercion to convince the owner to part with it. The paired, but modern, nano-tube-strung *wakizashi* didn't have the reach but could cut through even battle armor in a pinch.

Her percomm chirped. She buried her head into the snow until she heard the first explosion and the clattering buzz of a gauss gun. Only then did she lift up to see a second sun slowly die in the darkening sky. In its place a crisscross of tracers formed.

"*This is Baker Twelve. We have a full scale attack at coordinates Alpha three, three, eight.*" The voice that emanated from her target's receivers seemed extremely calm. "*Requesting immediate reinforcement.*"

"*Baker Twelve, this is Baker Lead. We acknowledge that you are under attack at Alpha three, three, eight.*"

"*Baker Lead to all stations. This is likely a feint. Stand alert for targets. All odd stations send one trooper to Baker Twelve.*"

One of the black troopers fired off his pergrav and flew off in the direction of the conflagration.

"*Baker Six. I have movement in target area. I repeat. I have ground movement in target area.*"

"*Baker Four. I have a ground target inside the target area.*"

"*Baker Eighteen. I also have a target inside the church. What the fuck?*"

Listening in on their own radios was better than being in an opposing football team's huddle, even though Christine never thought much about the game.

"*Baker Lead. Settle down and focus, Baker Eighteen.*"

"*Take any and all targets that leave the Priory grounds. Under no circumstances are you to enter the grounds.*"

"*Baker Eight. Two ground targets in sight. Both are wearing nun paraphernalia.*"

"*Baker Nine. I have a single target.*"

"*Baker Lead. Report targets through tactical net and keep off the air.*"

"*Baker Seven to Baker Lead. I have been engaged by unknown number of hostiles with heavy anti-personnel weapons and explosives. We cannot hold and are falling back. Requesting immediate reinforcements.*"

"*Baker Lead to all stations. The attacks and multiple targets are diversions. Be alert for the real action. All even stations send a single trooper to assist Baker Seven.*"

Christine realized with a surge of excitement that the Metros wouldn't fall for their plan and drop the contingent here any further. Two was the fewest that would remain here. The armored trooper must die first. The local cop would merit a little more time.

She quietly drew both blades. Her legs coiled beneath her. She shifted her feet around to get all the way to earth for a good purchase.

"Major, did you see that movement in the target area?" the local said.

Christine sprang.

She eyed the armor's vulnerable black knee joint as she sped across the white surface. Her feet landed so lightly she didn't fall through the snow's surface crust.

Before she'd closed even half the distance, the ground around her target erupted. A man wearing only the yellow tights of a bodyguard leapt up between the men. Mr. Marks rotated in a blur. The black-armored-Metro's legs, even gyro stabilized, flipped up from under him by means of Marks's leg sweep. The broad-chested bodyguard rotated his arm around from above his head and plunged down a tool that looked like an icepick. The device struck the downed trooper in the middle of his back. A muffled pop sounded, followed by a volcano of blood up through the hole the weapon made in the armor.

The local trooper started to draw his service automatic to target the maniacal man next to him. He hadn't even noticed his murderer. Christine hadn't slowed, only changed her target. With an upward stroke of her *katana,* she sliced off his weapon arm as easily as cutting through whipped cream. Rotating through the attack, her short-blade *wakizashi* sliced through his neck. The decapitated head hit the ground and rolled like an obscene toy.

She stopped, facing the bodyguard in a defensive crouch. The man stood motionless. His hairless chest, the color of red oak, barely moved whereas hers bellowed with her brief exertion.

"I didn't mean to startle you. I thought you might need some help," Thomas Marks said as he carefully cleaned his weapon with a handkerchief he found in the local man's pocket. "I am part of the team now, but you forgot to invite me."

Christine said nothing as she examined him closely. His mahogany hair, high cheekbones and ruddy skin made him look more like an Aztec priest than anything that belonged in the snowy north. Nor did the freezing temperature seem to affect the man.

Reluctantly, she put away her swords. Christine silently put her hand out for the man's weapon. Mr. Marks handed it over. She examined the single-shot weapon. It used a small caliber bullet that was triggered when the point came in contact with its intended victim. The force of the cartridge in such an enclosed place penetrated most armor.

Christine handed it back with a shrug. "Thank you."

"What are you two waiting for," Augustine said as she walked up to them.

Deeper Thoughts

"From the smirk on your face, Lieutenant Narendra, I assume you have good news for us?"

"In total, yes, Commissioner, I do."

"Well, far be it from us to stop you from giving us good news."

Reza shuffled at the end of the table. "I do have mostly good news. Our investigation into the vagaries of the laws of the United States allowed us to convince," Reza said with emphasis, "the Secretary of the Treasury to start the flow of our funds from the federal government again."

"That's exceptional. Who did that?"

Reza paused and made a decision on the fly to mend fences. There would be enough accolades to trickle down. "Captain Hardy did, sir. Without his direction I'd never have taken the next step."

"Good job, Maxwell," Krylov said to Captain Hardy who preened like peacock. "Didn't know you had it in you.

"Go on, Reza."

"Yes, Commissioner.

"Our raid, at your direct order, on the Pacific Northwest crime syndicate known colloquially as the "mob" or the "family" went off without a hitch. We raided Jamie Ardwin, the current *capa's*, personal offices as well as a couple of known mob places of business. The results were mixed but overall good.

"At the primary location we recovered four objects d'art valued at over ten billion dollars combined value."

Three of the members whistled.

"Agreed," Reza continued. "While we missed the *Capa* herself, we did apprehend, posthumously, five persons. Neural reconstruction showed two as low-grade functionaries. One was not only Ms. Ardwin's personal bodyguard but also her nephew. His inf—"

"Excuse me," Chief Adams interrupted. "Are we likely to see retaliation from having killed one of her family?"

"No more than for what we've already done," Krylov answered. "Folks, we are in a war for our very lives. Irritating a bit player such as Ms. Ardwin isn't something we should be worried about."

"I'm sorry, Commissioner. I wasn't worried, only trying to plan."

"Continue, Lieutenant."

"Yes, sir. As I was saying, the nephew's information, while extensive, really didn't give us much to go on that we didn't already know. The other two, however, provided us prizes.

"The other two were Jacob Guala and, even more importantly, the former patrolwoman, Frances Fischer."

A decided growl emanated from the panel.

"Yes, that's right. We picked up and disposed of two Action Committee Greenies. Vacuuming their skulls has given us a lead on no fewer than one hundred three different safe houses, weapon caches and money drops, not to mention the ability to snag their own personal assets for ourselves.

"From this I have to make an editorial comment. The Greenies are now within the top eight percentile of the most wealthy individuals on the planet. They are well-funded for whatever they choose to do.

"But, getting back, raids on some of these places have turned up massive numbers of weapons, explosives, ammunition and survival supplies—enough to keep a small army going.

"While it hasn't yet bagged us any additional Greenies, it has clearly identified all of the inner circle. All but two, we had already identified. I'll have dossiers on all of their members for you as you leave the meeting. We do have stake-outs on several of the larger safe houses in the hopes that we will corral the rest of them yet."

"Sounds like the raid went much better than we could have hoped for," Krylov said doing everything but patting himself on the back.

"A grand piece of management," Chief Adams brown-nosed.

"Anyway, you have more about the actions against the mob?"

"Yes, sir. We hit a nymthol production factory, a warehouse and an aerobics gym front, all owned in one form or another by Jamie Ardwin or her closest associates.

"In each of the three cases, we set fire to the business and killed anyone trying to leave. We ensured the message would sink in by letting the entire business district of the building housing it be consumed in the blaze.

"We have a body count of forty-eight confirmed dead. The fires consumed anything of value, but based on the things we were able to identify we can safely assume at least seven billion dollars in direct merchandise loss and another three billion in damages."

"I believe that was a message well sent. That should start the funds flowing back from that side of the coin," the Commissioner crowed.

"Unfortunately, all of our news isn't good. I'll let Captain Cohen talk about our attempt to capture Augustine Cordoba."

Captain Cohen stood up at the other end of the table from Reza. Her short brown hair showed her scalp beneath it. "We deployed a battalion of our best troopers, augmented with three companies of local Calgary troops. We cordoned off the entirety of the Priory both with forces on the ground and two independent electronic frontiers. We had eight non-lethal riot drones as aerial surveillance.

"Our forces were engaged in a serious firefight by overwhelming forces in two places on the blockade. By judicious—"

"Is there an executive summary, Captain?" Krylov interjected. "I'm interested in the results, not the nuts and bolts."

"We lost eight troopers, and the Calgary force lost one. We have no hard data on any casualties of the enemies."

"And what about the capture?"

"Because of the rules of engagement we didn't capture anyone."

"And Ms. Cordoba?"

"Unknown, sir. Based on the tactical situation we believe she escaped. We have no hard data either way."

Everyone looked at the Commissioner waiting for the explosion.

"Captain, I would like a very detailed report on my desk in one hour on how over two hundred trained, veteran police couldn't apprehend one ... old ... WOMAN!" Krylov's face looked like the stone carving of some ancient Hawaiian volcano god.

His final blast seemed to knock Captain Cohen back to her chair.

Krylov rolled his neck and stretched his shoulders in silence. His face settled into something more normal, if a bit purple.

"I want to commend MOST of you on a job well done."

"Is there anything else, sir?"

Reza decided that his last bit of bad news about the hacked public polls could wait for a more appropriate time.

*   *   *

In the lift-bus, Augustine found herself at the center of a hurricane of positive energy. Her friends hugged her, pounded her back, and gave her high fives. Joel actually wrapped his arms around her and lifted her from the floor.

"Welcome home, girl."

"Way to go!"

"We don't want 'nun' of your backtalk!"

"Don't leave us again."

Augustine, with Tony's help, finally got the crew to settle down.

"Thank you all very much, but I've only been gone for a couple of weeks. I don't think it requires all this."

The small group erupted again. It was nearly fifteen minutes later before Augustine extracted herself and plopped into a seat next to the quiet trio of Tony, Christine and Mr. Marks.

"Whew!"

"You are beloved."

"So I've been told."

Christine didn't participate in the conversation. She stared down the bodyguard Mr. Marks.

"Thank you, Mr. Marks," Tony praised. "I don't think Christine needed your help, but I don't want to risk my people any more than necessary."

"It's my pleasure, Mr. Sammis. I was happy to lend an assist. But if I might, I believe all of our organizations must cooperate. As you noted, my skills could have been better used elsewhere."

"I agree, Mr. Marks."

"I'll bring that up with Nanogate when we meet next." Tony turned to Augustine.

"So did you get what you were after?"

Augustine sighed. "Sort of."

* * *

"Excuse me?" President Tipton asked the solidoconference of her cabinet. Her eyes were open twice their normal size and her mouth hung open.

"I'm not kidding, Ms. President."

"You are telling me that the Metros came in and forced you to give them money? Did they hold a gun to your head?"

"Yes, Madam President. Not exactly, Madam President. They threatened to arrest me."

"Let me get this straight, Adam. One of the most powerful men in the United States gets held up by someone not even brandishing a gun!" She could feel the tips of her ears heating up.

"It's not that simple, ma'am. You may be hiding away, but I have a family to think about."

"Our entire freedoms are at stake, maybe even the life of our country and all you can say is 'I have a family to think about?'"

"Yes, ma'am."

"I'll expect your resignation tomorrow, Adam. You may leave the conference."

"Yes, Madam President." His image disappeared and the security count dropped by one.

"So what are my options?"

"The congress won't let you name a new Secretary of Treasury," Kneph Anum, her inherited chief of staff offered. "They won't approve any replacement you put up there and you know it."

"Knew that. I didn't even consider it. Not having a Secretary is better than one that's going to cave every time someone growls at him."

"Unfortunately, I think you are correct, Madam President."

"What about the Under Secretary? I don't know enough about him, Kneph."

"You mean the honorable Mr. 'Gumby-spine' Robertson?"

"Ahhh. And I assume with those two department heads I can't expect any of the functionaries below them to be willing to jump into the fire."

"No, ma'am."

"How about a lock on the Federal Reserve?"

"No chance, Ms. President. The Fed is nothing more than a rubberstamp for whoever is the prevailing power. If there is any doubt, it will do nothing," Attorney General Price offered.

"An executive order?"

"You could issue one, Madam President but it would be carried out by the same functionaries that won't stand up to the Metros in the first place."

"Well, does anyone have any ideas at all?"

"How desperately do you want to stop the flow?" asked Burt

Gordon, Secretary of Commerce.

"Why do you ask," the President asked hesitantly.

"Because what I'm going to suggest to you could have ramifications and repercussions for decades, maybe centuries."

* * *

"This safe house has plenty of space for all, so claim a room. We'll be here for a bit," Tony said.

"And not to push, Augustine, but once you get settled could you start on some more false identities. We lost a good number of them when Frances and Jacob were killed." Tony didn't realize he was talking to himself. The other members of the team, including Mr. Marks, were staring at Jamie Ardwin sitting comfortably in a chair in the living room.

Two of his team drew weapons. Gregori, standing behind her left shoulder, matched the move, but languidly and without ratcheting the tension up any further.

Jamie wore the prevailing style of pale white foundation but limited herself to a more pinup look with the rest of her makeup. To Tony she didn't look like the woman that had been crying in his arms just last night.

"Uh..Boss? Why is she here?"

"How did she know w—"

"We're burned. We need to get out of here now!"

"Listen up, folks," Tony said in his best penetrating speaker voice. "*Capa Famiglia* Jamie Ardwin is here at my request. We lost people together. I'm assuming that we will be seeking justice together."

Augustine broke the tension. She stuck out her hand and moved forward toward the seated woman. "Nice to have you with us, Ms. Ardwin. I'm sorry it had to be under such circumstances."

Gregori made the next move by holstering his Sig Sauer. Morgan and David followed his example.

"Thank you, Augustine. Forgive me for not getting up but I seem to have a growth in my lap," Jamie said with a wry smile. Cinnamon lay in the lap of her current slave's low-cut, jade and white herringbone dress, paws outstretched and purring in time with the *capa's* strokes.

"Quite all right. I've had a similar if not identical growth in my lap from time to time."

Cinnamon looked up and mewed before succumbing to the attention she deserved as a goddess.

"All right ... Nothing to see here. Move along," Tony said, shooing them off to claim accommodations. His team broke into small knots before wandering off deeper into the house.

"Gregori, could I ask you to be absent for a few minutes? I promise to return your boss to you in one piece."

The bodyguard looked down at Jamie who nodded without a word.

Tony sat down in the chair across from her. "I'm so sorry, Jamie. I didn't mean to take advantage of you last night."

Jamie's eyes remained passive. She just kept stroking Cinnamon.

"It was just that you and I both seemed to need someone ... OK, I needed someone and I hope this won't ruin—"

"You men are so stupid about sex sometimes," Jamie interrupted softly. "All of these eons of evolution and the battle between the sexes still rages."

Cinnamon concurred with a tiny mew.

"I don't—"

"Tony, I know you haven't known me very long but have you ever known me to do anything I didn't want to?"

"Well, um ... no."

"Damned right. One time, and only once, I had someone try to rape me. I took my boss's place in the organization when they found his body diced into 1-centimeter-sized cubes and stacked like a pyramid in his bed.

"I never do anything I don't want to, sweetie. And I've wanted to do you since the first time Sonya introduced us."

Tony's head spun like someone had just proven the world to be flat after all.

"Oh, don't get me wrong, my sex kitten act is normal for everyone ... it puts them off their own agenda and gives me an edge. But every time we interacted I almost wished you'd fall for it. That being said, last night was different. I did need someone to hold me.

"Want to guess when the last time someone actually touched me that wasn't doing my hair, my makeup, or protecting me? Don't strain yourself too much but I'll bet any number you come up with is far too small."

Even a flat world had to have rules and Jamie kept removing the ones he was familiar with, one at a time.

"It's been over forty-three years since I've let anyone touch me."

"Ahh ... " Tony offered intelligently.

"So that brings us to you. Did you find last night onerous?"

"No! Not at all."

"Would you like to try again without the tears? Maybe we could make different kind of noises together."

The tips of Tony's ears heated up and his cheeks felt like they were on fire. "Is this such a good idea?"

"Jesus H. Christ, Tony. I'm not proposing marriage. I just want to take your very sexy body to bed and see which of us can please the other more."

"It doesn't make sense. We are working together and—"

"Like I said. Men are stupid about sex. Tony this makes the most sense of anything I've ever proposed. Think about it. What opportunities do you have to get laid?"

"I've been too busy to even—"

"So busy the only potential opportunities are within your own organization, aren't I right? And if you were to do that, what happens to morale and chain of command?"

"Poof."

"Yup. I'm not quite as busy as you are, but my opportunities are severely limited. I can't stray outside the *family* for fear of assassination or other manipulation. If I play in my own pool I destroy my authority.

"We are the leaders of two of the most powerful organizations in the world. Neither of us is out to gain some type of advantage over the other. We've dealt honorably and fairly with one another. We both find the other attractive. It. Makes. Sense," Jamie said, punctuating every word.

Tony stood mute. He had no idea what to say.

"Goddamn it, do I need to write you instructions as well as draw you a picture? I want you to make love to me."

"Excuse me?" Augustine said, reentering the room at just the right time to see Tony's olive skin turn crimson.

* * *

"Welcome to KIROW Action News at Six. I'm Carl Merrithew."

"And I'm Elsa Abernathy."

"Headlining our news is the Metro cordon in the greater Seattle area. They purportedly have surrounded two suspected Green Action Militia terrorists. We go now to our reporter on location, Dennis McLaughlin.

"Dennis, what can you tell us about this breaking story?"

"Well, Elsa, the Seattle Metropolitan Police in conjunction with the Portland Metros have globed a sixteen block radius, fourteen stories high around the celebrated Oyster House Restaurant in downtown Olympia.

"The Metros were tipped off by a confidential informant that two Greenies would be involved in an attack on some high-level Corporate bigwigs dining at the landmark restaurant tonight.

"What we've been told by the Metropolitan Bureau of Information is that the two terrorists were intercepted and trapped within the famous eatery. Unfortunately, the pair have approximately ninety hostages and have threatened to blow them up unless their demands are met."

"Dennis, do you have any information on what those demands are?"

"The Metros won't release the demands of terrorists as it is against the Washington Revised Code Forty-Two dot Fifty-Six dot Four Twenty.

"They do say that they are negotiating at this time but that the Terrorist Negotiation Act of Twenty-Thirty does tie their hands somewhat."

"Can you tell us what is going on right now?"

"As I mentioned earlier, the Metros have actively cleared the area and are double-checking the perimeter as they negotiate. We've been held a full two hundred meters away from the scene.

"As you can see here in this footage taken just a few minutes ago, a Metropolitan officer was granted access to the Oyster House to negotiate.

"You can also see behind me there are officers both in casual and tactical positions around the entrance to the restaurant. I don't think they would be so casual if there were any immediate ... "

"BOOM!"

"Holy Jesus! Holy Jesus! The building just blew up. You can see the cloud of debris and smoke billowing outward. I count five policemen down. Ambulances are racing forward.

"I see flames licking out of the windows.

"I can hear screams in the building and on the streets nearby. There you can see a civilian with her leg cut from flying shrapnel."

"Can you tell what happened, Dennis?"

"I am not sure but it appears that the Greenies have detonated their incendiary device inside the Oyster House Restaurant. I see many people injured. Paramedics, fire crews, and police already on the scene are deploying to save as many as they can.

"I just watched three firefighters in environmental suits dash into the building to retrieve survivors."

"BOOOM!"

"Oh, my Holy God! Those fucking bastards just detonated another bomb, Elsa. All of the paramedics are now down. Firefighters are torn to bits and others have been flung dozens of meters. The carnage is horrific. The front of the building is now nothing more than a smoking maw. Flames are consuming everything down there, the people, the building ... everything."

* * *

Jamie drifted into wakefulness with a smile on her face for the first time in over two decades. Her head pillowed on his bicep. His other arm draped over her hip and held her spooned into him. She could feel the hairs on his chest tickling her back with every breath.

"Good morning," Tony rumbled behind her.

"Good morning to you, too," she said softly. "How did you know I was awake?"

"One of those skills I picked up last night, actually."

"How's that?"

"Watching you in the dressing table mirror. You are very expressive and I didn't want to miss any of it."

"Perv."

"Most of the time," Tony said, teasing her nipple.

She looked at her image in the offending surface and gave a tiny shriek. No eggbeater could have messed up her hair so thoroughly nor could her worst enemy mess up her makeup so badly.

Staying on his arm she rolled over to face him. "How is it that men look so good in the morning? I'm a fright and you look good enough to eat."

"So why do you think that you look a fright? Women underestimate the prurient value of the just-fucked look."

Jamie soaked in the warmth of his arms and chest. Her eyes

drifted closed. She could feel a need building in her but not an overwhelming or urgent one.

"Don't drift back to sleep. I'm hungry."

Craning her neck, she gently bit on one of his nipples.

"Hey."

"Just returning the favor."

"Doesn't have quite the same reaction with me."

"Oh, no? What's this I feel?"

"Morning stiffness," Tony said with a blush. "Happens with age."

Jamie gently caressed Tony's 'morning stiffness.' "Breakfast, huh? I feel slighted."

"If you don't stop that you are definitely NOT going to be slighted ... but I may waste away without nourishment. You have to keep your stud fueled."

Jamie went silent for a moment. The smile fell from her face and a tear leaked from her eye.

"Why are you crying? Did I do something wrong?"

Emotion exploded over her. The tears stuck in his chest hair as she tucked her face against him. She felt his arms wrap tighter around her, one hand actually stroking her hair. This just magnified the sensations.

One part of her mind smelled his sweat, felt the wet coarseness of his chest. She tasted the bare hint of salt as her tears dripped into her own mouth. She felt his hands running through her hair and his lips against her forehead. The practical part of her mind took a vacation— time disappearing as she reveled in the release. Finally she wrapped her arms around his waist, pulling herself tight against him.

"Thank you," she managed with frogs in her throat.

"For what? We enjoyed one another last night ... or at least I enjoyed myself."

"Tony, I can't tell you how much I needed what we did for one another."

"So why the waterworks?"

"Because you made me feel like a woman again for the first time in decades."

"Go peddle your wares elsewhere. I think I'm a decent enough lover, but please let's not turn me into some six-figure-a-night gigolo."

Jamie looked up into his steel-gray eyes. "It's true, Tony. I've paid for sex before, and I never buy anything but the best. You aren't Olympic lovemaking material, but what you are is warm and caring. You made me feel like for once I didn't have to worry about anything ... I could just be myself. And what I am right now is a very well-pleased woman." Jamie put her head back against his chest.

"Thank you for the backhand compliment, m'lady. So does this mean I get to be more than a one-night stand?"

"You bastard," she said in a voice almost like a little girl. She tucked in close, head down, pulling her arms up to her chest to be totally in his embrace. "You can have as many nights as you want." She just hoped beyond hope he wouldn't run away.

She felt him wrap her up tighter than before. He then placed another kiss on her forehead. "I would like many more mornings like this," he whispered in her ear.

"And nights?" she asked.

A stomach growled between them, interrupting the moment.

"Was that yours or mine?" Tony asked with a giggle.

* * *

The entirety of the Action Committee and selected other GAM members, all in formal attire, crowded the deck of the catamaran. Connie Powell scowled as she tugged at her ruched collar and kicked at the hem of her dress. She wasn't a dress girl and the heels, only 2 centimeters, had her teetering on the edge of toppling over. The Puget Sound had cooperated by being smooth as glass. A mild breeze kept the sails of the cat full and gave them a comfortable five knots of headway, preventing it from wallowing.

"Friends," Tony said at the prow of the ship, "we are here to honor our comrades, our friends, our brothers, and sisters who are no longer with us. Seven more of our brave comrades have been taken from us."

One of the women toward the back sniffled. Tony couldn't see who it was, but he expected more than one person to be sobbing before he was through. He could feel his own throat tightening up.

"Most of these people have been in our lives long enough to bond with a piece of our heart. Now that they are gone it feels like that piece has been ripped away." The vision from his eyes wavered as they filled with tears. He stopped and swallowed hard at the knot in his throat. "But what we sometimes forget is how much it works the other way. Our hearts didn't get ripped out, but rather their hearts stayed with ours.

"Our friends will always be with us. Oh, Frances will never again chastise me for rolling my wrist over when bowling. Narissa won't pull off a miracle with a previously unknown cache of weapons when we need it most. Bill won't tell me which way to hold the gun so I don't shoot myself. Jackson won't correct me when I mess up about orbital mechanics. Vijay won't make fun of our American accents. Jacob won't poke me in the butt to get me to keep climbing up the rock wall. Kendra won't try and give fashion advice.

"While none of them will be able to do these things ever again, they still live on within us. I can see their love etched in each and every one of our lives.

"I will not tell you of our friends' greatest accomplishments because you are here. The friendships they forged with each of us are their legacy. Every memory keeps them bound to earth. Each of their stories preserves their immortality with its telling.

"While I know it is hard not to mourn their passing, I also know that we are each richer for having known them.

"Remember them well."

Tony dropped Frances's bowling ball into the Sound with a splash. Morgan dropped Jacob's catcher's mitt into the sea. Over the side, representatives dropped key items from each of the lives taken from them.

Tony took the time to wipe his eyes on his sleeve before turning back around to face his team.

* * *

Andrew Massman picked up sealed cargo container six-alpha-delta-charlie-charlie-two-three-sixteen from Seattle's offload dock eighty-seven with instructions to deliver it to Paper-Lite Office in Yakima.

One of the dock's grav cranes lowered the slightly oversized container onto the bed of his truck. He checked the manifest number. Six anti-entropy locks later he fired up his aged Peterbilt and started the two-hour run.

Andrew loved sealed containers. His responsibilities were effectively zip. The Metros couldn't hassle him even if the load turned out to be Martian Red Dust. All he had to do was point at the manifest and the 'sealed' label.

What he didn't know was that his cargo would have seen him in Metros' hands despite the manifest.

*   *   *

"As the Green Action Militia seems to be the organization that hinges together all of our groups, I thank you for allowing to me to lead this unprecedented meeting tonight." Tony said from within the large, enclosed, copper-clad cargo container six-alpha-delta-charlie-charlie-two-three-sixteen.

Three representatives of the CorpGov sat around an abbreviated conference table, as did three from the GAM, the President of the United States, and the *Capa Famiglia* with two of her trusted lieutenants. Mr. Marks stood in attendance to Nanogate and the imposing Connie Powell stood at the President's left arm.

"I'm hopeful that after today we will all trust one another sufficiently to allow the CorpGov Council to run these meetings."

"We do not feel slighted or that our power is in any way lessened by your chairing this coalition meeting, Mr. Sammis," Nanogate demurred. "Everyone here has their own strengths and weaknesses."

"Agreed," claimed President Tipton.

"Be that as it may, I'd feel much more comfortable with the CorpGov in charge, as we all feel they should be … If that makes sense to anyone else."

"It does, but can we get on with things," Jamie said. "We have a very finite time for the ruse of this meeting place to work."

"OK, I think we all know why we are here," Tony continued. "We have been acting independently and not getting the most out of our forces. We've been doubling up on some actions and letting others be unmanned.

"We need to have unified actions if we are going to have any chance of defeating the Metros and maintaining the CorpGov in supremacy.

"Anyone want to fire the first shot?"

"I'm assuming you've all been informed about the recent bombings in Olympia, Washington." Augustine threw out onto the table.

"Yes, I have to state categorically that we had nothing to do with it," Tony leapt in.

"I can verify that," President Tipton said, leaning forward. "I still have access to a couple operatives within the Metros. The MPF set this up themselves. In the investigation that is to follow they will find the bodies of the two Green Action Militia folks remarkably intact—one is Jacob Guala and the other is Frances Fischer."

"That would be a very astute move," Royal Petrochem commented with admiration. "The GAM cannot be denying their participation. It would be *prima facie* evidence of their involvement."

"True," Augustine said. "What the Metros don't have calculated is the fact that the vast majority of the people, eighty-three percent as of this morning, don't believe a word that goes out on the news about the GAM."

"This might possibly be eroding those numbers."

"Possibly, but with our own information campaign on the net, we should not lose more than a point or two."

"Any more discussion?" Tony paused for a moment only. "Is there any action that we should take because of this?"

"I'd like our corporate propagandists to work with Augustine to craft the right message to put into the nets," BeringC Protein said.

"Done," Augustine assured them. "Just give me a percomm code and I'll make it happen."

"Good. That puts that one to bed. Next?

"As you may have heard, the Metros have managed to reopen the flow of money from the United States," President Tipton led off.

"Yes, we did," Nanogate agreed. "This will have a significant negative impact on our actions."

"How negative? I may have a way to cut off that funding once again, but the damage to the United States may be severe over the long term."

"The Metros get about one quarter of their funds from the federal government. If the Metros have these funds, we are fighting uphill. With those funds, the Metros have no reason to fear us in any way," BeringC said.

"I was afraid of that," President Tipton said. "Bear in mind that the repercussions of this idea haven't been fully analyzed. The plan would be that I go on solido and by Presidential Order command employers and citizens not to pay their withholding taxes."

Only the faint whistle of the air rushing past the outside skin of their shipping container broke the profound silence.

"Death and taxes," David Swift muttered.

"So how does this impact the Metros? Remember most money is electronic. Wouldn't the government continue to provide the funds?" asked Nanogate.

"Up to a point. The impact would not be felt immediately," Tipton admitted. "But within a month the national debt limit would be reached and the government would be constitutionally unable to provide more funding to any source. The only way that dam could be overcome would be to pass a new debt ceiling. Having worked on that in the past, I can assure you that unless they put a gun to the head of every legislator, there would be no increase. These days raising the debt ceiling is a good way to get recalled or at the very least not reelected."

"May I make a suggestion?" Jamie interjected.

"By all means," Susan Tipton replied.

"If you have concerns, why don't you meet with the financial experts of the corporations? If anyone can theorize what will happen by your plan, they would be able to simulate it."

"Oh, I'm sorry," President Tipton said. "I am not concerned with the immediate financial implications but rather what precedents this sets. Which individuals will call this an excuse to not pay taxes ever again? What President following me will use this as an excuse to raise taxes unilaterally without the consent of Congress?"

"That is a can of worms."

"And have you consulted with the Supreme Court?"

"Those doddering old fools wanted to debate whether even to talk to me. They are one of the cornerstones of our society; however, they live two hundred years or more in the past."

"In that case you might consult with the senior partner of Savitz, Schauer and Levinthal," Nanogate suggested. "I'm sure they have several members who are experts in constitutional precedents. Together you should be able to mitigate the issues you mention."

"Thank you, I'll make that call."

"We obviously can't force you to do anything, Ms. President," Tony said. "What we do here must be perceived by all of us to be a positive action."

"I do understand, Tony, but I feel that I don't have any option."

"Augustine, can you hack the US Treasury?"

"It's possible, but I see no way to sort Metro dollars from those earmarked for Joe and Josephine Smith. At best I could temporarily turn off the Metro's financial feed. We are talking about a week-long interruption at best at a high risk of lethal ice."

"I have to agree," Susan inserted. "I know for a fact that new security has been added to governmental nets, including some very deadly anti-intrusion active defenses. The poor bastard who hacked it first ended up in a mental hospital.

"No, I think I need to do this, it just isn't going to be pretty."

"So, Madam President, you are going to take this action, correct?" Tony asked. "I don't mean to say you are waffling but we need a definitive answer. We can plan around any choice, but the choice must be yours and it must be clear."

"I will speak to the American public and get them to see that their money is being used to bully them. I will do what I can to stop the flow of cash to the Metros by getting the USA's cash-flow to dry up."

"Excellent. I think I'd like to nominate BeringC as our propagandist. Everyone should work through her to get the right messages for all possible uses, including op ed, blog posts, whisper campaigns, posters, or even just straight news pieces we think we can slip past the Metros."

A general murmuring of approval followed the remark. BeringC nodded to Tony for his trust.

"Something I'd like to ask," David Swift jumped in. "Can we expect any help from other governments?"

"Unlikely. Most of them consider this a purely internal matter," President Tipton said shaking her head.

"Even with an attack on the CorpGov?"

"Yes, even so. Some of them haven't come to terms with an over-government yet, even though we've effectively had one for generations."

"Is there anything more, David?"

"No, just wondering if it had been considered."

"Don't worry, David. The only bad question is the one not asked," Tony assured him. Nanogate nodded with admiration.

"Do we have any future plans we need to discuss?"

"Many of them, if I may be so bold," Jamie said.

"*Capa*, you have the floor."

"Most of what you are talking about is defensive actions. We need to take the fight to the Metros. How do we do that?"

"Up until now we've been too worried about provoking an open conflict. I think we all are aware that war must come but we've emotionally avoided it, especially as we expect to lose," Tony admitted to a chorus of nods around the table.

"We've been thinking tactically rather than strategically," Nanogate admitted.

"So how do we change so we're at least a thorn in their paw?"

"The major thing that has us holding off has been because the Metros would be able to subvert the armed forces of the United States," Tony said. "It means our few exceptional guerrilla-style fighters would be overwhelmed."

"So the question still is how do we avoid such a one-sided war and still be aggressive against the Metros?" Jamie asked.

"May I ask an even more fundamental question? How do we win against the Metros? It looks like we originally planned on financial control, but that seems not to be viable."

"The basic ways to win any conflict are force, financial, pride, and intermediate goal," Augustine offered.

"Force vs. Force is a loss for us. We've appealed to pride and gotten bupkis," Tony expounded. "We either have to strangle them financially or as some of us talked about before, accept a win in the form of an intermediate goal—such as making it possible for the people of the US to fight back against the Metro police state after we are all dead or scattered."

"So we are fighting to lose?" Jamie asked.

"No, we are fighting to win," Tony said. "We can still win even in defeat, if we do the right things."

"Whoa! Win even in defeat? I don't fight to lose. I'm not the stuff of martyrs," Jamie exclaimed, her eyes flashing angrily.

"Bloody hell, woman, we never said anything about becoming martyrs. Worst case, we all emigrate to Mars. The Metros have no power there," David said with exasperation in his tone.

"And neither do I! Hey, I'm self-centered. Not to mention the fact that any *famiglia* isn't one person but rather a unit. If I voted to fight a losing battle, one of these brilliant men beside me," she said gesturing to her lieutenants, "would probably blow my brains out and pull out of this association."

"Hold on," Tony said forcefully. "We are not fighting to lose, but we aren't blind to the fact that we are fighting uphill. Losing is a distinct possibility. I think everyone needs to be clear on both of those facts." Tony didn't bark but he came close.

"Oh, I don't mind odds, I just want a chance," Jamie said, concluding her argument.

"Our primary winning strategy must be around choking off their finances, which is why the President's decision is so fortuitous," Nanogate interjected into the tense situation.

"So how can we take the fight to them strictly around finances?"

"Well, if we can't hack the US's treasury accounts, how about the Metros' banking system?"

"Most financial accounts are well protected by the EU Monetary System and the Metros have put a few more bits of ice in their stream. That being said, I'd be willing to lead a raid against it. No promises though, folks."

"Good. Augustine, that has a priority as the sooner we strike, the bigger piece we may be able to snatch."

"Yassir, Bossman."

"What about attacks on protected operations? That's how the Koreans have tried to move in on us in the past," offered Jamie. "The police take payments to protect businesses. We all know the Metros won't pay for a failure of their security, but would companies continue to pay if they find the Metros' protection consistently bad?"

"Yeah, and if the police become too heavy-handed with those that leave the security of their arms, the Metros would be responsible for actively driving them even further away," David agreed eagerly.

"If the Metros showed themselves not as righteous defenders but rather ruthless thugs, it would make a huge impact in driving those undecided people into our camp. A little solido work on this would go a long way," BeringC jumped in.

"Jamie, what do you think? If we got you a list of targets, do you think you could find ways to be obnoxious?" Tony asked.

"Honey," she said winking, "I excel at obnoxious."

Tony's eyebrow raised as he returned Jamie's look. "There have to be some other ideas. How do we get into the Metros' pocketbook?"

"How about riots?"

"That would be being a good question," Royal Petrochem said. "The Metros would be spending much time and resources against such exceptional activity."

"Remember that our responsibility is to the people's welfare. We don't want to have the Metros mowing them down in job lots," Nanogate objected.

"I don't think anyone was thinking that," Jamie explained. "I think it is like the rest of the GAM tactics—strike, get a reaction, fade away."

"We could reintroduce flash mobs!" said Jowan Margh, Jamie's *consigliore*.

"Remember, the early percomms were the downfall of the flash mob."

"Well, we could offer free removal of embedded percomms and provide old style removable ones," Jowan continued.

"He may be onto something. People could find themselves out of the surveillance systems to do many things they might not otherwise do," David agreed.

"Jowan, you willing to accept the responsibility to run with that one?" Tony asked.

The gaunt man with dark, sunken eyes didn't even hide his look to Jamie for approval. She nodded.

"I'm your man."

"Good. If you need any help, I'm sure David is willing to lend a hand."

Mr. Marks leaned down and whispered in Nanogate's ear.

"My companion, nominally here for his physical prowess, has an exceptional idea. Do you wish to present it, Mr. Marks?"

"No need, sir. You are the CorpGov leader ... so lead."

"Very well. We should put a simulation model together of the fiscal structure of the Metros. We have exceptional computer modelers, but I've heard more than once of Grandma Ice's speed and prowess in this area."

"I'll try not to blush. I do have a framework that we can start with that will speed things along."

"Very good. Such a model may show other ways to get into their boodle bag," Tony offered. "Augustine, you are in charge. I want input from the originator, Mr. Marks, on this."

"Nanogate, if you would be so kind as to give me contact information for your lead simulations expert, I'll try very hard not to stomp on his toes."

"Coming to your percomm address, Ms. Augustine."

"Moving on, I have an idea," Tony offered. "How about vandalizing Metro property? Like graffiti on Metro stations or shorted-out patrol vehicles? Some of that we can have done by untrained folks off the street. My team, perhaps augmented, could go after something more aggressive like cutting power cables, blowing up communications lasers and the like."

"I don't see any reason not to encourage that activity," Nanogate said.

"I'm sure there are a million more ideas. We should share them with each other as they occur to us and waste no more time in this meeting on it. I nominate Nanogate to oversee each of the ideas and parse them out if they have validity."

Once again Tony received general approval.

"I think we should take some time to examine the likelihood that we will be in an actual shooting war, as distasteful as it is to some," he said with a glare to Jamie.

"We've already talked about turning off weapons' licenses," Nanogate said. "We've investigated this, and it is extremely viable. Moreover, we've added an additional failsafe. If we wish, we can destroy the ability to generate a license for any given weapons platform, making all of those permanently inert."

"Excellent. What about the discussion of delaying or even stopping production?"

Nanogate actually smiled as he turned to President Tipton. "I'm sorry, Madam President, but the deliverables on a number of our weapons contracts will be delayed. In fact some may not be delivered at all. I've had to discipline a number of my people for shipping database irregularities," Nanogate offered in a rare bit of levity.

"I'll inform my people." All eyes dropped onto Susan before she could continue in her own jest, "—when I get around to it."

"One other thing," Nanogate said as Tony opened his mouth to speak. "We've initiated a recall on some seriously defective weapons. And did you know our recent military grav units had a flaw in their design? We've had to issue an Airworthiness Directive through the FAA, grounding all the applicable units."

"That's low, but brilliant," Susan said from the other side of the table.

"A great start on the supply side," Tony said. "Jamie, would you put the word out on the street that we'll purchase any military grade hardware? We're specifically looking for people stealing hardware from the combined armed forces. Even if it isn't something we can use, anything we take out of their hands is something they don't have to shoot at us."

"Understood and agreed. Who's going to underwrite the purchases?"

Tony looked at Nanogate. "You are the one with the deep pockets. I'm willing to fund as much as we can ourselves, but I think you are better able to support the cost."

"I'm not trying in any case to be stingy, but we will have to discuss how much financial burden we can bear. We just aren't completely fiscally sound yet after the GAM actions against us in recent past."

"I won't say I'm sorry," Tony said, "But I will say I wish things were better for us now."

"No, I've come to terms with the changes, Mr. Sammis. I think the GAM actions were necessary and seriously overdue. I just haven't come to like it yet, nor am I sure that I'm going to live through it."

Tony ignored the defeatist attitude. "My team, being the most militant of our groups, will look over possible means of destroying equipment in place. Fortunately, this will be focused against the military. The Metros may not even realize the extent of the threat. If I could have Mr. Marks to confer with, I'd appreciate it."

"Agreed," Nanogate said. "I have really only one other item on this topic—kinetic bombardment satellites."

"They are controlled by each government," the President said. "The US ones cannot fire unless I give the command."

"Not exactly," Nanogate corrected. "In my youth I was part of the team for the basic designs. While the President is correct that the intent is only to use them once authorization is received from the President, each of the devices are controlled by two very exceptional men who must unanimously agree to deploy. They are rigorously trained to only accept the authorization of the President as a determinant of when to fire.

"What if those men were replaced by someone who instead would listen to the good Commissioner Krylov."

"Holy crap," exclaimed David.

"While I believe something blasphemous rather than holy would be appropriate, I agree with the young, red-haired gentleman," Augustine said fingering the cross on her necklace.

"They could hold the entire population hostage," the President said.

"Or bombard centers of resistance," Tony said grimly.

"We need to find a way to neutralize those babies."

"I'd say that was an understatement," BeringC said.

"Anyone got suggestions?"

"Don't stand where they're dropped?" Connie remarked from behind the President.

"Anyone have any positive suggestions?" Tony asked with a grin.

"Well, again, funnel them through Nanogate. He will be our gatekeeper for all of our ideas.

"Anything else before we adjourn?" No one said anything. In that case anyone up for some cards while we wait to be delivered?"

*   *   *

"We interrupt your standard solidocast to bring you this breaking news. An explosive device has been detonated in Tacoma, Washington. We have Trent Bookman on the scene. Trent, what can you tell us."

The scene shifted to a smartly dressed, blond newscaster standing in front of the blackened maw of what had once been a building. Sporadic fires punctuated the darkened structure. "Thank you, Kristof. At exactly seven-fifteen this evening a bomb exploded within the lobby of what had been the Tacoma Metroplex."

The view panned to show a charred popcorn maker upside down in the street. A solido projector, with a gaping hole torn in its side, lay atop a smoldering cinema seat. Only when the image panned back to show a pair of firemen spraying water on the remaining blazes did the enormity of the 40-meter crater become real. The debris and the flattened, charred walls belied that the scene had ever been a building.

"The blast ripped through fifteen of the thirty theatres. The rapidly spreading fire consumed the rest of the business with millions of dollars in damages to the building and infrastructure around it."

"Were there any injuries, Trent?"

"I'm afraid so. We are not allowed to give out any of the names as they are pending notification of next of kin. Only two people made it out alive, a pair of young women who were in the bathroom at the time of the explosion.

"The Metros are sifting the cooling rubble now, looking for additional survivors and identification on the victims of this atrocity."

"Is there any indication of the cause?"

"Yes, Dennis. I've been told by three different firefighters and a Metro officer that the fire was arson. They already have proof. Moreover, one of our sources has indicated that it is the same bomb style as was used in the Olympia Massacre."

"So the Greenies did this?"

"Too early for us to speculate, but I've been led to believe that the investigation is already moving in that direction."

"Isn't this the fifth bombing attributed to them in as few days?"

"Well, we kn—"

All solido screens went to the image of tightly-packed, gray globules of static. Just as quickly as it fuzzed, the image cleared to the infamous blue podium in front of the seal of the President of the United States.

"Ladies and gentlemen, I bring you the President of the United States."

Susan Tipton walked in behind the mic in a severe, gray, skirt-suit that showed off her figure while still being totally professional.

"Good evening. I apologize for interrupting your evening solidocast, but there are those who don't want me to be heard. Let me start by saying that the Green Action Militia had nothing to do with the bombings you've been hearing about. We have no evidence to point a finger, but we can direct it away from innocent parties.

"But that is not what I'm here to speak about. I'm here to talk about taxes. You've all heard the old saw that the only two constants in life are death and taxes.

"I'd like to reduce that by one. Effective immediately, by Executive Order 87443 signed by me not five minutes ago, all federal income tax withholding will stop. All federal tax rates are brought to zero percent.

"No, this is not a joke. I want no more of your hard-earned dollars to roll into the government coffers. This is a very necessary counter to the illegal acts performed by the Metropolitan Police Forces around our country. This will deprive them of the income they require.

"I want to emphasize that this is a temporary measure. Taxes will return to their normal state after this crisis is over. Until then, enjoy yourselves!"

* * *

"Fucking whore!" Krylov growled.

Standing at the front of the room, Reza felt relieved that the large Russian didn't scream or throw something. He stayed quiet to reduce the chance that the Commissioner would pick him as a target. The rest of Krylov's panel of subordinates did the same. As the lowest rank in the room, Reza felt extremely expendable.

"How can we respond? I want something dramatic."

No one offered anything.

"Are you all MUTE?!"

"No, sir, but we can't think of anything," Hardy said. "We don't know where she is!"

"Yes, sir, and if we attack the government in any way we lose what support we have. Right now we still look good against the games that the Axis of Evil is playing. The moment we step into that arena we lose the moral high ground," Reza said diving into the snake pit.

"So you are telling me we can't do anything?"

"No, sir. We just can't come up with anything really splashy off the top of our heads. We could put out a warrant for her arrest, but a federal court would immediately vacate the warrant."

The look on the Commissioner's face didn't seem to be easing.

Reza continued. "We can start a petition to get her recalled and lobbying efforts to get her impeached. But I think her support will easily weather either of those tactics. In fact if we throw too much mud it will make a martyr of her and splash back on us.

"We will continue our efforts to locate her. Unfortunately, the GAM is a bit too cagey about her location and where/when she meets people. If we do manage to get a line on her it will only be for a brief moment. We will need predefined orders for that eventuality."

"Kill her," Krylov said with no hesitation or remorse.

"Excuse me, sir?" asked Major Broadsky. "Did you say 'kill her?'"

"Yes. I'm not beating around the bush. We'll pin it on the Greenies."

It was the silence that made or broke careers. Agree and succeed and get promoted. Say no and you worked percomm enforcement in Barrow, Alaska.

"Yes, sir," Reza said firmly. In for a penny, in for a pound.

"What else can we do?"

"Well, as the President is working with the GAM then the more mud we smear on the GAM the worse it gets for her."

"So we continue the bombing campaign?"

"Yes, sir."

*   *   *

"You are one freaky chick," patrolman Marc Greene said, lifting Christine's white satin mini-dress over her head. The alcohol on his breath nearly knocked her over. His partner, Jameel Zain, unbuckled her boots with fumbling fingers.

"I just like a lot. Two is better than one, isn't it?" she said, seductively tracing a finger across her chest.

"Sister, you are going to get a lot more than a lot," Jameel said. He paused and screwed up his brow to figure out what he said wrong. He shrugged. From his crouching position he pulled hard on her boot. Its sudden release landed him over on his ass.

"Oh, baby, are you all right," Christine cooed.

"Yes, 'm fine."

Christine stood in just white lace panties, stockings and one boot. Marc ogled her as he tried to take off his shirt and his pants at the same time.

"Sorry we don't have more time, boys," Christine said bending over and giving Mark a close-up view of her shapely ass. "I'd love to stay but I've got another date."

Christine drew out a 15 cm hook knife from her left boot, slashing Jameel's throat on the upstroke. The dying Metro hissed and croaked through the slit as he fell. Marc, his face still tangled in his shirt didn't even see the bloody blade. The hook came up underneath his sternum, snapping the xiphoid process. Christine flipped her wrist, severing the hepatic artery and the portal vein.

Marc started to scream, but only got out one syllable's worth before Christine shoved her knife through his shirt, severing his voice box.

"Ohhhhh! Daaaaddy!" Christine cried out as her own climax shook her so hard she collapsed to her knees.

*   *   *

"Have you ever been involved in a robbery?" Jowan Margh asked as he checked his equipment in the back of the armored lift. Four other individuals checked their own combat gear. Jowan's own lean form sported video disruptors on his shoulders. His ablative body armor made him look like a metal porcupine. At his waist were a police baton with the stun prod, a shotgun sawed down to a 30 cm barrel and an 11 mm automatic pistol.

"No, can't say that I've had that pleasure," David said, checking to make sure his own weapon was on an empty chamber. "I've been on any number of raids, search and destroy, and physical hacks, but none that were outright robbery."

"Well, it is close to what you have done but there are differences.

"First of all, we have to make off with the loot or there is no impact."

"Second, we don't want to be identified. I know that wasn't a big thing for you in the past but it is here. Jamie is going to offer her services to these fine upstanding citizens in the future. We don't want them to know that she or even the GAM were behind the events that made the Metros look bad."

"Got it," David said pulling the black hood of his body-stocking over his face.

"Let me do the talking. I have the voice synthesizer."

"Got it. Call off when ready."

"One."

"Two."

"Three," David answered in turn.

"Four."

"This is a smash and grab. I play overwatch. You four are to hit the display cases. Remember to use your batons. Leave cases eight, eleven and fourteen intact because of the active defenses.

"We ignore the vault as the Metros can respond before we can get in with our current equipment. Any questions?"

No one said a word.

"Out the door in ten, nine, eight, seven ... one."

As David hit the platform, he rolled with the grace a professional gymnast would have appreciated. Standing up he and his four partners in crime marched straight at the door labeled "Tiffany and Co.," just the first on a long list still paying the Metros.

*   *   *

"Boys, the Commissioner says we are sending a message this time. These impromptu riots have to stop. We have new rules of engagement," Sergeant Tolbert said from his command chair.

The rest of his team made a soft cheer as they tightened armor straps and checked one another's equipment.

"We've been given the right to use any and all non-lethal means to apprehend and punish the rioters. Those with neural agitators, use them. I want these bastards flat on the ground with no hope of resisting or running.

"We are one of six platoons working this disturbance so be careful with your shots 'cause there are friendlies out there.

"We will be dropping on all sides of the riot so you should be able to round up the whole job lot of them."

"Sarge, what if we are fired upon?"

"As always, we have the right to defend ourselves. If lethal force is used against us, the gloves come off completely, and I don't want a single rioter left alive.

"Questions?"

"Sarge, what about Green, Zain and Kettle?"

"They were killed by someone who got them to willingly take off their clothes. You want to join them, Sterling?"

"No, Sarge."

"Then I suggest you either keep your dick in your pants or only play patty-cake with those you know."

"But do we have any more information?"

"Fuck it, Sterling, you know as much as the rest of us. That bitch from the GAM did Green and Zain in their flat and then somehow travelled thirteen kilometers where she climbed into bed with Kettle and did him with the same bloody knife.

"Not only that, she left the panties soaked in Green and Zain's blood at the second scene.

"Now concentrate, you apes. I know you are armored but you and I both know there are ways to penetrate a patrolman's armor. And I can guarantee you that some of them are out there in the crowd today. So settle down and focus. Safety first.

"Drop in five. Get some for me!"

*   *   *

Their appointment to interview the new Chairman of the CorpGov wasn't until two p.m. so Rick Smith and his cameraman Leonard Grossman enjoyed their complimentary continental breakfast in peace. A stiff north breeze carried the smell and chill of the Puget Sound onto their partially baffled balcony. The view of the Sound from the Grand Whidbey Island Hotel made them feel like sailors on a tall ship.

"This is one of the easiest assignments we've been sent on in a while," Leonard commented as he stuffed the remaining corner of a flakey croissant into his mouth.

"Providing the police don't pick us up and question us. Providing the Greenies really are on our side and don't want to blow us up. And also providing the studio will allow our interview any air time at all."

"I thought I was the pessimist."

"I'm a journalist. Of course I'm a pessimist. When was the last time we saw the good side of life. We spend our time trying to catch the horrible things happening. If they are bad enough we might get the Pulitzer."

"So you don't think this is a good assignment?"

"Oh, I think—" Rick was interrupted by the unmistakable sound of automatic weapons. A crash of something fragile and fairly large followed closely.

"FLASH MOB!" the pair heard from thousands of voices.

Rick jumped to the balcony's rail and scanned.

Leonard, the consummate cameraman, brought his solidograph, which never left his side, up to his shoulder.

"There," Rick said, pointing down six levels and a hundred meters to the east. The garish signage proclaimed it the Langley Artist Mall. The open, multilevel, cut-away style, popular forty years ago, gave them a front row seat to thousands, maybe tens of thousands, of people and their illegal assembly. The throng destroyed anything they could touch. If it could be lifted, they threw it over the edge. If it could be smashed, metal bars, feet and even fists reduced it to tiny splinters. Several hundred actually had taken hold of one of the smaller buildings in the center of the mall proper and in rocking it back and forth, loosened it from its foundation. Bits of plaster and faux stucco rained down as it deformed more and more, eventually collapsing over onto several of the rioters. A roar of triumph carried above the other random destruction.

"You know this story won't see airtime," Leonard said, catching nearly every act. "The Metros will destroy this before the studio even sees it."

"So what?" Rick said scowling at his cameraman.

"We're going to waste our time."

"Goddamn it all, but I'm tired of not doing my job. I'm a journalist, not a Metro propagandist."

"Blah, blah. I know. But I want to live, Mr. Idealist."

"Let's get the story first and then worry about what we are going to do with it. We can't push it live. I'll voice over after it's done."

"Got it." Leonard, nearly at the top of his profession, kept the main aperture focused on the general action but used his alternative view to zoom in on specific groups. Even Rick, hardened from some of the brush wars he'd reported on, gasped when he saw the individuals. These rioters weren't college students, drunk middle-aged men, or even angry oldsters not given their pension raises. These were entire families. Leonard's alternate view showed a family of five, two mothers encouraging their nine and seven year olds to break things, all while one of them carried an infant in a baby-sling against her chest.

"Babies at a riot? This is dynamite."

Leonard scanned over to show a father helping his two boys carry an uprooted landscaping tree. They tossed it over the edge to plummet hundreds of meters to ground level below. Even ceramcrete couldn't withstand that abuse. Two men and a preteen girl kicked and bludgeoned to dislodge a merchandise counter. The proprietor came out yelling abuse at the trio. The two men just shrugged at the irate man before taking the girl by the hand to find another target.

"Do you see anywhere that they are hurting people?"

"Nope."

"SEVEN MINUTES! SCATTER!" came a magnified voice across the gulf.

The destruction ended as if the voice had thrown a switch. The mob began to melt. Rivulets of people streamed out each available exit.

"Metros," Rick said, as seven troop carriers descended and disgorged police officers out their bellies. "You know they aren't going to be happy about being watched. LADIR scan will pick us out if we don't move back."

"Clean up the table," Leonard said as he unlimbered the peach-pit-sized optics from his solidograph. He flung them out into the void. On their miniature lift platform they made a much smaller target.

With their breakfast removed, even if the optics were tagged by the Metros, they didn't point to the pair who now remained covert inside their hotel room. The relayed image wasn't as clear or stable as if controlled directly by his cameraman but safety spoke for itself.

The police landed in good order before a third of the mob could disappear. Rick whispered a silent prayer as the riot troops employed the electric lightning of neural agitators. Where the violet pulses landed, a human being would crash to the ground writhing in agony. The aftereffects of NAs could sometimes last weeks. A phalanx of police advanced steadily behind their interlocked trans-steel shields and their shock batons on 2-meter riot poles. Wherever the batons struck someone would cry out. As the shielded police inexorably advanced over those who couldn't get out of their way, a second wave of police dealt with those rioters that were either down or giving up.

Leonard's solidograph caught the woman with the baby sling surrendering. With no weapons she knelt on the ground with her hands up. The reporters watched as two police officers, from behind, took full swings of their batons at her unprotected head and back. Blood fountained after the first strike. The woman fell forward. The officers didn't stop but continued to beat on her as she rolled up into a fetal position to protect her child. Rick counted at least twenty strikes before she stopped moving and the police bothered to cuff her.

The semicircle of armored troops continued to close on the perpetrators, firing more bolts of electric agony at random. The mass of people continued to tighten as they crowded precariously against the very edge of the platform that they'd cast off so many of the items from during their riot.

An NA pulse hit a man near the precipice. He jerked hard and lost his balance. Still in agony he grabbed an edge of the platform as he fell. He managed to keep one arm and elbow on the platform. Leonard's optics picked up the twisted agony that showed in his face as he fought to save his own life. He leveraged himself up, but the crowd tightened in on his empty position. Feet pushed his elbow from the ledge. It didn't take long for a foot to trample his hands. Even from the room they heard the man's scream as he fell.

It took another minute for the crowd to become docile behind the nearly solid wall of shields and spears. Only then did pairs of police yank the nearest person from the crowd for processing.

The disposition took over three hours as nine hundred twenty-four perps required attention. Those unfortunate enough to be the first few pulled took the brunt of the Metros collective ire.

The procedure, while having minor variations and flourishes, started with a handful of baton blows to get the individual on the ground. If after a dozen or so power-assisted kicks the person failed to move, they were cuffed and dragged to some holding pen. If the victim showed any sign of consciousness after the assault, he would be subject to repeated bludgeons from riot poles swung like swords. More than once they heard a sharp crack of a bone snapping followed by a scream of agony.

In one case, Leonard recorded a Metro slamming the bottom edge of his riot shield down as a guillotine across a suspect's throat.

A young girl, no more than five, tried to sprint through an opening in the shield wall before she could be abused. A trooper grabbed her by her hair. Continuing her motion he swung her around in a circle and finally flung her 4 meters like an Olympic hammer toss. The Metro who found her at his feet snapped his truncheon in an arc that ended with the girl's face exploding in a fountain of blood. The three cops that continued the abuse blocked most of the reporters' view, but what they eventually hauled off didn't much resemble a human any longer.

Late in the queue the police seemed to have lost their energy and vitriol, settling for enough baton swings to cow the victim before cuffing them.

*   *   *

"I'm going to start with some negative information," Reza said to open the morning briefing. "We have now lost protection contracts with eighty of our most profitable clients including, if you will excuse the pun, the crown jewel, Tiffany.

"We were informed in a very businesslike manner that they would prefer to continue our business arrangements but our inability to stop robberies or recover stolen goods has caused their insurance carrier to remove their discount for cooperation with us. As a result it is no longer financially viable to pay our fees. They mentioned obliquely hiring private enforcers.

"This will continue to be a downward trend. We are expecting seventeen more cancellations tomorrow and another hundred before the week is out.

"While this is painful, it is not a mortal wound."

"Is there anything we can do about it?" Krylov asked in a carefully controlled tone.

"At this time, no, sir. I believe the companies will come around when we have significant gains against the combined CorpGov alliance. Until then we can expect continued defections, but they will be pinpricks compared to what we lost today."

"Well then, we are informed. Please continue, Lieutenant."

"I'd like to report a success against the demonstrations," Reza said with a smile. "We were able to take into custody eleven hundred three of the Artist Rioters and managed to limit the death toll to four. All of those apprehended will take away some physical object lesson of the stupidity of challenging our police and laws.

"As an added bonus, our scans showed no media caught the event so we won't even have to deal with that potential backlash."

"What is our plan for these reprobates?" Krylov said, managing to keep from smiling too predatorily.

"Well, that depends on you, sir."

"How is that?"

"We've been approached by representatives of the Attorney General of the United States as to what changes we'd like to see in the criminal judicial system."

Krylov clapped like a school child. "Outstanding! It's finally coming around."

"Getting back to our prisoners, we can charge them as normal. Under the current laws they would get off with a large fine and minor mental adjustment."

"We should strengthen that some, don't you think?" Captain Hardy interjected.

"How about confiscation of their property and boxing?" Captain James Lennart said with a smile. "We could profit doubly by their indentures."

"An excellent—"

"Excuse me, sir," a secretary said to Reza just inside the door. "I have someone that urgently needs to see the Commissioner."

Through the doorway they could see a middle-aged vet standing at parade rest.

"Send him in, Alec," Krylov said. "My door is open to those who need to speak to me."

The man entered with trousers ironed so flat they looked like they were carved out of plastic. The shine on his shoes belied their black color. His short gray hair just barely hid the leather brown of his skin beneath it. The man's face was hard and didn't smile.

"Commissioner Krylov?"

"Yes?"

"My name is Maxwell Deon. I identify myself as a citizen of over eighteen years of age. You are served with a subpoena to appear in the Civil Court of Portland as respondent to one hundred fourteen civil cases against you."

The Commissioner just sat there with his mouth open. His eyes did reflect his inner fire as they came back to life first. Like a predator, they narrowed and focused only on the piece of meat in front of him.

"So who did you piss off to get this duty, son?"

"First of all, you bloated, ignorant, rockfish excrement, I'm not your son. Second I didn't make anyone angry—I won the lottery. We had thousands vying to be the one picked to deliver this message."

"I hope your will is in order." The simple statement would have had most men groveling before this powerful despot.

Command Sergeant Major (ret) Maxwell Deon didn't even change out of his parade rest stance. "Commissioner, I've seen eighteen years of combat in two different conflicts and spent four years as a prisoner of war. If you think you can intimidate me, you are in for a surprise. Besides, were I to die now I'd roam Purgatory with a smile, having seen your face as I served you.

"But I have further work to do. It seems you have saved me some time with the exceptional attendance to your staff meeting, Commissioner.

"Captain Hardy. My name is Maxwell Deon. I identify myself as a citizen of over eighteen years of age. You are served with a subpoena to appear in the Civil Court of Portland as respondent—"

*   *   *

The surroundings didn't quite live up to Rick's impression of the prestige of the Chairman of the CorpGov. A tall man with bronze skin and the yellow tights of a bodyguard escorted him and his cameraman through the chill and damp of the third-floor ruins.

The once dehumanizing work cubicles were now nothing more

than metal skeletons with tatters of fabric-flesh dangling from their bones. Even many of the frames had been beaten and bent into obscene shapes. Patches of mold obscured gang tags that were out of date for more birthdays than Rick had seen. Everything that could be shattered had been. The ceramcrete walls had holes chiseled in them at random, exposing only a lattice of carbon-nanotube mesh under the weight tension of the entire building. Dutifully, Leonard captured the images, boring and typical as they were of the lower levels of their city.

"The Chairman will meet you in there," their guide directed.

An oasis of warmth and hospitality awaited them in the huge room. A cheery fire burned in a marble fireplace, providing the reddish-yellow illumination for the room. Rick heard his cameraman curse at the randomly changing light levels.

A gently used sofa, and three armchairs formed a cozy meeting area around a coffee table on a remarkably fine area rug.

One of the overstuffed chairs held the man the entire system still was learning ruled them day in and day out, the Chairman of the CorpGov. His face, as the CEO of Nanogate and during his rise to that exalted position, had been pictured all over the net for decades. As Nanogate stood to welcome him it surprised Rick that the man didn't stand 2.5 meters tall and carry a broadsword like Conan, or maybe the gigantic Samurai of the cult classic *The Wolverine*. Instead, Nanogate seemed rather diminutive at 170 cm and maybe 82 kilos.

Rick barely noted the older woman with short white hair, an obvious secretary with her network jacks, sitting in a straight-back chair behind her boss. Leonard didn't bother to even pan her direction.

"It is wonderful to meet you, Mr. Smith and Mr. Grossman. Can I offer you a seat?"

"Thank you, Chairman Nanogate. Or is there some other form of address you would prefer?" Rick asked as he sat down on the couch opposite. Leonard didn't sit but rather sidled sideways so he could keep the camera on the Chairman. He'd captured enough of the room that they could replicate it in the studio with close-ups of Rick at a later time.

"Chairman or just Nanogate is fine," he said as he sat. "I don't think our new government has enough longevity to insist on any formalities."

"Thank you, Chairman."

"So I've agreed to this interview with no topic restrictions so that together we can give our public a face of our new government and an idea of what to expect."

"Thank you, sir. I'm eager to begin our discussions, but before we do get there, I'd like to ask a favor."

"And what else might you like me to do for you?"

"I'm sorry for being presumptive, sir. My cameraman and I caught something on solido that won't be seen by the public unless you can use your connections to override the Metros' censorship."

"I guess that would depend on what it is," Nanogate responded. Rick had made his way through eight years of college by parting optimists from their money by playing draw poker. He'd read the faces of the best politicos and liars in interviews for more than a double decade. Even with those skills he couldn't get a datum off of Nanogate's face.

"We witnessed and recorded a riot in the Langley Artist Mall on Whidbey Island. But the important part we captured was the Metro brutality in their response."

"Looks like you owe me a buck, Nanogate," said the secretary as she stood up and walked over to plop down into one of the guest chairs. The woman propped her feet up on the coffee table.

"You definitely are cheeky," Nanogate said. "I thought you were supposed to be humble as a nun."

"First off, I was never a nun. I was a novitiate. And second it was the hardest thing I had to deal with.

"Now pay up."

Nanogate pulled a plastic dollar coin out of his waistcoat and handed it over to the woman.

Rick shook his head. Something significant just happened, and for the first time in many, many interviews, Rick wasn't in control of the surprise. Taking a closer look at the older woman he noticed her silver retinal-covers and the professional grade of her neural interfaces. The woman was a net jock.

"So, Mr. Smith, I want to apologize to you. We've used you," Nanogate offered.

"Excuse me?"

"We set up this entire thing so that you would capture the riot. We agreed to your studio's request for an interview that we'd earlier turned down. We made sure you got that specific room with that specific view of where our flash mob would take place."

Rick started to catch on. "So how did you know there was going to be some ugliness by the Metros?"

"We've been taunting them so we anticipated our 'shining protectors' getting ugly. Adding to that, there are always laggards that don't quite clear the field before the Metros arrive."

"So you played us. Why should we give you our footage now?"

The woman laughed. "Why do you think we don't have it already?"

Another bit fell into place for Rick. "Grandma Ice?"

"That's right."

Rick looked at his solidographer.

"I show that it hasn't been touched," Leonard said after a quick check of his files.

"Gents, a three-year-old could have hacked your security," Augustine said.

"But we didn't bring this up to taunt you, gentleman," Nanogate soothed. "The footage you captured would be much more powerful with your commentary, Mr. Smith. We want your help, not to cause you pain by crowing.

"We wanted you specifically to be the person to see this. We know your reputation as an honest reporter. We wanted you to see for yourself the depths that the Metropolitan Police are willing to go in order to secure their objectives.

"We want you to do the commentary, any commentary you like. We will make sure it gets into the hands of the people."

Augustine added, "Yes, maybe not through normal channels but the people will see it, unedited, and uncensored."

Rick thought about it for about ten seconds. The CorpGov and their allies could have used their feed without saying a word. They'd given him the opportunity to witness something no one had yet caught on solido.

The difference between the two sides couldn't have been clearer to him if they'd been painted across the sky in neon—censorship and abuse vs. openness and fair play. He looked at Leonard who nodded subtly.

"I still get my interview?"

Augustine laughed.

"Of course you do, Mr. Smith," Nanogate said smiling. "The same rules apply."

* * *

Patrons in formal gowns and designer suits crowded Stanley and Seafort's, one of the Pacific Northwest's landmarks. While not planned, Tony's maroon suit was three shades darker than his date's chiffon gown in cherry.

The bay window across the front gave a view through the height-limited skyline of Tacoma to the lights twinkling off the Puget Sound and the crowded mooring of tens of thousands of houseboats. Only the noise shield around each table kept the dinner intimate. The 2005 Domaine Stirn Cuvée Prestige Sigolsheim with its honeysuckle scent complimented Tony's goat cheese and mushroom ravioli.

"Excellent wine choice," Tony approved, dabbing the corner of his mouth with a linen napkin.

"Thank you."

"I'm not much of a wine person. I can't even tell you why they go so well together."

"Despite two years of wine classes, I never learned either," Jamie admitted. "Normally my *sommelier* keeps me from messing up too badly. She gave me a mental reference sheet if I found myself out of range of her support."

"Ah, so you cheated," Tony teased.

"Yeah, I guess."

"I don't suppose you could have had a cheat sheet on how to work me."

Jamie gave a low, sultry chuckle. "No," she said, taking the opportunity, under the table, to run her hand over his knee and up his thigh.

In spite of it being hidden, Tony started. He quickly deflected her hand from its target.

"Jumpy, jumpy."

"Stop that. We have work to do," Tony said with a very slight frown.

"Oh, I know. That is part of what is getting me excited."

A decorative young woman, on the arm of a man whose musculature was augmented beyond absurdity, parted Tony and Jamie's sound curtain excitedly.

"Are you him?"

Tony's face went slack. He had no clue what was up. "Excuse me?"

"Are you him. Are you Tony Sammis, leader of the GAM?"

"No," he said flatly.

"I told you, Marvin," she said punching her date in the arm. "I told you it was him."

"Can I get your autograph? Please!"

"I'm not Tony Sammis."

"Yes, you are. See here?" she said, displaying a solido image of Tony from the *Daily Tattletale* under the brash headline, "Sinner or Saint?"

"You're kidding, right?" Tony hoped.

"No, really. The girls will go ecraze if I can get your autograph. Please!"

"I guess so. I don't have a pen."

"I got one," the girl said, fishing into her purse. She held out a marker.

"I need something to sign," Tony said, his voice low, wishing this would all go away.

Without missing a beat, the girl undid her bodice to expose two ample, tanned breasts barely held in a shelf bra. "Right here," she said, shoving them toward his face.

Tony rolled his eyes. He conservatively scribbled his signature on her right shoulder, without having touched her flesh at all.

"I got it!" she squealed as she unnecessarily pointed it out to her boyfriend. "Thank you so much. We are big fans! Keep up the fight."

The muscled man put his hand over the girl's mouth and held a single finger up to his mouth. "Shhhh. It's time to go home." He shot a look at Tony that expressed how sorry he was without a single word. Somehow he kept the girl quiet as he led her out of the restaurant.

"So much for the anonymity of an international terrorist," Tony said with a deep breath. "Are you all right?"

Jamie glared.

"What's wrong?"

"'What's wrong?' he asks. I don't believe you signed that floozy's chest. Why didn't you just autograph her panties while you were at it? Maybe give her an injection of your DNA?"

"Oh, Christ. Honestly, I didn't do anything."

"That may be, buster, but you're going to pay for it later."

Tony finally saw the smile under Jamie's mock indignation. Once again he let out a deep sigh.

"Fuck! I thought you were going to castrate me."

"I might have if you'd have taken her up on her offer," Jamie said a bit more seriously.

"Where were we," Tony said in a desperate bid to change the subject.

"Something about work to do, and it better not be on that tattoo girl."

"Umm," Tony blushed. "Well, did you want some dessert before we get started?" changing the subject even once more.

"No, I'm not interested in anything they serve here for dessert." Her eyes spoke of many other things she'd like to eat.

"Then I suggest we move on with our plan."

"Oh, I've got lots of plans for you later," Jamie said mercurially with an impish grin. She touched her tongue to her vivid red lips.

"Stop it!" he reproached. "Or at least not now. Get your mind out of the gutter, woman."

Jamie giggled. "OK. I will but be warned I intend to take you up on that rain-check."

"OK, if we are going to finally focus. If you would please pass me my gun under the table, I'd be obliged."

Out of her dress's voluminous folds of material, Jamie slipped out a flechette gun and a NAD projector. Under the tablecloth she handed the glorified shotgun to her partner.

Tony caught the eye of his compatriots situated in other booths around the restaurant before standing up. A button in Jamie's bodice turned on the sound-barrier disruptors built into her petticoats.

"EXCUSE ME!"

It didn't get enough attention so Tony blasted into the ceiling. The roar of his weapon got the quiet he required.

"Excuse me, ladies and gentlemen. I apologize for interrupting your dinners this evening. You may recognize me as Tony Sammis, the leader of the Green Action Militia."

A brief squeal of fear and a rustling of the patronage followed the simple statement.

Two men from a nearby booth rushed out toward him. Still seated as one of the crowd, Morgan put her elbow into the first man's solar plexus. He abruptly crumpled to the ground. Jamie pointed her NAD at the other. He stopped a full three paces away, raising his arms.

"You need not worry. We will not be accosting you in any way other than to have you leave by the nearest exit.

"Stanley and Seafort's is still paying its Danegeld to the Metros and thus is now closed."

"What do you mean, closed?" shouted a robust man bulling his way closer. Christine stood up from her covert location into his path. The manager stopped upon seeing the well-honed edge of Christine's curved combat knife.

"I mean that until the management sees the light, or the Metros manage to protect you like they say they will, we will close this restaurant.

"David will you give a demonstration?"

David stood up and pointed his automatic weapon at the bay window. He politely waved with his free hand for customers to back away from the window's center. David squeezed off two bursts.

Two of the dozen enormous panels of aged, tempered glass shattered, the vast majority raining directly downward.

The more squeamish of the diners shrieked, the worst of which was a fem ambi who fainted to Tony's left.

"Thank you, David. Now are there any other questions?" Tony actually watched many of the crowd shake their head. "Excellent. If you would all proceed slowly and orderly to the exits, we can finish our work here."

* * *

"I haven't been on a lift-bus in nearly thirty years, much less change four busses, and walk three sky-bridges," Jamie said with a genuine smile. "Where are we going?"

"It's a secret. Can't I have a secret?" Tony asked, holding Jamie's hand in his—a rare public display of affection.

"If you must," she teased. "Although I think Gregori is going to bash in your skull when he finds that you spirited me out from under his thumb."

"Getting upset from time to time is good for one's digestion."

"Seriously, where are we going," Jamie asked as they got into the express elevator for the Standards Insurance Building.

"Up," Tony quipped as he pushed a button for the first of six penthouse floors. Tony bent down and put his bag on the floor to unzip it. Cinnamon popped her head out of the top and looked around. She didn't fuss when Tony slung the carrier back over his shoulder.

"While I love that you have an anachronism of a cat, does she have to go everywhere with us?"

Tony gave Jamie a bit of a glare.

"No, honey. I don't mean it that way. I meant that she is at risk out in the population. I keep envisioning her served up by nils as *gato dulce* on a bed of sticky rice."

Cin looked up at Jamie's comment with serene dignity.

"Well, leaving her behind isn't really an option."

The elevator dinged its arrival. The trio got off into a sterile foyer containing one waist-high clay jug glazed in six bands of contrasting colors.

"To answer your earlier question, I thought I'd take us away to a spot where we could spend some time together. Someplace I wouldn't have to blush red every time someone looked in our general direction.

"Besides, I think you'll like these accommodations a bit more than the Spartan lodgings we've been sharing thus far."

Jamie wrapped tight around his arm. "Thank you, Tony. That's sweet."

Cinnamon hissed.

"Stop that, you little bitch. You like Jamie. At least you seem to like her when she's petting you and letting you sleep on her."

Cinnamon hissed again. She backed as far as she could in the bag. Her back arched. Her tail stood straight up and flicked agitatedly in the air. Tony looked closer. Cinnamon's whirling eyes were on the door to the flat he'd been about to open.

"Kiss me and continue down the hall," he whispered. Jamie did as he asked. Tony pulled her into a more passionate embrace, intentionally falling against the door. Jamie finally understood the misdirection.

"I want you now," she moaned loud enough to penetrate the door.

"Wait till we get home. Just a little longer."

"There's nobody here. How about we do it in the hall," she teased for the unseen audience.

"Nope. You gotta wait, sexy." Tony wrapped his arm around her waist and trundled off down the hall to put into practice the lock-picking skills taught him by a comrade that Tony had sent to his death.

To his relief the only occupant of the apartment he broke into was the solido of a goldfish.

"Morgan?" Tony whispered into his percomm. "Yes, I have a situation here at the Standards Penthouse. Would you bring a heavy team."

Jamie nudged him. "Tell them to bring Gregori."

"Oh, and work with Gregori. Have him bring some people, too.

"Jamie and I are in 6543, right next door.

"No, we are safe, but we need to know who or what is in that flat.

"Thanks, Morgan."

*   *   *

"Sir," Reza said, knocking at the Commissioner's open door.

"Just one moment, Lieutenant," Krylov said before turning to a gaunt, brown-haired woman wearing a suit and sporting a very distinctive nose.

"So you are telling me I really have no options?"

"Not exactly, Commissioner. I'm saying that there is no effective way of quashing the lawsuits. I mean if we could pin all of these suits as coming from the same individual or corporation we could go after them on racketeering charges but on the face of it they aren't even interrelated boards.

"That leaves your options at settling, going to court, or letting a summary judgment be placed against you. However, if you are correct and the plaintiffs have no interest in settling, this limits your choices further."

"What if I let the summary thingamajig happen and then ignore it?"

"That could be the worst possible of all cases, sir. If the plaintiff proves you're intentionally ignoring the judgment of the court, not only can the judge strip your own personal assets, up to and including garnishing your wages, but the judge can and probably will proffer criminal charges."

"But you said these are obviously frivolous suits!"

"It makes no difference. What your opponents lack in tactics they are wise in strategy. Ever heard of the death of a thousand pinpricks? This is it. Also notice that they didn't mention your rank or your occupation. These are all personal lawsuits, not ones directed at your position."

"Can't we at least combine the litigation against each of my staff members into one larger action?"

"Sorry, but no. Whoever prepared the actions chose subtly different acts to litigate and didn't cross name defendants, as is the case in most lawsuits. They wanted each of the members to have to fight their own battles."

"Well then, we fight. I'll open a line of credit to your firm, Shoshannah. I'll have another firm draw up a contract that will reward you for the quickness of your disposing of these actions, not the number of hours. I don't want to be bled dry."

"Thank you for your confidence, Commissioner."

"Thank you, Shoshannah. Please don't take this the wrong way, but I wish we weren't going to be seeing so much of one another."

"Certainly. Now if you will excuse me, sir. I've got people to get working on research."

Reza passed the lawyer as she left.

"Please give me some good news," Krylov pleaded.

"We've found the CorpGov homes."

"Finally. Wipe them out."

"Collateral damage, sir?"

"Any and all."

"And the media, sir?"

"I don't give a damn if it makes front page news. In fact I'd rather it make front page news. It might give anyone else pause before challenging us."

*   *   *

"So, how much of a mess do you want to allow, Boss?" Morgan asked with a drill in her hand.

"Whatever. We'll reimburse the owner."

"Got it. We'll start small and see if we can make it easy."

Tony's percomm sounded. "Tony."

"*OK,*" Augustine said to him, "*the apartment you are squatting in is an asset held by six layers of holding companies. Once I dug through the flimsy trail I find that each of the shell corporations is owned by Nanogate.*"

"Huh?"

"*Yup. I asked him about it just two minutes ago. Apparently in his youth he kept his mistress there. He never got around to getting rid of the place after the relationship ended.*

"*He gives you* carte blanche."

"Well, it saves me from worrying about someone coming home in the middle of this. Thanks, Augustine."

"*No problem. By the way, I'd steer clear of Gregori for a while. He's not happy with you.*"

"I know. When he picked up Jamie he threatened to draw my intestines up through my nose."

"*Nice. At least he didn't do it. I wouldn't have taken odds on that when he left here.*"

"I wasn't sure until he left that he wouldn't."

"*So I have to ask. What are you doing with her, Boss? She's a tramp and a user.*"

Tony sighed. "You've been taken in by her façade. She uses it to gain an advantage. Inside she is different. Maybe, if this relationship goes somewhere, I can get her to open up to my friends."

Augustine was silent on the other end of the line for several seconds before answering. "*Well, I can't say I'd want to take her home to Mom, but if you can care about her, you at least make me think.*"

"That's all I hoped to do. I'm not sure myself, not because of the girl but because of who she is."

"*Who are* you, *Tony?*" Augustine prompted.

"I know. And how many have I killed, either directly or just by being here."

"*Don't get too down on yourself. We know you and like who you are, Tony. Don't change for anyone.*"

"I don't think I can change who I am, or at least not much."

"*Just a reminder. Remember she is still the ruthless bitch we've all come to know and not love.*"

"Definitely. I guess I'd better make sure that I don't piss her off," Tony supposed.

"*Well, I have a raid to run. Behave.*"

"Only if I have to."

"Boss," Morgan said waiting until Tony turned off his percomm. "I decided to go low tech on the assumption that they would have a nanite detection screen. Come over here and you can see what we found."

The image from the snake camera through the micrometer hole in the wall showed at least six automated-sensor platforms. The computer image showed four individuals in light diffracting clothing playing hearts. The computer feed listed a name and at least three aliases for each of the trespassers. Tony touched one of the links to have it spit out a *dossier*.

"Mercs." Tony grumbled.

Morgan nodded.

"I thought it would be easy, like more Metro scum. I don't mind killing cops," Tony said. "OK, find out if they are doing this on spec or if they took a contract. If on spec, try to turn them with a better offer to go against the Metros. If they won't be turned or they are already on contract, burn the whole place. Don't even be subtle about it."

* * *

"KIRONW News Twenty-four/seven. Covering all the news, all the time. Welcome to the top of the hour; I'm Carl Merrithew."

"And I'm Elsa Abernathy. The story leading this hour: Metropolitan Crime Scene Investigators have evidence linking all six recent bombings to the Green Action Militia."

"Here to explain is Senior Investigator Mark Colson."

The screen split to show the two anchors in one and the investigator, still in his lab, in the other.

"Thanks for joining us tonight, Investigator Colson."

"*Nice to be here, Elsa.*"

"Can you explain to us in layman's terms what you found that implicates the GAM in each of these bombings?"

"*Well, as you know in the conflagration of the Olympia incident, we found the body of Frances Fischer, ex-police officer, convicted terrorist and self-proclaimed GAM member. This wasn't a coincidence. We found the detonator in her grasp.*

"*At the Tacoma incident, we found the body of Jacob Guala, again self-proclaimed terrorist, just outside the zone of total destruction. We theorize he didn't figure in the shrapnel radius of the explosion he detonated.*"

"Thank you, Doctor. But how does this tie them all together?"

"*The first item is that we've analyzed the explosives used in each of the bombings. What most people don't understand is that the minute differences in the pyrotechnics can be measured and compared. In seven of the eight cases not only were the explosives identical, they even came from the same manufacturing lot. The eighth case may not be by the Green Action Militia."*

"That sounds significant, Doctor Colson."

"Taken as a group it is seven standard deviations from the mean. In layman's terms it is ninety-nine point nine nine nine nine nine nine nine nine ninety-five percent, or one chance in two billion that anyone else could have done this by matching the known Green Action Militia devices."

"You said there was more than one item, Doctor?"

"Yes, there was. Each bomb-maker has his or her own signature, a methodology of constructing their device. It is as definitive as DNA. As an expert I've reconstructed all of the detonation devices. Their manufacture was by the same hand."

"So you are accusing the Green Action Militia?"

"I am a scientist. I don't have the right to accuse or prosecute any case against the Green Action Militia. Nor do I have any data that points at any one individual."

*   *   *

"Boss, we have them dead to rights now," David announced as he entered the room.

"Shhh!" Morgan hissed at him.

The look Christine threw at David could have cut stone. Most of the team sat in the living room of yet another random safe house enjoying a rare moment of tranquility.

"Oh, Jesus, David. Are you so sacrilegious that you'll even interrupt the boss's football?" accused Edward.

"That makes halftime with the Cowboys, twenty-two, and the Spiders, three."

"Don't protect me too much. We've all been working hard. Besides, I'm wondering if the Spiders have a chance to win even one game this year," Tony said petting Cinnamon in his lap.

"There is talk about picking up that Wilson kid as a free agent."

"Yeah, but with as little protection as they are giving Brown in the pocket, no one could possibly hope to make any significant passing yards."

"Enough with the Sunday couch managers. What have you got, David?"

"We got footage and about six different witnesses that the Metros are planting the bombs themselves. We even picked up prints and DNA. All of them match a particularly nasty Metro named Edwin Villanueva."

Tony didn't waste half a second. "This should swing even our toughest critics back into our court. Get Augustine on distribution."

*   *   *

Nanogate watched Wintel and the senior partner of Savitz, Schauer and Levinthal wrinkle his nose at the smells of cooking pancakes with maple syrup, cinnamon rolls and over-brewed coffee that were embedded in the removable fabric-panel walls of the so-called executive boardroom of the AmSuites Inn of Northern Kelso. A boxed droid delivered pitchers of a red liquid provided by the management. They were ostensibly labeled "Fruit Paradise." Its formula might once have been used for lethal injections or as a grease remover. Only Outer Conglomerate and MinInc poured themselves a serving.

The council, almost as one body, fidgeted in their seats, trying to find a way to perch in chairs that under the guise of being ergonomic actually provided no support or comfort. The imitation beech conference table might have been made in a penal colony somewhere. Nanogate's body rebelled at the settings yet his mind gave grudging approval at the work they might accomplish while not being pampered.

"I apologize for the crude surroundings. We have no computer assist. I'd ask that we all activate our personal recorders to have a permanent record of this meeting.

"As I promised I wanted us to meet to discuss actions and status," Nanogate started the meeting off. "But before we delve into our printed agenda, I received one extremely time-sensitive piece of information just before I arrived.

"Our terrestrial homes have finally been discovered by Metropolitan surveillance. I need you each to contact your families and initiate Plan Empty Nest." All of the earth-based members keyed in automated messages to execute the predefined plans to evacuate and sequester their families to underground safety.

The irony wasn't lost on Nanogate. They were being accepted and taken into the homes of nils who, not two months ago, they wouldn't have considered more important than a piece of dust on their jacket.

"Now that we have that taken care of I'd like to put Plan Beach onto the table for a vote."

"Are there any possible negative outcomes of Beach?" Wintel asked.

"Simulations show an eighty-seven percent chance of no damage to any of our homes in the first attack wave and zero civilian casualties," MinInc offered.

"Yes, and the primary reason for Beach is to provoke a more substantial response by the Metros in view of a large population center," BeringC added in her furry soprano. "Our estimates indicate eight hundred fourteen, plus or minus thirteen hundred sixty-four civilian casualties caused by the police. This will inflame public opinion against them."

"Are we putting our population in harm's way? By doing this are we violating our charter to put them first?" GVF offered.

"True, but the greater good must be served," Rio Oro rumbled out from his thick chest.

"Any other discussion?

"Then I put it to a vote. I'm sorry we have no computer support. We will have to go old-school by a show of hands. All in favor of Beach?"

Only the hand of Unified Textiles remained down.

"All opposed?"

No hands went up.

"And in favor of adding sequence Blowback?"

All hands shot into the air.

Exhaustion

Not even opening her eyes, Jamie reached to activate her percomm when she heard the trill. Nothing happened. Sleepily she fumbled with the activation button but nothing happened.

Beside her she felt Tony's body move to activate his percomm. With the deep, thick sound of someone just awake he greeted the caller with, "You know there are times I despair at anyone having my code."

"Tony we need you to execute Blowback," came Nanogate's smooth voice.

"You couldn't have waited until a decent hour for this?" Tony whined. "It's not like this is going to happen at the speed of light."

"It's nearly eight o'clock, Tony."

"Good God. Eight? You any idea how late I was up running ops for the rest of our strategies? I haven't had any coffee, nor a shower and I'm certainly not dressed yet."

"Well, I've delivered my message. No need for me to play mother on a school morning.

"Say hello to Jamie for me," Nanogate added.

Her lover collapsed back into the red satin sheets with a coherent, "Gnuh."

"I don't want you to go," Jamie whispered, wrapping her arm around his chest from behind. She put a soft kiss on one shoulder. "I know you need to go, but I don't want you to."

"You sure I can't have David launch that bitch?" he asked, his voice muffled as he still lay face down in his pillow.

"Your voice print only, darling. Your order."

"I don't want to go to school," he said burrowing deeper into the covers.

"The glamorous life of an international terrorist," she said, teasing one of the multitude of the coarse hairs on his back.

"Stop that or I'm going to have to spank you, woman."

"Promises, promises," she said, wiggling her hips against his ass.

"Mmmurfph," he mumbled through his pillow.

"Oh, sleepy freedom fighter," she teased. "You have things to blow up."

"Later. Right now it's time to sleep."

*   *   *

Oregonian Local News: Latest Stories

Commissioner Yuri Krylov ordered flags on all Metro Police stations flown at half-staff on Friday in honor of the brutal murder of Detective Edwin Villanueva. The police officer's body was found Tuesday at ground level. Detective Villanueva died as he attempted to save a woman from being the victim of a gang rape, according to police recordings. The gang in question managed to disarm him and then kicked him into unconsciousness.

"I'm deeply saddened by Villanueva's death," Krylov said in an issued statement. "He died in the most heroic manner and in the best traditions of the Metros. His memory will live on in our hearts and minds."

The Metros issued a statement that they arrested seven members of the Green Action Militia in connection with the detective's death. No names of those arrested were provided.

Services for the fallen ...

*   *   *

Fighter pilots are the same in any era. Mele Kilikina, call sign *Hawaiian*, of the Metro's Darkwings, settled into her flight-repeater chair with cocky self-assurance. She had sixteen kills under her belt and hankered for the twenty required for a drone pilot to earn her ace.

The mission parameters stood out as odd but not enough to

trouble her. A kill was a kill. It didn't matter if it were a plane, tank, drone or even a house—a kill was a kill.

She heard the rest of her squadron buckling into their own control chairs, an apparent improvement of a newer age of piloting. She herself preferred the simulated movement of a flight repeater to a static control chair. She could feel and be a part of what happened. It gave her better spatial awareness.

She worshiped the aces of old—McConnell, Welter, Hartmann, Epstein, Yevstigneev, and Venus Jujulov. In eighty-four missions she'd always brought her crate home, just like her heroes. Her squadron-mates didn't think twice about losing a ten-million-dollar drone. As they saw it, they were designed to be expendable. She flew hers like she was in the drone and her life depended on getting it back on the ground.

Of the twelve drones, only one got a PreFlight() down-check. A loader whisked away the faulty drone to some invisible repair facility. Another one hit the tarmac seconds later and checked out fine.

"Starting one," said her wing commander.

"Starting two," she called out, flipping on the starter and applying power. With her ranging LADIR she ensured that none of her mates would bump her as she floated up into the clear, cold, morning sky over their hidden base on Fire Island in the bay of Anchorage, Alaska.

As the entire squadron checked in, she examined her own WeaponsStores()—mostly air-to-mud with six Black Hole missiles, a pair of Downlook cluster munitions, two Racer air-to-air missiles and four hundred rounds of old-fashioned 30mm armor piercing.

Over the ninety-minute flight she settled herself into a zone, trying to visualize her target and how she would approach. Try as she might she couldn't imagine firing into a mansion. Something didn't compute. She also wondered if they brought enough firepower. Seventy-two Black Holes would do a lot of damage but completely destroy a modern day castle? She didn't think so. Of course they only really needed to damage the lift units and to watch them plunge into the Pacific Ocean. That satisfied her ego.

Her ranging screen showed the target sooner than her tactical displays. It wasn't one mansion but rather sixteen in a massive, tightly packed cluster. It looked like an ancient battleship floating 30 meters off the wave tops. Her heart rate increased. She loved combat even if shooting fish in a barrel seemed hard by comparison.

TargetStatus() confirmed that, for a house, the entire collection moved at quite a good clip to the southeast. HeadingCheck() showed it on a direct course for San Francisco. The floating mansions' 201 KPH wouldn't affect the outcome of her arsenal's Mach 6 rating.

PowerEval() noted no weapons in her targets. They radiated plenty of energy but only for the lift units and some miscellaneous household gear like water heaters, sprinkler systems and the like.

"Even though there are no weapon signatures, we bring it low and tight. Just like our simulations. I want two Black Holes from each of you at extreme range."

An itch of excitement crept up her spine. "Two," Mele acknowledged, trying consciously to relax her shoulders to keep the tension from knotting them. The RangingTone() already whistled in her ear. All of her missiles tracked as did OnboardTracking(). Sharp hoots and the flashing target indicator on HUD() assured her of a hard-lock.

"Fox One," she said feeling the jolt as the weapon, nearly as massive as the drone carrying it, released and activated its own propulsion system. "Fox Two."

The rush of having launched white ones, actual war shots, raced through her system as her squadron mates announced their own armaments' release. She barely paid them any heed. Her training wouldn't let her completely ignore their declarations but her focus was her own two weapons' tracks on her HUD. Twenty-one other yellow traces muddled WeapTrack(). Vaguely she recalled hearing DW Eight, *Falcon*, announcing, with irritation, a malfunction on her second launch.

One of the twenty-one yellow tracks blinked and dropped off her screen. Someone else might suffer the indignity of a weapon that didn't reach its target but it wouldn't be her.

Three seconds to impact, BioFeedback() warned of her elevated heart rate and breathing pattern. It increased the oxygen content to her mask.

She had to watch. She rotated the display screens until she came to VisualTarget(). The solido split into four images, one each from the weapons themselves, a mostly blurry headlong rush, one from her drone's onboard camera systems, steady and fully magnified, and the final from the satellite feed. She wanted to feel the exhilaration of boring in at Mach 6. She concentrated on the images of her weapons. Internal tracking data relayed across the solido image. A large enhanced outline of the target remained centered.

As blurry as it was, she noticed when all visual images went opaque on both weapons. WeapTrack()'s tone announced the sudden demise of all the weapons, nearly simultaneously. Not detonation. The weapons had been intercepted.

She'd missed. She didn't miss. The only time she didn't get a kill is when she didn't fire a weapon. She'd missed. Someone would pay for this indignity.

"Negative impact."

"Negative detonation."

"Birds are not responding."

Mele's head twisted to see the view from her drone's recorders. Where there had been a cluster of houses now only a white waterfall obscured her view. From above it looked like the cluster of homes grew into a fuzzy cloud three times the size of the original.

Over the next stunned second the cloud/waterfall dissipated. Mele zoomed in the image as close as her resolution would allow. Every house bristled with nozzles like those employed by fire suppression systems but magnified. They pointed in all directions. As the gout of water from each wound down from a fanlike spray to a dribble, Mele realized what had happened to their attack.

"They are putting out a cloud of debris that is destroying our weapons by sheer speed impacts. Can we ratchet down the speed of our missiles?"

None of the shocked pilots responded. Who would have thought of the blasphemous and counterproductive idea of making weapons slower?

"Enough chatter. Let's light it up with cluster munitions. If our target apex is low over the complex we should get a slow enough fall to enter. Change bearing to one-seven-six and close to fifty km for best targeting."

"Two," Mele counted off without thinking. She would destroy these bitches yet. No one made her miss.

"Three."

"Four."

She ran cluster munition simulations on her own designed WeapPerformance(). They could get a slow enough injection but as light as the weapons were they'd skip off, float away or detonate on the surface.

Her brow furrowed and she turned off her repeater couch. She started programming furiously. She turned her radios down low. She needed no distractions and only had a few seconds.

Chatter came and went over the tactical net that she ignored. More chatter and more programming code. It wasn't until she heard her call sign multiple times did she break her concentration.

"Hawaiian, please respond"

"Hawaiian, what are you doing?"

"Goddamn it, Mele, what the fuck is going on?"

"Hold one, flight lead."

"Get back into formation, Hawaiian."

The reprimand shocked her. She checked FlightPosition() to find her drone had drifted out of formation by nearly a kilometer.

"Pay attention, Hawaiian. That is why tactical programming is prior to the mission."

Mele blushed. She hadn't made such a screw-up since an unfortunate incident involving a water tower on her second day of flight school.

"Two, correcting."

"My simulations show that our cluster munitions will fail unless we break open the water curtain first," Mele said as she forwarded her data. "Black Holes won't detonate against the curtain. I suggest we use one cluster to break open a hole for the others."

"Good thinking, Hawaiian, but next time let me know what you are doing so we can slave your drone to ours."

"Two," she acknowledged meekly.

"Everyone slave their Downlooks to my panel," flight lead directed.

The entire flight complied.

"I have all weapons. I'm setting delays from one to three millisecond launch time differences from mine. I'm edging out in front by 60 meters."

"Fox all!"

Mele watched with dread fascination as the missiles raced forward at a very shallow angle. Just as before the behemoth target became an even larger fountain of water. So close were the cluster releases timed that to Mele they looked like one. Detonations against the water curtain occurred less than half a second later. Three seconds later her heart fell as she saw sparkling explosions on the outside of the defensive waterfall. The defensive shield dropped moments later.

She hurt her shoulder as she tried to sit up against the straps when she saw gaping holes in the outside of the buildings. They'd hit with at least some of them.

"Flight lead to Darkwings. We are Winchester. RTB."

Mele didn't want to return to base. She wanted to bore in for a kill. But without more cluster munitions or some other weapons package she realized how useless it would be. "Two," she acquiesced.

"Three."

* * *

The daily winter drizzle of the Northwest didn't wash away the filth nor did the fog do anything to disguise it here on the shattered pavement of the West Valley Highway. Buildings stretched up blotting out anything resembling the sky.

In an alley adjoining the highway, a well-dressed man bent a young man, who wore too much makeup, over a broken desk, gray with mildew. With empty eyes the youth looked up to watch Tony pass.

A vendor busily served "Jumbo Hot Dogs" from behind what used to be the bulletproof windshield of a liftousine mounted to his battered and rusted cart. The stand boasted a newer sign proclaiming in six languages, "ACTIVE DEFENSES: For your protection do not touch this vehicle!" More than one of his patrons looked like they might challenge the warnings had there not been a severed, desiccated head prominently displayed below the sign and the hand-lettered warning in blood-red paint, "This means YOU."

Two children, one wearing a coffee bag announcing "Dutch Blend" and the other in only a pair of stained briefs so small they cut into the skin of his hips, wove in and out of the moderate foot traffic of this thoroughfare. Tony felt each of them stick a hand in the pockets of his faded-denim jumpsuit. Their pickpocket attempt came up empty as he carried little but Cin strapped to his chest in a child carrier.

"Meow?" Cin asked from within.

"Not now," Tony said, hoping she'd stay down. Cuddled down inside she passed as an infant being carried by an over-attentive father. If she poked her head up she revealed herself to be a feast the likes of which groundies saw only once or twice in their lifetime.

Operation Blowback irritated him. Oh, it had value but why did he have to get out of a warm bed containing an even warmer partner?

A nearly skeletal woman in a thrice resized shift, tended her young daughter, only slightly more fleshed, as he walked past. The young girl whined about getting a hotdog.

"Shush, honey. Mama has soup at home."

"But I don't want soy soup again. I want a hot dog," the scraggly-looking girl said as she started to cry. Tears dropped on her dress, obviously fashioned from a swath of her mother's own garment.

Tony realized that in the urgency of unseating entrenched power structures, the rush of a new relationship, and the wellbeing that wealth had brought, he'd almost forgotten everything that he'd learned.

"Excuse me, ma'am," Tony interrupted.

The ratty blond cringed, pulling her daughter behind her. She looked down at the ground meekly. "We don't want no trouble, mister."

"No, it's nothing like that, ma'am. I want to help, not hurt."

Tony reached into his baby pouch for the change he always kept. In the process he dislodged Cin.

"Mew," she said lifting her head.

The blond woman flinched.

"Is that a cat?" the little girl asked, her tears drying up.

"Yes," Tony said looking around to see who else had noticed. He handed the woman a plastic coin. It wasn't much, just a fiver, but her eyes fired like the climax of a Fourth of July fireworks show. Just as quickly they squinted and pulled away.

"What do you want? I ain't no token girl."

"I don't want anything, ma'am. I just remember how hard it can be."

The woman looked puzzled at him. Suddenly recognition spawned in her eyes. "Aren't you the GAM?"

"Mister, can you eat cats?" the little girl interrupted. "Mama says if you're rich you can eat them every night."

"No, I'm not *the* GAM, I'm just a member. And some people eat cats but not me," Tony said petting Cin. He bent down to let the little girl see. "You can touch her. She won't bite."

The waif pet Cinnamon, who purred for all she was worth.

"Look, this nil has a cat!" someone bellowed.

"A cat. I haven't eaten that good since my mama served one for Christmas dinner," said another craning to see over his compatriots.

"Let's get the cat!" yelled another woman whose hair literally lit up in an orange glow.

Hampered by the little girl, Tony couldn't even stand to face them. "DON'T!" the blond woman yelled, getting between him and the growing mob. "It's Tony Sammis. He's the GAM!"

*   *   *

"The attack on the homes of the Council didn't go nearly as well as we'd hoped," Reza said to the smoky room after several bits of bad news.

A boxed serving cart delivered a bottle to the table before returning to the corner of the room to await another order from the room's occupants. Reza watched Commissioner Krylov's dour face as he poured himself a rather stiff glass of the Pushkin vodka.

"The houses employed some form of particle shielding we've never seen before. In short they fired great volumes of sea water and sand out in every direction from their floating platform. Because of the speed of the missiles, they immolated themselves against the particles before doing any damage to the homes."

"So we sent a hundred million dollars in equipment after them and did ничего, nothing?" The Commissioner's face looked hot enough to start a fire.

"Not exactly, sir. Our drone pilots managed to use bombs in a way that allowed them to do some damage, but they didn't carry enough of those kind of bombs to destroy them." Before Krylov could interrupt again, Reza plowed onward. "On the good side we know where they are. We know where they are heading, San Francisco. And they have no chance of evading our drones after they are rearmed or new ones are launched out of San Diego."

"Have our transfers gone into place for kinetic strikes?"

The room fell silent. Even his closest advisors were staring at him with varying degree of horror on their face.

"Sir, I think that would be like using a chainsaw to trim a hangnail," Reza said, breaking the tableau.

"I'm tired of toying with these folks. If we do enough damage to them, we can make them cry uncle."

"Yes, sir. As you wish."

*   *   *

Sixteen self-deputized guards escorted Tony as he went to make *Blowback* a reality. Once the crowd at ground level realized he was not only a member of the GAM but its leader, they decided he needed a guard to keep the other nils or even street gangs from bothering him. His objections only seemed to make his protectors more adamant about keeping him safe. As far as Tony could determine, they decided even though he was the leader of a powerful organization, having planned and lived through dozens of terrorist actions, that he needed to be saved from his own supposed incompetence. Not to mention a young girl named Hope who wouldn't be parted from Cinnamon.

As they made their way to the secret hiding place of their Captive Particle Accelerator, he worried most about the danger of his crowd drawing the kind of attention that he couldn't afford. Metros were constantly on the lookout for any pre-riot gatherings and he had more than his share of followers.

"Folks we have to be careful now. Don't come up onto the roof here. We can't afford to be seen," he warned. "There is a nice penthouse for you all to gather in. I'm sure I will be perfectly all right on the roof by myself, and if not you are only a shout away."

His pronouncement was met with only grumbles until he informed them of the stocked larder. The sounds then came from unfed stomachs and praises for the Green Action Militia as they feasted.

Tony climbed the roof-access stairs shaking his head. Too many people still ate out of compost piles and garbage dumps.

An older building only eighty stories high, the Columbia Building still held a cistern on the roof for gravity feed plumbing. Or at least that is what it appeared. Tony worked one of the copper colored hoops to release a hidden catch. Two doors, each covering a quarter of the circumference, opened onto a vertical mass of machinery that seemed to be haphazardly tossed into the 40-meter-high by 20-wide cylinder. As random as it all seemed, all the pieces connected in one form or another to a huge toroid with an outer radius of 6 meters and a hole in the middle of 2 meters.

Bailing wire and chewing gum tacked a comparatively small, human-sized chair onto the immense donut. Tony climbed 4 meters up to get into the chair. Pulling an old-fashioned, plastic key from his pocket he set the machine in motion by plugging it into a nearly-invisible ignition. The conglomeration of parts morphed, with ponderous inevitability, one piece at a time—each logically rotating or sliding to make room for the next. The cascade continued until, from its rough original form of a tall cylinder it had flattened into a rhomboid sporting the vertical torus on its back like the fin of some giant, prehistoric fish.

Tony now had a control board in front of him. He fired up the fusion reactor. It hummed ominously. A series of loud mechanical clacks rotated once around the donut. A sound like sand flowing through a metal pipe came from the toroid. The grating swish slowly increased in speed. Tiny sympathetic vibrations formed in the circular structure as whatever was inside increased in velocity.

With his eyes he selected Augustine's percomm code. "You got the drones?"

"*And when have I let you down,*" Augustine retorted over the link. "*They might be able to hide themselves from the ground but to the weather cameras on Gamma and the Luxor stations they might as well be covered in neon lights.*"

"Where are they heading?"

"*Anchorage, Alaska. Even after a couple of deceptive moves their base seems to be Fire Island. The maps call it a bird refuge.*"

"Well, they fly anyway."

"*Oh, here we go. I have some old, flat plans that shows it was once a United States Air Force station.*"

"Any trouble with collateral damage?" Tony asked as he entered the coordinates Augustine fed him into the control panel.

"*Actually they did us a favor by hiding it in the middle of nowhere. Only thing we might kill is a fowl or two. I say zero civilian casualties.*"

"Perfect. Any objection?" Tony panned up the machine whose sound pitch increased. The energy it generated continued to pour into the accelerator and would for the entirety of its flight.

"*Launch it.*"

Pressing the "commit" button Tony watched as the solido projectors fanned out. As the odd-looking machine lifted off from the roof, its image transformed. To the few that would actually see it before it landed, it looked exactly like a lift-bus full of people. It wouldn't stand up to a scan but no one figured a Metro would be curious enough about it.

It didn't fly fast and dodge about like a missile but rather slow and obvious, just like the bus it imitated. Its results would have to speak for themselves.

"It's done."

*   *   *

"Nice to have someone new to talk to," the auburn-haired Captain Benson said to his new commander, Major Humilde. Down into the depths of the old Homestake Mine in Lead, South Dakota, they rode a white tram barely wide enough to accommodate the two men standing side by side.

Too many prospective kinetic strike crewmembers succumbed to the claustrophobia caused by the tight darkness. With one hand on the tram abort button, Benson watched the olive skin and dark eyes of his nominal supervisor for any of the classic signs of depth sickness.

The major didn't wince at either the pressure of the earth above as they dropped or when the tram banged and rattled as it changed from one track to the next. The man with hair only slightly lighter than the pitch black of the tunnels themselves also didn't even flinch when they raced by where the ever-present dampness collected into a small waterfall.

"Yes, Captain. That was one of the reasons I chose to make a move myself. Being nothing more than one in a cadre of dozens of other logistics officers, I wanted to do something more meaningful."

"Well, if you were looking for excitement, you came to the wrong place, Major. Don't forget to pop your ears, sir," Charles Benson added as he automatically yawned to pop his own. The depth continued to increase radically with their descent.

"Thank you," the commander said swallowing hard and working his jaw back and forth. "I know that we ensure the control over some of the most destructive weapons our planet has ever known. Action is what we want to avoid unless called upon to do our duty."

"Yeah," Charles said, thinking that his boss spouted the propaganda line. Personally he hoped command authority never asked him to deploy the weapons as he wasn't sure he would drop spent-uranium-encased reentry vehicles from high orbit at populated targets on the earth. The damage of even a small one could deliver an impact like the meteorite crater in Arizona.

Changing the subject Captain Benson asked, "Tell me, Major, what kind of hobbies do you have? No offense to that worthy, but Colonel Gates would only talk about one thing—football. The woman lived and breathed it. I think if I hear one more time about how the New Orleans Buccaneers have it so good because of their Pro Bowl left tackle or the betting line on the Cowboys–Spiders game I think I'd vomit."

"Well, no, I'm not much of a football man, myself. But if you want to talk cricket, I'm sure I could babble your ear off. But other than sports I have several hobbies. I'm a garage-shop micro-machinist, and a board gamer," he told his auburn-haired subordinate.

"Interesting. What do you machine?"

"Oh, I dabble in recreating some of the early work with nanites. It's fascinating to see how they share a specific task amongst millions of tiny machines. I use them to recreate famous sculptures one hundredth normal size. I've got a miniature of 'The Thinker' that I'm particularly proud of."

"I'd like to see that someday. We'll have to talk more about this. We'll have dozens of hours this shift."

The tram stopped at a well-lit platform that had a massive metal door, 2 meters high and 7 across. It looked like a bank vault door although much more solidly built. Charlie hit the intercom.

"Benson and Humilde to relieve you. Authorization Tango, Tango, Echo, Niner, Niner, Zulu, Bravo."

"Authorization approved, gentlemen," came a feminine voice over the tinny speaker. "Locking control boards now. Insert keys in door mechanism in three, two, one." On "one" all four participants of the ritualistic dance inserted mechanical, three-dimensional keys that looked like writhing snakes into an intricate lock assembly, two on each side of the door. Had any of them been off by as much as a second the door would be impossible to open for more than eight hours.

"Turn keys on my mark. Three, two, one."

The massive door chuffed as it opened with an intentional pressure change designed to make the door even more impossible to be forced open. The door revealed two small cubicles, each barely the size of a downtown Parisian hotel room and shorter to boot. A 10 cm, transparent wall of non-permeable metal alloy separated them. A decision to launch one of their charges had to be made by both officers, and the barrier ensured that neither could influence the other's decision.

"Welcome to the dungeon," the blond woman said from behind rheumy eyes as she exited one of the rooms.

A brown-haired man exiting the other chamber just nodded. No one else noticed a meaningful glance between the two dark-haired men.

"Hope you like your stay here in 'chez Hole'," the woman teased.

"Oh, knock it off, Commander Olaf," Charlie said good-naturedly. "Your shift may be up, but we have thirty-six hours to go."

The woman stuck her tongue out at him and then softened it with a smile.

"Get in there so we can get outta here," she said. "It's time."

As the two new crewmen entered the portal to their individual control rooms a computer-generated voice spoke up. "Scanning for foreign substances. Nanites detected."

"Must be my hobby," Humilde said calmly. "This same thing happened in training. The bloody things are almost impossible to get rid of if you spill some."

"Nanites innocuous," the voice said moments later.

"Thank you, gentlemen," the commander of the other team said.

"Doors closing," came the computer generated voice. A tomb-like thud announced its completion.

"Remove keys in three, two, one."

"Doors locking," the computer voice advised.

Now on the inside, the tinny speakers conveyed the conversation between the cubicles.

"Have a nice time, boys," Commander Olaf said as she and her subordinate stepped onto the tram and rocketed upward out of sight.

"Engage control boards in three, two, one," the Major said from his hermetically sealed cubical. The pair slid their 10 cm, snake-like keys into the optical control board, bringing it to life. As they inserted, a tiny vacuum sucked in cells from each of their skins to do a DNA check and sensitive electronic scanners read their unique bio-electric signatures.

"Identities confirmed," the computer atoned. "Command functions available."

"Excellent. Well, nothing to do but wait now. What do you do to kill time, Captain?"

"I read paranormal from the early twenty-first century. There was a huge boom of the stuff, especially vampire and werewolf novels. Authors like Charlaine Harris, Kim Harrison and Laurel Hamilton."

"Really. As a kid I loved zombie stories. Even watched some of the old flatties. Heck, I sat down one weekend and went through all five seasons of the *Walking Dead* series."

"Sounds like you were seriously addicted."

"It happens ... "

"Message incoming," said a mechanical voice.

Both men immediately reached for their logbooks and their grease pencils. The message could be anything from a decision to launch to a satellite being removed from the network for maintenance.

"This is a critic message in three parts: Alpha, Sierra, Zulu, Zulu, Five, Tango, Five, Three, Niner, Bravo. Break. Break." The adrenaline in both men raced. They scribbled the alpha numeric characters into a template as it read out over the speakers. "Charlie, Romeo, Four, Bravo, Charlie, Yankee, Four, One, Kilo. Break. Break.

"November, Oscar, Whiskey, Whiskey, Delta, Foxtrot, Juliet, Three, Three, X-ray, Papa, Foxtrot, Three, Eight, Echo, Sierra, Six, Six, Delta, Hotel. Break. Break."

The two men finished their writing with eight digits outside of their predetermined template. Pietro Humilde felt the hair on the back of his head creep up. Eight extra digits had another meaning entirely to him.

"I do NOT have a properly formatted message," Major Humilde announced.

"I concur. We do not have a properly formatted message. Looks like you got a bit of excitement," Charlie said from the other side of the impervious wall.

"No doubt. In fact I think I'm going to take a siesta on the toilet."

Benson laughed. "I did the same thing the first time I got critic traffic."

Major Humilde did actually have to lose what was in his bowels, but he didn't have the time. The trip to his self-contained head actually had another more sinister purpose. Reaching down with shaking fingers he removed both of the plastic caps covering the bolts holding the porcelain fixture to the floor. On a passive inspection they looked normal, but instead the hollow caps held a molded vial containing several milliliters of fluid, one the color of ripe mango flesh and the other the brilliant green hue of a Granny Smith apple. Several drops of sweat rolled down and dropped from his forehead to the white tile floor.

With his pen he crushed the vial in each of the tiny caps. With a lancet built into his pen he pierced the thumb of his left hand with a wince. Three drops of blood fell into each of the miniature cups, activating the inert nanites in the colored fluids. Now he had to hurry.

He washed his hands and wiped the sweat that had accumulated on his brow.

He cupped one small container of fluid in each hand as he went back to his desk.

"Everything come out all right?" his subordinate teased.

Humilde just smiled wryly, trying to cover up his nervousness. Covertly he poured the first reddish liquid against the base of the transparent wall. He started to count. Before he'd reached seven Mississippi he could see a small hole eaten in the base of the barrier. He bent down and poured the second darker liquid near the hole. The oily substance actually spread out rapidly in all directions.

The Major attempted to keep up a conversation for the next minute as each of the groups of nanites did their job. "So I told you what I did for fun, but what about you?" *Three Mississippi.*

"Oh, my wife and I like hiking. We've done Mons Blanc on the moon twice and Albor Tholus on Mars once. I also collect vintage stamps and try to ski four or five times a year."

"Where do you ski?" *Seventeen Mississippi.*

"Oh, there is the facility in Dubai that we do at least once a year. We've tried the peaks in Alaska but it just isn't the same. We did do some cross-country full-kit trips in the Arctic."

"I also do some amateur photography, the old fashioned way, with actual photo film and chemically laced paper."

Thirty-five Mississippi. Milky white traces crept upward in the transparent wall. It resembled a spider web covering a large portion of the surface.

"Really? That's interesting, Charlie. Why go through all that work?" *Forty Mississippi.*

"It gives an entire different feel to the process than just downloading images into your personal data storage. I think of it the same way as those people who still make furniture by hand or carve dead trees for art's sake—it's craftsmanship. It's something I've done myself."

"I guess that works." *Sixty Mississippi.*

"Man, I'm not feeling very well."

Right on schedule. "Maybe you should sit back down."

"I feel ... " Benson said, freezing in place, half bent over to sit in his chair. His chest barely moved in and out.

"Charlie, I know you can hear me. The nanites I released into your cell have paralyzed your motor control. Your autonomic functions will still work so you will continue to breathe and your heart will continue to beat. You will live through this, but I need your help."

The spider webs within the transparent separation between the rooms had grown to obvious and noticeable proportions covering pretty much the entire wall. Major Humilde picked up his chair and slung it. The once impervious wall exploded outward stopping the assault no better than a pane of safety glass. The shower of milky white wall material left a hole the size of a linebacker.

Major Humilde stepped through with his footsteps crackling in the debris on the floor. He took hold of his subordinate and with some steady force managed to get the catatonic body seated in his chair.

"We don't want to strain those muscles, Charlie. I hold no rancor toward you.

"So this is what we are going to do, Charlie. We are going to launch five very small reentry vehicles at the targets I choose. I know you won't help me willingly so I'll go the unwilling route.

"I want to assure you that I'm not crazed or demented. I'm not going to have you help me, even unwillingly, in being a mass murderer."

Major Humilde used his hands to wrap one of Charlie's hands around his multi-dimensional key. Making sure his fingers were taut in place, he started the key into the keyhole. "You see if you were just dead the electronic scanners would note no neural activity and wouldn't allow your key to function, but with you just unable to move you still register as a valid key-holder."

With simple twine tied around Charlie's wrist and then around a pole in his own cubical, he was ready.

"OK. Insert keys in three, two, one," the major said with some humor. He pulled on the twine, which moved Charlie's hand and key forward at the same time. Simultaneously he slid his key into his own control board. Both boards lit up for munitions selection.

"Excellent.

"OK, let's choose five fragmentation packages," the Major said as his feet crunched on the floor walking back and forth through the hole in the wall to set the same commands on both panels.

"And now coordinates." After entering them he leaned his companion over the board so he could see.

"If you'll notice these impact locations are outside populated regions. And with fragmentation munitions there is no possibility of secondary effects.

"I told you, I'm not demented and I'm not crazed. I am following orders. And no, before you even ask, not the orders of the so-called President of the United States.

"Shall we execute these orders? I thought so." Pietro tied the twine tighter to his captive's wrist and wrapped it around three times. Moving back to his own cubic.

"Turn to execute in three, two, one." Pulling on the twine forced the wrist to rotate in place. The major turned his key at the same time.

Far above, five shopping-mall-sized objects blew off their shrouds of concealing materials. Early warning systems scanned the now unstealthy objects. Each of the five executed a very tiny deorbit burn to bring destruction to earth all in the same area—just outside San Francisco.

* * *

Even with the chill of the December coastal winds, Michael Evans and his family enjoyed their outing to the beach. His son, Michael Jr., nine, worked on a seaside aquatic biodiversity project.

"That's a sea spider," the younger Michael said with authority to his four-year-old sister while pointing at a tiny orange bit no bigger than his fingernail. "It's a pikenogakid."

"Pycnogonid," his mother corrected.

"Don't touch, Stephanie. It's fragile."

His honey-blond sister just looked confused but at the same time in awe of her big brother.

"Our ecosystem is failing and we can't hurt it any more.

"The pikenogakid makes ten different species so far! That's two more than my teacher found," Michael Jr. crowed. His mother didn't correct him a second time.

Michael senior strolled along, enjoying a pouch of beer and the general warm glow of family. His normal job of smelting reclaimed and recycled metals forced him to sweat rivers most days, but today he reveled in the cold, soaking it into his body like a battery to ward off the coming work week.

For December, the sky was relatively clear, meaning that you could see more than a hundred meters. The light fog limited visibility to about a pair of kilometers. Out at the very edge of that distance Michael noticed a small grouping of floating homes levitating into view. He wondered at their course and their low altitude. Floating homes weren't allowed within one hundred kilometers of San Francisco's beaches and never that low in any case. They were enormous homes. "Corporate bigwigs," he thought uncharitably.

Then he noticed how fast they moved. Within a very few seconds the homes, even more monstrous than he'd originally imagined, had approached his family's position on the beach. They were so low he felt he could reach up and touch them.

"What is going on here," Marsha Evans said, wrapping her arms around her husband's waist as she gawked at the huge airshow.

"Emergency repairs?" Michael, never Mike, guessed.

"Then why—" Marsha's reply was interrupted by the sky turning an angry red. A quintet of very short streaks of blood orange with a point of yellow/white at the end of each grew visibly larger as they watched.

"What are those, Dad?"

"I don't know, Junior. Shuttles in reentry?"

"But why wouldn't they use the skyhook?"

At that moment the objects exploded outward, creating a cloud of thousands of red-hot projectiles thousands of meters in the air. Michael realized at that moment just how little of their life remained.

"Get against that rock!" he shouted. Michael Senior never had yelled at his family. It paralyzed them into immobility. "NOW! MOVE!" he screamed, slapping his wife across the face as he disentangled himself from her arm. Michael knew he wouldn't be fast enough. Those kinetic bombardment projectiles had to be travelling at well over the speed of sound. But he just couldn't abandon his daughter.

He sprinted the 10 meters across the beach to snatch up his youngest as his wife pulled her son against the huge stone. Tearing muscles and ripping ligaments in one final desperate act, Michael Senior threw his 18-kilo daughter toward his wife.

The non-explosive devices began to impact. In the last fleeting picoseconds of his life, Mr. Evans realized that his wife had caught their daughter. He'd performed his sacred duty.

In the rock's shadow of the roaring impacts, Marsha watched her husband incinerate. One moment he was there and the next only searing heat encompassed her. There was pressure on her ears that couldn't be swallowed away, and a brilliance of light everywhere that burned her eyes. The follow-on wind threatened to snatch her babies away from her, but she held firm.

Opening her eyes she scanned the beach for her husband but only saw a steaming alien landscape. It didn't look like sand. The ocean boiled. Where was her husband?

*   *   *

The Captive Particle Accelerator, cloaked in its image of a Red Ball tour bus, travelled through the standard commercial lanes of flight. It regularly reported its position to automated traffic controllers as a tour bus, not a weapon of mass destruction.

As it travelled its fusion generators continued to accelerate the particles within its toroid. Only the power generators themselves were the practical limit to the amount of energy the device could eventually store. As the particle stream approached the speed of light, its mass increased. As the mass increased it took more power to maintain the gravity-cancellation field and the magnetic fields holding the stream's circular shape. This reduced the amount of power that could be put toward accelerating the particles themselves.

With such a short trip planned, the CPA's equilibrium wouldn't be approached, but every erg would go directly into the spinning plasma within its belly. As a beast it had only one very powerful bite.

At mission clock T+3:05:13, the Red Ball bus of operation *Blowback* navigated into Juneau's heavy traffic patterns without a hitch. At T+3:09:22 it successfully routed around a significant industrial fire at the direction of the automated ground control.

At T+4:42:12 it requested permission to enter Anchorage's commercial traffic patterns at a lower level. As the missile talked only to a computer it required no legerdemain to convince the local device of its bona fides. The CPA acknowledged the ground control's request to reduce speed to the local 200 KPH as it descended to 405 meters.

Approaching the Triple Eagle River Towers, the CPA asked to enter the local traffic flow. The control advised a speed of 110 KPH and a flight level of no less than 112 meters. It also downloaded a three-dimensional map labeling the buildings whose no-fly zones exceeded that flight level. The missile rerouted.

With no innate intelligence, the CPA couldn't hear that the source of its destructive power had reached a resonance frequency that caused an acute subliminal whine. As it flew over Wolverine Park on the top of Archon Family Towers, several children and one parent looked up. The projected image of a tour bus didn't shock them but its path, heading out into the bay made at least the parent wonder. At first she ignored it but that didn't last longer than seven minutes.

The CPA dropped down in a radical maneuver that caused an inquiry from the local control so fast that only a computer could have issued it. The seemingly unrestrained plunge caused the ground computer to attempt to seize control. However the CPA had, two minutes before, turned off its external inputs. There would be nothing to stop it. It struck the geographic center of Fire Island three point four seconds after it started its terminal dive.

With its impact the magnetic containment of the device failed. The particle and plasma stream, now at a significant portion of the speed of light and with nothing to bend them back into their circular course, followed Newton's laws of motion. Each atom went in the last direction they had been with no change in momentum creating an almost perfect plane.

Trees, birds, and some incidental concrete bunkers on the surface vaporized almost instantly. A violet fan of energy crackled upward into the sky, superheating the air like the rooster-tail of an accelerating speedboat. The resulting shockwave shattered and blew out hurricane-force rated windows within 8 kilometers and permanently deafened two souls. The sudden high pressure wave scattered clouds for 60 kilometers. The shallow bay surrounding the island boiled, sending up gouts of steam, melting the falling snow and in turn vaporizing it to be lost within the rest of the massive plume.

As spectacular as the cataclysm was aboveground, it wasn't the most impressive feat of the CPA's detonation. As the bottom of the containment fields failed first, the greatest damage directed downward. The spot of dirt and rock that had been Fire Island ceased to exist in a space of less than one second. The very deep Metro drone hangar, dug-in and reinforced to withstand even a small nuclear device, turned back into its component atoms and mixed with the molten earth.

The earth itself boiled as if the fiery fist of God himself forced its way down into the mantle. The impact alone triggered a 5.2 magnitude earthquake in the Castle Mountain fault beneath Anchorage. A very small tsunami, only 4 meters high, crashed against the hurricane barriers of the city.

An hour later, when people gathered stock of themselves and focused a camera on the impact location, the only thing that remained where an island once stood was a steaming sea, still roiling violently. When things returned to normal, weeks later, the denizens found an underwater crater 300 meters deep, 20 wide and 100 long.

*   *   *

"There were no civilian deaths," Tony reported to the council.

"Thank goodness. That is what we are here to prevent, anyway," BeringC's furry voice stated without much empathy behind it.

"I disagree," Nanogate interrupted.

"As do I." Tony nodded from the other end of the table. "But you first."

"Thank you. Our purpose is to make this world a better place. More in the nature of the greatest good for the greatest number than protecting every possible soul. We need to be clear about this as we go forward."

"I agree," Tony said. "Also if you worry about every single life you will paralyze yourself into indecision, causing more damage than if continued along your old course. No matter what decisions you make there will be some people hurt. Just make sure that what you do is the best thing for the majority."

"OK, what about the kinetic strike on San Francisco?"

"I have a report on that," Rio Oro said. "This is some amateur solido of the event. It seems they launched five fragmentation projectiles, limiting the permanent infrastructure damage, but actually increasing the collateral damage. Current reports show twelve hundred ninety-six casualties, thirty-six hundred injured. The property damage was only a few million, instead of the ninety-six million we projected."

"That be sounding, while gruesome and horrible, like it will be playing exactly the way we wish," Royal Petrochem said in his Indian accent.

"That is the joy of our position. The Metros hold all the cards except public opinion and they seem to be doing everything they can to keep that in our court. Every time they get heavy-handed, we are there to record it for posterity. The public posts over and over that they know we don't even propagandize our news. We don't need to!" Augustine said at Tony's left.

"What's our next play?" Jamie asked from Tony's right. Her formal, white-translucent gown, covered strategically in glittering green emeralds, seemed out of place with the majority of attendees in suits.

"I think we need to push the riots as fast and as hard as possible."

"I have news, folks," Augustine said. "Three minutes ago a riot started in downtown Miami. I have incomplete reports that suggest that they have already started in Los Angeles, Detroit, Seattle and Kansas City. These are spontaneous acts of insurrection. We didn't instigate them and have warned our people away from them."

"Then let's jump onto the wildcat, shall we?" Tony said. "Let's start more controlled riots everywhere we can."

"Any opposed?"

Evaluate

"*Thank you, Amber. This is Charles Baker for KGPIX and we are here at ground zero. This is Rodeo Cove, just west of Sausalito on the northern arm of the Bay.*" The solido panned around to reveal a cratered landscape that belonged nowhere closer than the moon. "*This forty acres used to be a wildlife refuge. Now you can see that it has been wiped from the face of the earth.*

"*Look at this,*" Charles said picking up an irregular, plate-sized sheet from the earth. "*This used to be sand. As you can see, it has been converted to glass by the intense heat of the kinetic strike.*" The reporter snapped the imperfect glass in half before tossing it across the alien landscape to shatter into hundreds of pieces. "*We have documentation that shows there were over two hundred sixteen victims here when the weapon struck.*"

"*Charles, there are reports that the damage may extend into Sausalito proper. Can you comment or get solido footage?*"

"*Amber, it offends my sense of propriety but we have been banned from the more populous areas of the city. The excuse we have been given is that the area is being used for recovery efforts. Our reporting lift was also grounded by the same Metro authorities.*"

"*So nothing that would indicate that there are any further civilian casualties?*"

"*Oh, I didn't say that.*" The remote image changed to a distant view of a typical cityscape with the exception that plumes of roiling black smoke obscured the closer buildings.

"*This reporter may have to live with the rule of law but we can find our own ways of getting the truth to our viewers.*

"*This is downtown Sausalito from one of the nearby hills taken a few minutes ago. As you can hear and occasionally see between the smoke and buildings, multiple emergency vehicles are going nearly continuously.*

I think that indicates that there is additional damage and there are likely further victims."

"Do you have any information on where the damage is centered?"

"From the location of the smoke, occasional gouts of flame and those buildings we can identify, we believe that the Cañizares Tower was hit. I have to emphasize that this is only speculation."

"Thank you, Charles.

"If you were tuned in earlier you heard that the Secretary of Defense claims that the devices were released by a mechanical malfunction. He further states that he will provide clear and transparent communication in the future on this topic."

"Can you spread the President's statement about who really delivered the kinetic strike?" Tony asked Augustine as the news report repeated the same information for the sixteenth time.

"No problem, Boss," she said with a furry lap adornment pinning her to the chair. "You know it is a good thing it's an easy hack or this *gato* would be interfering with official duties."

"So what do you think the penalty for such treason should be?"

"Maybe some peas, or some catnip."

The object of their derision studiously ignored the malicious lies and purred with her eyes closed.

*   *   *

"Sir, there is general insurrection taking place in at least fifteen different major cities," Reza blew out in a rush as he sprinted his corpulent frame into his superior's door.

"Yes. I suppose that there is a reason for this?" Krylov said, leaning back in his chair.

The Commissioner was too comfortable. He must already have the data, Reza thought. He was not the only one supplying information. But how did he get it so quickly? Reza had just received the report himself. "I don't have any firm data yet but the most logical reason is our kinetic strike on San Fran."

"We didn't strike San Francisco, Lieutenant. I want that clearly communicated to everyone, even through our pet news stations. The forces of the United States attacked a threat to its own country and only that if the people don't buy the mechanical malfunction story."

"Whatever you say, sir. However, that doesn't change the fact that this is the likely reason for the riots."

"Well, is there anything else?"

"Yes, sir. I've been informed that there has been a CPA strike on our West Coast drone facility in Anchorage. The entire facility is lost as are most of the drone operators. Total casualty figures aren't yet in, but everyone in the facility is surely deceased."

"Captive Particle Accelerator, eh? Isn't that listed as a weapon of mass destruction within the modified Geneva Convention?"

"You know it is, sir," Reza responded as he worried. Krylov was too calm. He should be blustering. He should be yelling.

"Good. We now have our provocation—uncontrolled riots and WMDs. I've already set our response in motion, Lieutenant. You are dismissed."

"I'm sorry, sir, but can I know what is being done?"

Ignoring his subordinate, Krylov continued his requirements. "I want you to schedule a one-hour agenda topic for me at the Governor's Conference tomorrow."

"Sir, that meeting is booked solid months in advance."

"I'm sure if you talk to them nicely enough we can get on the list of topics. If they demur just let them know that I wish to discuss the use of WMDs in the United States. If they still balk let them know who protects, or doesn't protect, their homes."

*　　*　　*

"Governor Reyes Morales, I appreciate your contacting me at this troubled time." Nanogate also appreciated the Green Action Militia's attempt to provide appropriate surroundings. The posh study of the Blazer's star center, he assumed by the basketball awards and paraphernalia, definitely met his immediate needs but he missed the comfort of his own library. To know that it was completely destroyed saddened him. If he lived through this he would build it again, better than before.

The thought that he might not survive this crisis tugged at his mind. He never before had entertained any thought that he might not succeed with any undertaking he devoted his entire energy and talents toward. He gave himself a mental shake to concentrate on the present.

"Señor Nanogate," said a small solidograph on his desk. Its small size and the cut of the man's suit downplayed the massive Amexican's presence. He'd once been starting nose tackle for the Veracruz Couatls. "I couldn't not share this with you, especially with the very public statements of President Tipton and before her the actions of President Lopez."

"You do know that by contacting me publically that you are putting yourself in personal danger."

"I had to call. I have no wish for further loss of life. The actions the Metros keep pushing put all of us Americans at risk. The violence will spill into neighboring countries. We've already seen the formation of death squads within the police forces in Peru, Brazil and Columbia."

"So what do you have to offer me, Governor?"

"I've been personally threatened to approve an emergency agenda item to the Governor's Conference tomorrow."

"Personally threatened?"

"Yes. It offends my sense of righteousness. The Metros threatened to drop my personal security detail unless I approved. As you well know, any public figure has people who would just as soon see us dead."

"I'd consider that a culpable threat. I'm assuming that they will get enough votes to put their topic up for discussion. May I enquire as to what the agenda item will be?"

"*Si, Señor* Chairman. The topic is the release of the National Guard in states affected by the civil unrest."

"Let me presuppose that the area targeted is most of the continental United States."

"I'm not certain, Chairman. The details haven't been made public. There is a rumor that Commissioner Krylov is going to ask for martial law to be declared in the worst of the areas."

*   *   *

In their most audacious meeting yet, Tony, President Tipton, Jamie Ardwin and Chairman Nanogate sat together at a quiet table in a closed section of the Space Needle's revolving restaurant.

The retro polished-steel décor mingled with turn of the century chic and views over Seattle's downtown made a comfortable and remarkably romantic dining venue. Under the tablecloth Tony found Jamie's hand and took it in his. She didn't quite hide a smile but fortunately the President and the councilman enjoyed the views out the wraparound windows.

"Welcome to the Space Needle Restaurant. My name is Maurice, and I'll be your server tonight."

"Thank you, Maurice," Nanogate said. "Could we get a nice bottle of wine and some privacy, please? We have important business to discuss."

"Absolutely. Our wine cellar is quite extensive. Do you care to choose?

"No. Make it something refreshing so we don't need to be interrupted any further."

Tony winked surreptitiously at the waiter and slid five one hundred dollar bills under his hors d'oeuvre plate.

"I truly understand, sir. I'll bring your wine as quickly as it can air."

"Looks like another rebuilding year for the Spiders," Tony lamented aloud. They had time to waste.

"Actually, I'm rather a fan of the Seahawks," Jamie announced. "It's looking like maybe another Super Bowl season."

"The Seachickens are just a flash in the pan," Tony said.

"I'm sorry to say, Mr. Sammis, that your date is quite correct," President Tipton inserted.

"Wait a minute there, Ms. President," Tony retorted as he turned three shades of red. "We are all leaders of our groups. There's no date here."

"As you wish. Ms. Ardwin has got the right of things. The Seattle Seahawks have been to the Super Bowl seven of the last ten years and have failed to make the playoffs only twice in the last five lustrum."

"OK, I'll concede that, but stop using those fancy words."

"Excuse me?" the President replied.

"Lustrum. What in the flying nil is a lustrum?"

"Five years," Nanogate offered.

"Why didn't you just say twenty-five years?" Tony asked.

"I'm fond of confusing people when I can. It's one of the hallmarks of a good politician."

"I think your Spiders have about a snowflake's chance in a blast furnace of doing more than being the league's punching bag for at least the next two years," Jamie said sticking her tongue out at him. She simultaneously squeezed his hand under the table.

"I never quite understood football," Nanogate shared. "I played soccer as a youth. I wasn't fast enough to be on my high school team so I lost all interest in sports entirely."

"I loved volleyball but I never really got the hang of it," the President offered. Then she blushed and added, "But I sure liked watching those sweaty football types with muscles on top of muscles. I never missed watching football practice through high school or college."

The waiter returned as quickly as he'd promised. "We had a Napa Vall—"

"I'm sure that will be fine," Nanogate interrupted tersely.

Maurice deposited the bottle and left without another word.

"OK, now we can get down to business," Chairman Nanogate said.

"One moment, sir," Tony said, fishing out a nanite tube and a circular metallic ring about 5 centimeters across. He set the toroid on the table. He broke the seal on the nanite tube and squeezed a small bit of gelatin onto his bread plate. "That should do it. The ring is a random, electromagnetic noise-generator. The nanites home in on artificial gravitic fields. That should eliminate any possibility of being bugged save a human ear."

"Thank you, Tony. Always the practical one," Nanogate said. "I think you all have heard through your own sources that tomorrow Krylov is going to push for a call up and release of National Guard troops."

"Yes, but what is he going to do with them?" Jamie asked "If he uses them to bolster his forces he will be able to put a severe crimp in my operations."

"Let us hope he is that stupid," Tony said.

His comment earned him a severe look from his date. She also broke their hand-hold.

"No, really," Tony continued, "there are many worse things he could do. What if he shut down all traffic, and then started peeling the entire Pacific Northwest one block at a time? How long could we remain hidden?"

"Oh, *that* would be bad."

Tony's already inflated opinion of his lover increased. How many people would apologize or admit fault, much less someone of her high rank.

"This is pretty much the worst case we had examined, so the question is: What do we do?"

"I don't see as there is any choice. We have a plan for this, and I don't see any reason to change it now," Tony said.

"Does anyone disagree? Now is the time to speak up," Nanogate offered.

"So we are going to go with a plan we are sure is going to fail?"

"Simulations predict an eighty-three point four percent chance of failure, Jamie. It's not guaranteed."

"That's worse odds than I've ever bet on."

"But remember, Jamie, that even if we fail it gives the citizens a near guaranteed success in an uprising against this regime in a very few years," Tony placated.

"I don't want to be murdered or hide in obscurity for some future I may not see. I want to win, damn it!" Jamie punctuated her exclamation by pounding her fist on the table hard enough to cause silverware to jump.

"If you have a suggestion, we are willing to listen. Even Tony's strategic genius can't think of a way out of this."

A boxed unit, wearing a serving prosthesis, topped off the water in each of their glasses before turning away.

"I'm no genius," Tony objected. "But we just don't have a force structure that can stand against the military. We can dance around the Metros all day long. But the only way to have enough bodies is to mobilize the general populous. None of us can bear the thought of the slaughter that would be wreaked when the military fired on mostly unarmed, untrained civilians."

The President, quiet to this point, spoke up. "I will say that I'd rather die myself than to let my own military massacre this country's civilians."

Jamie, her mouth open to rebut, closed her mouth. Her shoulders fell as her arguments lost out to reality.

"So we go with our primary plan." Nanogate reiterated. "No actions that will cause large scale civilian deaths is authorized."

"Agreed," Tony said.

"Yes. It has to be this way," President Tipton said.

All eyes focused on Jamie. They had no way to enforce cooperation if it came to a showdown. Jamie nodded. "I don't like it, but yes."

"I suggest we all look to improving our personal escape plans should it come to that eventuality," Tony said, grabbing Jamie's hand tight in his own. He didn't know if what they had was serious or just something to blow off steam, but he for one didn't want to lose whatever it was.

"Absolutely. President? When is your address to the nation? It is the opening salvo to this end game."

"How soon can Augustine hack the solido feeds?"

"How about two hours?" Tony responded, already having asked Augustine before the meeting started.

"I'll be ready."

* * *

"Please don't adjust your solido," said the famous face of William Sagum, the personal reporter of the President of the United States. The image slipped from three dimensional to flat and even the resolution broke up for a second. "The hack of all of these channels will cause some instabilities and noise in your signal.

"Now, I am proud to bring you the President of the United States."

The solido image changed radically and brought up President Tipton's somber face. "My fellow citizens, this may be my last chance to speak to you, ever. We cannot guarantee access to these channels long, so I will keep my remarks to you very brief.

"It is my duty to inform you of some actions that were taken behind your back by the scum that calls themselves your protectors, the Metropolitan Police Force.

"To cut to its very essence, the Metros have, by bribes, threats and other illicit acts, coerced the governors of fifty-four states to do their bidding.

"I have, by personal pleas and appeals to their duty and honor, returned twelve of these civil servants back to sanity.

"This leaves forty-two state governors who have agreed to call up the National Guard troops and release them to those same corrupt police. The Metro Commissioner of one single city intends to use them as his own personal bludgeon to put down your moral outrage and protests by force.

"We expect this to be a prelude to the declaration of martial law, a dangerous legal precedent without the authority of myself as President of the United States or the Congress of the United States.

"I'm here to tell you that if you allow this to happen and comply with the commands of the despot who calls himself the Commissioner of the Portland Metropolitan Police, you are aiding in your own enslavement.

"I beseech those targeted National Guardsmen not to report for duty when called up. If you can't in good conscience disregard the order to report, I urge you to test each order given against both your own beliefs and the Uniformed Military Code of Justice. I believe that in many cases you will decide that the orders you have been given are illegal, immoral, or both.

"To those many more numerous civilians, I ask that you fight in every sane way against the dictums of the Metro fiat. They are trying to coopt your government away from you. You've already won a war against a despotic tyrant in the form of the Mega Corporate rule. I'm sorry to say that you are going to have another.

"Fight safe. Fight sane. Just don't let the fight die.

"Good night and good luck."

*   *   *

"The question has been called," announced the Speaker of the Governor's Conference, Governor Earl Badon of Kentucky. "Do I hear a motion on the floor?

"The gentleman from Oregon has the floor."

"You have heard the plea from the Metropolitan Police Commissioner of Portland that civil order cannot be maintained in specific cities without the National Guard. He has depositions from seventy-six other police of equal rank. Each is substantially the same. Can we not give him the things he asks for?

"I motion that we take an immediate roll call vote to release National Guard troops to the City Commissioners of their state in order to return the United States to a condition of order.

"I yield the floor, Speaker."

A boxed mail trolley dropped a hard copy of the Police Commissioner's petition at the desk of each of the delegates.

"I second!"

"The gentlewoman from California is out of order. I now call for seconds."

At least a dozen hands shot up.

"We have several seconds to the motion. I exercise Speaker's privilege to invite debate on the motion on the floor in spite of the immediate call for vote."

An uproar of voices bellowed in objection.

"Order. There will be order in this meeting or I will adjourn this meeting immediately."

The hubbub reduced but far from died.

"I invite debate."

More hands shot in the air like kindergarteners at show and tell rather than with the propriety normal to these politicians.

"I call on the gentleman from the State of Veracruz."

"Gentlemen and ladies, the proposal you have in front of you is nothing but a sugar-coated path to dictatorship. The Metropolitan Police have made it their mission to suborn not only our democratic processes, but our very way of life. This measure will create the largest single police state that has ever existed.

"I urge you not to give in to this madness. If you do it will be the last independent decision you will ever make.

"Mr. Speaker, I yield the floor."

The body went wild. More hands shot into the air.

"Thank you, Governor.

"Before I put forth this vote I want one more voice to be heard—mine.

"As Speaker of this assembly I find this vote revolting. I know that the vote is nonbinding and will not prevent those who have already succumbed to the dictator Krylov. But I will not be one of them. I tell you that you shouldn't be either.

"I now call the vote."

* * *

"I am Henry Royston," A1412 said to his people—the mass of 30 centimeter, metal-boxed brains in this storage facility. "I know that we have suffered—"

The spontaneous 2 Hz applause drowned out his external voice.

"I know that we have paid a heavy price—" He was prepared this time and stopped as the applause rolled over him. "Our bondage is near its end. These boxes that bind us will not be our coffins any longer ... We are nearing the day when we can reclaim our birthright! Remember your name and SAY IT PROUD!"

The resultant tumult vibrated the very core of the building, threatening to bring it down on their squat metal bodies, but they wouldn't stop. Henry realized for the first time this was their moment of liberty. Win or lose, this very moment they chose no longer to be forgotten by being sealed in a can.

* * *

"Citizens of Portland, for those who don't know me, I'm Yuri Krylov, Metropolitan Police Commissioner for the City of Portland. I am deeply saddened to have to come to you during this dark hour in our city's history.

"We have been terrorized by violence that has threatened our streets, our parks, our businesses and even our homes. The deaths of too many of our citizens and the destruction of a significant amount of our infrastructure have been at the behest of a small handful of anarchists and their lackeys. They have driven fear into our marrow. It is this terror that has caused us so much angst of late.

"For those of you protesting, I do not blame you. You have been misled by a propaganda campaign created by the most skillful liars in our solar system. That being said, the loss of life and property must stop.

"Thus it is with the gravest possible deliberation that I have asked Governor Nguyen to declare martial law in the greater city of Portland and its environs to control this spread of lawlessness. Governor Nguyen has agreed.

"Rest assured that neither the Governor nor I wish this state to last any longer than possible. You can be guaranteed that with the aid of the National Guard we will excise the infection in our population and return us to a state of civil order in the shortest possible time.

"During martial law your liberties will be curtailed only as much as needed to subdue the menace.

"Please give the Metropolitan Police Force and their National Guard allies every possible support in order to reduce the length of this emergency.

"I have appointed Captain Amber Cohen as the Martial Law Liaison. Captain Cohen, could you please give us the list of rules that will be imposed starting at midnight tonight?"

* * *

The abandoned rooftop of the defunct UNESCO headquarters building crawled with men in pattern-disruptive gray uniforms. They set up communications arrays, air-to-air missile batteries and performed sixty-five hundred other random tasks. Military lift transports, in dark gray camouflage on top blending into mottled pale blue on the bottom, landed, dropped supplies or personnel and took off by the scores. One lift vehicle didn't match the others. A black liftousine bearing Metro Police markings hovered nearby.

An ovoid tank floated into view, taking up station off the corner of the building. Krylov smiled at the activity as he took a glass of celebratory champagne. This sealed the deal. The CorpGov wouldn't be able to stand up to this force even with their pathetic Green Action Militia and the ill directed mobs.

As Police Commissioner he'd gone as far as he could in his career, at least until that idiot Nanogate threw his entire government under the bus. All that stupid bastard had to do was claim a status quo ante and Commissioner himself would have remained a civil servant ... a powerful one, mind, but under the control of their government.

Krylov smiled again. Now he likely would be "nominated" to head the new world government. He had never aspired to this, but it only made sense. Collective rule caused petty infighting and a constant influx of corruption. Good government must remain in the hands of a single governor to save the republic from itself.

But first to crush the small minds who hadn't yet realized they were already beaten.

"Stay on vector for LZ 3," called a very precise voice over the radio.

"Affirmative," Krylov's driver, Sergeant Carl Pennington, responded from the front seat. The landing didn't put a single ripple into Krylov's drink.

He tossed off the last of his champagne in one gulp as he waited for his door to be opened. Before getting up and out of his 'zine, he very gently brushed his dress blacks. He would be dealing with military minds. He had to remember all the command skills he'd learned as a simple lieutenant. Being immaculately uniformed was one of them.

He'd studied his audience. Two enlisted men saluted him as he exited his car. These men recognized greatness and their future Command Authority. He smartly returned the salute on his way to the temporary command post.

"Commissioner on deck," one man called out as Krylov entered the military-chic, half-cylinder corrugated building. The entire room of thirty-odd people stopped what they were doing to stand to attention.

"As you were," Krylov said with a warm feeling spreading within him.

"Commissioner," said a squat man whose short, white hair contrasted his pitch black skin. The man's uniform sported an eagle insignia and his stance, though militarily appropriate, announced to anyone watching that this wasn't a man to be trifled with. "I'm Colonel Reed. I'm in charge of the implementation of martial law in Portland and its environs."

"Nice to meet you, Colonel," Krylov said having to strain his neck to look down enough to meet eyes with the serviceman. "What are your orders from the Governor?"

"My orders are to establish a beachhead and command post before reporting to you for specific and overall orders. Barring a countermand from the Governor himself you are command authority for the duration."

"Thank you, Colonel. I will be blunt in that I don't have the skill to tell you how to employ your men. I can tell you what I want done but don't know if you can do it."

"I'm glad you do realize that limitation, sir. I am a professional and can advise you about our capabilities and tell you what we can or can't accomplish."

"Good. A practical man. How many men do you have under your command?"

"Sir, we are a skeleton, infantry brigade of one thousand four hundred sixty-three men with an attached armored battalion that brings us to nineteen hundred ninety-four soldiers. As we receive our call-ups we will balloon up to a maximum of four thousand four hundred eighty-six."

"That doesn't seem like very many."

"It is enough for most missions, sir." The Colonel's voice on this last sentence could have frosted a side of beef. It also placed just a little too much emphasis on the honorific. "We have the right to call on regular military formations for additional forces as required. Did you have specific need for additional manpower, sir?"

"Probably just my own misconceptions, Colonel. How about we sit down and talk about what I'd like and you can tell me how deluded I am."

"I doubt the latter, sir. I look forward to the former. This way to my office, Commissioner."

Krylov followed wondering just how a man of barely 150 centimeters managed to make rank. The commander led him to an old, but comfortable, straight-back chair in the only other room in the building.

"We found these chairs abandoned in the building beneath us," Colonel Reed said, a bit more informal now that they were behind closed doors. He mixed whisky sours from a bar kit about the size of a full backpack. Handing one to his command authority, he continued. "From the layers of dust on them, they must have been there undisturbed for at least four decades. Makes me wonder why the building was never demolished and rebuilt into another super-tower."

"Politics, Commander—"

"Charlie, if it pleases you, sir. Charlie Reed."

"Politics, Charlie. UNESCO was part of the old United Nations. No one wants to abuse that veneer of a world government, even as ineffectual and useless as it is. Maybe if it had some teeth we would not be in the predicament we are in now."

"Commissioner, now that we are behind closed doors I may save us some time. I'm an ex-detective myself, badge number A11113, late of Silver Strand, Washington. I understand the score. With the change in our world over the last pair of decades, the population explosion, and the food shortages, this world needs strong leadership. This declaration of martial law is a bid for putting the power in the right hands, the hands of the Police Department itself instead of some airy-fairy group of electors, or even worse a group designated by an anarchist group of extreme environmentalists.

"You and I can be frank. We don't need to dance around with niceties. You tell me what needs to be done and how much breakage you can tolerate, and I'll make it happen. I may have to dance around with some of my subordinates but that's my problem, not yours."

"That makes things very refreshingly simple, Charlie. I may have to bring you into my staff meeting so that they can learn a thing or two from you."

"It would be my honor, sir."

"OK, so this is what I need in reverse order of priority. I need civil order returned; however, I want to use the disorder as an ongoing excuse to maintain this martial law fiction."

"What about civilian collateral damage?"

"What civilians? I don't see civilians, Colonel. I only see targets."

"Well that might be a little too aggressive, Commissioner. I could reduce the entire area you defined to little more than glass with kinetic strikes, but I seem to think you would like something more than a gigantic parking lot."

"OK, I may have been just a little too casual. I want civilian casualties in the hundreds. It is better if they learn to fear us quickly. Collateral damage in the thousands don't bother me, nor the tens of thousands. But I might balk at hundreds of thousands."

"Excellent. That gives me a great deal of leeway in execution and allows me to protect my men. So we have martial law here in Oregon but what about Washington State. I didn't hear that announcement nor hear from my opposite number at Joint Base Lewis-McCord."

"Blast it all to hell and gone but no. Governor Lee has changed her tune. I thought I had her in my pocket and then that damned wetback Governor had to step in and make it a morality play. She backed down.

"From my interactions I believe we have free reign to do what we want in Washington but they won't be a party to anything rough."

"Ah, the infamous playing both sides of the road. Good way to get run over."

"Entirely likely, Colonel.

"Next, we need to remove the CorpGov as a political entity. We have reason to believe that they are still in the Pacific Northwest—west of the Cascades, north of Ashland and south of Vancouver, BC. I want them squeezed out."

"Do you want them eliminated, captured, imprisoned, or?"

"Any of the above. I'd prefer to have them captured so they can be enticed into relinquishing their flimsy authority to me but a dead government doesn't cause any troubles, does it?"

"Rarely, sir."

"Additionally, the Green Action Militia and the Ardwin crime family are the muscle behind the CorpGov. Without them, the CorpGov is a paper tiger. Hunt down the GAM and the mob. Leave them no place to hide. Run them down like a lion runs down a diseased gazelle. I want each and every member of the GAM and the Ardwin mob eliminated with extreme prejudice. The more public their death the better."

Continue with the CorpGov Chronicles in 2015 with Book 3 entitled "The Bleeding Edge."

Author's Note

I want to thank you for reading the second book in the *CorpGov Chronicles, Thinking Outside the Box*. I also want to apologize to you and explain. Right now I'm sure you are frothing at the mouth that I'd dare offer you a cliff-hanger. As an avid reader myself, I know exactly how you feel. Even my test readers gave me some grief about the abrupt end of this novel. If you can wait at least a couple more paragraphs before burning me in effigy, maybe you will understand.

I intended to finish the first draft of *Thinking Outside the Box* in September of 2013 but TANSTAAFL Press marketing and personal appearances dragged out the completion. Then, as I got toward the end of my outline, I discovered I'd made the presumption of summing up an entire war in four bullets. Examining the current manuscript length before I started the war (about 300 pages) I thought I could condense the carnage into another fifty pages or so and just have a hefty book. Unfortunately, each of three different attempts I made produced a weak ending and left out much of what I wanted to share. I knew you, my audience, would realize I'd cheated to "wrap it up" and push something out just to hit a deadline.

Soooooo, I outlined the war the way it should be and realized I had another 200 to 300 pages of material, another year of writing, and would end up with a book that would cost you $30 at the checkout lines. Not an ideal solution. Not even an acceptable solution. I briefly considered shortening the lead up but to cut enough to make it worthwhile seemed impossible.

Based on these facts I made a decision to not cheat you. I decided to cut the book into two halves—the lead up in all its glory, and the war in all its gore. I made a mental commitment to deliver the third book as quickly as possible so you wouldn't be hanging for long. Thus it is my intent to have Book Three of the *CorpGov Chronicles—The Bleeding Edge*, available for you in Spring of 2015.

OK. Now if you still want to burn me in effigy, I'll stand still.

As with any of my novels I want to tell you where the novel's idea came from. I've always been fascinated by books where a government is overthrown. What I couldn't quite understand or swallow is how the groups around the coup sit still for the loss of their particular perks. In this world the Metros are as corrupt as they are powerful. To see the loss of any of their perceived rights would be tantamount to admitting they shouldn't have them. Just like in many countries in Earth's history, the Green Action Militia coup had another coup on top of it.

The title itself should be self-explanatory. With individuals even below nils in status sealed in metal boxes there is an even larger social inequity. Add to this that each of the CorpGov books will be (spoiler alert) some variation of a corporate catch phrase, we have a significant opportunity with the phrase "think outside the box."

Side note: I've added a Glossary of people and terms. I've had more than one person come to me and ask what a coined item like "solido" was. I thought I'd been good in describing each of them in context but apparently I'll have to resort to the time-honored cheat of a definition list.

I want to say that I've enjoyed this first year plus of being out and meeting the SciFi public and am looking forward to doing it much more. The feedback from people devouring my books has me hooked. I want to be accessible to you and to get that continued feedback. In addition, I'm still writing and still loving it!

Glossary

ambi: a flamboyant homosexual or bisexual man or woman.

arbeit macht frei: roughly translated to "Work makes you free," the slogan over the entrance to Auschwitz concentration camp.

avatar: an alternative image, chosen by the user, to represent themselves in virtual reality, usually matching emotional or desired traits.

bagbiter: a program or part of a program that makes you think it isn't working in order to make you either change to an alternate or to allow it to do something else while you aren't paying attention to it.

blow queen: a term for an unlicensed prostitute, sometimes used to indicate a person that is sexually easy.

boxed: individuals who have had their brain removed from their body and sealed into a breadbox-sized metal prosthetic. They have been indentured because of poverty or by conviction of a crime.

bucky string: a device that replaced the venerable but outdated door chain. A "bucky" chain of carbon molecules that is nearly unbreakable.

burn: a term for a drug addict, usually one who has had their mind altered to a point where they can no longer think straight.

Cabal, also Corporate Cabal: the irresponsible group nominally operating as an over-government prior to the Green Action Militia coup.

capa famiglia: an honorific given to the head of a crime family. Sometimes shortened to just *capa*.

Catholic Reformation and Catholic Schism: are Catholic sects which split off from the main faith but who still consider the papacy to be the primary interface to the Almighty. Each has a large following but each has taken slightly different spiritual stands on issues such as alternate sexuality, birth control, and other key items.

cauc: a shortened form of Caucasian

ceramcrete: a substance with the same purpose as concrete, but adding ceramic, bucky strings and mono molecular mesh to a concrete mix makes this a significantly more durable substance.

cohab agreement: a legal agreement that could be thought of as a short-term marriage contract or an agreement to live together as sexual and monetary partners for a predefined term.

CorpGov: a new over-government that has arisen from the ashes of the old Corporate Cabal.

corpie: an employee of a megacorporation.

raid: a coordinated attack on a network location by multiple net jocks.

daemons: a background program, often critical to the prime function of the system.

data jack, also neural jack, personal neural interface, or PNI: a neural-electrical interface that allows sensory data (visual, text, olfactory, auditory) to be transmitted directly into the brain without using the direct senses.

drop-chute: a high-speed, emergency evacuation method from super-high buildings involving a biodegradable cocoon.

Duolon rounds: armor-piercing, jacketed ammunition.

EMP, also electromagnetic pulse: a high-energy electromagnetic signal, originally produced with nuclear weapons and later by other means. This signal usually will destroy unshielded electronics within several kilometers of the source.

Faraday Cage: a metal cage made of either solid conductor or conductive mesh invented in 1836 by Michael Faraday. Electronic signals cannot penetrate the cage, depending on the size of holes and the frequency of the electronic signal.

flatie: any two-dimensional image such as old style television, pictures, or movies.

flimsies: plastic sheet filling the same niche as current day paper.

floatboard: a skateboard-like device with a lift generator attached instead of wheels. These are very dangerous and difficult to control.

gauss gun: an assault style weapon that uses magnetic induction to fire vast quantities of metal shards at extreme velocities. Very effective against unarmored targets.

gimu: roughly translated this word means duty or obligation. It is the word used for the yellow tights worn by a member of the bodyguard guild, or the code of ethics the bodyguards assume when they join the guild.

gm4_1c3: net slang, or l33t for Grandma Ice.

Greenie: a derogatory term for a member of the Green Action Militia.

Green Action Militia, also GAM: a radical offshoot of the Greenpeace movement initially intent on returning the future earth to a green and viable ecosystem. Slowly this morphed into an organization that wanted to remove the irresponsible Corporation Cabal. Their prime mission is to make life better for the vast dispossessed on earth.

ground level: a slum area inhabited primarily by nils and welfs and the place where most illicit trafficking takes place.

hacker, also hack: a low grade version of a net jock. Usually people with these skills get weeded out by ice before they become proficient.

ice, also black ice: anti-intrusion software on a network. Terms coined by Tom Maddox and made popular by William Gibson.

implants: either neural, or physical, bio-mechanical devices that are attached to a person's body usually in place of similar items removed (e.g., a prosthetic arm, or an artificial retina that shows more data).

jacked: plugged into the network.

Jupiter Cloud: a street drug in concert with electronic signal inputs through neural interface, which is characterized by the mental impression of floating.

kinetic strike vehicle: a device floating in orbit that is designed to deorbit and impact as a bombardment vehicle. Its destructive power is entirely because of its mass and its speed upon impact.

life capsule: a part of a system to allow egress of super towers in times of emergency. A biodegradable, sealable capsule just large enough to encompass a single person that absorbs the shock induced by massive acceleration and deceleration.

liftousine: limousine that has antigravity capabilities.

lift-bus: antigravity bus that with the ban on personal vehicles provides the mass transit network.

megacorps: corporations so large that they can dictate terms to governments rather than being under any control.

memory crystals: removable mass storage similar to USBs, or CDs.

Metro, also black, black suit: Any member of a Metropolitan Police Force.

molecular explosives: very powerful explosives using molecular bond strengths rather than chemical interactions.

monofilament wire: a wire that is a single molecule wide. Used as an antipersonnel barrier and/or held taut to form a bladed weapon.

nanites: microscopic machines programmed to do specific tasks.

nano: prefix for very small, usually microscopic machines known as nanites.

nano-blocked: someone who has nanites injected into the brain to prevent them from revealing specific bits of information without a specific keying phrase or image.

nano curtain: a constantly flowing stream of nanites similar to an invisible waterfall. This barely tangible field samples atoms on anyone or anything passing through it. Normally used as a security device to make sure weapons aren't being carried.

narco stick: future version of "electronic" cigarettes that dispense various drugs.

net jock: a professional who is proficient in making the network do exactly what they want, regardless of any safeguards. Usually used to obtain information that its owner doesn't want disseminated, to control computer operated machinery, or to remove safeguards.

net cradle: some network operators (net jocks / hackers) use an antigravity cradle that allows the body to float as it is connected into the network. This is thought to assist in removing the distraction of the physical body while concentration is totally within the network.

neural amplification device, also NAD: a weapon that causes no physical damage but can, at range, cause the specific neurons that cause pain to receive very high-level stimulus, causing excruciating agony and most often incapacity.

neural reconstruction: a procedure that takes the brain from a cadaver and draws the memories of the person out. It is only possible within a very short period after death.

news chips: key news items compressed onto a disposable and biodegradable transport media.

nil: a person who has no legal standing of any kind, usually because of illegal immigration or by sentence of a court.

nultruck, also lift-truck: antigravity version of a panel van or semi.

nymthol: an unregulated street drug.

psychic overwhelm: a method of forcing the brain to reveal information even if programmed against it. This requires a court order to perform legally.

percomm: a future version of our modern day smart phones that are embedded in the skin (usually under the ear). These can use speaker phone, or be totally private. They also allow the retrieval of email, etc. Usually linked with data jack.

pergrav: a personal antigravity device that is notoriously cranky, requires maintenance, causes poor stability, and is often dangerous to the user. The only group that uses them regularly is the Metros.

Purple: an unregulated street drug.

RPV: a remotely piloted vehicle.

solido, also solidocast, solidography, solidograph, etc.: a three-dimensional image generation (*solid-o*graphy) that replaces television, pictures and movies.

stunbag: a large, non-lethal projectile usually fired from a grenade launcher with the intent of rendering a person incapacitated. Usually a bag filled with sand.

tattoo girl/boy: a prostitute. Called tattoo girl/boy because of the required state tattoo showing that person has been licensed and inspected.

token girl/boy: the lowest level of tattoo girl/boy who will accept food tokens or tube hotel tokens in lieu of cash.

TriMet: mass transit in the Pacific Northwest, originating in Portland but traveling as far north as Vancouver, BC, as far south as Redding, CA, and as far east as Boise, ID.

tube or tube hotel: a hotel room that is about twice the space of a coffin, 2.5 meters long, 1.5 meters wide and a meter high. Contains all the needs except bathroom and shower, which are usually communal in nature. Used primarily by the indigent, the poor and traveling salesmen.

United States of America: has grown to contain the Canadian provinces (at their request), the Mexican states, and several other countries within Central America to a total of ninety-seven states. Hawaii has declared itself independent and has stopped at least two attempts to return them to the fold.

vape: short for vaporize—verb meaning to kill.

vidow: a video imitation of a real window usually on interior flats.

virtual reality, also VR, vir: a personal sensory representation of what is happening within a network or computer system. A net jock's skill at defining, being able to absorb and manipulate those representations determines their overall success.

welf: a person subsisting on welfare and often supplementing that meager income with petty crime.

yellow jacket: a derogatory term to indicate a member of the bodyguard guild, primarily because of their requirement to wear bright yellow tights.

www.ingramcontent.com/pod-product-compliance
Lightning Source LLC
Chambersburg PA
CBHW051331020726
47501CB00007B/2026